PATH OF
DESTRUCTION

ROCK AND ROLL DREAMS SERIES – BOOK 2

Cassidy A. Storm

The story, main characters, and incidents portrayed in this production are fictitious. No identification with actual persons (living or deceased), places, buildings, and products are intended or should be inferred.

If you encounter a contradiction or slip made by a character, know that it was intentional.

The Rock and Roll Dreams Series – From Book 1 forward, follow Christmas Angel Devito from childhood into adulthood as she experiences relationships, fame, and fortune.

The Always & Forever Series – Book 1 & 2. Follow Elijah Blu Xiong and Tian Lee Yong as they meet in college and develop an inseparable bond. Continue to Book 4 of the Rock and Roll Dreams Series, "Unexpected Circumstances", where they meet Christmas Angel Devito.

www.CassidyStorm.net

CHAPTER 1

September 2004

I looked over at Kevin, my best friend who was asleep in the passenger seat of my Ford F250. His blondish hair which he kept swept to the side had gotten long and was covering one eye as he slept. He had hazel eyes and was considered short at five foot five. We were both sixteen and Kevin was on the run. He was normally a bubbly guy but he had run into some bad times. His parents had been abusing him in the past year and although they'd gone to counseling, the abuse had only gotten worse. He was traumatized so I had given him a Valium that I had stolen out of the medicine cabinet before I'd gotten behind the wheel. In all truthfulness, we were both running.

We were leaving behind Whitmire, South Carolina where I had lived with my dad and he had lived with his parents. It hadn't been planned that way. My dad had owned a ranch. I wasn't sure what line of work Kevin's father did, but that didn't matter now anyway.

Daddy had adopted me when I was five. I called him Daddy but I was his niece by blood. I had been a challenging child to him, having psychic abilities as well as being an alien spirit in a human body. Although he loved me, he had never truly understood me. Even I didn't understand me. The aliens had said that I was one of the spirits who held the energy to stabilize the grids in the earth. All I had to do was to live, oh and to heal people too. Kevin knew all of this but he was a non-believer.

To say that I'd had a lonely childhood was an understatement. I'd lived in a foster home for about six months before Daddy had found me at the orphanage. The foster family had abused me which in turn made me bitter and angry. School was a place where I took out my anger by being a bully who beat up people. I never thought of myself as such because I was only being a super hero to kids that were being picked on by others. I'd met Kevin when we were fourteen and he became my first true friend. He had introduced me to some kids who were forming a band. Rick was lead singer, a bass guitarist, and the oldest of us at twenty-one. Carol, his girlfriend, was the keyboard player and also twenty-one. David, lead guitarist was eighteen.

Daddy had died two weeks before of a massive heart attack. It was a blow to me and I had temporarily checked out in my mind. I was made to come back when a vision of Kevin dying by his mother's hands screamed inside my head. I had saved him by busting into his house where his dad had just beaten him. I held off his mother while he quickly gathered a few things and got into my truck. She had peppered the back of my truck as I spun out of their driveway. At that time my dad's friend and neighbor Bob, had guardianship over me. He had taken Kevin to a safe place then reluctantly signed guardianship of me over to Rick. Rick, Carol, and David were headed to New York to try to become famous as a band. Bob didn't know of a way to save Kevin and neither Kevin or I wanted to stay in South Carolina. So here I was with Kevin following our friends to New York to start a new life.

Two days later we arrived in New York. I was guided to a house in New Rochelle that we would rent on our first day there but Rick thought we could do better and we spent two more days looking. He didn't know the power of the voice in my head. None of them were happy because we would all be living in the same house. Part of this arrangement was because of an agreement Rick had made with Bob, but mostly it was the reality that none of us could afford a place on our own. There were two other houses that we considered but the people that owned them wouldn't rent to us because of our ages.

We rented a big house with four bedrooms and two baths. Rick and Carol would share a room, and Kevin, David and I would have our own rooms which were a lot smaller. I outlined a budget for us which they all scoffed at, then we went job hunting. Carol easily landed a job as a waitress and Rick found a job as a manager of a small clothing store. David searched for two weeks before he was hired to work at a department store. Kevin had the hardest time both because he was suddenly timid and because he was only sixteen and without a high school diploma. He was hired as a stocker at a grocery chain. I found a job within a week modeling clothes for Harris Company which was a mail order company. I also did general office work for the company when we weren't doing a catalog. Rick had registered me at the local high school where I would leave at noon two to three days a week to go to work. Kevin planned on taking a G.E.D test instead of attending school. Another change was that Rick had changed the name of our band to "Rebel". It was one thing that we all managed to agree on.

Being in a new place with new lives was quite an adjustment for all of us. Between the stress of adjusting to living together, working at new jobs and finding new friends, it was an experience. We found the weather in New York, and its people to be colder than that of the south. Another side of the coin was that the others felt freer to do what they wanted to do and act how they wanted to act. Kevin and David had shrugged off all modesty and could be found walking around the house naked from time to time, especially in the morning. At least they did that until the weather got really cold. I think Carol would have liked to run around naked too but Rick wouldn't let her. He was sure that she would sleep with Kevin and David. In the same respect, Carol was sure that Rick was going to sleep with me. About as naked as I got was a long t-shirt which I wore to bed and which I never ventured outside of my bedroom in but as it got cold, I wore a thermal top and bottom instead. Carol wore skimpy lingerie. She added a big velour robe as it got colder. Another thing that most of the others did was drink openly and sometimes smoke pot. I guess they had always done some drinking but now they weren't hiding it. They'd never smoked pot in front of me in South Carolina but now that we'd moved it was a common sight. I wasn't interested in either. I had never felt restricted at home and this setting didn't feel any different in that way. The only difference was that it wasn't a team effort. It was more like everyone was doing their own thing. We didn't even practice as much as a band as we should have.

Another adjustment was Rick's mood. He had

decided to quit smoking since it was a big expense to buy cigarettes but it was killing him. He was constantly in a foul mood. He also warned Kevin and David not to get me pregnant, and he warned me not to get pregnant. I didn't think he needed to be in my face with his attitude but I bit down my anger anyway. I was still grieving for the father and home I'd lost so I wasn't interested in sex anyway.

Kevin had more trouble adapting than any of us. He had always had to watch anything he did or said when he lived at home which now made him timid. I knew he could be bubbly and outgoing if he could overcome his past. His mom had called Bob threatening him to tell her where Kevin was, but Bob kept denying he knew anything. Everyone who didn't know the real story and even some who did, thought he had run away. I knew his mom would never have the police pick him up. She was having less problems with his dad since Kevin had left. I told Rick that but he was extremely angry at me about the situation especially since every time Bob called he gave Rick the third degree about taking care of me. Then Rick would hand the phone to me so Bob could chew me out about Kevin going with us. Every time his mom called; Bob called. After about three weeks she quit calling Bob, and in turn Bob toned his calls down to once a week then once every two weeks.

At first Kevin cried on my shoulder because his parents didn't love him and never would. I'm sure that I didn't help him too much because when he cried about lost family, I did too. The only helpful thing I may have told him was to try to forget, because Rick, Carol, David and I were his family now. Sometimes he slipped into my bed at night even though I told him not to. We held each other but never did anything else because all I could think of was how we had done things in my bed when Daddy was still alive, and that time was gone.

David snapped at Kevin one morning of how he wasn't the only one with family problems. David was still having trouble with his parents too which came as a surprise to him. Daddy had warned him that would happen. The difference was that he was of legal age to be on his own. I knew he hated his little brother but then the rest of us did too. I also found that I wasn't totally right about his mood when he cried with me one day over the loss of my dad. He and Kevin had come to think of my dad as their second dad. David told me that he had shared several confidences with my dad and now he didn't know whom he could turn to as his own dad didn't relate to him. I wondered if anyone would ever love me as much as they loved my dad. Surely, I had some of my dad in me, right? "You can talk to me. I won't betray your confidence." I assured him. It was something my dad would have said. I worried suddenly of how I could fix any problems he had but I needn't have worried.

"No offense, Angel but your belief is that no one should have any problems. You're not very compassionate." He told me. "And it's hard to talk to someone who is the best at everything they try and who doesn't have any problems."

I blinked in amazement as he turned to leave my room. "I have problems!" I replied loudly.

David turned back to me as he reached my bedroom door. "Then tell me one of them."

I'm the only responsible one of this bunch. Y'all need to grow up! I don't know what to do with all the attention I get at school. I hate having to lie about how we all ended up living here. I hate that my dad died. I hate that I'm so different from everyone! I hate that y'all can't mind read and see that I'm hurting! I fucking hate New York and its cold ass weather! I hate Carol. I'm tired of Kevin asking me for sex. I hate that y'all take whatever you want out of my room and you don't give me the privacy I used to have at home. I hate that Kevin and y'all are my responsibility! What are we doing here anyway? None of you want to practice as a band! But mostly, I MISS MY DAD! HE WAS MY DAD NOT YOURS!

"Yeah, like I said." David continued as none of my thoughts had made it out of my mouth. He turned and walked out.

Oh my God, what was wrong with me? I had never been able to tell my dad half my problems let alone anyone else. And sometimes I could see spirits. Was my dad ever gonna visit me? It hurt that he wasn't around as a spirit. What had happened to him? How was I going to survive without him?

Since Rick was trying to quit smoking, David decided to do the same. It was just too expensive, they said. I was glad because I hated the smoke. Somehow, they both managed to quit, except for smoking pot.

School was different for me now. New Rochelle High School had close to one hundred students in the eleventh grade compared to the thirty in Whitmire. On my first day, I had nearly every boy in my homeroom gathered around me asking me questions because I was new to them. I was careful how I worded all of my answers. I'd never hung with any clique in my old school because people were mean to me. It was weird in my new school when I sat by myself at lunch, it was never a moment or so before a boy asked to sit with me. Then all of his friends were pulling up chairs. They were telling me that my southern accent was so sweet and that I was so cute. I thought it was a curious situation that I'd never expected. Yeah, I'd been told all my life that I was good looking but, in my hometown, the school boys didn't want to deal with me. It was all the older guys, ten or more years older that wanted me. Several had said that they wanted to tame me, whatever that meant. I wasn't a wild animal. Dad ran every one of them off that approached me or came to the house. He said they were nothing but trouble and he was probably right.

Oddly, no one in this school seemed anything but accommodating to me although a few of the girls weren't happy with me because their guys were paying attention to me. But there was no fist fighting, just words which I ignored. Rick had warned me about fighting even though I already knew I'd be back in South Carolina if I slipped up. It's funny though. The fun of fighting which had always been second nature to me, rarely ever entered my mind anymore. The fight had drained out of me when my dad had died. I had nothing to prove here and I was no longer interested in being a super hero. And maybe that's why no one seemed to have the need to fight with me.

Work was a different experience too. It was a small company around fifty to seventy-five people. Everyone was older than I was. The girls that modeled for the catalog were in their twenties. They were all pretty. I still received a lot of attention from everyone regardless. A few of the older guys seemed to think they should watch out for me as if I were a little kid. They hovered showing me my job and sometimes doing my administrative duties for me. I was cool with that. My desk was in the back but somehow a lot of employees made their way back there for some reason or another. I talked to them as if I did that with everyone although everything I said was in general, never about the specifics of my life or my past. When they asked about boyfriends, I told them I was too young. And the work wasn't hard. We answered calls, typed up letters and reports, sent faxes, kept track of inventory in the computer and whatever else needed done.

As David had complained many times before, I learned quickly and was (mostly) good at everything I'd learned. I'd taken typing in eighth grade and had always been proud of how quickly and accurately I could type. So work was another place where people liked me and I excelled. I wondered where all this friendliness and belonging had been all my life, why it hadn't found me sooner.

***

I found out there was a stomach bug going around when everyone in the band was suddenly sick. They stayed home while I went to school. I came home but then ended up going back out for more Ginger Ale and crackers. They knew that I'd be sick next. In the meantime, I felt sorry for them and even washed some sheets for them as well as got them glasses of water and Ginger Ale. It was gross but farm work had sometimes been gross too. I drew the line at fluffing up pillows for them.

I went to school and then work, the next day as they recovered. One of the guys that sat with me at lunch asked me if I'd called to see if they needed anything. The thought had not occurred to me. I called them before I left school. They were thinking they could eat something. I bought eggs and bread, then made scrambled eggs and toast for them. I couldn't believe I was cooking when I hated it so much. I also reconsidered doing anything else for them because they were griping about the menu.

At work, one of the girls was out sick so I did most of her job too. She was someone who helped the boss a lot with everything he didn't know. By the time I left that day I'd shown him several short cuts and ways to do things in the computer software they used as well as shown him how to text on his cell phone. He was quite impressed with me but then I was good with technology, at least at work. At home I preferred to be clueless. It was my private joke.

By the third day, all but Rick was feeling pretty good. I never did get sick. There was griping about that too from the band. I wondered if any of them would have catered to me had I become sick.

When I was in school those first two weeks I'd think of how Kevin and I had met and that he needed to be in school too. He was beginning to look happier but I knew it was hard for him. He hadn't met anyone his age or with the same interests and he missed Wendy even though they had broken up before we had moved. He usually had a day off during the week so I suggested he hang out with me at lunch time and right after school so he could meet people his own age. He'd borrow my truck to drive me to school then show up at lunch, then he'd pick me up after school. Sometimes I got on the school bus with the kids down the block. I still had tons of guys that followed me and wanted my time and so he got to meet a lot of guys. Some of the girls thought they'd steal Kevin away from me so he got female attention too. I was glad for him.

We had a fun conversation the first day he'd met me at school. "Damn! How many guys do you have chasing after you?" He asked me in awe as he drove us home.

"The whole school, I think." I replied in a disinterested voice.

"And you don't even care." He said as he caught my eye. "Do you know how many people would give their right arm to have that kind of attention?"

"Guys are trouble if you ask me." *And sometimes it's overwhelming.*

"But you finally have friends at school. Doesn't that make a difference? Remember how you hated school before because everyone was so mean to you?" He asked as he brought my truck to a stop at a traffic light.

"I'd go back to school at that hell hole if I could have my dad back." I mumbled as I looked out the window. But I was just depressed at that moment. My new school was refreshing and I enjoyed the attention, and for the most part I felt and acted normal around my classmates.

***

A guy named Jordan who was on the football team had wanted me to stay after school to watch the football team practice. He said he was a quarterback. I had no idea what a quarterback did. Several of the football players had sat with me at lunch and agreed with him when he'd asked me. "I hate to be a bummer, dudes, but I hate football." I had replied.

They laughed their asses off at that and then described how great it actually was. Football was the highlight of school. What was I thinking? I still hadn't acquired their viewpoint by the time our lunch break was over but I'd agreed to witness the senseless sport when school let out for the day.

I was sitting in the bleachers gazing out at the field wondering how my life had become such a charade when some of the cheerleaders appeared in front of me. "All the players date cheerleaders. I don't know why you're wasting your time. You're not a cheerleader and you'll never be one." Sandy, the head cheerleader informed me. I too wondered why I was wasting my time watching guys practice a sport that I didn't care for and that made no sense. Some of the other cheerleaders snickered while a few just stared at the guys. I also knew that I could be a cheerleader if I wanted to. Maybe if I'd been a kid, I would have, but as it was, I was too old for it. I'd lived a hundred years already it seemed.

I saw Kevin walking the edge of the field headed towards me. "I probably should go practice with my band." I remarked in an unfazed tone as I stood up.

"Yeah, go play with your instrument." A few giggled.

"Don't leave mad." One of them taunted.

I turned and regarded them. "If I ever get mad, you'll damn well know it." I replied. They continued saying mean things as I walked away. I didn't give a fuck. The guys would just tell me that they were jealous and to ignore them even if I never mentioned anything the cheerleaders had said to me.

I knew that Kevin noticed all the girls because he made a point to hug me as we reached each other. When he felt intimidated or unsure, he was like my shadow, sometimes a clinging shadow.

"Why are you walking this way? I thought we'd stay and talk to the kids." He asked as he surveyed the situation.

"Nah, I've had enough." I replied.

He glanced longingly at the kids for a moment then reached out to hold my hand as we turned to leave. I glanced over at him wanting to be aggravated but knew that I shouldn't. I understood his uncertainty. We were living a totally new life where the rules hadn't been established yet. I just really didn't give a fuck about it. I was a guardian, I let him take my hand. "Are you sure you don't want to stay? We have time." He remarked as he looked back again at my classmates.

"Nah, let's get the hell out of Dodge." I replied.

"Okay. I'm starved anyways. We should eat Chinese. Surely, we could find a good place around here." He remarked to me.

"If we eat out you know we have to take food to the others." I replied.

He huffed at that because when they ate out, they never brought food back for us.

"Wait!" I heard one of the cheerleaders calling to us. We stopped walking and she sprinted over to us, pompoms bouncing in her hand. I remembered that her name was Gabby and I figured she had a crush on Kevin.

Kevin smiled at her and she smiled back.

"Don't mind those jerks." She advised. "They're just jealous of you."

Kevin scrunched his face up, partly in confusion and partly wondering what I'd gotten myself into. In the past I'd gotten myself into a LOT of things. I saw Gabby glance at our hands. A look crossed her face that made her think twice about Kevin and my relationship. We had told them previously that we were just friends. We sure didn't look like "just friends" at that moment.

He dropped my hand at that point evidently noticing what she'd noticed.

"Do you see me caring about their bullshit? They don't mean jack shit to me." I told her in a bored voice.

"Angel!" Kevin said in a low warning tone.

I gave him a weird look. I didn't think I'd come across as being angry.

"Hey! Where are you going? I thought you were going to watch us practice." I heard Jordan ask as he was sprinting towards us.

Kevin smiled in amusement but I knew his smile was for me. He'd tease me later about the guys that ran after me. He and Kevin did a fist bump and a "hey man".

I noticed then that several of the players, and cheerleaders including Sandy were right behind him.

"We have twenty minutes left of practice then we're all going to David's Burgers." Jordan continued. "You'll go with us, won't you?" He glanced at me, then Kevin who agreed with him.

It was fun to see the anger on Sandy's face as the guys were now all assuring me how great it would be. I had yet to say a word.

I observed it with interest. Guys flocking after me and they were my age. Huh. Kevin bumped his shoulder against mine to get me to respond.

"Yeah, cool." I agreed. I didn't even have to give a fuck or say a word and they all wanted me. And it was all positive attention now. Huh. I totally didn't fucking understand it but I also didn't care. All I felt was this deadness inside of me knowing my dad was dead and that I was now responsible for the immature clan I was living with. How had I suddenly become the oldest? I hadn't signed up for this.

"Well, it's settled then." The guys smiled. The coach was yelling at them by that time to get their asses back on the field and they sprinted back to practice.

"Why the fuck do they care about her?" Sandy griped loud enough for me to hear as the cheerleaders turned to walk back towards the bleachers. Gabby was smiling at Kevin over her shoulder as she walked with them.

"You're going steady with Mark. Why should you even care?" I heard another cheerleader ask.

"Whatever it is, I wish I had it. At least I'd put it to good use." Kevin mumbled just loud enough for me to hear.

I smiled at him and reached out to grab him. I'd wrestle him to the ground at home. He jumped out of my reach and ran. I ran after him. I restrained myself from taking him to the ground in front of our peers.

***

"I don't have a ride." Gabby remarked to Kevin as we walked towards our vehicles to head to the burger joint.

"You're riding with me, right?" Jordan shouted to me as he neared us.

"No, I'm riding with Kevin." I replied back.

He tried to persuade me.

"No, this is my truck, and that's how I'm getting there."

"But you're gonna sit with me when we get there?"

"Yeah." I agreed. That seemed to pacify him and he walked towards his dad's truck. Sandy trotted after him. It occurred to me that everything I owned was mine. Daddy hadn't paid for anything I had while our peers still had their parents behind their possessions. I wondered if I hadn't ended up in the abusive foster family's care if I would have had a real childhood. My conclusion only made me angry. I stuffed that feeling down.

I stood at the passenger door and so did Gabby. Kevin had already assured her that she could ride with us and that we'd take her home. He hadn't asked me, but I didn't care. I didn't care about much at all anymore. "Aren't you driving?" She asked me.

"Nope. Get in." I replied as I clicked the fob and unlocked the doors.

She gave me one last look and got in the truck so she was between Kevin and I. He smiled at her. "Angel doesn't like to drive." He told her. When she asked all kinds of questions about us, I stayed quiet.

"Do you live close to each other?" She asked.

I wondered if Kevin would lie about that. He'd slept in my bed curled around me the night before. It had been comforting to the both of us although he had wanted to talk half the night. I'd fallen asleep on him. "She has a guardian and I live with them." He finally replied.

That took her by surprise and she stared for a moment. "Please don't tell me you sleep together."

"No. I have my own room. She's just my friend." Kevin quickly replied.

Gabby looked at me to confirm. "He's not my boyfriend and he's not my lover, but he is my best friend." I told her matter-of-factly.

I could see she wasn't in love with the situation. I certainly wasn't in love with it either, not because of Kevin, but because of Rick and Carol.

As she asked other questions like why were we holding hands, I realized that the whole situation was not going to work out well. I knew Kevin didn't want to admit that he was a scaredy cat, and neither of us wanted to talk about the fact that we were both minors and living in a fairly toxic environment. And, that there wasn't much we could do about it. He couldn't live with his abusive parents, and I couldn't stand to go back to a town where I was hated.

"I guess it's silly but this move and all the change that has come with it has been hard and she gives me strength." I heard Kevin admit. I hated that he'd had to admit that. I probably wouldn't have. I didn't like people to see any weakness in me and I didn't think other people should show weakness either.

So that brought up why we had moved. I was glad we'd reached the burger joint and I was able to get out of that conversation. There was no way that I wanted to hear Kevin talk about my dad dying or his parents being abusive assholes.

There were three football players that didn't have girlfriends and they all intercepted each other vying for my attention. They rushed around buying my meal and refilling my drink and just about feeding me while Kevin glanced over a time or two shaking his head at the situation. I made a face at him at his last glance because he had two girls and two guys sitting with him. It wasn't like he wasn't getting any attention. But then I had a table full of guys sitting with me as two more random guys from our high school had squeezed into our table.

The guys sitting with me wanted to go somewhere after we ate. I bugged out telling them that my guardian was expecting me home. Gabby had to go home anyway so it was just as well. Rick wasn't really expecting me home, it's just that I didn't feel a spark with any of them and I didn't want a boyfriend anyway. Plus, they had asked several questions that I had already opted out of by diverting the subject. I wasn't interested in becoming anybody's booty call.

"Those guys are into you, and it's no wonder. You're gorgeous! Do you like any of them?" Gabby asked of the football players as Kevin was driving.

"I'm not girlfriend material. I gots too much independence." I replied, evading her question.

"Well, you're so beautiful and smart. It's no wonder they like you." She continued as she ran her fingers through the bottom of my long hair. On an average day I would have laid her out flat or at least blinked in surprise, but I did neither. Kevin knew a dangerous moment and he quickly averted Gabby's attention to himself.

Her and Kevin chatted while I tuned out. He kissed her before she got out of the truck.

"I got a kiss and that was the first time I've ever talked to her. Na na na na na." He gloated as we watched her walk to her front door. They'd made eyes at each other before but had never talked.

"Whatever. I could have gotten fucked by any boy there, including you." I countered.

"Braggart!" He replied in mock aggravation. "I'm ready right now." He added but I wasn't going there. "Next time, Kev, walk her to the door, huh? That's what real men do."

"Yeah, I should have." He replied. I knew he was beating himself up now that he'd messed up. He'd learn. I'd continue to teach him as Daddy had taught me, and I should have nudged him to do it as Gabby got out of my truck.

Later, I was sitting on my bed reading a chapter in my history book. Kevin was lying with his head on my lap disturbing my reading. He didn't seem to care that my book was resting against the side of his head. "So, this is what it would have been like to have had a normal teenage experience of friends in high school." He murmured thinking of our outing with the high schoolers. He was happy. I shook my head to myself. It's not like he hadn't had friends in school like this before, or a girlfriend for that matter. I was the one that never had them. Yeah, I couldn't even say that school felt normal. I felt like I didn't belong there, that I had already graduated. I was beyond school.

"Kevin, I don't see this lasting for whatever reason so don't get too attached to it." I replied.

"Why?"

"I don't know." I grumbled. "You know how life has a way of jerking your world apart. It just seems like it's gonna rip this apart too."

"Shit."

"In the meantime, I don't think we need to bring anyone from my school here or talk about the band. And we don't want people knowing your situation. I'd hate for your mom to find out where you are and jerk you back so the less people that know, the better."

"Oh my God! Do you think that's going to happen?" He asked as he jerked into a sitting position to look at me. My book closed and fell off my lap.

I felt a huge wave of fear shoot through me which jerked my insides. Sometimes it amazed me to feel other people's emotions. Sometimes I felt emotions but didn't know they belonged to someone else. I realized that I was automatically diffusing the fear. Huh. Didn't know that I'd learned to do that automatically. "Um, no, I really don't think so at this moment but she would have that right if she chose it. I didn't mean to scare you. But let's just be careful, huh?" I should have kept my mouth shut because then I had to listen to him fret about something that I just wanted us to be careful about.

Around 9pm I was by myself in my bedroom. The door was closed and I was lying on my bed with my favorite white Gibson guitar across my chest. I could hear Carol downstairs screeching at Kevin about whatever. I knew David was home but I had no idea where Rick was.

I hadn't planned to play but then I'd plugged in the amp. I closed my eyes and heard "Freebird" in my head. My fingers began playing it. I rocked my shoulders and head back and forth to the rhythm of my playing.

I felt the atmosphere change as someone invaded my space. I imagined it was Kevin and I'd had enough of him so I ignored him and continued playing. But as he sat at the end of my bed, I smelled David's cologne. "What the hell are you doing?" David asked over my playing.

Without missing a note or opening my eyes I answered, "What the hell does it look like? And who the hell invited you in my room? The door was closed."

I'm gonna be on the front of this magazine soon." He remarked.

I opened my eyes and stopped playing. He was holding up a guitar magazine. "I'll be on the cover of that magazine soon but there's no way you'll ever be on it." I informed him.

"You think you're hot shit." He scoffed. "I can play better than you can."

"Whatever you need to believe to like yourself." I muttered.

"I'll prove it. Give me your guitar."

As he reached for my Gibson, I batted him away. "No. This guitar is sacred. I'm the only one permitted to play it. Daddy bought it for me for our first gig, remember?"

He argued with me about my possessiveness over my Gibson but in the end, he left to go get his own guitar. I lay back on my bed, closed my eyes, and began playing another song. I was kind of tired and I was hoping he wouldn't come back. There was no need for him to try to outdo me on guitar. I was the best.

I grumbled a moment later when I heard him come back and plug in his amp. He'd unplugged my guitar and it fell silent. He let a note whine for me. "Go away." I told him as I looked over to see what he was doing. I was glad he'd brought his own amp rather than using mine.

He sat at the bottom of my bed with his guitar and started playing some damn simple song. I grumbled again and sat up to lean against the headboard of my bed. "At least play something hard." I told him.

"Oh, like "Freebird" he scoffed. "I can play that song. You're not the only one. Plus, I can play it better than you."

He launched into the guitar solo of "Freebird".

I shook my head in the negative as he played as if he was awful but he could play the song. I'd already known that he could. I liked to tell him that he sucked at guitar. It helped him to practice more and play better.

I think we both jumped as Carol suddenly stormed in my bedroom screeching. "STOP PLAYING THAT DAMN SONG! Why do you have to be a bitch and play that song nonstop?"

David abruptly stopped playing.

"Yeah, what the hell, bitch?" I asked him with a straight face.

"Oh, it's you." She said as she realized that David had been playing rather than me. "I don't know why you have to stoop to her level."

"We're playing music. That's what we do." He replied in a cold voice.

"You know, the both of you are a pain in the ass. Dumb fucks."

"Like you're not?" He shot back. She was exiting my room at that point. We heard her mutter more cuss words at us. We shared a look and I nodded at him to plug my guitar back into my amp. I picked up my guitar and the both of us began playing the Freebird solo, smiling as we did so.

A while later after another dramatic scene in the house, peace had been restored and I realized that David had videotaped the entire thing. He'd set his video recorder on my dresser when my eyes had been closed. He still had this idea that he would make a few DVDs of stuff I did before I became a star, then he'd sell it and make millions of dollars. I wondered how I would feel when that time came.

CHAPTER 2

Since Kevin hardly made any money working at the grocery store, I helped him look for another job. I felt good about a construction site I passed on the way to school. I told him about it, gave him a pep talk of what to say and he applied and got the job. It was hard work and he had to toughen up his personality but it worked out for him, plus he now made enough money to pay his own bills. The job was also within a mile of where we lived so he didn't need a car to get there.

Several times I had walked in on Rick and Carol having sex in some room of the house. They seemed to get a thrill out of being caught by the rest of us. I hardly felt any reaction to it. Mostly I just felt numb and generally cheated by life. Yeah, I was taking care of Kevin as I had promised but who was taking care of me? There was no longer anyone to hold me and assure me that everything would be all right, like daddy had always done. There were a few times I was tempted to shift into level two or three in my mind but every time I had the thought, the cherub would whisper in my ear that I had to keep a clear mind or my life would be so much worse. So maybe what I ended up doing became a worse solution. When I couldn't stand the stress of the household, I retreated into a story in my mind where my parents were still alive and I'd had a normal childhood. It made me feel better because in the fantasy I had lots of agreeable friends that thought I was the coolest chick ever and my parents loved me. The two people I thought of being my parents were a young couple that had tried to adopt me when I was a toddler. They were killed in a car crash and I ended up in the orphanage. The fantasy would have been about my dad but the pain was just too fresh from it. I also started listening to "Still the Same" by Bob Seger. I set it on repeat on my CD player sometimes. Both things became habits.

I had people I talked with at school and work but none of them were good friends like Rick, Carol, Kevin and David had been before we moved in together. It was harder to be friends when you lived together and people became lazy. We fought about whose turn it was to do the dishes, clean house, pay bills, etc. After one particularly nasty fight about housework, I went down to the park to run it off my mind. Running had become another stress outlet. I would rather have ridden my motorcycle but Bob, my former guardian, refused to let me bring it with me. It didn't matter though, there was no place to ride a dirt bike where we lived now anyhow. I ran for a while and then began walking home. I had a term paper to write and I didn't know how I would be able to finish it before it was due. Out of the corner of my eye, I saw something small running toward me. It wasn't so small as it began to jump on me, hitting my waist. It was a reddish colored Chow puppy. "Arf!" It barked happily. By the way it moved and barked, it eerily reminded me of Yellow, although it looked nothing like him. Yellow had been a handsome Golden Retriever that I'd confided in as I was growing up. He had died the year before.

"Yellow?" I asked as I knelt down to dog level.

"Yer-Arf! Arf!" The dog exclaimed as it licked my face and put on a real show.

"Biscuit!! Biscuit, get over here!" Yelled a male voice, followed by the male himself. He was a brown eyed, brown-haired guy about five foot eleven who looked a bit older than I. "Sorry, she usually doesn't act like this around strangers. Actually, she's usually skittish. She yanked out of her leash to run to you." He told me as he pulled her away and put the leash on her.

That's because she used to be my dog, I thought to myself although it seemed impossible. Besides, Yellow had been a male. This was a female dog and a different breed. "I like her." I replied. At that moment she was still bouncing around and not following his commands. She seemed very happy to see me. "Sit." I told her. I held the vision in my mind of the dog sitting down.

The dog looked curiously at me and then plopped down in a sitting position. The astonishment on the guy's face made me laugh. "How'd you do that? I've been trying to teach her commands but she hasn't learned any yet." He exclaimed.

"She likes me. Can I have her?" I asked although I doubted he'd give her up and what would I do with her anyway? The landlord wouldn't allow us to have any pets. I mean, she wasn't Yellow anyway, she just had some of his characteristics.

"No. She's my dog." He replied, taken aback.

"Well, okay. I'm C. Angel Devito. What's your name?"

"Jace Hart." He said after a moment. "What's the C stand for?"

25

"Christmas." I smiled back. I liked his manly short haircut and the way he looked so comfortable in a black baseball cap, blue jeans and a black sweatshirt, those were my colors.

He laughed. "Sorry, I didn't mean to laugh. Christmas is an unusual name. I like it though. I was heading to the park. Do you want to tag along?"

I agreed. He told me that he lived a few blocks away and liked to walk Biscuit in the park. He said he was a singer and a lead guitarist in a band called "Streethart". He said he worked at a pizza shop but really hoped one day to make it big with the band. For some reason I opened up to him. I felt a connection with him. I explained about daddy's death and the odd way that the band and I ended up together. It seemed apparent now that as a band, we really had come to New York on a whim. Rick's friend really couldn't give us any help. But we were here and I felt that this is where we were supposed to be.

Jace seemed understanding. He told me where his band had started playing and suggested that we try those clubs too. Streethart was at least well known. He told me to meet him outside a certain club a few hours later and I could meet his band if I wanted to. He started singing one of the Rolling Stone's songs they would be playing later that night. I usually don't sing that much but I joined right in. I thought we sounded pretty good together and I knew that I had impressed him even though he didn't say so. I was kind of surprised at myself. He asked me for my number and I gave it to him.

I went home and started writing my term paper. I wondered what I would tell Rick in order to get out of the house to meet with Jace. Neither Rick or Carol were home when I left so I didn't have to explain anything. David and Kevin were drinking and watching a horror flick and barely acknowledged me leaving the house.

I popped my CD of "Still the Same" and my other favorite songs into the CD player of my truck. I was fifteen minutes late pulling into the parking lot at the club. I'd listened to "Still the Same" over and over as I drove. I spotted Jace and some guys leaning against a van. "I didn't think you were going to show. We were about to give up on you." Jace remarked as I approached them.

"I got lost." I replied, glancing at the others. I had looked up the directions but somehow it had taken me other places first.

Jace introduced me to his band. There was Jimmy, who was quiet and serious; Smith, who was tranquil and brilliant; Curt, who was spontaneous and an avid dreamer; and Greggie, who was cute and cuddly like a teddy bear. As they walked with me into the club, and asked me questions, I took an instant liking to all of them. I found the attention very flattering, although I had a suspicion that they were all a lot older than I was.

As if reading my mind, Greggie asked, "How old did you say you were?"

"Sixteen." I replied hesitantly. "And you?"

They eyed each other a little warily (I thought) before Greggie smiled and said, "Twenty-three."

I looked at the others. Each answered with an age in their twenties. Jace said he was twenty-one.

"No wonder you're all so well behaved." I grumbled.

"She doesn't know us that well, does she?" Smith laughed and the rest of the group did too.

Jace pulled me aside and said, "I didn't realize you

were that young. I thought you were eighteen."

"Oh, so you were only wanting to pick me up?" I asked with sudden realization.

His face reddened slightly. He looked towards the rest of the guys and then replied, "This is a club. You're underage first of all, then there are all these guys who are older than you. Don't let anyone sweet talk you into anything, including my band. And don't get drunk."

I felt pretty stupid at that moment and wanted just to bolt out the door. "Is every girl a piece of meat to you?" I asked.

He grabbed my arm as I was turning to leave. "You took that wrong. I'm just telling you how it is. I just want you to be careful in here. You're not with your band and I'll be on stage in a minute. I won't be able to watch out for you then. New York is a different atmosphere than South Carolina. I'm just trying to protect you here."

Before I could respond the rest of the band yelled at Jace to get with it, and he left me to go to the stage area. I just kept thinking about what he had said. I wondered if he and his band would want me around since they'd decided I was too young for them. Jace was already taking the role of protector. I didn't want to be protected. I just wanted some friends. I went into the crowd and watched their first set. I had to admit that they were good. They would be good competition for us. I wondered if Rebel could be better, if we ever got our act together.

And he was right. Several guys asked me to dance and gave me different pick-up lines but I handled them.

Nothing really was said after Streethart finished playing. I complimented their performance and we said goodnight. I got home about midnight. Rick didn't even know that I wasn't home. I let myself in the door with my key and went back to writing my term paper. I figured that him and Carol had probably been out drinking and had passed out after coming home.

The next day I told Rick about the clubs that Jace had mentioned. Surprisingly, he didn't ask me where I had gotten the names at, he just went to check them out. We auditioned for Club Nine but it didn't seem to work out. Two days later Club Nine called us and agreed to let us play that Friday, only because their regular band had cancelled out.

I was surprised a few days later when Jace called me.

"I didn't think you'd call me. I thought I was too young to hang out with you guys." I told him.

"Normally you would be, but it's not often I meet someone who performs like we do. You know, someone who can sing and play an instrument on stage. Everyone in my band likes you. The other night I was just trying to warn you. I'd give that speech to any girl that just moved here."

"So does that mean you want to be friends?"

"Yeah. Are you into basketball? There's a court nearby. We can shoot some hoops."

Hmmm, I thought, now I'm one of the boys, but I guessed that was okay. It was still friendship.

"You don't have a motorcycle, do you?" I asked.

"What? No. No motorcycle. Why?"

"I had to leave mine in South Carolina." I replied.

"That's funny." He laughed.

I didn't correct him. "Well, let's just play basketball then."

We met at the park and played a few games.

"We can run together sometime." I told him.

"I don't go for running or jogging." He said sinking another basket. He was beating me pretty badly. "I guess foot races are okay, though." He added.

I debated over that and decided we could race. I wasn't that tired after playing basketball and Jace claimed he wasn't so we decided on one race for the road. I pointed out a tree that would be the finish line.

"Piece of cake." He remarked.

Well, he wasn't saying that as I made it to the tree and he was still several yards behind me. I thought he might get mad but he said that he guessed he was "tired" and that we should call it a day.

***

Our first gig at Club Nine had all of us nervous. Jace had given me some pointers of what and what not to do so I felt a little better about it. He said that he and Streethart had a gig at another club that night and wouldn't be able to come watch us perform. He sounded disappointed and I wondered if it was because he wanted to know how much competition we were going to be for his band.

Our gig turned out to be one of our better performances but even so I knew that we were only filling in for the one night that their regular band couldn't be there.

Jace and I began hanging out together when time permitted. At times we'd walk Biscuit. Jace would tease me that I hung around him just to visit with his dog. At times that was the case, but I didn't tell him that. Mostly we'd go play basketball. If it was a cold or rainy day we'd go to the YMCA or to the gym. I wasn't that crazy about basketball but I had nothing better to do either. Jace was also teaching me to play racquetball so whenever a court was open at the gym, we'd play a few games. I felt like one of the guys and that was okay. One day I was telling him about a book I had read and he asked if he could borrow it. I had never brought him to my house to meet the band and only talked vaguely to the others about him. They rarely told me what they did with their time and I didn't elaborate about mine. Life was rather tense at home.

Jace wanted to start reading that night so I drove him to our house. As we approached the front door, I wondered how bad of shape the house was in. I tried the door. It was unlocked. As we walked through the front door, I found the house to be what had become its usual untidy state, with Kevin and some girl named Shelley, passionately making out on the couch. Her bra was off and Kevin was sucking on her nipple. This was actually normal so I should have known better than to allow Jace into the house without first scouting out the area. Neither Kevin or Shelley even flinched knowing we were watching them. Ignoring them, I said to Jace, "Let's just go upstairs."

He gave me an uneasy look. "Sorry, but I don't make it with minors." He replied.

Laughter could be heard from the vicinity of the couch.

I just stared at him for a moment. "I meant to get the book." I finally replied.

He glanced once more at them and then followed me upstairs to my room which had posters on the wall, a made bed and nothing strewn on the floor. He sat on my bed and looked around as I rummaged through my closet looking for the book he wanted. "Does this sort of thing go on all the time around here?" He asked.

"Yeah, but I've seen worse. Like the time they were all drunk and had the place trashed or the time Rick's friend was trying to ride his motorcycle through the house." I answered from almost inside the small closet. I found the book and crawled out. Jace was staring at a picture of me and Kevin on my motorcycle. Daddy kept hoping that Kevin would become my boyfriend. He was even cool about the fact that Kevin and I had slept together.

"I thought you were kidding about the motorcycle." Jace remarked, now intensely looking at the photograph. There was another one beside it of me in midair on that bike. I couldn't remember who had taken that photograph. David was the photographer and I hadn't met him or any of the band at that point in my life. It had to be one of the dads that had taken them.

I spent a good thirty minutes telling Jace everything that had happened to me regarding the motorcycle. I even told him about Brad. Some of the story I sensed that he didn't believe. He could believe what he wanted to but it left me wondering why I had told him in the first place. I normally was all about the present and the future, not the past.

"So, Kevin isn't your boyfriend?" He asked, obviously puzzled by the photo of us and having just seen Kevin making out with another girl a minute ago.

"No. We just all live together. My dad really wanted him as a son-in-law though. He really loved Kevin, and David. I just wasn't into Kevin though." I replied as I gave him the book and sat on the bed beside him.

"Are you looking for me to be your boyfriend?"

I know I gave him a strange look. I was still pretty

depressed about my dad dying and everything else that had changed. "No. You're pretty conceited. Do you know that?" I replied. "I'm not into you. I have enough problems. If this closeness bothers you, we can stop hanging around together."

His face reddened slightly. "Uh, no. It's just that so many girls throw themselves at me. I know you better than that. It was stupid of me to say that. Sorry."

I managed to smile. "You're cute but you're not that cute." I remarked although I did think he was very cute.

"Thanks a lot." He replied sarcastically. "Do you have a boyfriend?" Before I could answer he looked intently at me and said, "You know I just realized that you don't talk about personal things much. You told me a lot the day I first met you about why you moved here, and today you told me about some of your life but in general you don't talk about yourself or the people you live with. You talk about my band all the time and what they're doing but all you talk about concerning your band is what your gigs were like. I don't know anything personal about them. I had no idea that you and Kevin had been an item, or that you could ride a motorcycle."

I began twisting the bedspread for something to do with my hand. "Kevin and I weren't an item. He was the first guy that wanted to hang with me and we became best friends. Look, I try to forget the band as much as possible. We used to be such good friends but anymore we are just individuals living in the same house. No one wants to do their share of anything around here. They don't even want to practice as a band anymore. I don't know how to get through to them. I'm just disappointed in it all. We supposedly moved here for our music. Jace, you're the youngest of your band and Rick who is the same age as you are the oldest in our band. We're just kids, and most of us are acting like babies."

"My band never lived together but we went through the same thing."

I really didn't think that he knew the half of it and I didn't want to talk about it anymore. "Yeah, well, let's go downstairs and get something to drink." I replied.

Jace hesitated. "What if your friends are buck naked now?" He replied almost seriously.

"Well, then we'll just watch." I grinned as I headed towards the door.

He stopped me before we left my bedroom. "Uh, are you serious? Do you watch them have sex?" he asked. He seemed surprised.

I hadn't thought much about that really. "Yeah, I've watched before." I told him. "Kevin and David walk around buck naked sometimes, and Rick and Carol like an audience, so yeah." I agreed.

He blinked in surprise. "Uh, wow. And Rick is your guardian, right?"

"Yeah, on paper anyway. Otherwise, he doesn't pay any attention to me unless he needs someone to take his anger out on."

"Do you run around buck naked too?" He asked.

"Oh, hell no, *it's far too cold to do that here.*" I replied as I scrunched my face up in distaste.

He eyed me with an emotion that I couldn't put my finger on. "I don't like that you live in a household of naked guys and where your guardian puts on a sex show." He finally said.

I suddenly realized that I should have kept my mouth shut about all of that. Maybe he would report us to the authorities. I shrugged my shoulders. "They're harmless. Are you going to report us?"

"No. But if I ever feel you're in danger I will."

I swallowed hard and hoped it never came to that. What he might think is danger might be a bunch of nothing.

He followed me downstairs. I glanced at the couch but Kevin and Shelley had disappeared probably to Kevin's bedroom.

"Hey, we're missing wrestling on channel 9." Jace said suddenly.

"You know, I'm a pretty good basketball player, the fastest runner, and I used to wrestle once in a while." I replied trying to change the mood. I clicked the tv to channel 9. Mostly I wrestled with Kevin and David, although not so much lately.

He laughed as if the mere thought was ridiculous. He commented on some of the moves the wrestlers were making on tv and then told me if I could wrestle, he'd take me on.

I smiled and tackled him. We hit the floor and I tried to pin him down. He was too strong for me and he proved it by throwing me off of him and gripping me in a hold that was hard to escape from. I relaxed for a second or two to catch him off guard. As I had expected, he loosened his grip. I sprung free and we tossed each other around, with him asking me now and then if I was okay. I had just gotten him into a good position that I thought I could hold him down in when Rick and Carol came home. They stood staring at us and Jace quickly and guiltily jumped to his feet. I slowly stood up. "You just ruined a great wrestling match." I informed them.

They nearly fell over laughing. "What a cool way to make a move on a guy!" Carol exclaimed.

I forced my face not to redden. "He's just a friend." I remarked and then introduced Jace to them.

"Hey, don't you play in the band, Streethart?" Rick asked him. Jace replied that he was and they began to talk music. As I noticed their instant bond, I knew that I'd never have to worry about Jace reporting us to the authorities.

Carol took me aside to tell me how cute Jace was. "He's just a friend of mine." I told her. "And he already has a girlfriend." I added.

"Doesn't mean you can't play dirty." She remarked. I wondered if Jace had heard her.

Soon after, Jace was ready to be driven back to the gym to pick up his truck and go home. When we were alone, he began happily chattering away about the talk he and Rick had had. He was obviously pleased that Rick was a fan of his. He thought they were really cool even if I no longer thought so. As he was getting out of my truck he paused just long enough to grin and ask, "So, are you going to play dirty?" He laughed.

"Might as well." I replied but he was already out the door.

The next day he was waiting for me as school let out. "Just wondering." He said. "You said you can play keyboard, right?"

"Yeah. Why?" I replied

He wanted to know if I could fill in for Smith during their concert that night. Smith was the keyboard player and although I was a master at keyboard, I'd never flaunted it. Carol would have flipped out if I did, but then again I wouldn't be playing anything complicated for their gig, and Carol wouldn't be around. Jace pointed out that our bands played a lot of the same songs. He wanted me to run over and practice with them. "I've got housework and homework to do." I told him.

"Talk your way out of it." He said. I called Rick and got an ear beating and extra chores to do. Even if I got home at midnight, I was to do these chores. I reluctantly agreed. He thought that I would be screwing Jace although I told him it wasn't so and he ended the conversation by telling me that I'd better not end up pregnant.

"What did he say?" Jace asked. "Can you play with us?"

I smirked at his wording.

"What?"

"Rick said I can play but I better not end up pregnant."

Jace burst out laughing.

We met up with Streethart at the club which wasn't open for customers yet. We gave it a trial run, our music echoing through the empty club. I told them what songs that our band usually played and we incorporated enough of them into a routine so that the performance was sure to be smooth sailing.

"That was great!" His band exclaimed after our trial run.

"Yeah Angel, quit Rebel and join Streethart and we'll fire Smith." Curt quipped.

"I'm really a drummer so if I joined Streethart I'd be taking your place not Smith's." I teased back.

"Good deal." Jace kidded.

"Personally, I'd love to have you join our group. You have a head for music and you're gorgeous to boot." Greggie said as he sided up to me and hugged me against him. I was rather intrigued by him and against my normal nature I snuggled right up to him. He was blond and blue eyed and I thought it was too bad that he was so much older than I.

Jace coughed at Greggie.

Greggie put his hands up in defeat and moved away from me. "What can I say? She is an Angel Babe. I can't help that she's still a baby."

"For being a drummer you sure can play the keyboard. Do you play any other instruments?" Curt asked, removing the awkward moment for me.

"Just about everything." I replied eyeing Jace's electric guitar.

Jace followed my eyes and handed his guitar to me. "No." He said wryly. "Tell me you can't play that."

"I'm a damn guitar legend. If you'd rather me not prove it you better say something right now." I grinned at him.

He laughed obviously not believing me then tossed me his guitar. It was a Fender American Standard Stratocaster Custom and it was pretty cool.

I launched into the Freebird solo and let it rip, partly to show off and partly because I was that good. And the thing was, that Freebird was like first grade for me and I'd long since graduated. I threw in a guitar riff afterward that was especially complicated but complimented the song.

There was almost a moment of silence after the last note sounded. It was awkward. They all looked amazed, even Jace. I remembered then, that Daddy had said not to come out with all my guns a blazing. Well, it was too late for that. I was armed with a machine gun and I'd let it rip.

"Shit. You're better than I am on guitar, and Jace

too." Greggie told me. "God, you're better than anyone I've ever heard play in person! How old were you when you could play that song?" His starry-eyed gaze wavered.

I stood there, cool and conceited. "Seven. I learned to play guitar when I was six." I smirked at his awestruck face. They were going to be shocked when I REALLY played keyboard for them.

"You've known me for how long and you never mentioned you could play like that?!" Jace burst out.

Everyone kind of stepped back in shock, even me. It only fueled my anger. "I didn't know it mattered!" I shot back. "For your information I'm good at a LOT of things!"

"Well, just name them." Jace replied. Now he was in my face.

The guys, who had just been standing in shock were now pretty much snickering.

I suppose I wasn't that angry because I caught hold of their snickering and it hit me as funny too. I turned and laughed with them.

"Now tell us what you're good at." Greggie purred fluttering his eyelids at me.

"I'm very good at 'that'." I replied seductively. "Not that any of you will ever know!" I added with a laugh.

"Dammit!" Greggie said slowly. I could see he was having a great daydream of it. Jace walked away without a word.

"Boy, you really floored him." Jimmy replied as we watched Jace disappear out the door. "Why did you do that? Couldn't you have just have plucked a few chords?"

"If you all have such fragile egos, I suggest you get

out of this business."

"Maybe, you should....." Jimmy began to say.

"I get it now." I interrupted as I stood in front of him. "You and Jace seem to think that women couldn't possibly do anything better than you. Well, most of us can. Get over it."

He began to tell me off but Greggie grabbed him by the arm and insisted they talk in private.

As all but Curt disappeared out the door, I turned to Curt. "Well, what do you think?" I asked him, just daring him to cross me.

He ignored my attitude. "You're cool with me." He replied as he lit a joint and took a drag. "Don't pay any attention to them. Wanna hit?" He asked as he held out the joint to me.

I jerked backward. "Uh, no. I don't smoke."

"Why don't you play lead guitar in your band?" He asked. He took a deep hit off the joint.

He had a good point. "They needed a drummer not a lead guitarist. I guess I should play guitar though." I replied thoughtfully. Although I was great on guitar and keyboard, I'd been happy playing the drums.

"We oughta get naked and fuck."

That remark jerked me back to the present really quickly. He had said it so smoothly. I had to just stare at him a moment. Even though I was good looking and guys hit on me all the time, I was still shocked sometimes by what they'd say to me. I was so stunned I couldn't even think of a reply. I guess I hadn't expected him to hit on me.

"I guess that's a no. Did I ever tell you about my friend Ruthie?" Curt was a story teller and he loved to talk. I knew he was trying to take away the awkward moment that he had created for me. Some of his stories were true but not many. He was an object of entertainment, maybe not to everyone, but he was to me. So, I listened.

It was fifteen minutes or so later when Jimmy, Greggie, and Jace reappeared. "Shit Curt! You didn't fucking get her high, did you?" Greggie growled as he smelled the pot smoke in the air.

Curt grinned. "Tried. She doesn't smoke, and she won't fuck me either." He replied.

Greggie shot Curt a dirty look. "Then let's rock," Greggie said to Curt and I. "We have a gig to play."

I must admit that I didn't think we'd pull it off but I was wrong. As soon as we started playing, the tension disappeared. Streethart was a more practiced and committed band than Rebel and I was able to pick up their signals to make the performance smooth. We ended up giving a very good performance.

Afterwards, I was struck that I didn't much care if Jimmy was still mad at me, but I did care what Jace thought. He was ignoring me. We were in the parking lot and he was ready to get in his truck. His girlfriend who had arrived sometime during the gig had already gotten in. "Hey, talk to me. Don't leave mad." I said as I came up behind him. He opened his door and got in. "You're better than me. What else is there to say?"

"Jace, what does she want?" his girlfriend demanded.

I ignored her. I couldn't even remember her name. "You shouldn't be mad at me." I told him.

"What, do you have something going on with her?" his girlfriend asked in alarm.

Jace turned to her and said something that I couldn't hear. Then he turned back to me. "I'm not mad anymore. Go home now."

I made one more eye contact with him before I moved back and he shut the door behind him and started up the truck. Then I turned and I walked to my truck. He was still angry. If that was the way he wanted to be then I guessed it would iron out sooner or later.

I was starting to unwind by the time I got home which was about 1 a.m. There was a note that Bob had called and wanted me to call him the next day. He checked on me about every two weeks. He still thought he was my guardian. He always gave me little threats and usually wanted to speak to Rick afterward. He thought that I would be ready to leave New York by now but I wasn't disgusted enough yet. What did I have in South Carolina anyway except my bike? Although truthfully, when things were so bad between me and the band, going back to South Carolina to ride my bike seemed like a good idea.

I sighed heavily and sat down. I really needed to do some work. I dragged myself back into a standing position and did over an hour's worth of housework before I even started on my homework. I fell asleep sometime after 3 a.m. I knew I would be dragging myself out of bed the next morning for school.

CHAPTER 3

Jace was waiting for me in the parking lot when I got to work. He was in front of my truck door as I got out as if I was going to go inside without talking to him. I kind of felt like it too. "Hey, I'm sorry about last night. I just wanted you to know." He said.

I moved forward so I could get beyond the truck and shut the door. I was surprised when he didn't move and that just made me closer to him. It also made me nervous, and I rarely got nervous. Since he wasn't moving, I started talking. It was hard for me not to move away but I was determined to let him know I would stand up to him. "Look, I'm not taking back what I said to Jimmy about the both of you. You both think that women can't do anything better than you. You need to get over it. I am who I am and I am very good at playing guitar. That's it, end of story." I pushed forward and he caught me in an unexpected hug. I lingered only long enough to look up at him, realizing my gift of guitar had now turned him on, then I pulled away. His erection had helped me to realize that.

"I don't think I'm that way." He replied as I shut the truck door.

When I didn't say anything he sighed and said, "What I came here to say is that I thought we were better friends than that. I thought that you might have mentioned something big like being great at guitar to me a while back especially since you know I play lead guitar. Why do you hold back so much?"

"Truce, okay?" I replied. "I don't think that I hold back information from you just like you don't think that women are the weaker sex."

He was leaning on my truck by then. "Then tell me something personal that no one else knows."

I leaned on my truck as well. "Actually, I already have. I slept with Kevin a few times in South Carolina. As far as I know, no one else knows. We've always been friends but we had sex when he stayed at our house. He was going to a foster home and he was really upset. He wanted to and I know I wanted to but we both went back to our girlfriend and boyfriend the next day. But the kicker is that my dad let me sleep with him during the whole week he stayed at our house. We never told anyone." I replied. "Now, you have to play guitar with me the next time we get together."

He shifted position to look at me closer. "Why would your dad do that?"

"Because Kevin's home situation had totally crushed him. My dad felt that I was the only one that could give him any comfort and he obviously didn't care if that comfort was sex. Don't get me wrong, it was fun for me, and Kevin is my best friend. It was just kind of weird knowing my dad let me do it."

"Have you slept with Kevin since?"

"No. It's only been a few months since my dad died and since his home life with his parents crashed. We kind of clung together when we first moved here but not so much anymore. I'm his sounding board. He tells me just about everything in his life and everyone else's.

We might fall asleep in bed together but we never do anything sexual anymore. He's seeing someone and there's this wall that's between the five of us since we started living together. It's just not as cozy as before..... But seriously, I want you to jam on guitar with me."

"But you would sleep with him..."

"Jace!" I said in exasperation. "Why don't you tell me how you're going to jam on guitar with me instead of asking me all this? I need to get inside before I'm late for work."

He smiled. "Yeah, I guess so."

I smiled at that and started walking towards the front door of my building.

"Would you sleep with me?" He called after me.

I was to the door by then. I jerked back around to him not believing that he had to nerve to ask me that, and to say it so loudly out in public where God and everyone could hear him. "No. And I can't believe you asked me that. I'm not a groupie." I replied angrily.

He smiled and shrugged his shoulders. I spun back around and walked into the building. That was the first time I did think of sleeping with him.

When I got home and no one else was home, I sat at Carol's keyboard and played one of Beethoven's harder pieces. Oh yeah! I still had it in me!

Club Nine called us before the week was over to see if we wanted to become their new house band. The former band had broken up and moved on. Hours after we agreed to become their house band, a club called Caterpillar Lounge wanted to know if we'd like to do a trial run of gigs on Wednesday nights for them. If it worked out, we'd be regulars on Wednesday nights. We agreed to that too since Club Nine would use us mainly on Fridays and a Saturday here and there. I was just glad we'd finally had some gigs.

On the Friday that started our stint as house band for Club Nine, I arrived at the pizza shop where Jace worked to tell him the good news. He was happy for us. Since it was an oddly warm day, he suggested that we play some basketball. He was just getting off work. We went to the park and were into our second game when it began to pour down rain. We ran to his truck and jumped in. We laughed at each other because we were both soaking wet.

"I guess we could go to my place." He remarked as he started up the truck. It was about dark anyway and we wouldn't have been able to play much longer.

I pushed my CD of "Still the Same" in the CD player.

He looked at me as the CD player started playing as if I should have asked him if it was okay to do that. But then he just chuckled and started driving.

I had never been to his apartment. It was just a small one bedroom apartment but it was far neater than Rebel kept our house. The furniture was dusty but nothing much was lying on the floor or cluttered everywhere. We let Biscuit out and she was quickly back inside. I waited for Jace to find some towels. He dug out a sweatshirt for me to change into and some clothes for himself. I was surprised when he began stripping right in front of me. I watched with interest and a little unexpected lust. He looked up suddenly. "Uh... if you want to get out of that wet shirt, the bathroom is that away." He said pointing the way. I must say that he looked pretty darn good in just his briefs.

I didn't look away immediately and when I didn't, I

sensed that at that moment Jace could lose his senses too. In the second my mind began to imagine what fun that would be, I was brought back to reality by suddenly also knowing that it would mean nothing to him afterward. He already had a string of women he was sleeping with and I wasn't even sure if he'd broken up with his girlfriend. I abruptly put myself in check and headed to the bathroom to change into the sweatshirt he'd given me.

When I came back the mood was gone. I made him get out his Fender Stratocaster and play. He argued a little with me but he did it. Then I made him get out an extra guitar that he had. I pressed him to play a song with me. It took a while but I finally got him to do it. Once that happened something seemed to click with him and we got to having fun with it. No longer was I the big threat. We were just two musicians playing music. I knew that he'd never forget that I could play better but he was at least more accepting of it. Later that night he followed me to Club Nine to watch me and my band perform.

Afterward we all went our separate ways. There were other clubs that were open most of the night and Rick and Carol went to one of them. I wasn't sure where the rest of them went, but me and Jace parted company and I went home to bed.

The next morning the phone woke me up. I grumbled because usually David or Kevin answered our phone, and neither of them were answering it. Rick was calling from jail and he wasn't happy that he'd had to call twice before I had answered. He and Carol had been arrested for drunken and lewd behavior. He wanted me to bail them out of jail. The bail was five hundred dollars. He was lucky the bank I used was open a few hours on Saturday but that left me to find someone who was of legal age to get them out of jail. I called Jace but he wasn't home. Greggie wasn't answering his phone either. I tried Smith's number and he groggily answered. It was about 10:30am but I suppose everyone had slept in that morning. I explained the situation to Smith and asked him if he would go to the jail with me to bail out Rick and Carol. He agreed and I met him there.

"I'm sorry about this, Smith." I told him as he got out of his car.

"It's all right." He answered.

I gave the money to him and we walked into the building. He dealt with the personnel there then handed me the receipt. "It will be a while before they get out of here." He replied. "Do you want me to wait with you?"

"No. I'm just grateful that you're helping me out. I'll wait for them. Thanks." I replied.

"No problem." He smiled.

I watched him walk out the door. I liked him for the parental vibe he and his wife had towards me. I'd wanted him to stay but my pride at wanting to appear so adult had gotten to me.

After about an hour later Rick and Carol appeared. They were sullen and angry, and hardly said two words to me as I drove them to the bar where Rick's car was still parked. They slammed the door shut on my truck as they got out. I watched that Rick's car started and he put it in gear, then I headed the other direction to the park to run it off. They hadn't even said thank you, and I knew they'd never pay me back.

At home, I slipped back into my fantasy world as I often did when I was alone or just stressed. I wished the fantasy life with my parents were real because life was so good with them. It kept my mind off all the pain I'd gone through with the abusive foster family and my daily life outside of my home with Daddy.

***

The boys at school had begun to realize that I wasn't interested in any of them but that didn't stop them from hanging around me. The ones that did stop following me were replaced by others thinking that they had a chance but the only guy I was interested in was Jace. He just wasn't interested in me, at least not as a relationship.

Kevin continued to come to my school to hang out with the boys that followed me, and the girls that followed them. He had borrowed my truck and taken Gabby out several times. Mostly they talked on the phone. It was a problem that he didn't have a vehicle to drive. He had ignored what I'd said and told her our story, and she also knew that we played in a band. "Kevin plays guitar. He played this really cool song for me yesterday!" She gushed to the others after school one day. One of the guys just happened to have an acoustic guitar in his car. He appeared with it. "Let's hear you play." He said to Kevin.

Now there were several guys and girls with us and Kevin wasn't comfortable being singled out for anything even if he was good at it. He'd never be a lead singer or a lead guitarist because it made him too nervous. And he also wasn't that good on the fly when someone asked him to do something spur of the moment if it put him in the spotlight. It could be a song that he had played perfectly every time we performed it at a club but in front of a few friends, he'd flub it up. "Angel can play better than I can. We're in a band together." He blurted out. Yeah, I had expected that. He liked to hide behind me most times.

I know my eyes bugged out because I had warned him not to go telling people our business. I hadn't told anyone that I could play an instrument. I gave him the evil eye but he acted like he didn't know what the fuss was about.

"Okay, you play, since you're in a band in all." The guy said as he reached to hand me his guitar.

"Play Photograph." Someone remarked.

Photograph was a Nickelback song and I'd played it a few times in the past. I ignored the snarky way he'd talked to me and accepted his guitar. I didn't play much acoustic guitar but I'd humor them. I sang "Photograph" as I played his guitar.

Everyone had a different attitude after that. "You really are good!" they gushed even though it was a super simple song to perform vocally and instrumentally. And now they had questions and more song requests. Kevin answered them. "We're playing at the Caterpillar Lounge Wednesday night." He said. I closed my eyes in frustration for a few seconds. If anything happened negatively because of it, it was his fault. I'd warned him.

At work, my co-workers were envious and my boss impressed when I told him that a manual process, we had been doing could be easily automated. I'd drawn up an outline of the fields that the system would need to reference and how the system should process the data. He had me work with the I.T. department, then called me into his office where he talked and talked about the vision of the company. He wanted my thoughts and so the voices in my head gave me conversation for him. Before I left for the day, he'd given me an unheard of two dollar an hour raise and a two-hundred-dollar bonus. I kept that tidbit to myself. He'd also had big plans for me; however, I hoped that by the time I graduated high school that our band would have become famous. Music would be my only job then.

Wednesday night, I was rocking out the drums on Sympathy for the Devil by the Rolling Stones when I noticed Jordan and some of the other football players stroll in. The Caterpillar Lounge was pretty packed that night with adoring fans. He was looking at me with a rather shocked expression on his face. I nodded nonchalantly acknowledging him. He looked over the rest of the band.

At break, they came over to chat, as did a few other guys that were in the club. I stayed by Kevin so he could answer all their questions. "Why do you let him talk for you when you're together?" Jordan demanded as Kevin walked away to go to the restroom. "Could you give us a minute?" Jordan asked the other guys standing around. They transferred their attention to Carol.

"Because he always has the answers." I replied. I mean, who cared if I ever said another word in public? Why were people so damn curious anyways?

"I thought you played guitar."

"I play several instruments including guitar."

Jordan went on to quiz me about the band and the instruments I played and if I'd reconsider being his girlfriend. We'd kissed before but I always had other things to do when he'd asked me out. I'd watched girls flock to him before because he was a good-looking popular guy. He didn't understand why I wouldn't be interested in being his girlfriend. I wasn't sure either.

"I can't be tied down. I'm a lone wolf." I replied.

"Do you not like men?"

"I'm interested in someone who doesn't go to our school."

"Woman or man?"

I cocked one eye at him. "Man." I replied. "Why do you even ask that?"

"You sure looked interested in Jenn when you were talking to her at school today."

I chuckled. "She was talking about big fucking trucks. I love big fucking trucks." Oh my God, that was funny. I had adoration for any person who talked about big fucking trucks.

Carol busted in on us at that point and started flirting. When he turned his attention to her, I exited the scene. She'd offer to fuck him and he would. That happened with any guy that talked to me. Who needed a guy like that?

I was angry after that and I fought with Kevin when we got home. If it hadn't been for him no one at the school would even have found us at the club.

***

At school, I had even more kids following me around because word had gotten around that I played the drums in a real honest to God band, and that I could play guitar too. Now kids wanted advice on how to get gigs at clubs like we were doing. Kids I didn't even know were bringing me gifts and asking for my autograph and wanting their picture taken with me. "I like McDonalds." I told a few of the gift givers. Yep, there was nothing better than an Egg McMuffin or a Big Mac, and so I was getting fed too. It totally blew my mind because it was a complete opposite of my previous school life in South Carolina. School had started out good here and had gotten better. Huh.

One guy brought out his electric guitar as several others stood outside of the school talking as school let out. "Play something cool. I got the power pack here for the amp. I can't play for shit but I bet you could tear this mother fucker up!" He said, his eyes bright with anticipation. The others agreed with him.

He plugged the guitar in to the power pack and the amp. I took the guitar from him but hesitated, mostly for stage effect.

"C'mon!" they urged.

So, what could I do but take a cool guitar hero stance, throw my hair back and burn that place down? I'd once stood outside the corner store and played guitar after the store owner had complained that business was slow. I'd gathered a crowd too until daddy had driven up and stopped my concert. It had gotten the store more business and he had wanted me to come back. Daddy told him, no, I was only eleven, and I had no business doing what I'd done. I'd been angry about that.

"Sharp Dressed Man" by ZZ Top was one of my favorite songs and I'd always liked the guitar in it so I laid it on them. I just loved how people's eyes always popped out when I played, and it was an easy song! Oh yeah! By the time I was into a second song, there were three times as many kids standing around as there had been. I had no idea that many kids loitered around the school after classes were over. Several of them assured me that they'd come to hear me play. Now that was the ticket!

All of us were really hating the cold and the snow when it came, and it came fast. The first really cold night I hardly took any clothes off to go to bed. I lay there thinking about the snow that was coming down outside and wondering why we couldn't have picked a warmer place to live. We'd been fighting about the gas bill and so the temperature was set at a mere 68 degrees. It just felt a lot colder than that. Plus, none of us had more than one blanket which was going to have to change.

Light from the hallway filtered into my bedroom as someone opened the door and came in. None of them seemed to know what privacy was since we'd moved in together. I jerked as Kevin crawled in bed with me without asking. Since he was with Gabby we weren't supposed to be sharing a bed. "What?" I asked him.

"I'm about to freeze my balls off. I need body heat." He replied as he moved to cuddle with me.

I grumbled. I liked to have the entire bed to stretch out on and I could hog the entire bed by myself. I further grumbled as his cold feet touched mine. Daddy never told me that there would be times like this. Well, maybe he had and I'd not listened.

"Stop being a bear." He murmured.

A few moments went by and I got used to his cold feet against my legs. It was warmer and I thought maybe I could fall asleep then. But then my bedroom door opened again.

"Stop it." I said as David was pushing me into the middle of the bed. The bed was only a double so it was a tight squeeze.

"I'm fucking cold. Hurry up and move over." He said.

I growled and he scooted me over because I hadn't

moved. He had his blanket with him and he spread it over us.

"This ain't gonna work! Seriously. One of you or both of you go back to your own beds!" I protested. "There ain't enough room in this bed. I didn't sign up for this. This is a chick's bedroom, you know. I can't be cramped up if I'm gonna sleep."

"Shut up." David replied as we were now all squished together.

"Dammit!" I muttered.

"Shut up and go to sleep, grouchy bear." Kevin replied.

I sighed in resignation. There was some nudging and shifting as we tried to get comfortable in that small amount of bed. Then they were warning each other and me not to snore.

"I'm gonna bop you both in the head if you don't shut up and go to sleep." I told them as I yawned a big yawn. My awake time was over and that was the last thing I remember. In the morning, they grumbled that I had snored the loudest. Ha ha.

***

I was sitting in music class not paying attention. Jordan had been on my ass about my not wanting to socialize with him outside of school. It had been my fault as I had let him kiss me in the stairway after lunch. Meanwhile Kevin had been on my case to have sex with him because Gabby wasn't putting out. Then there were all the other guys that wanted a piece of me in any way they could get it. I had guys drawing sketches of me in class and drooling over my guitar playing, and following me and wanting my phone number. OH MY GOD. Teachers wanted homework from me, Work wanted me to pose in a swimsuit and lingerie for their spring catalog and I wasn't agreeing with them. I was wondering if they'd fire me because of my refusal. Then there was Carol tie dying everything that didn't move. She'd tie dyed the one sheet set I had and two of my white shirts and my two pair of white panties. I was aggravated over the shirts. Kevin was just as into it as she was. Both of them were driving us all crazy with the tie dye. Then she dyed her hair pink and didn't like it. Her and Rick fought over it. Rick was having trouble at his job and taking it out on everyone. Then there was Jace being messed up by my bad ass guitar playing. David was about the one person not bugging me about something. Dammit, life was tough.

"Miss Devito, maybe you can answer the question."

I snapped out of my thoughts at the sound of my name. "What?" I asked.

The class snickered.

Ms. Lowe sighed. "Scott Joplin's musical piece "The Entertainer", what is it classified as?"

"Ragtime."

"Correct!" She smiled. "Since you seem to be so bored in my class, I should have you come up here and play it for us."

I shrugged my shoulders. I supposed she thought I couldn't play. "I'd rather play Beethoven's Moonlight Sonata 3rd movement." I replied. Lately I had been playing that piece when no one was home. I wasn't sure why I was suddenly so obsessed with it.

She blinked hard and laughed. "That's a very advanced piece."

"I AM the best." I informed her. A music teacher from the high school I'd attended in South Carolina had urged me to go to Juilliard. I'd just never enjoyed the piano as much as I did electric guitar. I'd never played any advanced piano pieces at home because I didn't want daddy to push me into going to school there.

She snorted and gestured to the piano. "In that case, play it for us."

So, with my peers staring curiously at me, I took a seat at the piano and played. I heard gasps and soft comments as I played, and several "holy shits!" I smiled at that. I looked up at Ms. Lowe as I ended it at around three minutes. The third movement was over seven minutes and people's attention spans tended to be short.

She shook her head in amazement. "You're amazing." She murmured. "How long have you been playing?"

"You should hear her play guitar!" Several people remarked.

"Since I was seven, but I don't play keyboard much anymore. I'm a drummer." I replied.

She shook her head again. "You REALLY should think about going to a school like Juilliard". Then she talked to me after class about practicing and what my plans were.

Word of my impressive piano skills got around fast. Several kids that played keyboard stopped to talk and play piano with me. The crowd I hung around with that knew me as a guitar legend, had to rethink their whole perspective of me. Teachers and kids I didn't know talked to me. It was incredibly surreal of how I was hated at the last school that I'd attended and here I was golden. So much about school was blowing my mind but in a good way.

Later that day I was at my locker as school was letting out for the day. There had been an out-of-town football game and so all the football players and cheerleaders had already been bussed out. I might have gone but we had a gig that night. I looked at my books as I paused to remember what homework I had to do. I was really conflicted about where my priorities were. On one hand I wanted to be a regular teenager and go to the game even though football didn't interest me. The kids accepted me at this school and that was a big thing. But on the other hand, I really loved playing music. I finally decided that I had math homework to do so I grabbed my math book, shut my locker and turned around. I almost ran smack dab into a guy that was just standing there.

I blinked and probably gave him a weird look. Neither of us said a word. He was a little taller than me, as thin as me, wore black glasses, and just looked awkward. "One of us has to say something." I finally told him as I did a quick analysis of him. He was a geek for sure.

"I, uh," He stammered, his face reddening.

In a past life, I would have just shrugged him off and left him standing there. "Whatcha need, dude?" I asked him instead. What I wanted to give him was a big dose of confidence. He was going to need it in this lifetime. He would go on to invent something important in the medical field if he had the confidence and drive to do so.

"I..I just wanted to tell you that you're like what super girl would have been like as a rock star." He stammered, then he turned away.

"Wait!" I called to him. I had liked his comparison. Kids had called me a rock star before but none had commented on my super powers. His had been the best compliment ever and so unexpected.

He turned back to me. He was such an awkward dude, no confidence at all and I wondered who'd beaten him down, or maybe his parents just had never built him up. Either way it was a damn shame. Kevin had some of that awkwardness in him. I wanted to stomp it out. *"Help him with that."* The voices whispered. I wondered what they meant. Sometimes the voices talked in circles that I was supposed to understand. Sometimes they only told me part of the story, sometimes they told me straight up what I needed to know, and sometimes everything was cryptic. It was a crapshoot at any given moment.

"I do have super powers. Wanna see?" I asked him. I was just being funny since I had no idea what the voices had meant.

He gave me a curious look. "Yeah." He replied, not sure of what would happen. Truth be told, I didn't know what would happen either because it actually seemed like something would.

"It won't hurt." I told him as he watched me bring my right palm up and place it on his forehead as I thought, "be all you can be". Then it was like I stepped into the middle of the universe as purple and blue light with white lightning flashed around us. The lightning startled me as it flashed through my hand through his forehead. I jerked but the energy held me tight. Then visions of his life flashed through my head. Him as a happy little boy, then watching his mother cry as a police officer came to the door and told her that her husband was dead. He looked about eight years old then. Being shuffled off to relatives as his mom tried to support the two of them, shame as he faltered in the confusion of it all, kids making fun of him and leaving him to his silence. His mom was exhausted as she tried to support them, and hadn't given him the love and attention that he'd needed. The kids at school hadn't understood his loss and they'd bullied him. I felt his pain and I understood it all too well. Then the vision suddenly disappeared and was replaced with the brightness of a thousand lights for just a second, then it faded like smoke dissipating. I wondered if he'd seen everything I'd seen. I wondered what exactly had been given to him, if anything. Had it helped? OH MY GOD, he'd tell everyone at school! Shit. I wasn't even sure why I had thought to put my hand on his forehead in the first place.

I removed my hand which felt rather hot and we stared in surprise at each other for a second or two until he burst into a smile. "That was AWESOME! Just like Captain Picard on Star Trek taking the Enterprise to warp ten!" He exclaimed.

"Yeah." I said rather warily. "I didn't expect that to happen. I was just sayin' stuff. I think it was you that did that." Yeah, this was going to be hard to explain to all my football friends when word got out. It was best to blame it on the geek.

"Oh no, it was you! I knew you were like super girl!" He exclaimed as he bent down and picked my math book from the floor and handed it to me. In the purple blue lightning explosion I'd dropped it and hadn't even noticed.

"I really didn't know that could happen." I stressed to him. OH MY GOD. Me and my big powers. Why had I done that? Now life at school was going to suck again.

People would laugh, and talk, and be mean, and I'd have to kick their asses. Dammit! It was my own damn fault. Why had I been so arrogant? I knew by hearing the voices that something would happen. Why? Why? Why?

He was rambling on about a Star Trek episode in all its greatness as I rambled inside my head about the consequences of what I'd done. How could I have been so stupid? "I gotta go. My mom just drove up." He said suddenly as he pulled his cell phone out of his pocket and looked at it. He suddenly hugged me, tightly I might add, and then he was sprinting away yelling, "thanks, Super Girl Rock Star"!

I stared after him. The last moment had happened so fast and I'd been mostly not listening because I was stressing in my head about how my life was about to take a big downward turn. Sigh. Dammit! Yeah, I was a Star Trek episode all right. Dammit.

He was gone but I still stared down the hallway. He'd somehow experienced some or all of the techno effects of the experience. Damn, he was right. It had been awesome just like a ride to warp ten on the Enterprise. I was thinking that I'd experienced spaceship rides like that before, maybe I'd even piloted the craft.

***

"You've been sulky since you got home tonight. What are you so mad about?" Kevin asked me as he helped me set up my drum kit at the diner we were playing at that night.

"I tried to give confidence to this guy at school and it went all Star Trekky. I put my palm on his forehead and bam! There was all this blue and purple light and white lightning. I didn't know that was fucking going to happen, I was just teasing him. But Bam! Blue and purple light and white lightning! And what was that about?" I grumbled.

He burst out laughing.

"What's so funny?" David asked as he stopped strumming his guitar. Carol and Rick looked over too.

He laughed as he repeated what I'd said.

"So did you whip out your light phaser and blow him away?" Carol laughed.

"Use the force, Luke." Rick said using a Darth Vader voice. Yeah, they were having a blast laughing at me. They obviously didn't know Star Trek from Star Wars either.

"Did I fucking say that was public knowledge? I swear you can't keep your mouth shut." I complained back angrily. I turned to Rick. "I'm gonna give you the fuckin' force." I threatened. They were laughing as I went over and popped my palm against his forehead. He jerked but laughed it off. Yeah, there had been a spark, nothing like the purple and blue light and white lightning but there had definitely been something. I saw him try to hide that he'd felt it too. Now Kevin and David were trying to play slap me and wrestle around. Maybe it was kind of funny. Surely the guy wouldn't say anything to anyone. If he did, he'd get the same reaction I had just gotten, right? I let my anger go, although they teased me for days afterward.

CHAPTER 4

I was standing at my locker thinking about other things I'd rather be doing than attending school. I had been sent on a mission by my science teacher to pick up excuse slips at the main office. I was stopping at my locker first. Some sophomore had said he'd put some chocolate chip cookies in my locker that his mom had made, all because I'd said that I'd liked them. I didn't appreciate that he'd gone into my locker, but hey! I was getting cookies! Lord knows that I couldn't wait until class was over to eat one, or two.

"Hi!" Said a male voice, scaring the crap out of me. I jerked towards the voice. "mmph." I said, my mouth full of cookie. It was a senior boy who I'd seen around but didn't know. He was dark haired, dark eyed and only an inch or so taller than me.

"Sorry. Didn't mean to scare you but I wanted to ask a favor. I'm Ken, by the way." He held out his hand. I shook it and managed to swallow the cookie down. "My brother Sully plays the sax and he was wondering if he could play a song or two with your band. He wants to get gigs and he needs some experience. I told him that I would ask you." He continued.

I blinked at him. He had been stealth, appearing out of nowhere, an empty hallway and then he was there. I wondered if he was a wizard. Maybe we had something in common. "It's not my band. I'm the drummer. Our next gig is Friday night at Club Nine." He could show up and talk to Rick. "We start playing at eight so maybe seven-thirty?" I replied.

"Okay, thanks. I'll tell him."

I wondered how Rick was going to feel about that. Maybe Sully would be a no show. Some people had dreams but when it came down to it they were just too scared to pursue them. I watched him walk away. I had expected a puff of smoke and then he'd be gone but he was still there. I guessed he wasn't a wizard after all. Huh.

On my way to my next class, I noticed the guy I'd gone all Star Trekky on. He was talking to another guy and they both glanced my way and smiled in a really happy way. I just knew that he'd told his friend about our little healing. He waved and I waved back. Huh. In a weird way I had been hoping that purple and blue light with white lightning would engulf us to a galaxy far, far away. It had felt like a good day for it too.

***

The band and I were setting up at Club Nine that Friday night when Gabby appeared. Kevin and she were still seeing each other. A little while later when Kevin disappeared to my truck to get something, Gabby stood there talking to me. It wasn't two seconds before Carol butted into our conversation. "So, you're her guardian?" Gabby asked her.

"No!" Carol replied quickly in distaste. "My boyfriend is her guardian. She's an asshole. I don't have anything to do with her."

I shook my head in aggravation. I really hated living with her and Rick.

Gabby's face reddened. "Oh." She replied. "So, the four of you live together?"

"There's five of us. David (she pointed at him) lives with us too. It sucks but it is what it is." Carol huffed as she gave me the evil eye. I really couldn't imagine that being my guardian was that distasteful. I never did anything wrong. I never got in trouble at all anymore and I kept a low profile at home, staying out of everyone's way for the most part.

I saw Kevin approaching.

"Do they sleep together?" Gabby asked Carol of me and Kevin.

Kevin walked up to us as Carol remarked, "Do they fuck each other? No, she's too much of a prude but he's always in her bed anyway."

Oh my God. What had she said? We were trying to keep our business private. She was just being an asshole at that point. She knew that Kevin really liked Gabby, and Gabby didn't need to know we sometimes shared a bed.

"I thought you said the two of you were just friends." Gabby remarked angrily to Kevin. "And here I find out that you do sleep together."

"We are just friends, and sleeping in the same bed happened before I met you."

"You're just a damn liar! She just said you're always in her bed!" Gabby insisted, and she was right. She turned and walked away with Kevin running after her trying to explain. I didn't figure there was any better way to explain it. And now that Gabby knew our situation, the whole school would know it by the next school day.

"Thanks a fucking lot." I said angrily to Carol.

She smiled a spiteful smile.

"Why'd you fucking have to do that?" David asked. He'd been eavesdropping.

"I didn't do anything." Carol remarked as she walked away.

Kevin came back in and dragged Carol outside to argue with her. He was so damn pissed at her and I couldn't blame him, but in truth, we were in a fucked up situation. It was going to be hard for the two of us to find anyone who would put up with our living situation.

Sully dropped by in time for our break between sets. I sighed to myself thinking that the night was going to get worse. Everyone in the band was angry at each other. But Sully hit it off with Rick and he let him play his sax with us on one song. I was grateful. Sometimes that tiny bit of extra stress was enough to wipe me out.

When we got home Kevin wanted to vent half the night about Carol. I listened for about fifteen minutes then I told him that he shouldn't have mentioned anything about us playing in a band in the first place, that he should have kept his mouth shut until he was in a deeper relationship with her. "I warned you about that weeks ago! Who knows how this is going to play out at school?" I continued. "I have to go to school there, not you. What if it ends up being the same damn situation it was for me when we lived in South Carolina? I'm gonna kill you if that happens. I'm at my fucking wit's end, Kevin!" I shouted at him. And so, it was a long night with Carol getting back into the argument and Rick taking her side, and David trying to referee.

"I'm sorry." Kevin sniffled to me after we'd calmed down. "You told me not to say anything. I didn't want to remember lies so I told Gabby the truth."

I was angry but I understood his point too. That's why I hadn't gotten involved with Jordan. I didn't want to have to lie. I just didn't need everyone to love me like Kevin did. I just needed acceptance and I worried that it was slipping fast with not a damn thing I could do about it.

At school the next day, I had just sat down with my lunch when Jordan approached me. "So the truth comes out. I knew you and Kevin were more than just friends."

"I'm not fucking him." I replied. I was already aggravated and expecting the backlash at some point that day. Even though I'd never gone out with Jordan, he was wanting sex from me, just like all the other guys. We'd kissed a few times, hadn't even made out.

"But apparently, he sleeps in your bed. Gabby said that your guardian told her that last night."

I shook my head in aggravation. She couldn't even get the fucking story straight; Rick hadn't said a word to her. "She didn't talk to my guardian, she talked to my guardian's GIRLFRIEND who is a spiteful, lying bitch. Who fucking cares if we've slept in the same bed before? I'm not fucking him, or anyone else for that matter! I'm nobody's girlfriend. I'm not having any kind of sex with anyone, not even in my damn dreams." I shot back.

He glared at me. "I don't get you at all. You could be my girlfriend if you'd give me a chance. What's so great about Kevin anyway?" He proceeded to take a bite out of his burger then.

I sighed in more aggravation. He wasn't listening to me either. "All I can tell you is that all me and Kevin have right now is each other. My dad, my only relative, died and so I moved here with my guardian, who I might add, just became my guardian. And Kevin had an even sadder mess with his family, and now he's here. He doesn't have any family anymore either. I hate my guardian's girlfriend and I'm not so keen on my guardian either but I'm trying to deal with it all. They are always taking their anger out on me as if I'm the cause of all their problems. I hate living with them. I'm at a new school, I'm still grieving over my dad's death, I have a job now, and I have a totally different life that I'm trying to deal with. If you can't deal with me and Kevin living in the same house, just go away. I can't take any more stress. I'm just fucking trying to deal with this new life when all I want is to have my dad back." I huffed to myself after I'd said all of that. No one needed to know. It was none of their business. I was just as bad as Kevin spouting out all of our secrets.

Jordan stopped in mid chew. "I didn't know. You never said anything." He said as he swallowed hard.

"I didn't say anything because I don't want to remember that my life is gone, that everything I knew and loved is gone. And Kevin just wanted someone to love, that's all. He really likes Gabby but our living situation is just weird right now. I wish she could understand. I just want to make something of myself musically but Kevin just needs a girlfriend in order to start over. That's all I can tell you." I added as I bit my tongue again at all I'd said. Dammit.

"I'm sorry. That's a lot to deal with." He replied as he started eating again. "I can help you deal with all of that if you let me."

What if instead of just being a boyfriend he became another problem? If I brought him to the house Carol would sure enough fuck him. She was a bitch in that way. She was already cheating on Rick although Rick didn't know that. "I can't right now. I need some time." I said as I looked down at my food. I felt like I'd choke if I ate it, and that was a shame because I was hungry. Jordan would be moving on and I wasn't sure how I felt about that either. I supposed it was just another day in my shitty situation. It still felt like everything was going to be ripped away from me again so there was no reason to get involved. At first, I had thought it was from my classmates finding out that Kevin and I lived together, but I now thought it was something else. Whatever it was, it was hurling towards me like a heat seeking missile. I only hoped that I would survive the attack.

***

I was in my own world as I sat staring at the tv in the living room with Kevin. He nudged me. "Hey." He said. "Carol just said the phone is for you." I hadn't even heard the phone ring.

It was Bob and he wanted to know if I was coming to South Carolina for Thanksgiving or Christmas. I told him, no. No one else was planning on it. Even if they wanted to, no one had the time off from work and it was an eleven-hour drive. Rick's and David's parents were angry that they weren't going to make the trip although they weren't footing plane tickets either. Bob wasn't too happy about it especially since he knew I had plenty of money to get there. After he was satisfied that I wasn't doing drugs or sleeping around, he ended the call.

Daddy and I had been talking about a possible move to another state a few months before he died. David and Kevin had wanted to go too. We were going to start over. Well, David, Kevin, and I had moved. I just hadn't expected to move so soon and without my dad. I wondered if we had all moved then if the transition would have been as hard as this.

"What's the matter?" I asked David as I saw him in the hallway. He was wiping his eyes. He looked up at hearing my voice and quickly looked downward. I'd just come home and I guess he hadn't heard me enter the house.

"Nothin'" He muttered, then he headed toward the stairs.

"I'll listen." I replied as I followed him upstairs to his room. He wasn't one to cry about anything and I was curious what the problem was.

"Get out of here, huh?" He said angrily as he tried to shut his door on me. My foot was in the way of him closing the door. I had my cowboy boots on so there was no way I was budging.

"Oh, let me be a friend, huh? We used to hang out sometimes." I remarked but I was really just being nosey.

He huffed in defeat then let me in. He shut the door behind us. I noticed that his room was neat and clean and his bed was made. I knew my bed wasn't made. He sat on the bed so I did too. I noticed that he had tie dyed pillow cases and I smirked at that. Hell, Kevin had tie dyed underwear. Crap, so did I. "What do you want?" He asked in an annoyed voice. He was dressed in jeans and a t-shirt instead of being naked. I kind of liked him both ways. He was so buff but it was too cold to be strutting around naked.

"I seriously would like to be your friend." I told him. "Kevin likes me, why can't you?"

He gave me a weird look. "We are friends, most of the time." He replied.

Several seconds went by in silence in which I read him. "So, what's your little brother done now that your parents are praising him about and getting on your case about?" I finally asked. I should have figured it was something that his brother had done.

He gave me a hurt look. "Why do you always seem to know everyone's fucking business?" He spouted, then a second later he looked ashamed. "Shit, they're just stressing me out. Alan's a math whiz and he just won the semi-finals in some fucking math contest. They're talking about him going to M.I.T. They want to know when I'm going to get serious and go to college."

"Oh, so what? He's only thirteen fucking years old and he's a dumb ass. He's gonna knock up some girl before he's seventeen years old. I doubt he ends up going to college at all. All he'll ever be is a moocher off your parents. I bet he'll have illegitimate kids all over the place." I spouted out without thinking.

"What? Why would you say that?" David said as he moved to take a better look at me.

"Because he's a horn dog. He's been after me and every other girl since he's been seven! And guys are so dumb! You'd think that sex was just discovered and no one has caught onto how a male shooting sperm into a female could cause pregnancy! But most of all, Alan has no ambition to do any fucking thing. And why do you give a fuck what your relatives say about him? You're gonna be a fucking rock star! You don't need to go to college. You can laugh in their faces when you're famous."

He gave me a doubtful look.

"And I also know things and that's what my mind is telling me."

"Oh, so you're psychic now. Okay, smarty pants, if you know so much then why isn't your life perfect?"

"Believe me, I'm just as frustrated about that as you are." I huffed. We stared at each other for a moment, then he laughed. "You really are a bullshitter, but thanks for making me feel better."

Kevin was the next one who was crying about losing everything and not having a good Thanksgiving. Gabby had made it clear that she was done with him. Jordan still talked to me but not as much as before. He had his eye on several other girls. I still received a gift or two of food or favors and conversation each week from the kids at school. Everyone still seemed to love me, although it puzzled them as to why I wouldn't go out with any of them. There were whispers that something was mentally wrong with me. I would have made more of an effort if I'd thought I'd finish the school year with them but I didn't think I'd even make it to spring break.

"Kev, I'll buy us food for a feast and we'll have our own Thanksgiving. Between me and you, we could figure out how to cook a turkey, couldn't we?" I asked.

"Are you sick or something? You don't cook and you avoid grocery stores like the plague." He snorted.

"I can't believe you'd say such an awful thing about me." I huffed in mock disbelief. Yep, I'd send him to the store. I wasn't going. Ha. Stupid males.

"Imagine me saying the truth." He said sarcastically as he opened the fridge and looked for who knew what.

"I'll cook if no one else is going to only because I want to eat. And I'll see if Streethart wants to come over. Why don't you invite a friend or two?" I remarked. I figured the whole meal couldn't be hard. I mean, David cooked all the time and he was just a stupid guy. We had a cookbook; I'd just follow some recipes. If worst came to worst, I knew how to make eggs and toast.

David stopped us before we walked out the door. "Where are you going?" He asked.

He laughed when Kevin told him that we were going grocery shopping because he knew I wouldn't step into a store to save my life. He decided to go with us. I was hoping he would because I didn't have a clue of what to buy except for the turkey. And just how big of a turkey was I supposed to buy? Yeah, I'd given in and decided to brave the grocery store, however I never had said I'd go in.

"Still the Same" started playing as I started the truck.

"Can this be a no repeat Monday?" Kevin asked me. He and David laughed about it.

"You just fucked that up, now, didn't you?" I asked sarcastically as I spun out of our driveway and hit the repeat button on the CD player. I loved the burst of power of my truck, a V8 engine was the bomb.

"You're getting just like Rick and his OCD, the way you always have to listen to songs over and over again."

"Am not, just one song." I argued, although I had been hitting the repeat button a lot on my CD player. Going into a store of any kind increased that need for repeat. Although I was wondering if I'd get out of the truck once we were there.

It was an ordeal shopping for the meal. I was willing to give fifteen minutes tops to shopping but David had to look everything over carefully before he decided that it was appropriate enough to buy. Then Kevin kept talking about sugar cookies even though everyone knew that you only made those for Christmas. And the people! There were so many people shopping. I started snapping at the twelve-minute mark and so they made me give them the grocery money and then banned me to my truck. So yeah, I was in time out, and I had paid for everything as well as provided the transportation. I thought it a small price to pay for them doing the shopping.

At the twenty-minute mark I was freezing and I started up the truck. Bob Seger sang for a few minutes. I tapped the radio/CD off and all was quiet. Even I got tired of that song sometimes. But most other times I needed it like an addict needed drugs.

A guy appeared at my window and told me that he liked my truck. We got to talking so I invited him into the cab. I found that he liked big fucking trucks and muscle cars too. We talked about Ford Mustangs and tall pick-up trucks. We were just getting into how we loved the sound of a good V8 engine when Kevin and David appeared at the passenger door. "Hey, good talking to you." The guy whose name I didn't know remarked.

"Yeah, enjoyed it." I replied. "Come hear us play at Club Nine one Friday night. Our band plays there."

"Oh yeah, I'm there." The guy replied as he eased out of the cab and said hi to Kevin and David. "Hey, can I get your number?"

"NO." David told him forcefully. "You're too old for her." He and David traded some more words, then he looked at me.

I helplessly shrugged my shoulders. "Brothers! They rule my life." I remarked in mock exasperation. I hadn't wanted to date him anyways. I hit the CD player so "Still the Same" would play then I hit the repeat button.

"Why don't you have enough sense not to invite strangers into your truck when you're by yourself?" David asked me as if I were the stupidest person on earth. "Especially guys. Guys will fuck you in an instant and take every other advantage of you." He and Kevin had put the groceries in the bed of the truck and were now climbing into the cab. Kevin adjusted the CD player so "Still the Same" wouldn't repeat.

"He seemed harmless enough." I replied.

"Yeah, they're all harmless enough until they hijack your truck and kill you."

"What are the odds of that really happening?" I asked as I put the truck in gear. I wondered how much gas I'd used with us sitting there talking with the engine running. I glanced at the clock in my truck and found that we'd talked almost twenty minutes. I was probably going to have to stop and fill up soon. It irked me that shopping hadn't been my intention and that I could have made it out of that store in ten minutes tops.

"You're really going to have to stop watching cartoons like a little kid. The world isn't all love and laughter like the tv show makes it out to be."

Hmmm. I couldn't remember ever meeting anyone dangerous before besides me. I made a face at him. He was the one that watched cartoons sometimes, not me. Well sure, I watched Speed Racer reruns but didn't everyone?

"You guys are harmless." I remarked as I pushed the back button on the CD player to the first song which was "Still the Same".

"That's only cause we know your dumb ass needs taken care of otherwise we'd a fucked you by now.

You're high maintenance with a capital H." David replied as he pushed my hand away from the CD player and hit the radio button. We batted each other's hands away from changing the CD player to play or the radio. I gave up and left it on radio. It was belting out a VanHalen tune. I glared at David and he glared back. "You'd have fucked me by now." I stated just so I knew we were on the same wave length.

"Oh yeah, Kevin would have too, right Kev?" David remarked.

"Oh yeah." Kevin agreed, smiling from in between us. "I'm about over that taken care of part so watch out. You're in for the time of your life."

I smirked at that. They were so stupid. Kevin and I had slept together before, not recently but in the past. David just didn't know it. "I'm not fucking either of you pansy boys." I informed them.

"Brothers, huh?" Kevin remarked.

"Yeah, Bros." I smiled back, then drove us home.

It was way too early on Thanksgiving morning when David bounced me and Kevin out of bed to help him cook. It's so annoying when you're made to do something that you never do even though you were the one that initiated it in the first place. David had me peeling potatoes. He had Kevin putting something together with sweet potatoes. I hated sweet potatoes so I knew I wasn't eating any of that. As I was making fun of Kevin, David saddled me with making a pumpkin pie. He said that the more I made fun of them or griped, the more I was going to have to do with our dinner. They laughed when I suddenly shut up. Kevin had purchased a few sugar cookie dough rolls and cookie cutters with the money I'd given them. As he rolled the dough out and started cutting shapes, I took interest and started cutting them out too. As I smelled the cookies baking and the Thanksgiving meal cooking, a vague memory surfaced of me helping my mother cut out cookies. Her name had been Cindy and she had been my foster mother until her and her husband had died in a car wreck. All my memories of her were good. I couldn't recall even one time that she'd been angry at me. I blinked back the emotion and the memories. It was several years after their deaths that I'd been told that they weren't my biological parents. I still remembered them as mommy and daddy.

David made sure the cookies didn't burn. "You just might turn out to be a Betty Crocker after all." He wisecracked. Yeah, ha!

Rick and Carol were grumpy once they finally got out of bed. They scoffed at us making the Thanksgiving meal but helped themselves to the cookies. They left at 11am to hang out with another couple they'd met. Supposedly this couple had money. They left and we all were glad to see them go.

The phone rang right after they left. "ANSWER THE FUCKING PHONE!" David yelled to me from the kitchen. I had been tuning my guitar. I never answered the phone but it was a holiday and I didn't want to be fighting all day. I huffed and answered it on the seventh ring. It was Connie, Carol's older sister. "Well, hey Squirt! Happy Thanksgiving." she said.

I had to smile. I liked her sister. "Hey Bonnie Connie." I replied back.

She giggled. "So, where's Lil Bit?" She asked. She was talking about Carol. She and I had a private joke about what Lil Bit actually stood for. She was calling Carol a bitch but had put "Lil" in front of a word that sounded like bitch.

"Oh, who the fuck knows and who the fuck cares?" I asked back in a bored tone.

"I know, right? But it gives us time to talk. Howya been?"

And so, the conversation went on and we laughed and talked. She put the call on speakerphone and their brother Donnie chimed in and teased me. As I hung up almost thirty minutes later, I couldn't help wonder how their family could have two great kids and one dud. Carol was pretty like their mother. Donnie and Connie were rather large and awkward like their dad. It was obvious who had gotten all the attention as they grew up.

We had time before our guests arrived so I sat at Carol's keyboard and rocked it with complicated pieces. I really had gotten tired of hiding my true talent on the instruments that I played. David and Kevin both appeared in front of me.

"What?" I asked.

"You're pretty damn good on that thing." David told me. "I had no idea."

"Now I know why you don't play anything complicated in front of Carol. She'd be fucked up until the end of time." Kevin added.

"Yeah, I'm aware of that. I can play bass pretty good too, and violin." I added. I hadn't played the violin since I was nine but I knew I could still outplay anybody on any day.

"Shit!" Kevin replied. He looked at David and they huffed and walked away. "Everything is so fucking easy for her." I heard David grumble.

"Walk a mile in my shoes." I grumbled back. If only my life were as easy as playing an instrument.

I had invited Streethart but only Curt, Smith and his wife, Carrie accepted my invitation. Jace had gone to see his mom in Florida. Kevin had invited a girl named Paula and a guy named Andy who he'd recently met, and David had invited a guy named Gary that he worked with. We had a good time with our friends. David was a fabulous cook and our meal was great, even the parts that Kevin and I had made. The guys watched football while the girls sat in the kitchen talking. "Kevin talks about you." Paula told me.

I was amazed that I was getting along with the guests, especially the girls. Usually only the guys talked to me. And I would have been hanging out with them if they hadn't been watching football. Football was stupid. "Why?" I asked, totally confused.

"You helped him run away." She answered.

"Oh, yeah." I replied as I reached to the plate of cookies we'd left on the table. I was sure that I could eat one more. It annoyed me that Kevin was telling people he'd run away. First, it sounded like something a baby would say, and second, what if someone took him seriously? It was the truth, but no one needed to know that.

"So, is he good in bed?" She asked in a serious but also teasing way.

Carrie looked at me too for that answer. I was trying to figure out if I had to respond to that question. "Yeah. No complaints here. But that was a long time ago. We don't sleep together anymore." I finally replied. It was true but I didn't think that was anyone else's business. I had to take a big bite out of that cookie then.

"Did he get you off?"

I swallowed hard and coughed. Then I took a swig of my coke. I saw that they were waiting expectantly for my answer.

"Uh, yeah. He waits for his." I hesitantly replied. I wondered if I needed to stop there. Yeah, I needed to stop.

They smiled and giggled appreciatively. "Then why aren't you still sleeping with him, girl?" Carrie giggled.

"I just can't. My dad just died and now I don't have any family, and the five of us are living in a city so different from where we used to live. And we hardly get along sometimes. It's just too much. I can hardly deal with so much change." I blurted out and then stopped.

But they weren't interested in my problems. "He said you were his first." Paula said.

I blinked at her. Why was she asking me questions like this? "Yeah." I lied. He'd done Wendy before he'd done me but history wasn't always set in stone if your company wasn't witness to it.

After she determined that I wasn't sleeping with Kevin any longer, her and Carrie started talking about the sexual encounters they'd had. "What about you?" they asked.

"Kevin was it, and that was only a couple of times. I don't have anyone else to talk about. I'm only sixteen, you know." I replied. Yep, history could be whatever you wanted it to be. I'd eaten two more cookies and was regretting it. I just didn't know the conversation was going to be so personal.

"What about David?" they asked.

"No, I've never done him. He's just a dumbass." I replied. They giggled.

"How about you and Jace?" Carrie asked.

"We're just friends."

"He'd do you in a minute, you know." She smiled knowingly.

Yeah, no doubt.

She wanted to talk more about it but luckily Smith walked into the kitchen and sat down with us. I made sure that I had other things to do when the conversation went places I didn't want it to after that. I was happy though, how our Thanksgiving was going.

Since most of us were in a band, we jammed a little. Kevin took the drums and I blew them away with my bad ass guitar playing.

"Jace would be so fucked up by you if he were here right now." Carrie remarked.

"Then I'm glad he's not here." I smiled.

Rick and Carol rolled in sometime after 2am and they were oddly happy the next day. "What's up with you guys?" Kevin asked them.

They smiled sly smiles. "We hit pay dirt." Carol giggled.

"What are you talking about?" David asked.

Their energy hit me in the pit of my stomach wondering what they had gotten involved in.

"I'm going shopping." She announced as she ignored his question.

"And since when do you have money to blow?" David probed.

"Like I said, we were at the right place at the right time." She gave Rick a kiss and giggled her way out the front door.

We looked at him. "What pay dirt?" Kevin asked.

"I think the question is, what the fuck did you two

get involved in? And are we going to have to go into witness protection because of it?" I demanded.

Rick snorted. "We just met the right people and they offered us a side job that pays easy money, so we took it."

Kevin and David didn't get much more out of him with their questions. "I don't like it. It feels bad." I remarked. "Daddy always said that easy money was dangerous money."

Rick patted me on the head as though I was a puppy, then went up to his room.

"What do you think they got into?" David asked.

Images of partying and sex flipped through my mind. I shook my head. "I don't know. But I think it's going to bite all of us in the ass." When Carol came back with about three to five hundred dollars' worth of clothes, jewelry, and shoes, I knew I was right.

***

I didn't know what to say when I got called to the principal's office from my third period class. I hadn't caused a lick of trouble since I'd transferred to New Rochelle. The receptionist had me sit and wait in one of the hard wooden chairs against the wall. The chairs faced the principal's closed door. I wondered if it was a tactic to scare kids. It was working.

I looked up as the principal opened his door and invited me in. The door closed behind me like a tomb. I had been wracking my brain trying to figure out what I'd done wrong and I hadn't been able to come up with one thing. I was such a little angel at this school, and a musically talented hottie so the guys at school said.

"Ms. Lowe tells me you're quite the maestro, and I've been hearing talk that you play in a band and are quite good." He remarked as he sat on the edge of his desk and

I sat in a hardbacked chair facing him. The chair seemed to get harder with each passing moment.

"Yeah, gonna be a well-known guitar legend in due time." I agreed. "But I play the drums right now in the band." I quickly added.

"It's good to have high ambitions." He agreed. "I'd like to give you the chance to play in front of the entire school the first Friday in December." He went on to add a few details, one being that we couldn't be vulgar which meant no cussing or sexual references in the lyrics or gestures.

"So, I can't give anyone the finger or tell them to fuck off?" I asked.

"You're pushing it, young lady."

I smiled. "I'll ask the rest of the band."

I talked to them that night. They tossed it around and then decided that it would be fun for me to fuck up in front of everyone in my high school. "Yep, I'll even let you take over for one song. You can play lead guitar and be lead singer." Rick decided as he laughed about it.

I didn't often mess up. In my opinion, I was the strongest one of the band, followed by David, then Rick, then Carol, then Kevin. Well, it was a toss up of who was better between David and Rick. Rick could sing and was pretty good on bass. David was fantastic on lead guitar but he didn't like to sing, and when he did it was never good enough to be lead singer.

CHAPTER 5

When I went to work on Monday, the girls in the office were excited because another one of our catalogs had just come off the press. We always received copies from the printing company before the public did and each one was like a new toy to us. There were six of us who worked as models for the catalog. Only three of us did the office work to have a steady job. Mostly we did outerwear such as slacks, blouses and coats. A few liked to pose for the lingerie ads but I wasn't one of them. They knew I'd never do that. They also knew I probably would never do swimsuits either and that was okay with them. In this catalog I was on several pages. The picture everyone liked of me was where I was wearing a clingy red dress with a matching hat, shoes and purse. They knew that I had posed for Cardello in jeans ads and they were impressed. Cardello was big time compared to a mail order catalog.

I didn't think anyone I knew outside the office actually received the catalog but I was wrong. Greggie called me to tell me how great I looked in the red dress. He hadn't known I worked for Harris Company and when he saw my picture in the catalog, he couldn't believe it so he had to show it to Streethart and everyone else he knew. He wanted me to autograph it and wanted to know if I could get any more catalogs for him and bring them over. I thought it was funny. When I told him that I had posed for Cardello, he about dropped the phone. He was truly impressed. I picked up some extra catalogs and arrived at his doorstep. He hugged me as usual and we talked a bit. Then he pulled me to him. "You are so hot." He told me as he was caressing my arms and brushing back the hair from my face. He kissed me and I enjoyed it.

I backed up just a bit. "You're living with someone, Greggie." I remarked.

"Yeah, I am." He said. "Don't you want me? I can make you feel good."

"Are you going to break up with her?" I asked.

"No." He replied dreamily, pulling me against him.

"I'm outta here." I decided as I pulled away. "See ya later." I added as I headed out the door. And that was the end of that.

My band was not impressed with the catalog. They also had seen the catalog since the company mails each model a copy of each catalog they appear in. They were jealous of the modeling I did and jealous that I always seemed to have money. Since I rarely had time to shop and I didn't blow my money on beer and other things, I did indeed have money. From the time we had moved into the house together I had been paying more than my share of the groceries and utilities just to keep peace. Sometimes I even cleaned up when it wasn't my turn. It seemed like all I did was give and all they did was take.

Lately the house was looking like a pig pen. I mean it had never had a neat moment but it was just awful lately. I wouldn't even invite Jace over because it looked so bad. Rick yelled at me as if it was my fault that the house was a disaster area. I wasn't the lazy one. Kevin was suddenly giving me problems too. Mostly he'd been taking advantage of the fact that I had a truck to drive. He had been borrowing my truck an awful lot lately. And I also never realized that we wore the same size clothes until I found why my jeans were disappearing out of my drawers. Kevin was wearing them, just going into my room, taking my jeans and wearing them. I yelled at him and complained to Rick about it. Rick yelled at both of us then.

I awoke about 3 a.m. that night disturbed about bad dreams and of how bad everything was. I wanted to just hang it up. Our music career wasn't too bad but the five of us were just not working out. I should have waited until daylight but instead I woke Rick up to talk to him about it.

"What did you wake me up for?" He yelled.

"I had a bad dream and we need to talk about things."

"Get out of here!" He yelled back.

"I hate you! You're a poor excuse for a guardian. You don't care about me or the band. None of you do!" I yelled back.

"I never wanted to be your guardian. I'm too young!"

Carol had awoken to our yelling and she began yelling at Rick claiming that he was screwing me on the sly.

"Damn you, bitch!" Rick shouted. Before I could react, he had pushed me hard and I'd fallen backwards.

I ran out of the room. I threw some clothes on and sped off in my truck. I went to Jace's apartment. He didn't mind being awoken. I was rather ashamed of my crying but Jace pulled me into a hug. I cried on his shoulder about all the problems in my life. He held me in his arms until I had no more to say. Biscuit was lying against me with her head on my legs just like Yellow used to do.

"Do you feel better now?" He asked.

"A little." I sniffed.

"Let's try to get some sleep and we'll talk about this in depth later. He fixed up the couch for me and Biscuit curled up with me. Surprisingly I drifted off to sleep rather quickly. I awoke with a start when I heard him rattling dishes in the kitchen. I relaxed when I realized it was Saturday and I was safe.

"Hungry?" He asked.

I took a minute to check. "Yeah. I didn't know you knew how to cook."

"Yep. I'm the best."

I cracked a smile. I was the one he always said was good at everything. I hadn't learned to cook that well. Daddy had done the majority of the cooking, although he had said that I should learn to cook more than eggs and toast and to reheat pizza.

I sat down at the table and watched Jace whip up pancakes, eggs and bacon. I didn't complain because everything was excellent just like he said it would be. Biscuit nudged me every so often hoping for something but Jace refused to let me feed her anything from the table. As my mind drifted, it told me to let them take me and not fight it and it would work out. As I was trying to figure what that was supposed to mean, Jace started going over my alternatives to solve the problem with the band. He said I could find someone else to share an apartment with or try to solve the problems with the band and if that didn't work, I had no recourse except to go back to South Carolina. He didn't say that he'd let me stay with him as a last resort but I knew that was what he was thinking.

I knew even if the band broke up because the five of us couldn't solve our differences that I wouldn't return to South Carolina. Bob would physically have to bring me back there. I could make a life here by myself somehow. And when Kevin and I turned eighteen we could move to Texas like we'd originally planned.

I looked at Jace. "I know that I have to try to work things out with the others. In order for our band to make it, we have to pull together and that means sharing living space. I have to try to straighten this mess out. If I mention anything to Bob that's happened with the band then he would have me back in South Carolina in a minute. We've really been lucky so far and the band is strangely unaware of that."

He agreed with me and we spent some time talking about what I could do to try to make the situation better. Afterward he blew off the plans he had with his girlfriend to spend the day with me. He said he'd go out with her later. We ran some errands, went shopping, walked a lot and went to a movie.

We were driving by an expensive new subdivision when I saw this house that was nearly finished and it was gorgeous. "Can you stop so we can look at it?" I asked.

He pulled over and I went up to the house and looked in the windows. I walked around the back and he followed. I tried the door handle but it was locked. "I really want to see the inside." I told him.

"You can't. It's locked." He replied.

I took my driver's license out of my pocket and

wedged it between the door frame and the lock. The door swung open. Jace had been looking across the back yard and hadn't noticed what I'd done until I'd swung open the door. "What did you do?" He asked me suspiciously.

"I used my driver's license." I replied as I stepped into the house.

"Should you be doing that?" He asked as he looked around to see if anyone had seen me do it.

"Jace, that excuse for a lock was just begging to be blown open. Let's go in." I told him and he reluctantly followed me inside.

The interior was gorgeous. I liked the way the rooms were laid out and it had a beautiful kitchen. I knew I would one day own a house just as amazing. Jace admitted the house was beautiful but he was too worried about getting caught inside of it so we left. "Sometimes you still surprise me." He remarked. Yeah, well that was good, right.

Much later I went home. No one was there. It was only about eight o'clock. The house looked worse than ever and it disgusted me. I sat down at my drum set and began beating out what I now liked to call the "odd rhythm". It still was a rhythm I'd never heard before in a song but sometimes it seemed to haunt me and I'd drum it over and over again. The band had gotten used to it but sometimes they just yelled at me to stop. I left my drums and started scrubbing and vacuuming and straightening up. About two hours later it looked acceptable. I lay down for a moment intending to only rest for five minutes, then I was going to read a while in my room.

I looked up and saw Daddy standing before me. I

couldn't believe what I was seeing. Tears rolled down my cheeks and I put my arms around him. "Dad, I'm glad you're here. It's been so horrible since you left." He jerked and the mist from my mind cleared for me to see that I was really holding onto Rick. It had just been a dream or hallucination. I heard myself gasp in shock, then I turned and flew up the stairs to my room, slamming the door behind me.

The next morning when we were all downstairs, I told them that we all needed to have a meeting. Nobody was cooperative so I told them my viewpoint. "I will no longer do housework when it's not my turn. "Rick, you are no longer my guardian. I refuse to take any more of your bullshit. I'll beat the shit out of you if you ever push me around again. I have followed all your rules, paid more than my fair share and I haven't gotten into any trouble. I don't deserve this. And Kevin, my truck is off limits to you and no longer will you wear my clothes. You've been taking advantage of me too much. I've been trying so hard to make this work. Why aren't you guys trying?"

They all began yelling at once. Rick called me a spoiled brat, a crybaby and a bitch. He assured me that he'd hit me anytime he felt like it. That did it for me. I swung at his face as hard as I could, knocking him to the floor. I quickly pinned him down because he wasn't expecting it and struck him another time or two. Carol knocked me off him but I regained my balance and slugged her hard. No sooner had I done that then Rick was slamming me against the wall. Pain went through my head as I hit the wall but I ignored it and belted him in the stomach. He hit me in the jaw and I fell against the wall again.

"Stop it! Stop it!" Kevin was yelling.

David was suddenly in front of me warding off Rick and Carol and saying, "Okay, okay. I think we get the idea. Let's try to calm down."

Rick struggled against him for a few seconds and then stopped. "You're supposed to be her guardian, man!" David informed Rick in case he'd forgotten. "You know she could have told Bob plenty of things already and ruined everything for us but she hasn't. You know we're really lucky we haven't been thrown out of this house too. The cops are here almost every weekend."

I picked myself up from the floor. It had been an awful long time since I'd been in a fist fight and it made me feel strong again. It also surprised me that David had stood up to Rick for me.

"I'm not her guardian." Rick insisted.

"I don't want you to be. I can take care of myself. That never was a problem." I replied steadily.

"To me it is." He said.

"To me too." Carol added.

"Well, let's sit down and maybe we can talk about this." David suggested.

We all went into the living room and tried to talk it out. Everyone was supposed to get things off their minds. Carol said that I always had more money than the rest of them. I told them that I did have dad's insurance money which Bob allotted me so much a month but that I did work part time and go to school all day too. I had housework and homework and the gigs and practices with them. That explanation seemed wasted on them. They, of course, had it harder with jobs and our music. Rick didn't want the responsibility of being my guardian over his head. Kevin said he had too much responsibility on him. David said he hated that he had no privacy. The conversation went back to the argument stage and we stormed off in our own directions.

I went to lunch at the pizza shop where Jace worked. He took one look at me and said, "Jesus! they beat you up! Let me bring you some pizza. I'll be right back." He pointed me to a back table. He was back with pizza for both of us.

"Rick and me got into it." I explained. "I started it, actually. I was trying to get us all on the same page about housework." I glanced at him to see his reaction.

"But he hit you! He's supposed to be taking care of you. If I'd known he'd hit you I wouldn't have let you go back there." He protested as he reached for me and hugged me as if it would take away my problems. I let him hold me.

"Fights are really nothing new. You didn't know me when I lived in South Carolina. I used to fist fight all the time. I was suspended so many times, it wasn't funny. My dad practically lived at the school for teacher/parent meetings to explain my behavior. But oddly enough I've not really had much of a taste for fights since we moved here. The band has needed to be put in line for so long. I may not look so good, but I feel much better inside."

He let go of me and his eyes got a bit wider. "Well, I know you're kind of a tom boy with the sports and motor cross and everything but I never knew you were a fighter."

I was silent.

"That still doesn't excuse Rick from hitting you. He's supposed to know better. I'm going to have a good talk with him."

"No! That's not why I came here. I can fight my own battles!" I got up to leave. He touched my arm and sat me down again. He said he wouldn't beat up Rick. We talked about the things that the band had complained about.

"You do know that they are jealous that you're a model, even if it is only in a catalog, right?" He asked.

I knew. "What do you think of me?" I asked.

"You're pretty cool." He replied as he put his arm around me and hugged me to him. I put my arms around him and hugged him back. When he kept holding me, I let him, then someone called his name and we let go of our embrace.

Eventually I had to go back home. Carol quickly pointed out that it was my turn to cook. "What am I supposed to make?" I asked.

She looked at me warily and replied, "Spaghetti, meat balls, garlic bread and something for dessert." I headed to the store and sweet talked a stock person to find the ingredients so I could pay and leave.

The dinner was satisfactory. Nothing was burned, nothing was broken. The sauce was out of a jar, the garlic bread only had to be taken out of foil and baked, as did the peach cobbler. The meat balls fell apart but tasted okay. I hadn't enjoyed a minute of it. Afterward I went to my drum set and drummed out the odd rhythm until Rick yelled at me to quit.

We had a gig the following night. I usually didn't pay too much attention to any one person in the crowd but I noticed a couple that came in right before our break. They sat where they could see us and the guy stared at me. All I could think about was hit men for whatever reason.

At the break, Rick and Carol greeted them. I got a Sprite from the bar and several guys were vying for my attention. Rick busted in between us. "I want to introduce you to someone." He told me. I already felt someone looking me up and down and evaluating me. I didn't like it one bit. And on top of that, his energy felt dangerous.

"This is Joseph Poplas and Katrina." He said to me as I stood in front of the couple's table. Joseph stood up and took my hand as Rick introduced me to him, then to Katrina. They were darker skinned and had accents. I couldn't quite place what country they were from.

"Do you like to have fun?" Joseph asked me as he smiled. I sensed that he was already having a fantasy of some sort in his head. His accent was intriguing and I could see how women could get infatuated with him. I also sensed that he had plans for me that I wouldn't like.

"I'm sixteen and I'm the guardian of this bunch." I told him as I saw that wasn't the answer that any of them wanted to hear.

Joseph laughed. "Very responsible. I like that." He went into talking some sweet talk and when I didn't bite, he aimed towards Carol who smiled and cuddled up to him. "Now, she knows how to make a man feel welcome. You need to learn the same." He murmured as he looked down at her cleavage. I glanced at Katrina but she didn't seem to care that he was flirting. I wondered what she was to him. It seemed like they were together but the vibe seemed like she was his property and that made my skin crawl.

I silently huffed to myself. Men needed to make me feel welcome not vice versa, the jerk. "We need to go back to work." I remarked and I exited that conversation.

"That was rude." Rick told me a moment later as we settled back with our instruments ready to launch into a song.

After our gig was over, he and Carol left with Joseph and Katrina.

"What do you think they're up to?" David asked me.

"Prostitution and drugs." I answered back without hesitation.

He and Kevin laughed until they noticed that I wasn't laughing. "Are you serious?" They asked.

"Yeah."

"Shit." David said, drawing the word out.

Yeah, that was a good response. The two of them drilled me about my conclusion and I told them how I thought it was going down.

"But why do you think that?" David pressed.

I shrugged my shoulders. "That's how it feels to me."

"She always knows everything. You know that." Kevin remarked as he helped me load my drum set into my truck.

"No, she doesn't." He replied. I was hoping in this certain case that he was right.

***

I was in my room after school the next day when Carol invited herself in. "That Joseph is a handsome guy, don't you think?" She gushed.

"He's old, and you don't know anything about him." I replied back as I pondered over some Algebra One. Math wasn't my best subject and I actually had to listen in school and study it.

"Old? He's only twenty-six!" She exclaimed as she sat on my bed with me. She went on to gush about him. He was rich, he was successful, he was a good catch. "We're going to a party with him and Katrina after our gig tonight. He wants you to come with us."

"NO. And I think you should lose them before the shit is too deep for you to get out of. I have a real bad feeling about them and whatever y'all are doing. And I definitely don't think they think of you as friends of theirs. He's seriously dangerous."

She got aggravated at me then. "You're just jealous because we found a good thing. Fuck you, if you don't want involved. You're lucky that we even asked you." She said, then she loudly exited my room. I thought about running after her and slamming her against the wall for slamming my bedroom door. I hated doors being slammed, especially when I was right, and I was always right.

When Rick came home, I tried to talk to him. I told him that he and Carol needed to lose Joseph before the shit it the fan and we were all running for our lives. He huffed that he was an adult and that it was none of my business who their friends were.

"He's not a friend. He's a mean sonofabitch who will hurt you whenever you stop cooperating with him. Please stop this now while you still can." I told him very seriously. Wow, I'd even said "please".

He snorted as if it were funny and dismissed me. I knew that I didn't want to live in witness protection with one leg, or in a nursing home with half a head.

***

We all had tension between us but we were speaking to each other most of the time instead of yelling. David had been bitching about a speeding ticket he had gotten, and Kevin had nearly been charged with drunken driving. He ended up with a warning since they couldn't prove he was intoxicated. He and I had a long talk about driving drunk especially in my truck. He was only sixteen, and was basically a runaway. If he got into serious trouble, they'd make him go back and live with his parents. That notion was enough to knock some sense into him.

The house didn't quite look like the disaster area it once had been and I noticed that every bill except for the gas bill had been paid. When things got tense at home, I went to check on what Streethart was doing. I found myself listening to yet another one of Curt's stories. He was telling us about the adventures of his friend, Terra. I had gathered from comments I'd heard that every story involving Terra also involved sex with animals. He had never told any stories about Terra when I'd been around.

I heard him saying ".....yeah, I never would have believed it either but you know how horny Terra is. I mean she jumped on that baboon not even wondering if he was dangerous and she...."

"Curt!" Jace interrupted. "Do you mind?" He thought I was too young to listen to the smut that Curt liked to tell, meanwhile I'd probably seen and heard far more than he ever had just by the things Rebel did.

"Oh, let him tell it. Then maybe I'll tell you one of my stories." I told him.

Jace shrugged his shoulders. Curt finished his story then asked to hear mine.

I didn't have a story in mind but I let my imagination run wild. "Well, as you all know I'm having some trouble with Rick. One night about a month ago we got along real fine. You see, everyone in the house was partying that night. He was sky high and everyone else was drunk. Carol was passed out on their bed. I was the only one not wasted. I saw Rick go upstairs so I followed him. I paused at his door but then went to my own room. He knocked on my door and when I opened it, he said that he had something he wanted to teach me. He came into my room and then locked the door. Pretty soon we were both undressed." I said as I watched to see if they were really interested. I had their undivided attention. I went on to describe exactly what kind of sexual adventures I'd had that night. I described them slowly and dreamily as though I was still there. As I finished the story, I acted embarrassed like maybe I shouldn't have told them. They stared at me in amazement. I had told that story well and without a script. I was pleased with myself.

Curt nervously lit a joint. "Now you're a good story teller." He remarked. They still didn't know if it was the truth. I could tell by their faces. I would let them wonder.

Smith noticed the joint, caught Curt's attention and motioned for him to put it out.

"I saw Rick a week or so ago and you did leave some bruises on him. He's twice your size and he got beat up by a pint-sized kid." Jace commented.

"Hey, you better watch out who you call a kid or you'll be next." I teased.

He laughed because he didn't think we'd ever fight about anything. He playfully punched my arm and I punched him back.

"Oh, come on. How could this Angel Babe beat up a grown man?" Smith asked.

I was annoyed. "I'm strong and I know how to

fight." I replied. I spotted Jace's bar bells sitting in the corner of the room. "I can lift sixty pounds over my head." I said pointing to the bar bells.

Jimmy and Smith laughed at me; they thought I was kidding. "Listen to that shit. She can't weigh more than 90 pounds. Between that story and this, she's a bigger bullshitter than Curt." Jimmy said.

"Of course, I can do it." I insisted.

"Well, five bucks says you can't". He shot back.

"Okay." I replied going over to the bar bells.

"You don't have to do this." Jace and Greggie told me.

Jimmy set the weights. I stalled for time just to humor them. Finally, I stood in front of the group and prepared to lift the bar. I got it to my shoulders and paused for a second or two. Jace and Smith jumped to my side as if I would drop it, but I brought it above my head. "I can get it down too." I told them but they helped me put it on the floor. "Pay up." I told Jimmy.

He disgustedly tossed a five at me. He liked for things to go his way and this hadn't.

"Wow!" Smith remarked.

"Yeah. Wow!" echoed Greggie. He looked at me with admiration reflecting in his eyes. "You're so unique. On one hand you're so sweet and on the other hand you're so tough."

I rolled my eyes dramatically and smiled.

He reached out and pulled me onto his lap. I liked him and wished we were alone, but we weren't and the other guys gave Greggie some flak and warned me that I was just causing trouble. I stayed put and ignored them.

A bit later they went home, leaving me, Jace and Biscuit alone.

"You need to leave Greg alone." Jace remarked to me.

"Someone will tell his girlfriend. He's too old for you anyhow."

"I like him. Maybe he'll get rid of her." I replied.

"Don't count on it. Find someone your own age. He's just playing you." He said as he cleared off the empty beer bottles from the coffee table. I'd already known that.

"That story you told about Rick, is it true?"

"Does it matter?"

"No." He lied. His thoughts were just the opposite. "Seriously." He asked again.

"No."

"Then why would you tell a story like that?" He remarked as he looked intently at me.

I didn't answer for a moment. I had kind of gotten into the story as I was telling it. It had been a long time since I'd done anyone and although I would have loved to have made it with Rick when I first had a crush on him, I had gotten over it. However, if he were to give me the chance, I knew I'd probably take it. That's just how it was.

"Angel." Jace said nudging me out of my thoughts.

"I'd sleep with Rick in a minute, if things were different. He was my first crush." I confessed.

Jace looked at me in amazement but said nothing.

I giggled at his reaction. "You asked." I said.

"I think you just need a vibrator." He remarked bluntly. "And to quit fantasizing about Rick, and Greg for that matter."

I considered that for a moment. "Nah! I think I'm going to go home now. Maybe Rick will be there." I smiled. Although when I arrived home Rick was in such a bad mood that I remembered why I didn't have a crush on him anymore.

It wasn't until a few days later that I found out why he was in such a bad mood. I overheard him and Carol talking. Carol thought she was pregnant. There was no telling who the father might be.

***

I was tuned out in my own world as I sat on the couch with Kevin and David who were watching some Christmas movie. We had a blanket over us because the temperature outside was only in the twenties and we weren't crazy warm inside. In my fantasy world, Jace was all about me and he worshipped the ground that I walked on. We were all startled as the front door opened and Carol stumbled in shrieking and crying. I jerked out of my world to find that somehow the three of us were laying all over each other. I had my head on Kevin's shoulder, and David was lying against me. We sat up and looked towards the noise.

"Oh my God! What happened?" Kevin and David asked as they jumped up, nearly dumping me on the floor. I recovered and muted the tv and picked the blanket up from where it had fallen. I tucked it around me.

Rick helped Carol to a comfortable chair. "That sonofabitch Joseph beat her up." He replied angrily. "I ought to kill him!"

"What are you guys into?" David asked. "This is some fucking serious business."

I observed Carol as the story spilled out. She had a black eye, her makeup was running, the heel was off one of her shoes, and her blouse was noticeably ripped. She had refused to go out with a client of Joseph's. I was thinking that she'd gotten off easy on the beating. I was sure that Joseph could have beaten her so much worse.

"So, you've been a prostitute just like Angel said." David stated.

"I was an escort!" She exclaimed angrily. "Yeah, I usually had sex with them but I was an escort! I was making three hundred dollars a night free and clear!"

"I'm calling the police." Rick said as he started towards the phone.

"Nope! You can't. They're gonna really hurt you, if not kill you if you do." I said as I jumped to my feet and stopped him.

"We can't just let him get away with this!" they all said.

"You have to. Do you really think crime lords want to be handcuffed and put away? Joseph is into drug dealing and everything else that's illegal. Do you think if they land in jail that you wouldn't be assaulted or killed by some unknown assailant as payback for reporting them?" I asked as the images flipped across my brain.

Rick opened his mouth to say something then shut it again and sat down heavily.

"Oh my God. What have you two done?" David asked, his eyes wide with so much fear that I could taste it. I felt myself trying to diffuse the fear in the room. Huh.

"Why are you listening to her? She don't know jack shit and y'all are acting like she knows what's going on. We haven't told her one damn thing." Carol spouted back. She was rubbing her arm and I noticed now how bruised looking it was.

Rick put his head in his hands then.

"Rick! This is ludicrous! Call the police." She said as she stared at him in shock. He always sided with her and now he wasn't saying a thing.

"I think she's right." He finally said, his head still in his hands as if he had a headache.

"Oh, fucking thanks! Now your crime lord's gonna kill all of us. Just fucking thanks!" David said as he stomped around the living room thinking about it. All of them were yelling at each other now. I watched and listened.

"What do we do now?" David asked me as suddenly all eyes were on me.

"Stay away from them, not that there won't be revenge. You're small change to them at this point and I think when they realize that you haven't called the cops that eventually they'll forget about you. It's gonna take a while though." I said thoughtfully.

"Revenge? Small change? They'll eventually forget? Oh my God. You don't know that." Were several of the comments. But I did know that.

Carol's cell phone was ringing. Everyone jerked at the sound except me. "Oh my God! It's him! It's that fucking asshole!" She cried. Yeah, her rich, young, handsome man was now a fucking asshole.

"Don't answer it." Rick told her.

"You answer it." I told him. If you don't, I figure that Joseph will send a few of his goons here." He hesitated. "Hurry. If they show up here it will be a bad, bad scene." I told him so he picked up the phone. I was glad because I didn't think I'd be any match for a crime lord and his goons, no matter how fierce I thought I was.

He didn't have to say anything. Joseph or one of his goons did the talking. "No, we haven't and we won't. Just leave us alone. We're done." Rick said to him. Then he looked at the phone. "He hung up. He said that if we go to the police that we'd regret it and that we should take his advice very seriously."

As the rest of them cried and carried on, I examined the energy of the situation to see how much danger we were in. I was really glad that it felt like Joseph was more bark than bite. He wasn't going to kill us. But still, it was going to be a rough ride.

It started that night when Carol had a miscarriage because of the beating. None of us had suspected she was pregnant. She would have had an abortion anyway but it was a sobering reality of what Joseph's goons had done to her. I was thinking of revenge.

When we found that Rick's windshield was busted to pieces it angered me more. After two of Joseph's goons sat in the section of the restaurant that Carol waitressed and threatened her, I had more thoughts of revenge.

"I'm scared." Kevin told me two nights later as he was putting away the clothes he'd washed of mine. I was glad he'd stopped wearing my clothes. I was sitting on the bed trying to read a boring story in my Literature book. "What are we going to do?" He asked.

I put down my book. I was wishing that I could have someone else take my Literature class for me so I didn't have to read boring stories that were supposed examples of great writing. Had none of them ever read work by James Patterson or Brian Freeman? Now, they were some great writers that would be a better read than what we'd been assigned. "It's intimidation, that's all. It will stop eventually." I replied as I yawned a big yawn.

David walked into my room then and Kevin brought him up to speed on our conversation. "Why aren't you scared?" Kevin asked me.

"The energy doesn't seem as dangerous as before."

"It seemed dangerous when they cornered me as I came out of work today." David informed me as he suddenly appeared before us. "Joseph's goons warned me that I'd better keep Rick and Carol in check or they'd break my legs."

Anger flooded my veins and I felt mean. "They threatened you." I stated as I puffed up in anger. It was one thing for them to threaten Rick and Carol because they'd gotten themselves into this mess, but David or Kevin? No way. They were my guys, my bros.

"Yeah, and I don't mind telling you that I'm fucking scared for my life." David replied. He went on a rant about how stupid Rick and Carol were getting us all into this mess as he paced around my bedroom.

"Joseph is going to pay for this." I informed them. "Not this minute or else it will point straight back to us, but in the near future."

"And what are you going to do?" David snorted. "You might have been a bully in school but these guys mean business."

"So do I. NO ONE is going to hurt or threaten my friends and get away with it." And I meant that.

He and Kevin dismissed me as just spouting off. That was okay, they didn't need to know what I was planning. It was best that they thought I was harmless.

CHAPTER 6

Ever since Carol had found out she was pregnant Kevin had been worrying about getting the women he slept with pregnant. "You use a rubber, right?" I asked him.

"Yeah, but what if it breaks?" He asked as he nervously chewed on his thumb.

I gently moved his thumb out of his mouth. "I don't feel like you'll have a rubber break. But if you're that scared about getting someone pregnant then I would always use a rubber even if the girl says she's on the pill. Carol is on the pill but she forgot to take two of them. She would have gotten an abortion anyways had she not had a miscarriage."

He huffed in exasperation. "Damn, this sucks."

"Yep." I agreed. If it had been up to me, I would have made it that you had to take a pill to get pregnant not the other way around. I wouldn't have been born had that been the case but whatever. The world's population would only be half of what it was.

***

As I came out of work a few days later I felt bad energy. It directed my attention across the property to the parking lot. I bristled because I knew it was Joseph and or his goons. Before I could huff myself up to the big bully I'd always been, I saw a spaceship appear and hover a car length from my truck. It was a huge spaceship but noiseless. I felt ten feet tall and bullet proof then so I walked straight up to Joseph who was leaning on my truck. "Get off my truck." I demanded. His goon who was standing a few feet away closed the space between us. I punched him as he intended on grabbing me. It hardly fazed him and he quickly grabbed me and had his hand over my mouth. They were going to kidnap me. I felt no fear. I was going to stop them somehow. I noticed two aliens standing a few feet away from us.

"*Hot*", the voice in my head said, and I understood.

The goon suddenly threw me backwards and was screaming as he shook his hands out as he looked at them. "What the fuck did you do to me? My hands are burning!" He screamed. I jumped back a few feet away from him but was amazed by what had happened. If I'd had any brains in my head I would have run.

"Jesus Christ! Do I have to do everything by myself?" Joseph exclaimed angrily. He moved towards me and I was ready to fight him but suddenly he was thrown backwards as if the wind had knocked him off his feet and thrown him against my truck. He'd hit pretty hard. He looked really dazed.

"Hey! Watch the fucking truck! I'm still paying on it." I exclaimed angrily. I was as angry with him as I was with the aliens. Sure, their aircraft was invincible but my truck wasn't. I stood there with my feet spread apart and my hands on my hips as if I were Supergirl. The wind blew hard whipping my hair behind me and I could imagine my cape flying in the breeze. "Leave me and my friends alone. They said they wanted out, now let them out." I snapped again. The goon was looking at his hands and whimpering.

Joseph rolled to his feet and came at me again. Before he got within my reach, he was blown back down to the ground.

"Fuck! She's the fucking devil! I'm getting the fuck out of here!" The goon exclaimed with a hysterical edge to his voice. He was already running through the maze of cars to get away from me. I felt the urge to zap him with electricity as he ran.

Joseph stood up and stared at me. "You don't scare me, little girl. You'd better watch your step."

"Just leave us alone." I replied back staring him down. I watched his back as he walked away. I had been about to add, "You don't fucking scare me either", but the voice in my head shushed me. I watched him walk to his sports car and screech away.

I walked over to my truck and stood in front of the dent that Joseph had made when he'd slammed into it. One of the aliens appeared beside me and touched the dent. I watched as it smoothed out as if it had never happened. I scrunched my face up and looked at him. "Be more careful next time." I remarked out loud.

A voice giggled as the person walked up behind me. I turned to face them. It was one of the guys that followed me around at work. "Who are you talking to?" He asked, smiling.

I looked towards the aliens but they had vanished and so had the spaceship. Yeah, they liked to go all cloak and dagger at times like this.

I shook my head and smiled. "I was just talking to myself. I was sure that a grocery cart hit my truck right here and dented it a few days ago but I guess it didn't." I lied.

I groused to myself as I drove home. Joseph's goon had called me the devil! I was an alien, dammit!

***

It was the first Friday in December. The band and I had set up in the gym of my high school. At 2:30pm the kids would be coming in to hear us play. We'd play for an hour and then school would be over for the day. All of the band except for me had had to take off early from work to play this gig and we weren't even getting paid. Most of the band just wanted to see my school and my demise in front of them, at least Carol did. Now that Joseph and his goons seemed to have stepped back, she had decided to blame me because she didn't have a load of cash to spend anymore. I was suddenly the reason that Joseph and his goons were after us. I really wanted Joseph to off her.

I felt a little exposed as I waited at the drums with the rest of the band. We watched the kids file in and take seats in the bleachers. Several people yelled out to me. I waved and gave them a drum thump. The principal had warned me that we'd better be respectful and that he wouldn't tolerate any vulgarity. We had yet to play in a club that tolerated vulgarity so it wasn't any big deal. As several more kids shouted "Rock on!" or something of the sort to me, I felt the energy of my band change. I didn't talk about my life in school to Rick or Carol or David. Kevin knew I had friends here but he didn't know half of the interaction that went on during my days.

"Where's all the booing and the insults?" Carol wisecracked to me. "I expected you to have the entire school brawling by now."

"And I thought you'd be sucking all of their dicks by now." I replied back.

"Hey! Hey! Hey! The microphones are on!" Rick shushed us. "Let's at least get one song down before we get thrown out of here."

I had to smile at that.

Ms. Lowe came out on stage and there were several wolf whistles. It was a typical high school for sure. Some of the kids stomped their feet on the bleachers. There were probably close to three hundred and fifty students that went to school here. Our audience count looked to be close to three hundred.

Ms. Lowe introduced each of us. When she introduced me, I stood up and a lot of the kids cheered, stomped their feet and shouted out to me. About half or so of the audience stood up and clapped, with about fifty being really loud. With sticks in hand, I gave them a triumphant gesture. Several whistled at me. Wolf whistles sang out too and I smiled. I wished that daddy could have been there to see it. I finally would have made him proud.

"Those kids are cheering for you. Hell has fucking frozen over." I heard Rick remark in amazement.

"We're not in Kansas anymore, Dorothy." David muttered referencing the Wizard of Oz movie.

When Ms. Lowe introduced Kevin, several cheered and shouted at him. There was obligatory clapping for the rest of the band since the kids didn't know them. "We're chopped liver. Seems anymore that she gets all the attention." David grumbled. I supposed that was true.

I started us off and we played Jumping Jack Flash first, then a few of the current rock songs. Towards the end of the hour, Rick announced that I was going to sing Joan Jett's I Love Rock and Roll. There was a lot of cheering and comments that were shouted. The clapping was loud and long as we finished that song. Then we could hear people shouting for me to play guitar. I expected Rick to be irked at that but he wasn't. "You want her to play guitar?" He asked them.

I smiled as the kids loudly affirmed that.

"Well, I guess." He said in a mock aggravation. "Let's give her more of a reason to be so full of herself."

The kids that were able to hear him laughed. I took Kevin's guitar and he took my place at the drums. David was the lead guitarist and I wondered if he'd fight me if I took lead. I caught his eye and said, "I'm lead".

"That's the plan, your majesty." He scoffed.

"What are we going to do?" Rick asked me.

"Billy Idol, Rebel Yell." I answered.

"Right, a show off song. Shoulda figured." He mumbled then relayed it to the others.

"I'm just glad it's not Still the Same." David remarked and they laughed.

Kevin hit the sticks and I started us off. "Rebel Yell" was an energetic song and it had an awesome guitar riff. Kevin could show off too with the awesome beat of the song. I just loved how people's eyes always popped out when I played, and it was an easy song! Oh yeah! And I could scream as well as Billy.

As I sang and played, several of the kids had stood up and were dancing and clapping. I focused on them. Yeah, this is what I wanted to do with my life, rock out on my guitar. The song went by too fast. As the clapping was ending, Ms. Lowe was walking towards us. She announced that the hour was over. The students were protesting loudly before she even had a chance to thank us for playing for them. Now they were stomping the bleachers. Since they were so loud, she glanced over at the principal and he held up two fingers. "Okay, okay, settle down. If they're willing, we'll let them play another two songs. But those of you that need to get to your buses are free to go." She told them. They clapped and cheered at that. I turned back and smiled at my band, uh, Rick's band. We all knew from previous experience that once I got ahold of a guitar that the audience wasn't about to let me go back to playing drums. It was also experience for us that you just couldn't end a set on such an energetic song. My fault, ha! We played Boulevard of Broken Dreams by Green Day with me singing, and then Rick sang Are you Gonna Be My Girl by Jet. We had played well. About fifty classmates or so came over to talk to us as the bell rang and there was a rush for the kids to get to their buses. I was back to feeling like a celebrity. Back in Greenville we'd had a following and groupies, here in New Rochelle we didn't quite have that yet. The kids talked to all of us though and within thirty minutes all that were left were those few that had driven to school and didn't have anywhere pressing to go. I even let Jordan kiss me knowing that the band would harass me about it later.

We began hauling our equipment out to our vehicles and we had plenty of help. It had been amusing to hear several of the kids gush about how cool I was and how great I was. Gone were the days where all the kids were scared of me and talking about beating me up. I liked the change. I noticed my band members giving me curious looks when the kids had said nothing but positive things about me. I gave my fans high fives.

"Well, THAT, was different." Rick remarked when we got home. "I didn't know you could act like a human being in school, well anywhere for that matter."

"Stupid New York! Done fucked me up." I griped back at him in mock aggravation.

They snickered at me. I realized at that moment too, that we were all getting along. Huh. When we played music, we got along no matter how badly we had been acting up until a moment before we performed. Yeah, I was feeling good. It had taken so damn long to feel this way.

***

About a week and a half before Christmas I got a call from Smith. He asked me over to his house. He said that the rest of Streethart was there and they had some business they wanted to talk about. As I drove over there, I wondered what they could want. It seemed so odd.

I couldn't help evaluating them when I got there. Every one of them seemed nervous. Then I found out why. "We have three gigs this week." Smith began. "We want to know if you'll go onstage with us those nights and play lead guitar. We'll introduce you and say that you're from the band, Rebel. We've been wanting to do this for a long time but you always have gigs the same nights we have gigs. Just by coincidence, I found out that your Wednesday night gig is cancelled because of some remodeling and Club Nine wants you guys to play on Saturday night this week instead of Friday."

"Yeah." Jace agreed. "We'd like you to jam with us."

Wow, I thought to myself, he was serious. "I don't get it." I replied. Actually, I did. They were hoping that I could help them draw a bigger audience. An impressive lead guitarist who just happened to be a model. That's what they were thinking. Even Jace was thinking that.

"There's a few songs that we've been dying to use and when you showed us how well you could play, we thought you would like working with us and doing us a favor at the same time." Jimmy told me.

I cast a wary look at Jimmy. He was kissing up to me. Usually, he only seemed to tolerate me. He was the bassist and for a moment the thought of showing him how well I could play the bass entered my mind.

I glanced at Jace. "Are you sure you'll be okay with this?"

"Yeah. This will be good for all of us. I'm cool with it. You're good on guitar. I admit it and I admire it."

"Wow, thanks." I replied drinking it all in. He really meant it. He'd come a long way in his attitude.

"We'll pay you like last time." Smith replied.

I knew that some lessons were about to be learned though even if they didn't. I would do what they wanted. "Okay." I replied. "It will be cool." I knew it wouldn't though. It would cause problems. I was up for it though.

The first gig was on a Wednesday night. True to their word, I was introduced as C. Angel from Rebel and a model from the Harris Company. We did some heavy-duty rock and roll with Jace as lead singer. We did some "Stones" hits and towards the end of the first set, I played the guitar solo from the "Rockies". The audience went wild on that one. But best of all, me and Jace jammed together with dueling guitars and that was worth it all.

We took a fifteen minute break. All of Streethart's girlfriends were back stage waiting. When I first met Streethart, none of their girlfriends steadily attended their performances but one by one they had started showing up. I imagined that Streethart talked about me sometimes and their girlfriends had decided that they better check me out and make sure I wasn't trying to steal any of their men. The only one I was remotely interested in was Greggie. He lived with his girlfriend and she continuously pointed out to me that he was her man. Tonight, was no exception. I didn't tell her that he cheated on her from time to time, but not with me.

When we went onstage for the second set the crowd was huge. By the time we finished the set, the crowd was standing room only. Streethart told the audience that I would be performing two more gigs with them and to join us then.

The guys invited me to hang out with them afterward and I really wanted to but I was going to do school, work and a gig another two nights in a row, I knew I'd better go home and go to bed.

I must admit that the next night at the gig even I was shocked at how many people were there. We started out just like we had at the first gig and then went on to some deeper stuff. By the middle of our second set, it was standing room only. Maybe it was the nightclub that we played at; I don't know. It was some performance and definitely an unheard of crowd for a Thursday night. The guys even let me be the lead singer on a Guns n' Roses song. I felt a rush from the crowd cheering for me after that song.

The guys were extremely wound up after we were finished. It was a bigger crowd than I had seen with Rebel, with me as a drummer and Rick as the lead singer. The next thing that happened was something that I figured would happen. Rick was suddenly backstage raising hell. He was yelling at me for trying

115

to underhand our band. Then he was yelling at Streethart. The guys tried to explain to him that it was just an agreed upon deal, that I wasn't trying to break up Rebel. He was in my face again and this time he was about to hit me. Jace stopped him and set him straight. I thought he was going to knock Rick flat. The rest of Streethart, Jimmy included, closed in on him. They told him that he'd better keep his hands off me because he would answer to them if he didn't. They said that his anger should be with them not me. Then they were all arguing. During the course of it, one of them said that I would be happier with them, that they knew how to treat a lady. Maybe they got to Rick a little bit. He calmed down and it became more of a discussion. I stayed out of it. A while later, he left. His parting words to me were, "We will talk about this later."

They watched him go out the door and then Curt turned to me and said, "And to think that you slept with him too."

I couldn't help laughing. "No Curt, I didn't sleep with him. It was only a story and you better not tell him."

I left soon after with their words of caution ringing in my ears.

Rick was sitting in the living room brooding to himself. The tv was low and the house was otherwise silent.

"Well?" I asked as I sat down on the oak coffee table which was almost directly in front of him.

"What are you doing, Angel? Are you trying to join their band? Did they talk you into it?" He demanded.

"No. I'm not joining their band and they didn't ask me to. They were just jiving you. They asked me to play guitar for them for three gigs. I knew it would be a lot of fun. I don't see it as a problem."

"It is a problem when you don't bother to mention to me what you're doing and I have to find out through the grapevine."

I gazed at him dreamily. It seemed like a dream. "But you said you didn't want to be my guardian and we scrapped that rule."

He stared at me with anger in his eyes.

"Look, I don't see that anyone else is home. It's just you and me. I'm going to be straight with you. Jace and his band are my friends and I was only jamming with them. I don't want to join their band. Keep in mind that I am pretty damn good on guitar maybe even better than on the drums and I think I could get into any band I wanted to. But I'm staying here with you guys because this is what we decided to do together. We need to get our shit together. It's not only that I'm a problem to you guys but we are all problems to each other. If we don't get it together, we'll never make it big as a band, or if we screw up in a way that Bob hears about, he'll haul me back in a blink of an eye. I don't want that to happen."

He listened to what I said and then got his coat and walked out the door without saying a word.

I figured he and Carol were fighting again when I witnessed an exchange between Carol and David the next afternoon. I had come in from work to find Carol and David in the living room. She was wearing near nothing and trying to seduce him. I said hi and went to the kitchen. I was warming up some leftovers when I heard him say, "I'm just not interested in doing you right now. Can't you let it go?"

"You never want to do me," I heard Carol whine.

"I get enough action from the rest of my women. God, you women about wear me out! Besides, your old man lives under the same roof. How the hell can you expect me to do you?" He said in an exasperated tone.

I stood in the doorway watching them then. She was as close to him as she could get without being on his lap.

"Another time, okay?" He pleaded.

"I guess." She replied.

David hugged her to him and kissed the top of her head. I couldn't believe a male was actually turning down Carol for sex. I moved back inside the kitchen so they wouldn't see me. I went to check on my food. David was beside me not two minutes afterward trying to pry my heated up spaghetti away from me. I figured I could make him leave. "You can do me, David." I smiled. Once the words were out of my mouth, I realized that I'd meant them. It had been so long since I'd had sex.

He rolled his eyes. "You damn women! You wear me out!" He said, then he stomped out of the kitchen.

I giggled but I also was somewhat disappointed. I had a different type of fantasy in my mind then.
***

Friday marked the last gig I was to do with Streethart. I stopped at Jace's apartment first. "I don't know if it's a good idea for me to go to your gig tonight." I told him.

"Why? Do you think that Rick is going to crash it?"

"Yeah."

"Do it anyway." He said.

It was an hour before show time and I was off stage with Streethart and their girlfriends. It looked like we would draw another large crowd. Curt had another tall tale to tell and was in the middle of it when Rick dropped by.

"Stopped to see the show, huh?" Jimmy smirked to him.

"It's going to be a good one." Smith told him.

"Angel, I want to talk to you." He said ignoring them.

He looked to be in a decent mood so I walked outside with him. We stood in the freezing air and I wondered if he was going to talk at all. He looked at the moon and then scanned the parking lot.

"Richard!" I said impatiently. "It feels like ten degrees out here."

"Okay. Let's sit in the car." He said. We got into his car and he turned on the heater. He looked into my eyes. We were sort of at a standstill where he wondered if I'd give in if he talked to me nicely. "I don't want you to do this tonight." He said.

"Why not?" I asked meeting his eyes.

"They're using you!" He said angrily.

I looked out the window. "I know. I'm giving them their fifteen minutes of fame. They just don't know it yet."

"What are you talking about?"

I knew he wouldn't understand but I'd tell him anyway. "We'll be stars one day – if we get our act together, Rick. I told you that a few days before we left South Carolina. Streethart never will so I'm giving them a moment of fame. Plus, I like being a guitar player so I'm doing it for some selfish reasons too."

"This is just nuts! You can't know that we'll be famous."

"I can't explain it so you'll understand but come watch us."

After some cussing, he walked into the club with me. He stayed for nearly the entire performance, which was a combination of the two previous ones. The crowd was great. The press showed up and interviewed Streethart. They turned to interview me but I only gave them my name and talked about what a great band Streethart was. This write up was their baby.

I went straight home afterward. No one in the house was very happy with me. Rick was drunk and tried to argue with me and then he and Carol were fighting about infidelity. I seriously thought about staying at a hotel but didn't go through with it. Eventually everyone settled down and was silent because no one was on speaking terms with anyone else.

The following day a small article came out in the paper about Streethart and me. They were thrilled but I had to deal with my band's anger.

CHAPTER 7

Things still weren't going all that smoothly at home by the time Christmas Eve rolled around. The house wasn't decorated and to my knowledge no one had even gone Christmas shopping. Jace was having a party and told me to come over. I looked for his latest girlfriend when I got there because she thought that Jace was much too friendly with me. I had been hoping to become friends with her because I didn't have close friends that were female but she didn't want me as a friend. Curt gave me a glass of punch and I drank about three glasses worth just listening to him tell me one space odyssey tale. Smith and his wife, Carrie joined us as I was about to get another glass of that delicious punch. "Do you drink much?" Smith asked me.

"No. I don't drink at all." I told him, which was funny because I was feeling rather hot and dizzy.

"The punch is spiked." Carrie smiled.

I guess I stood there with my mouth open. I had never considered that the punch would be spiked. Whenever the band drank it wasn't hidden in anything, it was all out in the open, in plainly marked bottles. I sat down again, my thirst suddenly gone.

Carrie distracted me with some gossip about someone at the party and I forgot about the spiked punch. I hadn't talked much with her before but I liked her. Both her and Smith were twenty-six which was really old to me. I asked about Jace's girlfriend and she said that they had broken up.

Christmas morning, I woke up with a headache. Jace was sleeping beside me. We were in his bed and I didn't remember how I'd gotten there. I was still in the clothes I'd worn the night before minus my shoes. I lifted up the covers to see what Jace had on. He was wearing blue jean shorts and a t-shirt.

I got up and almost tripped over Biscuit as I headed to the bathroom. I was unsteady on my feet but at least I didn't feel sick.

Jace stirred as I lay back down beside him, mostly because Biscuit jumped on the bed too.

"Merry Christmas." I said to him.

"Merry Christmas, yourself." He replied sleepily.

I stared at him. I wondered if in our drunken states we'd slept together. But I was dressed. Surely, I would have been naked if we'd done something.

"Don't look at me like that. I didn't do anything to you. You were on the couch when I went to sleep. I didn't put you here." Jace said to me.

"I was just wondering." I replied with irritation. "I hadn't meant to climb in bed with you."

"No big deal. You can stay put."

"Did I hit on you?" I asked.

"Go back to sleep." He replied groggily rolling away from me. I followed suit and we slept a few hours longer.

I awoke as Jace got out of bed.

"I'm hungry. Can you cook us something?" I asked hopefully.

"How can you be thinking of food when you were

too drunk to go home last night?" He asked.

"Don't know but I could use some aspirin too."

He grinned slightly, found some aspirin for me then went to take a shower.

During breakfast he was unusually silent and distant.

"You got a hangover too?" I asked.

"Yeah, I guess." He replied as he sipped some coffee. He had made us eggs and toast but he hadn't eaten much of anything.

"You're not saying much." I remarked as I finished off my toast. I always seemed to eat more when he cooked a meal.

The look in his eye suddenly scared me. "So....Biscuit can talk, huh?" He said slowly.

Oh, God. What else had I said? Surely nothing. But then.... I couldn't remember very much about the night before either. "Uh, if she could I'm sure that you would have known before now, right?" I replied.

Jace ignored that question and said, "She apparently knows and tells stuff that she couldn't possibly know about. For example, she knows that Curt's cousin is in jail for breaking and entering and that Jimmy's girlfriend scratched his car up last week when she hit a fence with it. Oh, and that you and your band will one day be rock stars."

My face reddened. Those things were true but nobody had told me. I just knew about them. Biscuit didn't have a thing to do about it although at times she'd tell me that she wanted to go on a walk or that someone had fed her something good that she usually didn't get. Jace surely wouldn't understand that. "How mad are they at me?" I asked.

"Not very, although it was apparent that both those revelations had been secrets. How did you know about them?"

"Oh, I just do, sometimes by dreams. And I keep the stuff to myself, except for last night."

Jace pondered on that for a moment. "What? Do you see things, hear things? What do you know about me that you're not telling?"

I hesitated on answering him. Would we still be good friends now or would this secret of mine ruin everything between us? All I could tell him was the truth and hope that things would still be okay between us. "It depends. Sometimes I hear things in my mind and sometimes I catch glimpses of things that mean something to me or I dream about something. At times the images or words don't make any sense until the time comes and then it all falls into place. Sometimes when I touch something I will know about it."

He began clearing away the dishes.

I started the water to wash the dishes. "Do you think I'm weird now?" I asked with my back to him.

"No." He replied as he came up beside me and laid the dishes on the countertop. "You've slipped up and told me many things you shouldn't have known before last night. I've more or less known all along. The guys and their girlfriends didn't know until last night."

"Will they forget?"

"Possibly." He replied as he reached past me to put away some dishes. "They were all pretty wasted."

I didn't know what else to say so I went back to the living room and sat on the couch staring blankly at the tv which was on but the volume was low. Jace came and sat beside me but I was afraid of what he might ask.

I could already feel his mood and it was a weird one. "Hey," he said as he took my hands in his. "Seriously, I want to know how much you can tune into me."

I took my hands back. I didn't want to be honest with him. What if I said the wrong thing and he didn't want to be friends anymore? Sometimes his friendship was all that held me together. After a moment I said, "If I really want to know how you feel, it will never come to me. The more I want to know the more it turns off. If it's just in fun I can know some things but it doesn't mean I hear your thoughts. Although on some subjects or at odd moments when we're really connected, I think I could. Things with strong emotions behind them I usually know too, like bumping into someone who is really terrified of someone else, I can feel that. Or someone who is really excited about something, I can know and feel why. Then sometimes random things just pop in my head like Curt's cousin or Jimmy's girlfriend. Every now and then I can read someone if I touch them." The last statement was a lie. Although I was able to read some people by touching them, it wasn't a prerequisite. All I had to do was look at them or think of them and if I was on the same wavelength, I could know what was on their mind. I didn't feel that anyone needed to know that I could do that.

He stared at the tv in thought.

"What's up?" I asked him.

He turned to me. "I don't know. I just feel cheated. I want to know things about you. I mean, you have to know things about me."

"I really don't have a wealth of knowledge about you, Jace. Really."

He looked back at the tv for a moment then turned

back to me. "Since I don't have your gift, I want to ask you a question and I want an honest answer."

I put my hand up as if I were warding him off. "Better watch what you ask unless you really want to know, okay? Sometimes when you know the answer it makes everything more complicated and weirder." I cautioned him. Yes, I already knew what he wanted to know. "I'll answer your question truthfully, whatever it is but before you ask just think about what response I might give. How is it going to affect you on different answers you might hear? But the big thing is, can you handle it? Can you handle it if it's not what you want to hear? Can you handle it if it is?"

Jace's face reddened and he rethought his question a little, then totally rejected it for another question. "What if I lied this morning when you asked me if we'd slept together?" He finally asked.

"Why would you lie about it now?" I replied back. We hadn't and I already knew that.

"Just to test you. To see if you really knew if I was lying or not. And to tell you the truth I feel a lot better now because I know now that you can't read my mind." He remarked as Biscuit distracted me by jumping on the couch and plopping on my lap.

He was bluffing. His recollection of last night had nothing sexual in it between he and I or with anyone else. I had been sleeping on the couch and just gotten up in the middle of the night, used the bathroom then climbed in bed with him since I was kind of dizzy. Then I'd fallen asleep.

"Whatever. I really can't read people's minds." I replied in a disinterested voice. "What was it you really wanted to ask me?"

"Nothing." He said with a little bit of irritation in his voice. "I already know the answer."

It wasn't the same answer I would have given him, that was for sure. "I guess I should be getting home. Maybe someone has missed me by now." I remarked as I nudged Biscuit off my lap and stood up. "Maybe me and the band can fight a little before the day is over."

He stood up too. "Hey, I'm glad you decided to spend Christmas Eve with me. Call me or come back over if you have trouble with Rick."

"I'll be okay. This was nice." I said as I stood by the door. I pondered on whether I should elaborate or not. Oh hell, it was Christmas, why not? "You know?" I asked as I leaned against the door. "You really are the glue that holds me together sometimes. Especially when life gets tough. Seriously. You're my best friend. I just wanted you to know that."

He looked surprised. I wasn't usually that forthcoming.

"See ya!" I smiled and started out the door.

He caught the door before I closed it. I turned around to face him. He hesitated and we just looked at each other for a moment. "Wait." He remarked. "What would you have answered?"

"Yes, is what I would have answered." I smiled. "Bye!"

Before I could move away, he grabbed my arm. "Yes, what? You're my best friend too, you know. You can tell me." He said seriously.

My smile faded and I said seriously, "Can you handle the answer?"

"Yeah. But you don't even know the question." He replied his eyes intent on mine. Oh, but I did.

"I am attracted to you but I'm not going to sleep with you just to sleep with you. I want a real relationship and I'd want you to be faithful."

I could tell I'd shocked him. He let go of my arm like it was burning him and the color drained from his face. He wasn't handling it well at all. Maybe he still thought I knew every thought he'd ever had, or maybe he was shocked that I'd admitted my feelings for him.

"We're going to forget this conversation. I can tell it's not what you want. And, I'm okay with it. But now you know the answer." Then I left, with him staring after me.

***

I arrived home about three o'clock after listening to "Still the Same" on repeat. I was surprised at how neat and orderly the living room looked. The band was watching tv and drinking beer. They greeted me rather warmly and didn't even ask where I'd spent the night. Even the air was less prickly than usual. It put me on high alert. "What the fuck?" I asked warily as I glanced slowly at each one of them.

Rick was the first to speak. "Well, Baby, we've decided that you were right. If we're going to survive as a band we have to learn to live together. If you'll sit down with us, we're ready to work out some things."

I was very puzzled by this change of heart but I sat beside him, ready to listen. I figured this was all too good to be true.

"We're all willing to give in a little if you're willing to give in a little." Rick continued.

"How so?"

He was silent for a moment as if he couldn't believe what he was about to say. "Okay, about me being your guardian. I am too young to be doing this but I did sign the papers and promised Bob I'd watch after you. From now on I'm going to live up to that agreement."

As I started in astonishment, Carol put in her two cents worth. "I'm taking care of all the major cooking for the household. You don't have to cook anymore. You hate cooking anyway." I wondered if she'd taken an acting class recently because it was a noteworthy performance.

Kevin spoke next. "I'm going to stop borrowing your truck so much. I won't wear your jeans again unless you allow me to."

There were some snickers all around the room about him wearing my clothes. What guy wears girl's jeans?

I looked to hear what David had to say.

"I guess I'll start doing my share of the housework." He said. I knew that Rick and Kevin were also pretty lax in their house cleaning chores.

"And what are you asking of me?" I wanted to know. I knew it would probably be big – like King Kong big, or at least monster truck big. I was thinking that I would like a monster truck though. I'd drive that thing over...

"Well..." Rick began. "If you'll pay the electric bill and the rent, we'll cut out your house cleaning chores. The rest of us will do more house cleaning from now on.

The electric bill was anywhere from one hundred and fifty dollars to two hundred dollars a month, and our rent was eight hundred a month. Money wasn't a problem. I paused for dramatic effect. "And you think this will solve our problems, huh?" I said. I noticed all of them looked towards Rick then as if the master plan they had created had failed. Earth was doomed. Hell and brimstone would rain upon them.

"Yeah." David replied.

"We're really trying here." Rick huffed.

"And what are the consequences if one of us reneges on this deal?" I asked.

"I'll take care of it if it's one of you guys, and you, Baby will put me in line if it's me that reneges." He said rather seriously. "Does that sound fair?"

"Why do you keep calling me "Baby" as if it's my real name?"

"It's your new nickname." He replied. I knew he was testing it out on me. "I'm your guardian and you're my baby."

I knew that was bullshit but whatever. I looked for Carol's reaction. There wasn't one. It occurred to me that something really strange or profound had happened while I was gone to cause such a change in Rick and the others. Alien abduction and replacement came to mind. I decided to let it go although I figured that his real reason for calling me "Baby" was to put me in my place somehow. Rick was one of the few guys that didn't call his girlfriend "baby".

"Baby. That's cute. I like it." I replied. "What about a clause for playing with other bands every so often? You guys were raging mad about me doing the gigs with Streethart. Did you forget about that?" I asked.

They traded glances. Carol spoke up. "That was low, Angel. But it wasn't just your performing with them that made us mad. It's also the fact that we didn't even know that you could play the guitar - I mean really play the guitar."

Maybe I hadn't played my best for them. In the time they'd known me I'd always been a drummer. Yeah, I'd played a fancy solo on the guitar a few times but maybe that was all. I had never really thought about it before.

"Show them what you can do." Kevin said. He knew how good I was. "Rick was the only one who heard you play with Streethart."

"Seriously?" I asked.

"Yeah." They replied. I checked David's reaction just to make sure. He was our lead guitarist.

He seemed comfortable with it so I went upstairs and found my favorite white Gibson. I stared at it a moment, feeling it's smoothness. I hadn't played it but once since our last gig in South Carolina, the night my dad had died. And all my life Daddy had said, "Don't come out with your guns a blazin', Pumpkin." Daddy was gone and I realized with a start that his reason for preaching that statement was to keep me small and living in our small rural town. He was afraid of ending up alone. I took in a deep breath and let it out, along with that sad memory, then I went back downstairs. From now on I'd always have my guns a blazin'.

I plugged my guitar into David's amplifier which was as usual in the line of living room traffic. I played the guitar solo from the "Rockies" and then the song "Brownstone" that I had written.

"See, I told you she was good!" Kevin exclaimed.

"Yeah. You are." Carol agreed

"Better than me." David admitted. He didn't seem upset about it.

"Rick?" I prompted. I knew he wouldn't admit I was good in a million years.

"I'm glad you can't play bass." He muttered.

"Thanks." I replied. "I'm glad you liked it." I could play bass whether he guessed it or not. I looked around at them and the good times of our friendship were so strong at that moment. It was almost as if it washed over me. "I have to tell you something." I told them as I noticed that one of them had broken down and bought a tiny Christmas tree that was sitting on the coffee table.

"What do you mean?" Carol asked suspiciously.

"I mean I'm going to be sentimental here. Remember all the good times we had together in South Carolina? I miss that." I lowered my head. "I really love you guys. Can we be friends again?" I asked.

When I looked up again everyone looked stunned. "Yeah, I want that too." Kevin replied, breaking the moment. He pulled me into a hug and then everyone was hugging each other, even Rick.

"Well, Merry Christmas!" David exclaimed. We all smiled sheepishly.

"What about our agreement?" Carol wanted to know.

I was doubtful of it. "Put it in writing and after we all sign it, I guess it's law." I replied.

Everyone was smiles after that. Little did we all know that the winds of payback were about to blow.

CHAPTER 8

January 2005

The first of January rolled in my seventeenth birthday. No one remembered it which was fine with me. Things had been going abnormally smooth around the house and that was a gift in itself. Everyone had the day off which was just as well because they were hungover from the night before from a little New Year Eve's celebrating. I would have liked to have had a great day but I kept feeling uneasy and there was no visible reason for it. My mind kept telling me to let them take me and not to fight it and everything would be just fine. I asked myself, "who?", and the answer came, "Bob and Nancy." I didn't welcome that thought and pushed it away but what I should have done was heed the warning.

I was wondering if Joseph and his goons had been harassing any of us. Rick said that he'd noticed one of the goons following he and Carol the day before but that they hadn't been approached. He said it seemed like the goon just wanted them to know they were being watched. Maybe Joseph was on his way to leaving us all alone.

About noon, I was in the kitchen with the rest of the band, playing poker. David was pretty good at poker and was teaching us how to play. I'd already known how but I pretended I didn't. The music was blasting, and a few of the band's friends were visiting. Several had joints and were getting high. The smoke was burning my eyes and I tried to fan it away from me. But I knew that in a few minutes the joints would be gone and they would only be drinking from then on. Someone knocked on the door and Kevin went to answer it. "Oh, God." I heard him say.

We all turned to see Bob and Nancy standing in the doorway. David ground out a joint as Bob started in on Rick and Carol. The neighbors took off as if it were a raid. Which I guess it was.

They had traveled to check up on me and to celebrate my birthday with us. Indeed, it was a surprise. I didn't think Bob was ever going to calm down. Finally, when he did, I found my room being packed up. He and Nancy took me to a hotel where they had a room. Bob told me that he didn't want to hear any protests because I was going back to South Carolina whether or not I wanted to. I said nothing. In the morning he went to school with me and withdrew me, then we went to my job where he explained to my boss why I was quitting without notice. Then he loaded my belongings into the backs of my truck and his. By the time we were leaving, Kevin was near tears and Carol was quiet for once. Rick's and David's faces were expressionless.

Before we left, Bob allowed me a minute alone with Rick. "I guess you don't know nothing." He told me. "You said we'd be stars. Now what? Did you tell Bob about all our drugs and drinking? How we screw each other and everyone else?"

I gave him a defeated look. "I never told him a thing. He walked in on it, remember? But you have legal guardianship, not him. Tell him, tell him I can't go with him."

Rick was too much of a coward to stand up to Bob. "You know Bob. It's his way or the highway. There's nothing I can do about it." He replied.

I sighed in aggravation. "You guys just buckle down and have Kevin be your drummer. You can manage the band like that. Have faith. I'll be back. We are not over." I gave him a last-minute hug and pushed all of the cash I had on me into his pocket before Bob beckoned me threateningly from the door.

Once outside, I asked Bob what I was supposed to do about Kevin. The cherub had said it was my responsibility to take care of him.

"What do you mean, what are you supposed to do about Kevin?" He asked me. "He's old enough to take care of himself."

"Can we take him with us? He's only sixteen." I replied.

"No, my only responsibility is you. I put my ass on the line smuggling him out of South Carolina and that's where it ended. You wanted him safe and here he's safe. Now let's go."

"But Bob, I just don't know if he's strong enough without me." I pleaded.

He sighed, then he paused to look at me. "He's going to have to be strong. If he comes back to South Carolina there will be nothing but problems for me, for you, and for him. I'm not going to jail for him and I sure can't hide him out. He's a minor and he has parents. The state will make them take him back and who knows what will happen to him then. His mother was shooting at the two of you, for God's sake! Do you really want him to go back to that?" He was looking at the ground now, shaking his head.

A moment passed.

"Let me at least say goodbye to him." I replied. Kevin was not happy at all that I was leaving. I told him to go to David if he had any real trouble because I felt that David would help him. "I'll be back, Kevin. Don't worry." I told him, but I was worried.

Bob drove his truck and Nancy rode with me in my truck. Nancy only dealt with me listening to "Still the Same" three times. I had really needed to hear it several more times.

We stopped one time to sleep and Bob had Nancy and I take turns driving my truck. We were in South Carolina before I knew it. Bob warned me that he would shoot and kill me if I tried to run back to New York. I told him that I had no intention of running away. I knew that wasn't the answer. It was far better if I stayed with them and they got tired of me, at least that's what the voices had said. I sighed inside and wondered how long that would take.

I pretended to settle in with them as if I were their own. I never said one thing about New York, however I missed Jace and Streethart badly. I did miss the others but living in New York had been hard without the trouble my band had given me. Maybe now they'd learn some lessons and that gave me some satisfaction, although I worried about Kevin. Well, I didn't plan to be gone that long.

I'd wanted to send them money but Bob had commandeered my bank account and wouldn't let me have access to it. I didn't know how the band was going to survive without my contribution to the household.

The first week back was really hard. Bob enrolled me in high school so I was back facing all the kids that I'd beaten up and antagonized. I had never wanted to go back to that atmosphere. I wanted the new school where everyone loved me. I swallowed a lot of sorrow over missing my classmates and the Goddess like status I'd just left.

And then there was Alan, David's younger brother. He was also a sophomore in high school but he was actually two years younger than me. He was following me around and feeling like he'd gotten one over on David by my coming back to South Carolina. He didn't care that I wasn't interested in him, he seemed to be in my face after each class that first week. I blamed that train wreck on their parents. They worshipped Alan for some ungodly reason, when they should have been despising him. No wonder David hated him.

It was also different living with Bob and Nancy. They were easily old enough to be my grandparents and they expected a lot more out of me than my dad had. They wanted me to help around the house rather than the farm. Nancy patiently showed me how to clean house and how to cook and although I wanted to freak out, I knew better than to do so. They also wanted me to wear more than blue jeans and t-shirts. Nancy told me that her granddaughter would come over and take me shopping. She was talking dresses and skirts. I was thinking that I'd really get in trouble at school with the kids teasing me because they'd never seen me wear a dress. I couldn't remember wearing a dress since the beauty pageant I'd competed in when I was nine. I didn't know how I was going to stop from killing the people that teased me. They also expected me to eat regular meals. When I'd been with my dad, he hadn't made each meal with a meat, two vegetables, a salad, and bread. Sometimes we just had meatloaf, or chicken, and nothing else but I never cared about that. Sometimes we just had a plate of vegetables, and sometimes we just ate popcorn.

Otherwise, my life was pretty much as it had once been when I'd lived with Daddy. But one big difference were the tears. I hadn't cried much about Daddy before I'd left but the tears were here now, often and at inopportune times. I attended school, although I steered clear of any fighting. That was especially hard with all the kids I'd once beaten up in that school. Many wanted payback but I couldn't jeopardize my future by indulging them. Cole, my first boyfriend, had moved away to college which surprised me. It was pretty empty being in South Carolina. All the friends I'd hung around with were now in New York.

School wasn't just harder now, it was hell. I missed all my new high school friends that I had made in New York. Going to school while I'd lived in New York had been the happiest I'd ever been in my life. The guys always wanted to talk to me and go out with me, and a couple of the girls liked me too. And the worst thing was that I didn't realize how great I'd had it until I had been yanked away from them. I wanted so much to believe that when I finally was able to break free of South Carolina that I'd fit right back in, in New York. I wanted to believe that so badly.

I asked Bob about Kevin's parents. I was really shocked to find that they had moved away. Word had it that they'd moved to Nevada. I thought about Kevin who didn't know that they had moved. It really upset me that his parents were so different from my dad, that they didn't love Kevin at all. If he ever contacted them in the future, he'd find out that they had moved. I wouldn't be the one to tell him. I was angry at Bob. He had said that Kevin's parents would make trouble for us but they didn't even live in South Carolina anymore. I argued that Kevin should be able to come back too but Bob wasn't giving in.

I did chores around the house without being asked, except cooking. Since it was January, it was rather cold to ride my motorcycle. Bob didn't want me riding it anyway. But I did manage to write a few songs. I redid some of the lyrics on my angry song and thought it sounded especially good. I also played my favorite white Gibson guitar a lot. And there was the "odd rhythm" that I drummed every so often. I was hoping that Bob would be so tired of it that he would want me to leave but instead he bought sheet music for the country songs he liked so I could play them on guitar for him. He'd found my violin too and expected me to play it. I hadn't played that violin in years but it wasn't hard to pick it back up again.

For the most part I wondered constantly how I could have lived without friends so long. What did I do before I met Brad, then Kevin and the others? It was just me, Daddy and my dog, Yellow before them. Now it was just me, and the loneliness was eating me away. Now the tears included these things too. I had never felt smaller before in my life. I had always been so tough and strong. It really scared me.

I talked to Bob about sending some money to Rick or at least to Kevin but he wouldn't hear of it. He knew about my other checking account and he cut me off.

He said that the band had to learn to deal with money matters without me, that maybe they'd straighten their lives up now.

Their granddaughter, Cathi, came over a few days after I'd settled in. She was twenty and going to college in the next town over. My impression of her was that she was a lot wilder than me. I guess if it came down to it, everyone was wilder than me. As Nancy explained to her that I needed to get some school clothes, Cathi looked me over. All I wanted to wear was black t-shirts and blue jeans. Daddy had long ago quit fighting with me about wearing something other than I wanted to wear. He was glad I wasn't wearing low cut blouses and short skirts.

Cathi took me to a mall in Newberry and we looked at the clothes. She was dressed in the latest college fashion which was a clingy knit top that showed her assets, leggings and boots. I grimaced as she picked up the same type of clothes for me. I had never worn a pair of leggings in my life, or the clingy type of top that she was wearing. We were in the dressing room with the first stack of clothes that she picked out and she was trying to dress me like I was still five years old. I was just wanting her out of the dressing room. "Good grief, I'm only trying to help you dress." She told me in an exasperated tone as she helped me out of a shirt and managed to also cup a feel of my breast.

"Stop it!" I told her. "You're doing a little more than dressing me here and I don't like it!"

"Sorry. Didn't mean to do that." She replied, but I wondered whether she was being truthful. Okay so she didn't outright molest me after that but she sure managed to be in my face and to be fixing everything from the collar to a shirt to helping belt a belt. It made me uncomfortable.

We argued a bit when she went to get another stack of clothes and when I wouldn't cooperate, she just bought what she wanted for me. I ended up getting the same type of outfit, cowboy boots, four-inch heels, several other tops that she considered cute, jeans in different colors, one short dress and a short skirt. I also got two dressy outfits of pants and a matching jacket. One was corduroy. I'd never bought even half that amount of clothes ever. I guessed that we were using my dad's insurance money to buy them.

Nancy was pleased with what she'd bought me and she wanted me to model everything for her. I sighed to myself and put on the first outfit. Cathi got Nancy's camera and took a picture. "Now it's just like you're still modeling clothes for that catalog." She was referring my job at the Harris company. She said to me with a glint in her eyes. She was making fun of me. Nancy didn't get that, she just thought it was thoughtful of Cathi to try and help me feel more comfortable in her home. Well, I wasn't about to make a big deal of it even though she was making me feel like an ass.

After I'd tried on all the clothes and Cathi had taken pictures, she decided she was going to stay the night with us. I was hoping she wouldn't because I knew she was going to prank me somehow. My bedroom was about as far away from Bob and Nancy's as you could get. Cathi was in another bedroom closer to theirs. I wasn't tired but Bob and Nancy being older, went to bed by 9:30pm, and more often by 9pm.

They were cold natured and it must have been like eighty degrees in their home. I was sitting on my bed in a tank top and panties with the fan turned on me trying to do my homework when Cathi came into my room. She shut the door and sat on my bed uninvited. She asked about the club scene in New York and wanted to know what it was like being in a band. "So do y'all get crazy with booze and sex after a concert?" She asked me with interest.

"Uh, no. I just turned seventeen and I promised daddy that I wouldn't do that stuff." I replied. I had seen some of the crazy stuff but had never been really interested in it. Rick and Carol were into it, and sometimes Kevin and David joined them in partying. Still, it wasn't anything I considered wild. Somehow, they still had that caution about doing anything worse than smoking pot. I just hoped it always stayed that way.

"I bet you're still a virgin." She replied in amusement.

"Sex gets you babies, and I don't like babies." I replied, avoiding her question. I had no idea what she might tell Bob and Nancy.

"There's a way it won't." She smiled at me. As I gave her a curious look, she put my books on the night stand, then clicked off the lamp by my bed.

"What are you doing?" I asked her in irritation, but then I felt what she was doing. She had her fingers down my panties. I jumped and went to push her away but she pushed me down on the bed. I had the strength to knock her clear off the bed but she knew where to touch me and it had been so long since I'd had sex that I just let her continue. She moved her hand up under my tank top and touched my braless breasts, lingering on my nipple. I just wanted to come after that, I was so aroused.

"No, you have to touch me too." She told me.

I wasn't really into it but I wanted her to keep touching me, so when she kissed me, I let her, and I touched her, and then she went down on me and I found that I could get off twice in a row if there was like thirty seconds after my first orgasm. I might have never learned that if it hadn't been for her. After she went to her room, I got myself off two more times. I'd really missed sex. I was glad she went back to college the next morning because now I was really disgusted with what I'd done with her.

Nancy had me wear a dress the next day for school. Yeah, that day was horrible. There was so much teasing and so many nasty comments, and kids laughing at me. I don't think I've ever felt so humiliated in my whole life. This whole situation was beginning to be so much worse than I thought it would be. It was worse than anything I'd gone through with the band in New York. I was really missing my friends at New Rochelle High School. Gone were all the boys vying for my attention as were all the adoration from the kids that were impressed that I played gigs with my band. I was back to the hell hole I'd endured since my dad had adopted me. All I could do was withdraw within again and deal with it.

CHAPTER 9

That first Saturday was a particularly lonely day. I found myself sitting in the cemetery at Daddy's grave. School had not gone well at all the day before. I had two near misses with guys who had wanted to beat me up because I'd beaten them up in the past. I had looked like a coward when I had refused to fight them and that made me feel bad because I knew I could have at least given them a good fight if I'd wanted to. I also knew that I couldn't get into any trouble if it was my intention to go back to New York. But then three girls with attitudes were teasing me about the pink jeans and top I was wearing and they pushed me into a mud puddle and made me miss the school bus home. I had to call Bob to come get me because it would have been too dark to walk home. I would rather have walked because Bob was on my case about him having to drive me home from school, and he didn't believe that I hadn't started the incident that landed me in the mud. That really angered me because I wasn't a liar. If I had been the instigator, I would have owned up to it.

"Talk to me, Daddy." I said to the air. "Tell me what I'm supposed to do now."

I really wanted to go back to New York. I waited but there was nothing, just the still cool air and the rows of tombstones. I closed my eyes for a while in frustration.

My whole life just wasn't worth it. There were obstacles everywhere and I knew I didn't have the tools to communicate with people the way others did. At one time I had enjoyed the quiet and the solitude. I loved looking and feeling like the bruiser that I was, the one that people crossed the street to avoid. Now, I wasn't even allowed to be that person. They were making me into someone else and I really hated that person. And now because of Cathi I was wondering if I was gay.

I was stressed so my mind drifted back into the fantasyland where my parents were still alive and we lived a very upscale, fun, loving life. Sometimes I liked the fantasy too much. I was so popular in my fantasy, and I was so damn good looking. I was the same age I was now but I was a cheerleader and all the jocks loved me. Hell, the entire world loved me and included me in their events and they talked to me and cared about me. My friends and I had a ton of fun together and it was so satisfying to be one of the gang. My mom was a home economics teacher and my dad, a lawyer. They encouraged me to do everything and to make friends. We went on lavish vacations of sun and fun. We were in some tropical paradise now where the breeze was the perfect temperature and we were tanning ourselves on the sand by the ocean. The breeze felt so good and I was lulled by the sound of the waves.

I opened my eyes suddenly, and jerked when something cool and bristly brushed by me. I stifled the urge to move suddenly or scream out as I watched a gray wolf turn and sit down directly in front of me. He was as tall as I, both of us sitting on the cold ground. He licked his lips and I hoped that he had eaten recently. I made a conscious effort to feel his energy. From now on

I decided that I'd always feel the energy around me to make sure I didn't end up in another situation like this. I didn't feel any threat from the wolf as I evaluated him. He made eye contact with me, gave a little grunt, then stood up and started to walk away. He looked back at me and I got up to follow him. I figured if that wasn't what he'd meant that he would either run away or attack me. I was curious to what he had to show me. He led me out of the cemetery and into the woods. We walked for about thirty minutes with him looking back every once in a while, to make sure I was still there. The brush had gotten thick and I was a little scared wondering if I could find my way back because the air was chilly, and the temperature would get down to below freezing that night. As he kept walking, I wondered suddenly if we would ever reach our destination. And what if he was just leading me into the woods to abandon me?

At one point we crossed a small stream which I wasn't happy about at all since the temperature was only about 45 degrees and my shoes and pant legs got wet. Now I was cold and wet, and still following this wolf. He stopped suddenly and sat down about ten feet in front of me. "I don't get it." I told him. We were in the middle of nowhere with nothing but woods and brush around us. There was hardly even a path where I stood.

The wolf suddenly got up and ran at me. I didn't know what to do and I ended up doing nothing. I went down hard as he jumped at my chest. "Owww!" I yelled as I hit the ground on my rump. Then I was busy yelling at the wolf as he ran away. I stopped yelling as the sound of a child wailing filled the air. I blinked in surprise and looked towards the sound. I followed it a few feet away and found a little girl about four years old lying in the brush. She was crying for her mama.

"I'll find your mama." I told her. She put her arms up for me to pick her up and I did. I began walking back the way I'd come as she sniffled and told me about the camping trip she'd been on. She didn't know how long she'd been lost. She was cold, wet, hungry, and thirsty but I didn't have any food or water on me. I wrapped her in my jacket, knowing that now I'd become bitter cold. Once I'd carried her over the stream, I was lost. I called out in my mind to the wolf to lead me back. I mean, he'd gotten me in this mess, he'd better be willing to lead me back out.

I stood there a moment with the child whimpering because I'd stopped walking. She was starting to get heavy in my arms. I wanted to whimper too because now that I had been standing still for a few moments I was so damn cold. Then I heard a rustle and saw the wolf ahead. He began walking and I followed him. By the time I'd gotten to the cemetery, my arm muscles were aching like they were on fire. I packed the little girl up in my truck and fired up the heater full blast. I stopped at the McDonalds drive thru to buy her some chicken nuggets and a milk. She ate as I drove to the police station.

The sheriff was really surprised to see me and the little girl, and when all was said and done, Bob had to come down to his office. I couldn't even tell them the truth of how I'd found the girl. She had been missing for almost twenty hours by then. She had wandered off from her family camp site. Everyone was stumped as to how she had survived the night before as the temperature had gone down to forty degrees and she hadn't been dressed for it. She told them that a big gray dog had stayed with her. Yeah, I knew that big gray wolf too. My butt still hurt from where he'd knocked me on the ground. I supposed that there was some moral to the story that I was supposed to understand but the truth was that I didn't have a clue.

In the morning however, I did. The news van was at Bob's house interviewing me on how I'd found the child. Then everyone in the neighborhood and at school was talking to me about it, and some continued to talk to me in the days afterward. Bob asked me later how I'd ended up in the woods and I told him. Daddy had talked to him many times about the things that had happened to me, and he knew that my dog, Yellow talked to me, so he wasn't shocked that a wolf had led me to the little girl. Instead, he walked me out to his barn and asked me to have a talk with his horse.

As he glanced at me and the mare, I couldn't help but have some fun with him. "That mare is sure fucked up." I told him. "What the hell did you do to her?"

"Hey!" he said in a rough voice. "What have I told you before about cussing?"

I smiled in amusement. "That me and you are the only ones allowed to say the F word." I replied.

He looked at me as he tried to keep a straight face. "Damn straight, and don't you forget it." He replied as he struggled not to laugh. He had said he wasn't going to tell me what the problem was with the horse, that he was testing my superpowers. I could only imagine how much he must have teased my dad about me when I wasn't around.

I was still smiling when I walked closer to the mare and regarded her. Suddenly a midget appeared sitting on her bare back. He was dressed to the max like a little cowboy and he looked absolutely ridiculous, but I managed to keep an expressionless face. What made it harder not to laugh was that he was bouncing up and down on this horse and yelling, "giddy up, giddy up, you old nag!" I really wished that Bob could see and hear him. Yeah, the aliens like to amuse themselves sometimes by trying to make me laugh. I was thinking this little show was because I'd done my good deed by finding the little girl.

"*What's wrong girl?*" I thought to the mare.

"*YOU'RE DOING IT WRONG!*" The midget informed me loudly.

"*How should I be doing this, Mr. Cowboy?*" I thought back to him.

"*You have to be the horse.*"

The only idea that came to mind from what he'd said was for me to synch with the horse's energy pattern. So, with Bob impatiently waiting, I felt the energy pattern and tried to hold it in my mind. Now I could see it in my mind and I turned it over and over looking for defects. The midget jumping up and down on the horse shouting "giddy up!" did not help my mission.

I couldn't find any defects.

"I thought you could talk to animals." Bob remarked.

"It sometimes takes a few minutes." I told him.

"*Give up?*" the midget asked me.

Before I could even roll my eyes in frustration over the midget's meddling, he blurted out, "*She fell into a pond when she was a colt and now, she's afraid of water.*"

I repeated his words to Bob.

"Hell, I know that much. Tell me how to fix her." He replied in irritation.

"How did my dad stand you?" I asked back without thinking. "I can't believe you were friends."

"Hey! Your dad was an asshole. He cheated at poker constantly, and he would never take my advice about anything. Does that remind YOU of ANYONE?" He smirked back.

Yeah, me. But suddenly I thought of Mary. "Can I go see Mary?" She had been the married woman my dad had been sleeping with on and off for most of my life. I never knew why she wouldn't leave her husband for my dad, but he had told me many times to stay out of their affair. But now I felt an urgent need to bond with her.

I watched the color drain out of Bob's face. Whatever it was, it was bad. Now he was trying to figure out what to say to me. "Honey" He began as his voice softened. I blinked at his endearment and his tone. He had never called me "Honey" before. "Mary died right after your father did. She was really upset by your dad dying. She was over here crying over him and saying she couldn't go on without him. I wasn't very sympathetic to her. I told her that she should have left her husband long ago if she loved your dad so much."

"*Learn from this*." the midget shouted at me. "*Not making a decision is making a decision.*"

"She killed herself?" I asked in shock, finally understanding what he had been trying to say.

"Yeah." He replied solemnly.

I was surprised when my legs gave away and I landed on my butt on the ground. Now I was bawling. I wondered if my dad would have still been alive if Mary would have left her husband. Had her inaction caused my dad to die? And now they were both dead? Fuck!

"Oh honey." Bob said as he knelt down beside me.

"It's so unfair!" I cried to him. "Why is there all this misery with relationships? I just wanted my dad to be happy and for them to get together. He never had anyone but me all these years."

As he persuaded me off the ground and we walked the mare back inside the barn, he tried to soothe me. For a gruff old man, he was really great. We went into his shop and he turned on the heat as he told me everything he thought might make me feel better. We probably talked for an hour before Nancy came out looking for us. She urged the both of us into the house to get warmer and to eat supper. "Why don't you try to find your biological dad?" She suggested.

"I really can't handle that right now. I think I'd absolutely lose it if I found him and he ignored me or didn't want me." I replied.

"You'll always have a home with us, Pumpkin." She assured me.

"Thank you." I said mustering a little smile. "Y'all are sweet old people.

"Hey!" Bob growled in annoyance and we all laughed.

***

School had become a little more bearable. A few kids actually talked to me. In Science class one of the nerds ended up being my lab partner. His name was Nathan. There had been a show about aliens the night before but I'd not been allowed to watch it because Bob had wanted to watch a cop show that aired at the same time. He didn't believe in recording shows to watch later either. Nathan was talking excitedly to me about the alien show. He had me in deep thought about things he'd seen on the show. We'd even laughed together.

Curly, Larry, and Moe, my enemies, plunked their bad selves down at the table I claimed at lunch time. I still sat with my back to the wall as so no one could come up from behind me. I couldn't believe they had the nerve to sit down with me. "Have you run out of helpless animals to torture?" I deadpanned as I glanced at them. In the past I would have squared up and my existence alone would have caused them to avoid my table.

"Saw you on tv." Larry told me as he broke open his milk carton.

"Yeah. That was so fuckin' cool that you rescued that kid." Curly added.

"You're a fuckin' hero." Moe added.

I scoffed at them. They were eating now. I had stopped.

"Are you glad to be back?" Larry continued.

"No." I replied with emphasis.

Miss Jones, a teacher I'd had the previous year, walked past our table with a nod and a smile to me. She knew I was a bully and now she had observed me getting along with my three worst enemies. I sighed to myself. Wow, where had my badness gone?

"Rumor has it that you ran away to New York to be a rock star but then Bob found you and dragged you back." Larry remarked with a little smirk.

I watched him spoon mashed potatoes into his mouth. I hated his big fat mouth along with the rest of him. I shrugged my shoulders. "Shit happens."

They laughed and wanted to know more.

"Well, I was living on the streets for a while in my truck. Then it got too damn cold and I moved in with a bunch of kids. I finally managed to get a gig at a bar and grill so yeah, I played some music. Bob found out and here I am." I lied. Yeah, I couldn't help myself.

I knew I'd strung them all in with my lie as they were all of a sudden hanging onto my every word. So, I lied some more. I let them talk as much as I could without adding anything.

I figured I'd just keep them all at arm's length. I just hoped I could keep the bully in me in check as they sometimes got on my last nerve. And I was just as glad that Alan didn't share the same lunch break otherwise, he'd been in my face.

"What happened to that dickhead that you used to hang around with?" Moe asked.

"The only dickheads I know are you three." I replied as I glanced at the clock on the wall. I was hoping that our lunch break was about over.

"Fuck you!" He snapped. "And you know damn well that we're talking about your bitch, Kevin. Word has it that he disappeared, amazingly around the same time that you did."

Hmm. I had to give the appropriate reaction on that one, a fake one, of course. I frowned and looked downward as I swiped an imaginary tear from the corner of my eye. I put some anger and huffiness on. "I think his parents killed him. They probably fucking buried him in their back yard!" I replied.

"I heard he ran away."

I figured I was a pretty good actress. "Well, he didn't! And I don't even think the police are trying to find out what happened. I went over his parents' house but they don't even live there anymore. If that's not guilt, I don't know what is!" I exclaimed with enough anger and outrage to be convincing.

Moe and Curly were buying my story now. Larry didn't look convinced but he said nothing as the others talked about the situation. The bell rang to end our lunch break. I was happy to walk away from that charade.

It was two weeks later and Rick had called Bob twice to my knowledge to plead for my return. Bob told him all the ways he had messed up and that I would never return to New York. He wouldn't let Rick talk to me. After Rick's second call, I asked Bob how he would act if he were in Rick's position, being away from home without any parents looking over his shoulder. He briskly told me that he sure wouldn't be doing drugs or tempting me to do things I shouldn't do. I explained that Rick's parents just hadn't taught him about life as Daddy had taught me, that Daddy had let me do most anything except drugs and alcohol and that I still didn't have a desire to do them. Bob insisted that I had to have done those things just by being with the others.

"Was I high or drunk the day you dropped in on us? Everyone else was." I asked.

"No." He admitted.

"How was my attendance at school and my grade point average?"

"Straight A's and one day missed." He reluctantly replied. These were things he had checked before withdrawing me from school, although he probably thought I didn't know he'd checked.

"How about my attendance and job performance at Harris Company?"

"Excellent according to your boss."

"So, does this mean I'm being punished for what the

band is doing?"

He stared a moment then said, "This discussion is over."

"Just one last thing, Bob. I've not caused one bit of trouble here since I've been back. But most of all, you cannot even imagine how lonely I am with everyone gone. I don't have any friends here. But mostly being back here reminds me that Daddy is dead. My life is dead. I can't stop crying. You know I never cried before. I'm not faking this." I replied.

"But I'm responsible for you." Bob insisted.

"But Rick is my guardian. He's the one that's responsible for me."

"Yeah, and what a great job he's done so far." He muttered.

***

It so happened that Bob's youngest daughter, Barbara, showed up with her two kids the next day. The youngest child, Ben, was eight months old and the older child, Stacey, was five years old. Barbara and her husband had had a fight and she was moving in for a while with her parents. My life in the past ten years had only included me and my dad, no cousins, no kids, and no elderly people except for Bob and Nancy. My nerves were shot the first day because I was sensitive to all the chaotic and negative energy that everyone was giving off. I'm sure that Bob and Nancy weren't expecting crying babies or a sad, crying adult. I mean, they were already trying to deal with a sullen teenager that had been thrust on them by my dad dying. Not that I tried to be a handful, but wow, I was just shell shocked to be living in an environment so different from what I had been used to. Even the atmosphere in our house in New

York was easier to deal with. Now they told me that I couldn't practice my guitar or my drums because the noise would be too much for the young children.

The day after Barbara and her kids moved in, she was trying to get some semblance of fun into the kid's lives. They were in the game room where my drums and guitar were at and she had turned on some kiddie song that Stacey was dancing to. Barbara explained to me that Stacey had been taking hip hop lessons. Nancy thought it was great fun to watch and urged me to dance with the five-year-old.

"No, Nanna, she's too old!" Stacey said putting her hands on her hips like a little diva. "She can't do this."

I just couldn't believe this little kid was saying I was too old at seventeen to dance. "I can too." I told her. Besides that, I wasn't big. I was only five foot two and about 100 pounds.

I got up and tried to copy this little kid's dancing as she pushed me away. Finally, she relented and I danced with her. I had to admit that she had some cool moves. I realized a few moments later that Nancy and Barbara were smiling at each other because I was playing well with others.

What I didn't realize was now that Stacey trusted me, she would wear me out. She was suddenly my shadow and I didn't have a moment's peace. She was always bugging me to do something with her. Could I read to her, could I fix the toy she'd just broken, could we dance, could we watch some stupid cartoon she liked, could we play with her dolls, and the list went on. And if it wasn't one of those things, she was into MY things, breaking them, dragging them all over the place, trying to dress up in my clothes, or bouncing on my bed. And in the background the baby would be screaming. Oh my God! I just wanted to hide.

Stacey and Ben were finally napping at one point and I was in the kitchen just sitting there staring. Wow, I'd forgotten what peace and quiet felt like.

"Makes you want kids now, doesn't it?" Barbara said in amusement as she walked into the kitchen.

"I don't think I was like that." I replied, trying to remember. No, I hadn't been. I'd been an angry mistreated kid, then I was a sullen, friendless, farm working kid, driving the tractor and bush hogging the fields at eight years old, although it had been my choice. I'd never played with dolls or anything else really. I'd hardly watched tv either. Daddy and I would play poker sometimes but mostly there was always something to do on the ranch and I was in charge of handing tools to him and learning how to work on farm equipment.

"You weren't like that. You've always been some weird little bruiser of a kid." Barbara informed me matter-of-factly. "I remember when your dad told my dad that the reason you could drive when you were five years old was because Speed Racer, a cartoon character, taught you." She laughed.

"He did teach me." I replied seriously. I mean, that was the truth.

She laughed harder. "See what I mean? You are so out of touch with reality! The situation you're in right now with me and the kids being here and living with my parents, that's normal, Kid. And you went to New York with those kids you call a band and you thought you were going to become stars? That's not reality. You really should face the truth."

I had a lot of things I could have spouted back

at her but I was still trying to control my behavior so I wouldn't cause trouble. "I guess everyone's reality is different, Barbara. Right now, I want my old reality back." I told her. If I couldn't have my dad back then I wanted to go back to New York to be with the few people that I felt a little bit of kinship with.

The baby started crying then and she left the room. I thought about what she'd said. So normal families had crying kids and little ones that monopolized every bit of time a person might have? That must mean that I had been given the solitude to accomplish my dreams, right?

A little while later, Nancy told me that Cathi was stopping by to take me to the VFW in Greenville with her and her college friends where they were going to sing karaoke. "I'm really proud of the both of you girls." She beamed. "I didn't think you'd get along because you didn't when you were little, but you're both doing so well now. I'm really proud that you're doing better at getting along with people. This will be so much fun for you!" She continued.

I didn't have the heart or the guts to tell her that Cathi had coerced me to have sex with her, and when I hadn't tattled on her, her intent was to corrupt me some more. I could feel the vibes in the air from her and she was having lots of fun causing trouble for me.

Cathi and two of her friends, Joann and Jaime, arrived about 7pm to pick me up. Cathi immediately didn't like what I was wearing and insisted that I wear a cute top, skirt, and heels.

Once we were in the car and Cathi was driving, her friends lit up a joint.

"*Oh crap.*" I said to myself. Her friends waited for me

to say something but I didn't.

When Cathi accepted the joint, I said, "No, no, no. You're not driving if you're gonna get high. Pull over and let me drive, I don't want to die tonight."

Her and her friends laughed at me. "I can drive when I'm high. Don't be a spoil sport."

There was nothing I could do to stop her either.

It took over an hour to drive to the VFW in Greenville. The girls were plenty wasted by then and I wasn't happy at all about it. I knew that if they didn't let me drive them home, that I would find another way. I knew I wouldn't let them drive drunk either and I dreaded how I was going to break the news to Bob.

We walked in and the place was pretty much packed. I thought the people there would be older but most looked to be in their twenties and thirties with maybe ten percent being older. The girls giggled as they found some of their friends and we sat with them. I couldn't help notice all the guys staring at us hungrily. As the guys crowded around us all trying to get our attention, I heard someone butchering a Bob Seger song, and that was just wrong.

Cathi pinched me hard about ten minutes later. "Quit scowling and have some fun, Miss Priss." She hissed in my ear. It took all I had in me not to smack the shit out of her. I was guessing that I had no choice but to relax. No one was driving and no one was dying at the moment, although the beer and alcohol was being drunk like water. I had a Sprite, which I drank half of but then knew that I wouldn't touch it again for fear of roofies. Yeah, I might be Miss Priss but I was also Miss Reality. Someone was now butchering a Pat Benatar song.

"Hey!" Cathi said loudly and excitedly, "You're in a band! Go sing!" Now she had everyone at the table agreeing and asking me about it. When I wasn't excited, she ran up and put my name on the list to sing "Like A Virgin". Her and her friends thought that was hilarious. One of the guys leaned over and told me that he'd take away my virginity. I betted to myself that he was lousy in bed. It was even worse when Cathi held her hand out to him with the car keys and a rubber. "Take it easy on her. She's never done it before." She told the dude.

"Oh, HELL no!" I glared back as they all laughed at me and joked at me being a virgin goody two shoes.

A few minutes later they called my name to sing. Her friends were all laughing and carrying on as I went up the stage. I stood up on the makeshift stage looking down at them. I'd never had stage fright or been afraid in front of a crowd and tonight was no different. As the introduction of the song started up, I was wishing the key wasn't so high. I had a good range to my voice but wow, that was a higher key than I wanted to sing in. I guessed I'd dial it down a notch. I'd seen the video before of Madonna singing the song, and I'd seen some of her other music videos so I knew how she moved when she sang so I did the same. My little performance had people doing everything from picking their mouths off the floor to just staring at me in amazement. Now, THAT, amused me. I smirked, put the microphone down, and stepped down when the last note ended. Then I had like the entire VFW coming up to talk to me.

When Cathi was finally able to get close to me, she said, "Damn! You really fucking can sing!"

"Kind of seems like it." I smiled. Sometimes I did like attention.

I loosened up after that happened and joked and laughed with her friends. I danced with some of the guys, and then everyone wanted me to go back up and sing. I sang "Paint it Black" by the Rolling Stones. As I went to step down after that song, I found that people had signed me up for three other songs. I sang some country song I'd only heard once, "Love Shack" from the B52's, and "Thriller" by Michael Jackson.

I was a little taken aback that I'd had such a big reaction to my singing. I liked playing my guitar more than singing and some of those songs I wouldn't have picked to sing at all. Well, most of them I wouldn't have picked.

It was about 1am when we left the VFW. Cathi and her friends were falling down drunk by then, and I was pretty sure each one of them had screwed their choice of a guy or guys in the car. Well, I knew that because the gas tank had a lot less gas in it from running the heater and several ripped open packages of rubbers were on the floorboard. I was glad the used ones were outside on the ground.

I wrangled the keys from Cathi and we started the drive home. One of them puked in the car about halfway home then the other two immediately rolled down their windows and puked down the outside of the car. I had to stop and clean them up, and that wasn't pleasant at all. I stopped somewhere along the road for them to pee two different times since it was urgent and there was no other place to stop. Yeah, they were on top of their games tonight.

Cathi thought she was going to drive back to her dorm room that night but I told her no. She got into a loud argument with me, and then Bob was walking down to the car to see what was going on. He had been waiting up for us.

"Dammit to hell!" He cussed at us. "You're all shit faced!" He said as he surveyed us. "Who drove?"

"Miss fucking Priss." her friend told him. "She doesn't drink. She's such a loser."

Bob glared at her. She was so damn drunk. Then he walked up to me. "Is that right?" He asked me.

"Yeah." I agreed.

He paused as he looked me over. "Go ahead in the house." he told me in a less irritated voice.

Bob had a temper and he was a lot stricter than my dad ever was. I knew he'd give Cathi hell, but it wouldn't be until the next morning, otherwise she might not remember it.

Nancy was waiting at the door when I came in and she asked me what happened. "They got drunk. Now they're all sick, and the one girl peed all over herself." I replied. I really didn't feel it was my business to tell about anything else that had happened.

"Did you drink anything?" Nancy asked as she looked curiously at me.

"No, I'm the weird one, remember? The one who talks about aliens and who learned to drive from Speed Racer, and whose dad lectured me constantly about not drinking or doing drugs." I replied wearily. "I'm Miss Priss." I felt bad then, taking out my frustration on her. She had always been so nice to me.

"Ah, Pumpkin, you're not weird. You're my sweet little girl. And you saved my heathen from killing herself and y'all tonight." She said as she went to hug me. And Oh my God, I burst out crying. At that moment I sure missed my dad. Nancy had always taken after my dad and called me "Pumpkin", starting when I'd been little. If I had known that I was going to have an emotional moment, I would have gone into level one in my mind where emotions didn't rule me. As I settled down, I wondered why I hadn't visited her very often when I'd been younger. She'd always been so sweet to me.

***

It was another school day where I wished I were anywhere else. When the bell rang for lunch, I found myself in the music room playing the piano. I wasn't supposed to be there. All good students on their lunch break were supposed to be in the cafeteria. For whatever reason I was playing Piano Man by Billy Joel. It's an easy song and I was looking for something to cheer me up. Mr. Walker who taught Civics appeared in the doorway as the song ended. He clapped and complimented me on my playing. He made chit chat for a moment and then asked if he could talk to me.

"Yeah." I agreed but my mind was in New York wondering what Jordan and my other friends were doing.

"I hate to tell you this." Mr. Walker said in all seriousness. "But a few of the people you don't get along with have started a rumor that you had run away to New York and were selling yourself on the streets, that you ended up homeless and addicted to heroin. They're telling people that Bob Anderson had to go to New York and drag you back here, that you totally lost it after your dad died."

I chuckled and he looked confused. I knew that they would add to the story. "I told them most of those lies, then they added extra drama to it. They think that they can just sit down and be friends with me after all the crap they've ever done to me? They're going to tell untrue stories anyway. I figured I give them a solid tale to tell. I would have busted their heads in if I'd had a choice but I have to behave for now if I ever want to get out of this town."

He looked confused. "So, none of that is true?"

"Well, Bob did drag me back here, that's true. He thought the people I was living with were a bad influence. I'm going back though. Maybe not tomorrow, maybe I'll have to turn eighteen to leave but I'm going back." I explained.

"What's in New York?"

"I'm going to be a guitar hero, a rock star. Somehow, it's all gonna start there."

He looked at me with sympathy and began to lecture me on how many people didn't make it as a musician or an actor, and of how hard it was to make it.

I thanked him for the advice but knew that I would make it as a star. I'd known it a long time ago.

***

Bob and Nancy happened to be at the grocery store the next night when the phone rang. I listened to it ring several times and then I grudgingly answered it. I thought that it was one of them calling to check up on me or ask me some grocery related question. I was actually expected to answer the phone when it rang. I was wrong about who was calling. It was David. He asked me how I was doing and when I was coming back.

"I don't know." I grumbled to him. "I guess this is real life here. I have a mother figure and a father figure and they're making me go to school and be a kid. It's nothing like I've ever known. I'm way too old for this shit."

"We're about to self-destruct here." He interrupted. "Rick and Carol might look like adults but they don't know what the hell they're doing or where they're going with the band. And we're all fighting about money because you're not here to pay the bills. Who knew it cost so fucking much to live? Is there any way you can foot us some money?"

I sighed. "No. Bob took away my bank access and I can't do anything about it because I'm underage."
"Damn. I don't know what we're going to do."

We were silent for a few seconds. "I'll think of something but you guys are going to have to buck up from now on. I can't save you from everything." I finally replied.

"We'd sure appreciate it."

"Has Joseph and his goons been harassing any of you?"

"They appear in places so we'll see them but so far they'd quit harassing us."

I was thankful for that.

I sat at the kitchen table and stared out the window. How was I going to get enough money to pay their rent? Our rent was eight hundred dollars and I was sure the utility bills would add three hundred dollars to that total. No ideas came to me so I turned on the tv. A commercial came on a while later about the lottery.

After Bob and Nancy returned from the store, I bargained my way out of the house saying that I had to go to the library for a few minutes. I stopped at the gas station and looked at the lottery tickets. There were some that had higher payouts but the drawings for them were a week away. I didn't have that kind of time. The only one that would payout today was a daily number. I had about ten minutes before they drew the number for the night. As I was pondering how I was going to buy it, one of Rick's high school friends walked in to pay for some gas. I asked him if he'd buy a ticket for me. "I'll give you two hundred dollars of it if it wins." I remarked.

He paid for his gas and bought a ticket with the numbers I'd picked. Then we waited to hear the results on the tv that was mounted behind the counter. I wasn't surprised when I won but he was having a fit. It was a one-thousand-dollar payout. I bummed his phone to make a call to New York. No one was home so I left a voicemail telling them I was mailing the rent to the landlord and that would have to do. From there I went to the grocery store and got a money order. I bummed an envelope from them and bought a stamp. The post office was in the same strip mall so I popped the envelope in the mail to our landlord. Lastly, I gunned my truck over to the library and hurriedly checked out a book. Bob and Nancy were none the wiser about what I'd done but Bob griped that I'd taken too long at the library. Yeah, the band was going to have to do the best they could moneywise. They were going to have to grow up and take care of themselves rather than relying on me as the adult.

CHAPTER 10

School still wasn't the best experience. I wanted to be back in New York at New Rochelle High School. I wanted to be adored by the football team and my classmates again. I wanted to see Jordan. I wished now that I had agreed to be his girlfriend.

It was that five-minute period between classes when I stopped at my locker to grab a book for my next class. A guy that I'd seen around school had a locker two down from me. He had also stopped at his locker. Larry and Moe walked up to him in a threatening manner. Moe pushed him. I slammed my locker door and stared them down. "Later!" Larry remarked as if they'd just taken enough of his shit and couldn't wait to exit the area. They turned to walk past me. "NO MORE. All that crap stops THIS MINUTE." I said sternly to them in a low growling voice.

"We'll do what we want to, bitch." Moe told me as they kept walking.

The guy looked over at me. "Thank you." He said. In the past most kids were too scared of me to even thank me.

I nodded to him and turned to go to my next class.

"You really are bad ass, ya know?" He called after me.

"Damn straight. Before the boogie man goes to sleep

at night, he looks under his bed for me." I replied back. Yeah, comments like that probably didn't help any. Ha.

***

On a Saturday morning, Bob's son Greg stopped over and the entire family was taking the kids to see a Disney movie. I couldn't believe that Bob was going too, but then again, they were going out to eat afterward and somebody had to pay for it. Greg had a son named Derek that was almost eleven and he didn't want to go to any Disney movie. Well, I didn't either. I wanted to have the house to myself and to play my guitar as loud as I wanted to. It had been a while since I had played and so awful long since I'd had the house to myself. Bob allowed Derek and I to stay home while they all went out. I was to babysit him. I grumbled to myself and so did Derek.

After they'd left, Derek was playing games on a play station and I was playing sweet guitar. I wasn't paying attention to him as I got into my music. I put down the guitar and was rocking with the beat of my drums. And I was really missing everyone I'd left in New York. I was going to have to go back there soon. I wasn't used to having all these relatives around that Bob and Nancy enjoyed.

I was doing some showing off on drums just for my own enjoyment when Derek walked in and just looked at me. When he was still staring a moment later, I stopped drumming to see what kind of trouble he'd gotten into because he looked kind of upset. "What's the matter?" I asked him curiously. I hoped he hadn't bothered any of Bob's guns. Even I knew not to touch his guns. Or maybe he'd broken some glassware of Nancy's. She loved her glass figurines.

His face reddened. "Do you know anything about boys?" he asked me.

Crap. I kept a straight face just wondering what in the world he wanted to say. "Yeah, I have some guy friends, so I know some things about boys." I replied. He was making me nervous and so I tapped out a soft beat. It took a lot to make me nervous but wow, where was this story going?

Whatever it was, it was embarrassing him and he just couldn't tell me. "What if you turn around and don't look at me? Can you tell me then?" I asked. Wow, this baby-sitting stuff was hard and he wasn't even a baby.

"Only if you don't tell anyone, especially Grandpa." He replied.

I agreed and he turned away from me. He went on to tell me how his wiener had gotten hard and he'd touched it. He'd been touching it for a few weeks. "I broke it today." He told me, his voice shaking.

Crap. How was I supposed to fix a broken penis? Staying with Bob and Nancy had put me in a whole new category of problems. It just blew my mind. Daddy had never told me that there'd be days like this. "Um, why do you think you broke it?" I asked him carefully. I really didn't think those things broke that easily, if at all, but I didn't have one so hey, maybe they did. It was really going to suck if I had to call Rick and ask him how to fix one. I'd probably never hear the end of his teasing, or yelling. Maybe he'd think I'd broken it. Dammit! Then the band would go around calling me "Dick Breaker." Damn, that would suck.

"Stuff came out. It never did that before." he mumbled pulling me out of my thoughts.

Oh, Thank God. I knew about that. His penis wasn't broken after all. "Oh, that's normal. You're just growing up." I explained to his back. "When you get to be about this age you produce sperm so that when you get older and have sex with a girl you can get her pregnant and she can have a baby. When the stuff comes out it means you came, you had an orgasm. So, when you jerk off like you've been doing, you do it in private."

Derek turned around and studied my face. "Are you going to tell? Because I don't think I was supposed to be doing that."

"No, I'm not going to tell. You can play with it if you want to, it's no big deal. Most guys do it, they just don't talk about it. Have your parents told you about sex?"

He said they hadn't but that he already knew everything. We talked about what he knew and he was really wrong. I figured that I might as well explain it. Stupid Boy and my dad had explained it to me and that was how I knew. We talked about sex, and how a woman got pregnant, and that he should use birth control when he got old enough to have sex, and that he needed to be a gentleman and never force anyone to do anything sexual. I also told him that no one, man, woman, or kid should be doing anything sexual to him that he didn't want done. He had a right to say no, even if they were an adult or a family member. He asked me about that and I told him about sexual predators, of how sometimes they were people you knew and trusted, in some cases they were family members. I was hinting around to see if Cathi had done anything with him but it didn't seem that she had.

About twenty minutes later after digesting all that we'd talked about, he said, "My wiener is pretty big. Do you want to see it?"

I really did want to see it. I was a fan of the male body. But my dad had taught me better. "No, that wouldn't be appropriate." I told him. "I bet it's pretty big though." I assured him.

He decided to go back to playing games on his play station and I picked up my favorite white Gibson. I wondered if that was the hardest question I'd ever be asked when I became a parent. Somehow, I doubted it, especially when the voice in my head laughed.

***

Towards the end of January, I asked Bob if he would reconsider letting me go back to New York. "Angel, you were going to school full time, working, doing gigs with the band, not to mention doing chores at home and homework. Why in the world would you want to go back? Quite obviously, you were working your butt off while the others did nothing but go to a job and play at your gigs. You can find some new friends here if you try."

"Being here has been comfortable, but our band will be famous in a few years if I go back. I'd like to have that chance. And Bob, I actually have some friends there besides Rick, Carol, Kevin and David." I told him.

"You mean your boyfriend, Jace?" He asked sarcastically.

I was taken aback. I hadn't mentioned Jace. I quickly regained my composure. "We're not seeing each other, and I haven't slept with him. He's just a friend. He's in a band too." I finally replied.

"He called here asking for you." Bob replied evenly.

I blinked in surprise. "He did? Wow. I didn't know."

"I wouldn't let him talk to you. You're not going

171

back to New York because of some kid."

"I like Jace, but he's not the main reason I want to go back. Our band has a future. I just want to be part of it. You know that I can see things. We'll be rock stars." I argued.

"Yeah, your Daddy told me that, but what happens when the rest of your band burns out from the drugs? I can't have your Daddy staring down at me knowing drugs are all around you."

I hated to think about it but if the band kept at it like they had been doing, who knows what kind of drugs they'd be doing a year from now. "I guess drugs will always be around. You know, drugs and rock and roll, but I honestly haven't touched alcohol or drugs even if the rest of the band has. I don't need it. If worst comes to worst, I can make it on my own. You know how good I am on guitar." I replied matter-of-factly.

"All of them have called but they need to learn to take care of themselves."

"Kevin too?" I asked as my eyes narrowed.

"Kevin too. He needs to grow up. They all do. No doubt you've been the adult of the bunch. You're more level headed and mature than all of them put together." He huffed.

I stood there holding my temper. "You could have let me talk to them, or at least to Kevin. You know that he doesn't have anybody." I said through clenched teeth. Wow, Kevin had needed me and I hadn't known or been allowed to help him. I wanted to call him but Bob wouldn't allow it.

"That's all we're going to talk about this right now." Bob replied.

I sat in my bedroom and listened to Still the Same on

repeat.

***

As I rode the bus to school the next day, I brainstormed how I could call Kevin. Bob wasn't going to allow me to call him from their house and I didn't have a phone, plus it was a long-distance call. I huffed to myself. I'd never had these problems when I'd lived with my dad.

I still hadn't come up with a plan by the time lunch rolled around. I grimaced at the slice of turkey over a slice of bread with gravy on it. Not that it wasn't good, I was sure it was, but all I could do was stare it as I stirred around the applesauce on my tray. I was angry with myself. Had I been a more intelligent person I would have thought of something by now.

"Are you gonna eat that or what?" Alan asked as he sat down across from me.

"Yeah." I grumbled. I couldn't believe he'd had the nerve to disturb me when I was trying to think. And what was he doing here? This wasn't his lunch break time.

"You're sure lookin' good. What are you so mad about?" He asked.

I glared at him. I really wanted to off him and bury him in the woods. His hair was blonder than I remembered. He was as tall as I was now and he could look right into my blue eyes. I had noticed that the girls adored him. I wondered why he couldn't be more like his brother, David. Although now that I thought about it, both of them were annoying. "Bob won't let me call New York. I need to talk to Rick." I blurted out. I mentally slapped myself because I'd almost said "Kevin" instead of "Rick". I wasn't supposed to know where

Kevin was.

Alan shrugged his shoulders. "Is that it? No biggie. Daddy has a cell phone with free long distance. If you go out with me then I'll ask to use it."

I blinked because I was so stupid. David's family still lived where they'd always lived and I knew that his mom called David sometimes. But I didn't want David's family telling Bob that I called New York. No doubt they'd bump into each other at the grocery store or gas station and mention me. That's the way it always seemed to work. "I ain't going out with you." I replied. "But I do want to use your daddy's phone."

"Let me feel your titties and I'll work that out for you."

I narrowed my eyes at him. "No." I replied.

"Too bad so sad that you won't be callin' New York." He smiled with that evil smile of his.

He rambled on as my anger rose and I saw red. I didn't know how else I was going to make a long-distance call without Bob knowing.

I know I was grouchy that night at Bob and Nancy's house but I couldn't help it.

Alan was standing at my locker the next morning at school. I wanted to punch him just for standing there. "Guess what I got, Snookums?" He asked with that evil smile of his.

I watched him bring his hand out of his backpack. I stared as if he were holding the crown jewels. It was a black flip phone.

"One feel, that's all it would take for you to use this baby." He said teasingly as he held the phone out of my reach.

"I would have to call right as school let out. Rick

would be home then." I answered as I continued to stare at the phone. "How would I get home if I miss the bus?"

He blinked in surprise but quickly recovered. "Mom is picking me up from school. I could talk her into driving you home."

At lunch, we snuck down the hall to the lone handicapped bathroom. I was totally grossed out and humiliated as he felt me up over my bra because I wouldn't let him touch my bare skin. He gave me the phone and I left the bathroom with it in my jeans pocket. I nearly ran smack into Mr. Walker as I rounded a corner.

"Whoa. Where are you going? You're not supposed to be in the hallway." He remarked.

"I was delayed at my last class so I'm on my way to eat lunch now." I lied.

He nodded. "Okay, get going."

I was glad the lie had worked. I could hardly think after having Alan's hands on my breast. I wondered if I'd ever stop feeling gross.

I called our house in New York as soon as my last class let out. I almost whimpered when Kevin answered the phone. I had been worried that one of the others would answer. David might not have given me any grief but Rick and Carol would have and that was the last thing I needed.

"Angel?" He asked.

"Yeah. Are you okay? Bob told me you called but then he wouldn't let me call you." I said in a rush.

"No, I'm not okay! When are you coming back here? All we do is fight since you're gone. This is a nightmare. I can hardly take it anymore!" He exclaimed and then he was crying but trying not to let me know.

"I know, Kevin. It's no picnic here either."

"Why haven't you called?"

"Bob took away my money, Kevin! And he won't let me call you guys! You don't even want to know what I had to do in order to make this call! You're not the only one who has it hard." I blurted out.

"I'm sorry." He replied. He went on to tell me the problems he was having.

"I want to leave Bob and Nancy on peaceful terms. I'm getting close to that. You just need to hold on for a while." I told him as I walked out of the school. The cold wind hit me and I pulled my coat tighter around me.

He was crying some more about something as I rounded the corner to where the buses parked.

"Where have you been?" I heard Alan yell. I sighed as I saw my bus pulling out into the street with everyone who had bothered to get on it.

"C'mon!" He urged.

I sighed again. "Kevin, I gotta go. I missed my bus and now I gotta endure a ride with David's brother."

As we walked a few steps and were standing by Alan's mom's car, Kevin reluctantly disconnected the call. I was so close to just hanging up on him but only because everyone else didn't want to give me any additional time to talk. I handed the phone to Alan. He opened the door and stuck his head inside to ask his mom if she would give me a ride home.

"I don't have time. Remember? We have to go to---" blah, blah, blah, I'd stopped listening. I now didn't have a ride home and I hadn't even had enough time to talk to Kevin. The wind agreed as it whipped around me and blew my hair into my face. I brushed a lock of hair away.

"Um, I guess we can't give you a ride." He told me.

"Surely you can call Bob." His mom remarked. "Now get in the car, Alan."

I sucked in a breath as he got in the car. I was still standing there as they drove away. It was getting dark, and exactly what phone did she think I was going to use to call Bob? I huffed out my anger and shook my head in disgust. I saw my breath in the air before the wind blew it away. The parking lot was deserted except for a car or two. I started walking. No doubt Alan's mom would bump into Bob and bitch to him that I called New York on their precious phone.

I relived the conversation with Kevin as I walked. I cursed the diminishing daylight and cold wind too. It would be dark before I made it home. It would take me over an hour to get there. In a few moments I would just run and maybe beat the darkness. Lord knows I didn't want to be stumbling in the dark to get home. Maybe this predicament was the universe telling me that I needed to get more exercise by running the five miles home. There was always a reason for the way things happened, or so they said.

I thought about everything that had gone on from me going to New York, the things that had happened there, being dragged back to South Carolina, then all the things that had happened until now. I wasn't sure what I was supposed to think, how I was supposed to feel, or what I was supposed to do. Bob wouldn't let me drive to school, and I didn't want him bitching at me so I was walking home. No one was making my life easier. It only seemed harder and more complicated as time went on. I jerked out of my thoughts as a car pulled up beside me and rolled down the window. I gritted my teeth knowing it was probably Curly, Larry, or Moe cruising for young girls to torment. "You're going to get run over walking on the side of the road at this time of day." Mr. Walker groused.

"I can't help it. My ride fell through." I replied. He was driving a 2002 silver Honda Civic. I wondered if it got good gas mileage. It was fairly clean but had a slight dent in the door.

"Get in. I'll drive you home."

He didn't have to ask me twice. He asked me where I lived and then began driving.

"How did you miss your bus?' He asked. He was listening to a radio station that played soft rock. I cringed inside.

"I didn't mean to miss my bus. It was just a bad day." I replied evading his question.

"Bob Anderson is your guardian, right? Was he not at home?"

Man, I hated all the questions. It was none of Mr. Walker's business, in my opinion. I was already in for the third degree when I got to Bob's house anyway for being so late.

"He's probably home but he was pissed the last time I missed the bus and he had to drive me home. I didn't feel like dealing with that tonight." Yeah, I probably should have just called him since I probably would be thirty minutes late getting home now. I wished that my dad was still alive.

"Are you okay? Sometimes it helps to talk." Mr. Walker remarked as I felt him taking a more detailed look at me in the near darkness.

No, I wasn't. I needed my dad for all the stressful and confusing things that were happening. Who was taking care of ME? Wasn't I still a kid? Why was I having to go through all this turmoil and stress? I'd just paid for a phone call by letting a boy I despised feel me up. I hated myself for that. The phone call had been important though. I had to make sure Kevin was okay. But I'd failed at that too. There was nothing I could do to help his life out in New York. Bob and Nancy wouldn't understand any of that. Hell, most of the things I did at their house were to take care of them and make life easier for them because they were old. Had I agreed to be a guardian to everyone in this lifetime? "It's just been a hard day." I murmured. Even I could hear the stress in my voice.

"I'm sorry. Try to let it go. Things will look better after a good night's sleep." He replied as he lightly squeezed my shoulder.

I glanced at him as he put his hand back on the steering wheel. We were pulling into Bob's gravel driveway. He had said those words in such a comforting way. I wished at that moment he were my dad. It felt like he was a good dad to his kids and that he helped them through their troubles. And Lord, I needed someone like that.

The car came to a stop. I paused before getting out and I said some words to him that I rarely said to anyone. "Thank you. You're a good person and you sound like a good daddy. I really needed my daddy today."

"I'm really sorry about your dad's passing. I know this has to be an incredibly hard time for you. Think about talking to the guidance counselor to help you through this, or if you're more comfortable talking to me, I'm here." He assured me.

I nodded as I stood outside the passenger door. I couldn't remember anyone ever being so compassionate to me, outside of daddy.

"I mean that. You can talk to me." He repeated. Yeah, it was just like hearing daddy talking to me now. I wished then that I had talked to daddy about my sorrows rather than keeping them all inside. It was too late now. And Mr. Walker couldn't be my dad as much as I wished he could be. Life didn't work like that. Besides, no one could really help me. I had a destiny that involved a different approach. I also had aliens and ghosts in my life. Who in the world would understand or believe that? Daddy hadn't.

"Thank you. You're very kind." I replied as I held his gaze for a moment. There was nothing he could help me with but I so deeply appreciated that he'd noticed my state of mind and that he cared to lend a listening ear. I shut the door and waved as he pulled away. A wave of peace from his words washed over me as I walked up the front steps. I kept that peace in me as Bob gave me the third degree a few moments later.

***

A few nights later, I went with Bob to the grocery store just to get out of the house. Barbara's kid, Stacey was driving me crazy and even though I hated grocery shopping, I couldn't stand one more moment with Stacey bugging me. As Bob pulled the truck into a parking space outside the grocery store, it suddenly hit me that he was no happier about Barbara and her kids staying with them. They had gotten used to the house being quiet. Well, hell, I wasn't even allowed to play my guitar now because of Barbara and her kids, or so that's what he'd said.

"Why don't you tell Barbara to suck it up and make it work with her husband? It was for better or for worse, right?" I blurted out before I knew what I was saying.

He shut off the engine and he seemed to want to say so many things. "I have told her. She won't go. She was the baby of the family and we coddled her, now she takes the easy way out. Now, you on the other hand, know what you want and you don't let anything stop you. I do admire you, Kid, and I know her brats are driving you crazy, but right now staying with us is the best thing for you. Your dad was rather unorthodox and he did the best he could for you but you never had the normal family environment like a mother and a father, brothers and sisters, aunts and uncles. Nancy and I are going to give you that so you can see what most of the world experiences. You deserve that."

"Don't talk New York, don't talk music. Just thank him." my mind said loudly although I really did want to. I also wanted to tell him that I didn't need all the relatives. I just needed my dad.

"Thank you, Bob, You're pretty cool for doing that." I found myself saying.

"You're welcome." He said. He actually smiled at me and gave me a one-armed hug as we walked into the store. It wasn't until I heard myself utter those words that I realized how much he and Nancy were sacrificing for me. It wasn't just my life, it was their lives too, and their time was dwindling. I was beginning to pay more attention to sensing energy these days and I felt that Bob's energy was lessening. It didn't feel like he was dying but something else was happening. They were really great people to want to give me a normal life and I would have stayed there if it hadn't been for the music career that was ready for me in New York. I realized that if Barbara and her kids were gone that part of me did want to stay and have Bob and Nancy be real parents to me. It also dawned on me that my dad, although well intentioned, hadn't given me the best home to grow up in. I hadn't known that because I had no other home to compare it to, at least until now. And that realization was rather sobering.

"Bob, tell Barbara you're giving her two months to get a job and get her own place. Keep on her ass about it, and she'll be gone so fast you'll wonder why you didn't do it sooner, because right now you're giving her a free ride. She's too old for a free ride." I told him as we put the groceries in his truck.

"Sounds like a plan. She needs to grow up and be as old as you." He agreed. I guessed that she was about thirty-five or so, since Bob and Nancy were about seventy. They were old enough to be grandparents to me.

Bob stopped at the gas station on the way home, and sent me inside to pay for the gasoline. They made you pay up front and he was paying in cash so I would have to stay inside until he was done filling the tank up. He was driving that big hulk of a truck of his and it was empty so it would take a few minutes.

As I stood at the counter, a guy about thirty-five was looking down the potato chip aisle.

"Tell him you like karaoke." the voice told me.

I sighed to myself. I didn't like karaoke but sometimes it was best not to argue with that voice. I went up to where the guy was looking and picked up a bag of chips. "Hey, do you like karaoke? It's like my favorite thing." I remarked to him, feeling so damn silly. I should have said it differently so that I hadn't sounded like a ten-year-old.

"Really, and I bet you can sing like a super star?" He smirked. "Like all the other teeny boppers."

"Belt out the chorus for "What it Takes". Really belt it out." the voice told me.

Oh crap! I didn't feel like singing. I just wanted to go home, lock my bedroom door, and put my headphones on to drown out the crying baby and Stacey pounding on my door for me to play with her.

Do it NOW

I just as suddenly belted out the chorus, feeling silly as all hell.

"Tell me what it takes to let you go
Tell me how the pain's supposed to go
Tell me how it is that you can sleep in the night
Without thinking you lost everything that was good
in your life to the toss of the dice
Tell me what it takes to let you go"

At some point I had shut my eyes while I was singing. When I opened them, the guy was staring at me smiling. I heard a few patters of applause from inside the store.

I suddenly smiled back, "I'm fucking awesome!" I told myself as well as him. Oh yeah!

"I told you to stop the Goddamn cussing!" Bob said loudly and suddenly from behind me.

Now it was just funny, with him catching me and I laughed.

He was really mad at me though and he grabbed my arm to yank me along with him and was growling to me that he'd kick my ass if I cussed in public like that again.

"Hey, hey! Wait a minute!" the guy said to us. Then he was telling Bob how my singing had impressed him and how he owned a club in Greenville and he wanted me to come down and sing. He really was wanting a band to play at his club sometimes but no one really had any talent. He said I was the first person who did. "It's too bad you can't play guitar." the guy remarked to me.

Bob glared at me as I replied, "I'm accomplished on guitar, keyboard, and drums but I can also play the violin."

The guy laughed again. "Can you come down to the club tomorrow night and audition?"

"She's only fifteen, mister. She isn't going to any club in Greenville." Bob informed him.

"I'm seventeen, Bob." I corrected him.

"Well, come with her. I want to see what she's got. She might end up with a job." the guy told him. He kept talking and finally Bob gave in because he wouldn't shut up.

On the way home, Bob said to me, "Now how did that interaction happen? I sent you into the gas station to pay for our gas, and you end up with an audition, and you didn't even pay for the gas. I had to take the money from you and pay for it."

"Shit happens." I replied casually.

"Will you fucking quit cussing?" He replied back in irritation. "If you don't, I'm going to have your aliens come get you." It was funny that he only said the F word around me.

"If you call the aliens, they're just going to make crop circles in your field and do hideous experiments on you." I lied. The aliens were only concerned with dealing with me.

He laughed his ass off.

CHAPTER 11

The next night, Bob drove me over to the club in Greenville that Norris owned. It was a Friday night and we were supposed to be there about 9:30pm. Bob was grumbling about how late we were going to be out because he was usually getting into bed around that time.

"If you get drunk, I'll drive us home." I remarked to him. Bob had wanted me to wear something decent but he said it was my parade and if I wanted to fuck it up then it was my choice. I had worn a black t-shirt, jeans, and my cowboy boots. Man, I was a sucker for cowboy boots.

He smirked at me. "I might want to get drunk after I hear you play." He wisecracked. "I'm sure this is going to blow my ears out."

I noticed that the place was crowded. There was still some room but wow, there were a lot of people here if I was supposed to be doing an audition. I was suddenly wondering what I'd gotten myself into. It was a Friday night. I supposed that answered my question. I clutched my favorite white Gibson harder for assurance, and I slipped into level one in my mind. We found Norris and he explained that I needed to get up on stage and sing a song karaoke style, then if I did okay on that, he was going to have me play my guitar and sing. There would be someone on drums. I noticed that the music that was playing wasn't super loud and I was thankful for that since Bob was with me.

"What's your first song?" He asked.

"Welcome to the Jungle." the voice told me.

"Welcome to the Jungle. Guns N' Roses." I answered.

"Well okay, take the stage." Norris told me.

I saw Bob look around at all the people and wonder how I was going to do it. "Can you sing in front of all these people?" He asked as I felt his fear. I just smiled at him in amusement before I walked up on stage with my guitar. Even though Norris said that I would only be singing the first song, I already knew it on guitar, and my favorite white Gibson was awesome, so I plugged it into the amp. As I looked out at the crowd, I also noticed that they were filming me. I was big time already. Maybe I'd even be interviewed afterward. Oh yeah!

As the karaoke machine started the introduction, I saw Norris give me a look that he wasn't happy because I wasn't listening to him. I didn't care, I just needed my Gibson, the guitar that my dad had bought me. I put it down for now. "Welcome to the Jungle" is a very high energy song all the way through. I'd watched Axl Rose many times in that video and I knew how he moved, and I knew where he wailed. So, I got into the zone and started with the wail he does in that song, then launched into the rocking lyrics. About halfway through the song Axl is down on his knees leaning back just a wailing so I did too, just a rocking it. I could hear the crowd then, cheering and singing with me. Then at the rather long instrumental, I picked my Gibson up and played along with the karaoke machine. I finished the song with the same intensity just a ripping it apart on my Gibson.

Okay, so I knew that song would have some impact but it was even more than the impact I'd had at the VFW. It's like these people had never been to a live concert and heard someone rip a guitar. I swear that everyone there roared as the last notes ended. There was whistling and every other noise too. I looked at them with a smirk on my face. I realized that the energy of the crowd gave me strength. "Y'all like my favorite white Gibson, don't ya?" I asked them as the noise dipped slightly.

"Yeah! Hell yeah!" I heard amongst the other comments and whistles. It made me smile as the crowd was wild again. Yeah, I was bad ass, so fucking bad ass. I noticed another guy approaching the stage now. "Do you know "You Light Up My Life?" by Debbie Boone?" He asked me.

I rolled my eyes in absolute disgust. "Yeah, I've heard it before." I replied. Were they seriously going to make me sing that song? Songs like that made me look like a wuss.

He nodded to the piano and put the sheet music on it.

I looked past it to the people who were now all crowded around the stage. I picked the mic back up and told them, "Y'all are gonna hate me for this next song. Sorry, it wasn't my choice. Mama wants to hear it. Feel free to cry if the song moves you to do so, but not so loud that you have trouble hearing me sing." The audience howled at that. They were mine now. I knew I could make them do anything I chose to. I smiled in amusement.

They laughed and cheered me on even though they didn't have a clue what song I was going to sing. As

I glanced over all of the people, I imagined this was what groupies were like. They were crowded against the small stage looking at me like I was the most awesome person in the entire world. Wow! I was all about that.

I placed the mic on its stand, put down my guitar, and went over to the piano. I knew Norris wanted to see if I had a soft side to me, and to see if I was being truthful about the instruments I'd said I could play.

I sang that soft song with clarity and strength even on the high notes all the while thinking that I didn't like it one bit. I didn't even stumble when I turned the sheet music to the next page. Interestingly enough, the audience seemed to focus on my every word and note, and they clapped and cheered loudly as I ended that song. I wondered at that point if the audience was made up of aliens. The aliens loved me, and if they wanted me to succeed at something and I was giving it my all, they'd make it happen.

"Now you pick a song that shows your guitar skills, and I'll be the drummer." the guy told me.

"Rockies." I replied easily.

"What? You'd have to be really damn good on guitar to play that guitar solo!" he said as if I were crazy.

"Yeah." I agreed back in a very satisfied and conceited tone. "I would have to be. Try to keep up."

"Holy shit." he murmured. "Well, it's your audition, fuck it up if you want to." He said as he went back to get in position to drum.

I went to the edge of the stage and grabbed my guitar and the microphone. "If y'all liked what I've done so far, you're gonna lose your mother fuh, ah mother freakin' minds on this song." I said as I smiled wickedly at them.

"Awe YEAH!" came the response of the crowd as they cheered loudly. I caught a glance at Bob and I was afraid he was going to lose it as I said that. I had almost said "fuckin" instead of "freakin". I was amused at the look on Norris' face too. Yeah, maybe I'd taken it a bit far but it was the first time the stage was entirely mine and it was freakin' awesome, I mean, fuckin' awesome!! I wished the crowd were one hundred thousand or so, so I could blow them all away.

I looked back at the drummer and he started us off. I launched into the song which isn't an intense song until around the middle of it when the guitar solo starts. I was just rockin' it and dancing as I belted that song out. Then on the guitar solo, I ripped into it as I had many times before when I'd wanted to impress. I must admit that I loved this crowd, because they were even louder when I finished that song. In that moment, I became a rock star. I had to admit that this had been the best performance I'd ever done. Uh, well, it was the only performance like this I'd ever done too. When I was with my band, Rick was the lead singer and I was the drummer, and we'd never had a reaction like this before.

I walked back to the drummer as the crowd continued cheering. "That was fucking incredible." He admitted to me. "Let me shake your hand and I need your autograph and to get a picture with you because I know you're going to be fucking famous one day."

I smiled in total conceit and shook his hand. He handed his cell phone to someone so he could have his picture made with me. As the shutter snapped our picture, I realized that I'd just met my first groupie and given my first autograph.

"Can I play?" I asked him as I nodded to his drums.

"Oh HELL, no. When you're hired here, you're never to touch my drums. I want to keep this gig." He told me seriously. I saw him look behind me as he finished talking. Norris was walking up behind us. "Can you play five more songs?" He asked me.

"I'd love to but I don't know if my guardian can handle any more. It's way past his bedtime." I replied.

"Go ask."

I was mobbed as I tried to walk over to Bob. They finally let me through. I told him what Norris had asked. "Only if you play something by Johnny Cash." Bob replied.

When I'd played five songs including one by Johnny Cash, and Norris had talked to me with Bob listening, we headed to his truck to go home. Bob let me drive. Norris had wanted me to be part of the band for his club. I half listened as Bob rambled on about everything that had happened including my almost slip up with the F word, and the crowd's response. "How can I let you work there when you're only seventeen? And dammit, you were so good! That crowd loved you!" He remarked to me. He had been talking for at least fifteen minutes nonstop and hadn't given me a chance to get a word in. I figured he was trying to talk himself into a decision, but it didn't matter because I'd already made one. I was going back to New York. He couldn't make me stay. Rick was my guardian now and music was my destiny.

"I more than appreciate everything you and your family have done for me, Bob, but what I want, is to go back to New York and be famous with my band. This little concert tonight proves that we can be famous. It's what I'm supposed to do. I can't do it here even though it looks like I'd have chances to perform."

Bob was suddenly silent. "What about the drugs and the alcohol?" He asked a moment later.

"They're everywhere." I remarked. "Case in point is your granddaughter, Cathi."

"Yeah, I know. She's headed down a tunnel of destruction. I don't know what to do."

"Every member of your family needs to cut her off. Six months, no contact, no money, no words. When she crawls back then tough love, her parents need to make her live at home, and abide by the rules. I guarantee she'll be better. But the question is, Can y'all do that for six solid months? I can absolutely guarantee it will be hell on you."

"Probably not." He replied.

We were silent for probably twenty minutes as the radio played softly on a country station, and I managed to find the right roads to go home.

"I'm sorry." He said suddenly.

"For what?" I asked. Bob was like me, never sorry about anything.

"You know, when I dragged you back from New York, I thought I was bringing you home to someplace safe but I found out that I was wrong. I imagine your dad hates me right now for what's happened to you in the short amount of time you've lived with us." He said as he stared straight ahead.

I sensed that Bob was talking about the sexual incident with Cathi and then having to deal with her and her friends being drunk and high, although he hadn't out right said anything about either incident. I knew that Cathi had told him about the sexual incident in her attempt to put some of the burden on me, because Bob had been so angry at her for getting drunk.

It hadn't helped her case any, it had only put more of a spotlight on the problem that she was. "I don't want to talk about any of that."

"I don't either, but I do want you to tell me honestly if you're okay after what Cathi did to you." He remarked as he continued to avoid looking at me.

"I don't seem to be any worse for the wear." I replied. Hell, I'd come twice that night with her, and I'd cleaned up drunken band members a few times. And she'd molested me once when I was seven years old. I supposed that Bob didn't need to know that.

"Are you being honest?"

"Yeah. Don't blame yourself. And no offense, but I'd keep her away from the younger kids - boys and girls. Her personality is prone to addictions."

"I'm too fuckin' old for this." He muttered.

"You can educate the kids on what's appropriate. It's a tough subject but let them know they can say no to sexual advances. If they know that, then they'll rat her out, and I don't think she'll force them."

"Then why didn't you say no?" He blurted out. "Oh hell, don't answer that."

"Because a person's sex drive can be a bitch that drives you to do things you normally don't do." I replied. I knew that he could relate to that. He'd gotten Nancy pregnant way back when and that's how they ended up getting married. "And Bob, if any of the kids come to you and say that she did something to them or wanted them to do something, believe them. Don't make them feel bad or wrong for telling. Why do you think that I always had something to do when she came to visit you when we were little? I went out of my way to avoid her. She had her hands on me way back then." I confessed to him.

"Holy shit! Are you fucking serious?" He blurted out.

"Yeah, I'm fucking serious. She molested me once when I was seven years old riding the rodeo circuit."

"Why the hell didn't you tell someone?" he demanded.

"You do realize that you're not the easiest person to talk to, right?"

"Hell, you should have told someone."

"I did. I told Stupid Boy and he kept her away from me, and I just always made sure I never went any place isolated with her."

"Stupid Boy? Ryan Connor, the older kid you couldn't keep your hands off of?"

"Yeah, him, the boy you thought was molesting me. He never tried anything with me. Man, I miss him!"

Bob was silent for a moment. "Girl, you know you just fucked up my world, right? I had the world all figured out, and now you're telling me everything I knew was wrong." He and my dad had always thought that Ryan had molested me even though I'd told them that he hadn't.

"I really owe you a big apology where Cathi is concerned. But with Ryan, it was better that he left and you didn't have any further contact with him. I know what I saw, and the two of you would have gotten into big trouble had he stayed around. He didn't have anyone paying attention to him except for you, and you were gaga over him."

"I'm going to look him up and go see him while I'm here."

"No, you're not. Leave the past behind."

He was wrong. I was going to try to find Ryan.

"And another thing." He added. "I should have talked to the school after that first incident with those girls fighting with you and knocking you into the mud. Instead, I busted your ears about it. You were being a good kid and even though your past caught up with you, you still didn't fight with those girls. I should have done better. Yeah, I'm gonna talk to Principal White."

I would probably have told him not to do that but a cop car was racing from behind us and I had to let it pass. It had somewhat surprised us and interrupted the conversation. So, I said nothing and pulled back onto the road to continue home.

"I'm going to miss you when you go back to New York." Bob remarked as he looked at me. We shared a smile. "You remind me so much of your old man. You are your father's daughter, that's for sure."

I was going to miss him too. He and Nancy were sweet old people and they would have provided a really good home for me. When I was older maybe I'd be able to provide a loving two parent home for my kid which would make up for the childhood I never had.

I did try to find Ryan but his mom had moved away and I couldn't find anyone who knew where he lived. I was disappointed. I owed Ryan my life and I had just wanted to talk to him.

CHAPTER 12

I thought it was going to be a bad day for me when I came to breakfast and Bob was sitting there drinking coffee. He usually was out in the field or down at the town diner talking shit with the retired farmers. "After you eat, we need to discuss something." He informed me. Yeah, him saying that didn't help either. I only imagined the worst.

I stalled on breakfast as long as I could. The baby was crying and Stacey had knocked over my juice onto my lap. Bob had closed his eyes and was shaking his head in aggravation. Barbara wasn't saying much of anything for once. I wiped up the juice, then said I was going to change into another pair of jeans. It was an in-service day at school so I didn't have to go but now I was wishing I could go just to escape the tension in the house.

"Meet me in the truck." Bob called to me as he walked away.

He was in his truck with it idling as I walked out of the house. He must have been trying to erase other sounds from his head because I could hear the country music even though the truck windows were closed. From the house I could hear Stacey wailing that she wanted to go with us. As soon as I got into the truck and closed the door, he put the truck in gear and we headed off. I wondered if he was going to take me out and bury me somewhere.

He turned down the radio. "I talked to Barbara this morning; told her she has two months to get her act together. She's pissed." He finally said.

"Good for you, Bob. That's tough love but it works. She's gonna try to manipulate you. If you give in, you're gonna have to take care of her and the kids the rest of your life." I replied.

"Yeah." He said slowly. "About that, exactly how do you and the kids you live with handle your money? What kind of arrangement do you have for the bills?"

Crap. "It started out with all of us chipping in equally for the rent and utilities and then we all had chores assigned to us but we had a big blow up at Christmas and that changed."

He glanced at me to continue.

"Daddy never made me do housework so we made a deal where I pay the rent and utilities and I don't have to do any housework, even my clothes get washed. And the rest of them pay for the groceries."

Bob was staring at the road but he blinked in surprise at my answer.

"Were you making enough at your job to cover that expense?"

"No, I usually had to dip into the insurance money for a couple hundred more a month."

"So, you were taking care of four Barbara's. Were you going to do that for the rest of your life?"

I knew he was right. "Only until we all got famous and started making more money." I replied.

He put on his turn signal and I saw that we were pulling up to the bank. He harped on me about when

I thought that would be and that the rest of them were a bunch of freeloaders. "I guess we both have to decide what we're going to do with the Barbara's in our lives." He finished as he calmed down. He turned into a parking lot in front of the bank.

I followed Bob into the bank wondering what he was up to.

We sat down with one of the bank staff. "We need to make a deposit and to put some money into stocks or some investments." Bob told the bank employee. I saw that her name tag said "Elle".

As Bob and Elle discussed the matter, I found that the insurance company had paid out the million-dollar life insurance policy that my dad had taken out on himself. Our house had sold after I'd moved to New York and Bob had put the funds in my bank account. The insurance policy didn't seem real until now. I guess my mind had been too messed up after my dad had died and a life insurance policy hadn't entered my mind.

Elle told us about the investments then Bob turned to me. "So where do you want it to go?" He asked. I knew he was waiting for psychic information. I thought about it for a few seconds and then told him. "I want you to take half of the money." I told him.

"No, ma'am. Your dad wanted this for you. He and I talked about it a long time ago."

He put the money in the investments that I'd advised him on and he had Elle put fifty thousand of it in an investment that could be easily liquidated.

On the drive home he asked me what I'd do with the money if I had access to the entire amount right now.
" Nothing." I replied. He hadn't given me my checkbook back. And technically I had a million dollars but it was

all in investments that I couldn't touch anyway.

"You wouldn't buy a new truck?" He asked.

"My truck is new. And I've had access to fifty thousand until you took it away when I moved back here. If I'd wanted to spend it, I would have already done so." I replied as I watched the scenery go by.

A moment of silence went by. "I'm impressed with that. The account still has close to fifty thousand in it."

I wondered why I didn't have anything in mind that I wanted to buy. I was going to have to consult "Still the Same" while I thought about it.

***

Two weeks later I was back in New York. Bob had had a long talk with Rick both on the phone and then in person after we arrived at our apartment. And the three of us had many deep conversations before that. Before Bob left, he said to me, "If you really want to go back to high school have Rick register you, otherwise don't worry about it. You can always take a G.E.D test. And here's the checkbook for the allotments I've been sending you. You know what you need. And when you need a vacation or decide you want to come home, our door is always open." I was amazed at the transformation in him from living with him for two months. I'd also had many talks with him in those past weeks of all the things that Daddy and I had gone through, and I also made it a point never to be whiny. I was always on my best behavior and acting like an adult. I think he finally realized that daddy was aware that if I knew I'd be in a famous rock and roll band that drugs would always be around me. And I think he finally understood that my life as I knew it in South Carolina was over for me.

I'd also talked to Bob about using some of my money to buy Kevin a car. Neither Kevin or I were old enough to buy the car ourselves and I knew that Rick would never agree to it. The band didn't know exactly how much money I had to my name. They figured I had a couple thousand and I wasn't telling them any differently, I hadn't even told Kevin. So once Bob packed my truck up and followed me to New York, he took me and Kevin out car shopping. Bob picked out a 2004 Toyota Yaris that had thirty thousand miles on it. He assured us that it was economical and would last. He put two thousand dollars down on it and then in order for Kevin to establish some credit, Bob's and Kevin's name went on the loan. I told Kevin that I'd help him pay the payment if he ran short.

He had a talk with Kevin in private and I'm not sure what he told him but Kevin bawled to me later because Bob had been so nice to help him and to put up the down payment, and that I had been so generous to help him pay for the car. "You left the bad life behind, Kevin." I told him. "Now you're about to live the good life." I had told Bob to let Kevin assume that he had put up the down payment when in fact, it was my money that paid for it.

"I love you, Baby. I'll never forget how you've been there for me. I'm gonna make it up to you." He told me as he clung to me.

Both the fact that he'd said he'd loved me and that I didn't think I'd really been there like I could have been jerked something inside of me. "And I'd do it all over again." I replied as I also realized that sometimes other people came into your life to do what your own people failed to do for you. Bob and Nancy had stepped in to right the failure of Rick as a guardian. I had stepped up and assumed responsibility for Kevin when his family had failed him even though I thought I needed taken care of just as much as he did. It only seemed fair to assume that other people would step in and help us with other failures as time went on. Thinking about the situation with that attitude eased my mind a little.

"Tell me you love me." Kevin murmured against me. We were still holding each other.

"You don't have to mean as a girlfriend. Just as my friend." He added when I didn't immediately respond back.

I didn't want to but it felt like he needed those words so I gently pushed him back so I could look at him. "I do love you, Kev. Daddy and I have always loved you as family. You and I will always be family no matter what." I told him sincerely as I met his eyes.

Tears fell from his eyes then he crushed me against him. Then he really bawled.

"Breathe his pain away. You need to learn to automatically do this as needed." A voice told me. I breathed away Kevin's pain as I told him soothing words and held him as he relived some of the hell with his parents. It reminded me of how I'd had to comfort some of the first graders when I'd been in school. "It'll be all right. I promise." I assured him as he wiped away the last of his tears. I was saying the words not only to him but to myself as well. He just didn't know that.

I unpacked the last of my things thinking that the situation was more stable than it had ever been and problems would pretty much be a thing of the past. I was wrong. They would just take a new direction. I knew the first order of business would be to get the household out of debt, which I could only guess that they were behind in the bills. Okay, so I was right about that. We were at the point of eviction from our house and utilities were near the shut off point. I paid our debt and that was settled. Rick then told me that Club Nine had fired us and that the Caterpillar Lounge wasn't far behind. He and I went down to Club Nine to see if we could set things straight. It was no use, we were out. We would just have to work twice as hard at the Caterpillar Lounge. I didn't understand how we could have gotten fired. Kevin could play drums as well as electric guitar which meant that Rick was no good at managing our band. I had to step up. *"Not only that, but the group dynamic couldn't withstand the pressure without you. Your strength helps them to have strength and confidence. You've been leading them. You are the guardian."* is what the voice in my mind told me. Well, that was certainly something to think about considering that I didn't feel any of that strength at all. How could I help them if I didn't feel what I was supposedly projecting? *"Strength is much more than what you think it is. Strength is having faith and following your inner guidance. You are pronounced in both of those traits."* And what could I say to that?

***

I soon realized that all of them were sick with colds. There was a lot of coughing, sneezing, and grumbling going on especially with Rick and Carol. "You're gonna be sick now too." Kevin told me. As far as I could remember, I'd never been sick. I wasn't about to start now.

I left the sickies and went to Harris Company where I used to work and asked them if I could have my job back. They had filled my position so I just started filling out job applications for different jobs. I contacted Cardello too. I told them that I wouldn't mind doing some jobs for them from time to time. They said they'd keep me in mind. I came back to the house with cold and flu medicine.

I thought about whether I should go back to school. I really wanted to see Jordan, and I'd missed all the attention that I'd once gotten. I thought I'd give Jordan that chance with me that he had been wanting. I appeared on the school grounds as class let out. The football players and the cheerleaders walked out of the school laughing and carrying on. "Hey! Long time no see! Where have you been?" One of the guys shouted as he noticed me. I looked past him to see Jordan wrapped around one of the cheerleaders. He blinked in surprise at my appearance. The kids crowded around me.

"It's a long story." I replied as some of the kids hugged me and I tolerated it.

We had a little reunion but the energy felt entirely different now. Although Jordan talked to me off to the side and was clearly angry with me about not calling him while I'd been in South Carolina, he had moved on. I could tell by the way the cheerleader hung onto him and how he didn't mind that. Even the others weren't so into me. It took a few days to process the heart break from that. It seemed like everything that was good would continue to be yanked away from me. I decided that school would only be a weight to drag me down if I returned so I wasn't going to. I found it true that once you left you couldn't go back even if it had only been two months.

I scheduled myself to take the G.E.D. I really didn't

want to but it seemed like if I didn't then somehow down the road it would kick my ass.

During my first visit to see Jace it wasn't any better. I found that he was miffed at me too. "I thought we were best friends." He told me. "Why didn't you bother to say good-bye when you left?"

"I had no choice except to pack and leave. Bob and Nancy hardly let me say good-bye to the band." I replied quite puzzled by his behavior.

"Why didn't you call me from South Carolina?"

"I couldn't. I didn't want to fuel my guardian's fire. I had to make him realize that I wanted to come back to be with the band. A long-distance call to you on his telephone bill wouldn't have conveyed that intention. And besides, I knew I was coming back."

Serious eyes looked at me. "I called you twice. Bob wouldn't let me talk to you. He said for me to get over you because you weren't coming back. I told him that we were only friends but I don't think he believed me."

"I'm sorry he was rude to you. He finally told me three weeks ago that you called." I sighed.

"You still should have called me, Ang. There are things called pay phones. Or you could have called collect. I can't believe you didn't call me after you knew I'd called." He huffed.

Things were worse than I had thought. "I didn't think you really cared. I really did miss you though."

"Yeah, me too, this much." He replied as he leaned down and really kissed me, and I let him. But then I was just staring at him afterward wondering what the kiss had meant. It was awkward and he suggested we go play racquetball. I supposed that the kiss was just a one-time thing. After all, he hadn't replied back that he did care.

CHAPTER 13

I was sitting in my room processing all the responses and moods regarding my return to New York. Maybe it was just me, but I had expected a more favorable response. It seemed like all the things that could have been and had been good were pretty much gone now. That was depressing. I stretched my legs out on my bed and looked at my brown cowboy boots. I loved cowboy boots. Nancy had insisted that I go shopping with her daughter right before I moved. She had paid for the new cowboy boots I was wearing. The boots had been expensive and cool but she had okayed the purchase. Yeah, maybe I'd had it made staying with her and Bob and I'd blown that to hell and back. Maybe.

"Hey." David greeted as he walked into my room.

I raised my eyes to look at him. My door had been open but even when it was closed the others walked in unannounced unless I locked it. It was annoying. I remembered back when I had been an only child and had my privacy. That was shot to hell and back too.

"You're kinda mopey." He remarked as he sat at the bottom of my bed.

Maybe if I ignored him, he'd go away. I smoothed out my jeans so that they were straight over my new boots. Nancy had paid for the jeans too.

"Yeah, I know how you feel." He said although I

hadn't uttered a word. At least I was finely dressed though. New jeans, new cool boots.

He had no idea how I felt, physically or emotionally. Maybe if I threw something at him, he'd leave. Hmmm, there was nothing in throwing distance.

"You can help me with something." He continued. "It will get us out of the house and make us feel better." He was feeling nervous now. Even a three-year-old could have sensed it. He reached over and smoothed out my jeans as I had just done. I regarded him petting my leg. Well, now he knew how my leg felt but that didn't make me interested in helping him.

"I want to get the guys at the gym to let me take pictures of them so I can put together a portfolio that shows I have experience photographing bodybuilding. If you went with me then I wouldn't feel so weird. And I think guys would jump at the prospect when they saw you because you know, guys are horn dogs. They'd all want to talk to you."

I had narrowed my eyes and was staring at him now. He wanted me to do what?

His face had reddened slightly which further confirmed that he was uncomfortable asking me to go along with his charade. "Will you please say SOMETHING!" he remarked in exasperation.

I made a face as though I was pondering his request. I looked over at my clothes that I'd tossed haphazardly in the corner. I didn't care for too much disarray in my room but somehow, I was still a slob. "Do we have any cookies, specifically homemade chocolate chip cookies?" I asked suddenly.

He huffed in aggravation then because my behavior indicated that I wasn't interested in the least in helping him. He looked toward the door wondering if he should just storm out of my room. He'd done that in the past but it had never gotten a positive result from me. It just put him out of sight, out of mind. That was a win for me.

He turned back to me. "If I drive to the mall where there's a tollhouse cookie store and then I go in by myself and buy a dozen warm chocolate chip cookies for you, will you help me? You can eat every last cookie too."

Oh my God, yes! Without expression I smoothed my hand down my face as if I was thinking about his offer. "Yes, that is acceptable." I finally said.

He smiled then. He stood up and opened my closet door.

"Hey, what the fuck?" I asked in annoyance. I hadn't given him permission to raid my closet. He couldn't fit into any of my clothes and there was nothing in it he could possibly want.

"Just change into a decent shirt rather than that ratty old Aerosmith shirt. We want to look a little bit professional."

I truly didn't feel like arguing although I wasn't acting like it. We left the house with me wearing a lavender knit top, not one of my top choices for a shirt, and Kevin's brown leather jacket because it matched my cool new boots.

After David had purchased a dozen chocolate chip cookies for me, and I had eaten four of them, we had arrived at the gym.

"Now what?" I asked him as we stood in the entrance to the weight area. I could see, hear, and smell several guys lifting weights. Other guys were running on a treadmill. A few women were scattered amongst them, using the machines and stair master.

David was staring into the room, his camera gripped in one hand. His nervousness kept hitting me and I kept releasing it. It was just a gym, nothing that would make anyone nervous. "We walk up to them and you ask if they would mind posing for a picture for my portfolio."

I shrugged and headed towards the nearest guy. I looked down at him lying on the weight bench attempting to lift an enormous amount of weight. He looked about David's age but weighed a lot more. I supposed he wasn't bad looking. Another guy, tall and skinny, was spotting him. He was in dire need of a haircut. I wondered how much weight I could press. David nudged me. "Hi, we're taking pictures for the paper. Would you mind us taking a shot or two of you?" I asked the guy lifting weights.

David turned suddenly to look at me then he remarked to the guy, "No, it's not for the paper, it's for a photography portfolio I'm building. I'm David and this is Angel. You'll have to excuse her, she's not a very good assistant yet – still needs training." I wasn't a bad assistant I had just been adding some spice to the conversation. You'd think he would have known that.

The guy looked irritated although he hadn't answered.

I tried another tactic. "You're pressing a lot of weight there. I'm thinking you'd look great on film." I remarked. "Actually, you have really big arm muscles already. I wouldn't mind feeling them to see how solid you are." I added as if that little remark had accidentally slipped out. (The pretend ditz that I was.)

"Uh, well yeah, thanks." He said as he reconsidered and sat up. "Yeah, you can feel my muscles." I saw that he was checking me out. I casually fluffed my gorgeous hair with my hand.

The music that was playing in the background was tolerable with a good rhythm. I fussed over the guy's muscle then remarked. "Cool music." I did a slow groove to it as I saw David shake his head ever so slightly in disbelief. The guy that was spotting him glanced at me with interest so I held out my hand and he twirled me around. I tossed my head back like one of those rock video dancers, or one of the Dallas Cowboy Cheerleaders. My gorgeous hair bounced provocatively.

Needless to say, there were a lot of guys that needed their muscles felt up in that room and who needed their pictures taken. All of them wanted to pose with me in a picture. I was laughing inside. Men were so easy. All it took was a serious hair toss and they drooled like dogs in heat.

I could see that a few of them were really photogenic because David was more social with them in order to take additional shots. I couldn't help notice that none of the guys that he took several shots of were old or ugly. His mood had improved considerably. We probably could have taken them all home with us. Instead, I told them where we'd be playing that night. That really got some quality conversation going about our band, and David snapped a hundred shots or more. I had to admit that he was pretty good with his camera, and not bad with the small talk either. I felt his approval that I'd brought up how we were bad ass guitarists in a rock band.

"Well, that looked productive." I remarked in satisfaction as David drove us home. He had been talking and talking and talking about all the great shots he'd taken.

He turned and gave me the look. I was thinking that he needed to keep his eyes on the road. He tended to get distracted sometimes when he was driving. "You were quite the little persuader." He remarked sarcastically. "Oh my God! I have to feel you out." He said in a mimicking tone. I hadn't said that, not directly. "And I thought I was going to bust out laughing when you had them dance with you." He was laughing now. It had been fun, putting on a show.

"Regardless, you got what you wanted, dude." I replied back as I dug out the bag of cookies. And I had gotten what I'd wanted too. Several of them had given me their business cards or their number just in case we needed additional photos. Ha. Stupid males. As we were walking to the car, I'd stuffed the cards and pieces of paper into David's front pocket of his jeans. He'd been startled as if it had been a really intimate gesture but I hadn't even brushed against his dick.

"Oh yeah. After your little acting production and them finding out that you were available, they all gave me their phone numbers for additional photo shoots! We'll do a couple more outings like this and I'll have a great portfolio!"

Uh, no.

***

Now that I was home more, I began to notice that Rick and Carol's relationship was beginning to strain. All along Carol had been accusing Rick of sleeping with me on the sly, and in turn, Rick had been accusing Carol of sleeping with Kevin and David. I had always ignored them. I knew for a fact that Rick's attitude had done a 360 turn around and he was cheating on Carol with every chick but me. I figured Carol was cheating too.

It was a miserable day where things kept going wrong that I arrived home earlier than expected. I had just slammed the truck door shut when I remembered that I'd left the mail inside, so I had to unlock the door, cuss a little, get the mail and slam the door shut again. Then at the front door, I fumbled with the keys and dropped them on the ground, which is when I noticed Jace's truck in our driveway. I puzzled about that as I opened the door. I dropped the mail again as I saw Carol tucking in her shirt and Jace fixing his jeans. She thought I was screwing Rick so she was screwing the guy I was closest to. I couldn't believe Jace would do such a thing. I was so naïve. I ran up the stairs and slammed my bedroom door behind me.

Jace knocked on my door a moment later. He told me that he was going to come into my room whether I wanted him to or not.

"I'll beat the shit out of you if you do." A threatening voice from inside me said to him.

He ignored my threat and walked into my room. I slammed his 170-pound frame against the wall, knocking the breath out of him. I stood there shaking with fury and unable to speak. He had betrayed me and was jeopardizing our future as a band.

"You know, you don't have a good reason to be so pissed off at me. Me and you don't have a thing going, I can fuck anyone I want to." He informed me.

"Yes, I do! Carol is part of our group. If anyone of us leaves, then our band is history! I want our band to go somewhere! We are finally getting along together! This is all I live for, you jerk! Just how fucking high are you?" I screamed at him.

All he could think of was sex. "If you're jealous because I'm fucking Carol, fuck me and I'll leave her alone. You know you want to. You said so at Christmas. You told me a lot of things at Christmas!"

I couldn't believe what I was hearing. He didn't even seem to be the same Jace I knew. I really snapped out and belted him one. I caught him off guard. I was about to hit him a second time when he caught me and tossed me backward. I fell against my bed. We had a shouting match and then he slammed out of my room. I just couldn't believe what he had said to me. But it was his remarks about what I'd said at Christmas that really got me. He wasn't referring to our last words at his door that day, he was referring to things I'd said while I was drunk. But I had no idea what I'd said, and frankly, I guessed that I didn't want to know.

I found Carol and I chewed her out too. She was so stupid sometimes. I don't think she had even thought about what she'd done. "You go ahead and tell Rick. He doesn't care." She replied back. I didn't dare. I would just hold my breath that Rick didn't find out.

The whole thing got me kind of crazy. I know I had said that Jace was trying to break up our band but then I was pretty jealous that Carol had tried to sleep with Jace. She had been right. I did want to sleep with him. So, on a night where oddly everyone had gone out clubbing except for Rick, I stayed home too. He was in his room practicing on his bass guitar. "Rick! Come in here!" I yelled.

The guitar playing stopped and Rick appeared in my doorway. "What?" He asked. He seemed to be in a pretty good mood.

"Shut the door and lock it. I want to talk to you in

private" I replied. I was sitting cross-legged on my bed.

"Why should I lock the door? No one is home." He questioned.

I gave him the evil eye. There was no telling when someone would arrive home and barge in.

"All right." He said in exasperation, then he shut and locked my bedroom door.

I patted a spot on the bed beside me. "Sit down."

He walked over and sat beside me without comment. "What's with all the cheating you and Carol do?" I asked.

He looked at me curiously. The room was heating up as I looked in his green eyes. Not many people had green eyes. "Might as well get it out of our systems now rather than later when we're in a more serious commitment."

"Oh." I replied not expecting that type of answer. I thought about it for a moment and wondered if I was fair game. I reached over and pulled him to me. He leaned with me easily enough and we kissed. I was fair game. It totally blew my mind plus made me horny as hell. We continued kissing, his growing hardness pressing against me. I couldn't even think straight by then.

Rick finally broke away and said, "So word on the street is that we've had sex before."

I grimaced thinking about the story I'd told Streethart, and of Curt's big mouth. "They were telling stories so I told one too." I said as I regained my composure. "But I wanted my story to be real."

Rick's green eyes stared at me. I knew he wanted me just as badly as I wanted him.

"*You will ruin everything if you do this.*" I heard in my head. God, I wanted to ignore that voice.

We continued to stare at each other. We kissed again. That time it was spoiled by my knowing exactly why sleeping with Rick would ruin everything. If we connected at an intimate level, it would ruin everything between him and Carol, and also the future of the band. I pulled away from him and he pulled back too. I shut my eyes just hating that I had to know things. Tears of frustration sprung at my eyelashes.

Rick lay back on the bed realizing that I wasn't about to sleep with him. "If it's any consolation to you, I can't do this either. I'm supposed to be your guardian. I'm supposed to keep you out of trouble not cause it. Besides, if you think revenge sex against Jace will make you feel better, it won't."

I sighed knowing he was right about me wanting revenge sex so I was silent.

He sat up and said, "I gotta practice."

"You do if you want to be as good on bass as I am." I replied.

"I'm better than you any day." He replied. He wasn't, but I wasn't about to argue.

I went downstairs a while later and noticed that someone had taken a phone message for me. I had a job working at a warehouse if I wanted it, the note said. That sounded good to me. I would call them tomorrow and accept. I just wished I could stop thinking about Rick. The universe really had a twisted sense of humor. How could you want someone so much yet hate them too?

I drove down to the local convenience store when I found we were out of soda. I had really wanted some coke but Carol sucked it down like it was water. As I got out of my truck, I bumped into Curt coming out of the store. We chatted a moment then I went inside and made my purchase. I was surprised to find him leaning against my truck as I came out of the store. Curt was a techie and he looked like a nerd which I supposed he was, but he was a cool one. He had light brown hair and brown eyes and when he wasn't telling tall tales he was talking tech speak. I smiled at him as possibilities entered my mind. He was trying to be cool as he smiled back at me. "What?" He asked because he could tell I had something on my mind.

"I want to go to the karaoke bar on ninth street but I'm not old enough. Can you get me in?" I asked. He was twenty-two and I knew he could probably make that happen.

"What are you going to do for me?" he kidded although he wasn't really kidding.

"Probably nothin'. Take it or leave it." I replied as I patted him away from the door handle of my truck so I could open the door. He stepped aside and I put the soda in my truck.

"Are you going to pretend to be my girlfriend tonight if I get you a fake ID?" He asked, looking interested.

"Do I have to put out?" I asked as I stood there with my hand on my truck door.

"It would be nice if you did."

"I'm not nice, and I'd better get home. I'm only seventeen, you know." I remarked as I got behind the wheel of my truck and shut the door.

He knocked on the window and I rolled it down. "Okay, okay, but I get to go with you and I need for you to hang on me even if we never do anything. I can't let you go to a place like that alone."

He was right so I followed him to some guy's house who made me a fake ID. It only cost me twenty bucks.

Now we were at the karaoke bar which was echoing with a song from Green Day, and whoever was singing was doing a pretty good job with it. Curt picked out a table for us and when the server came over, he went to order us both a mixed drink. "Uh uh, make mine a Sprite" I told the server.

When the server left, Curt remarked, "I can't put nothin' over on you, can I?"

I looked at him for a moment then replied, "Your best bet to make points with me is to just chill because hitting on me is just going to put a halt to anything happening. If I want to do anything with you, I'll let you know."

He was thinking of a comeback when two guys stopped by our table and started flirting with me. The one guy wanted to know if I'd dance with him. "I would, but he's pretty fucking jealous, and I'm with him tonight." I replied as I glanced at him then Curt.

"Yeah, what she said." Curt agreed and I could have laughed at him because he wasn't convincing at all, but the guys looked confused then walked away mumbling something. Curt and I talked about what songs to sing. He told me that he wasn't getting up there to sing so I wrote down a song for myself. As we waited for it to be my turn at the microphone I talked to Curt about his approach with women. "Don't come on so strong. Just talk to a woman for a few minutes, then work her into dancing with you or sitting at the table with you, and ask her what she's interested in. Then you can work a kiss or a squeeze in. Probably your best bet is to watch what the other guys do that seems to work. I think women want to get laid as much as guys do, but they want some romance first.

"So, what are you interested in?" He asked back.

"Screaming guitars and big fucking trucks." I replied back without hesitation, and we both laughed. I started talking the technical aspects of guitars then. Curt was interested for like two minutes then I saw his attention follow women that apparently were walking somewhere behind me. I stopped mid-sentence and he looked back at me. "What are you interested in?" I asked him. "Other than the other women you're watching? Which will not get you any points, by the way."

"Storm systems. I'm a storm chaser." He replied absent-mindedly, his gaze still looking beyond me.

As I was trying to comprehend that I heard my name called and I smiled. I was more than ready to sing. I walked over to the karaoke microphone. I listened to the introduction of the cool guitars that started "Gypsy Road" by Cinderella, then I laid into that song. Man, I loved that song! I wished I'd had my favorite white Gibson to rock it the way it should have been rocked but as it was, I just handled the vocals. The volume was loud and the music was ready for dancing. It was only a few seconds before people started rocking it out on the dance floor. I smiled when I saw that happen. When the song ended and I walked back to our table, people were smiling at me and telling me that I did great and some just touched my arm and nodded.

Curt just shook his head at me when I sat back down at the table. "Why. Aren't you the front man of Rebel? You fuckin' blew that song away!" He asked me rather angrily.

His anger surprised me. Yeah, I liked getting up

there on stage and having it to myself, and I'd liked performing in Greenville, South Carolina at that club, but I guess I didn't think I could keep people interested if I pursued it. Rick did pretty well on stage for us. My expression sobered and I unconsciously lowered my head thinking about it. He was still staring at me as I looked back up at him. The real reason had just hit me. "People don't like it that I'm that good. Jace is jealous that I can play guitar well, and Rick and Carol don't like it that I can sing well and that I have more stage personality." I replied slowly.

"Well, FUCK them, Angel!" He huffed at me. He was really angry.

I suddenly smiled at him because he was so right. I had money, I could live on my own. I could find another band if Rick and the others didn't want to cooperate. We needed to be gearing up for something big, not hoping that things might work out. And Jace could either get over his jealousy or drop out of my life. "You just taught me something really profound so I'm gonna teach you some things too." I told him as I reached over and grabbed the collar of his dark blue polo shirt and pulled him to me. He looked off balance until we'd stared for a second or two, then I kissed him. I was going to fuck Jace where it hurt. He'd deserved it for even considering fucking Carol.

An hour later after I'd sung three more songs and played with the crowd, I went home with Curt. I told him that it was a one-time thing and he'd better not say one word to anyone about it or it would be the last time I said one word to him. I meant it too. I taught him a lot of things that night that as a man he needed to know. The first thing was that in bed, he needed to be a gentleman. His technique was lacking and I taught him about that too. It was a mediocre night of sex but he'd seemed eager to learn. I'd gone home satisfied before the dawn broke. I also told him of another company that he should go to and apply for a job. It would pay a lot better and I thought he might enjoy it more. At that point he was just mesmerized by me and listening to every word. I had given him oral sex, and done him three times in five or more positions that night and I'd come three times. We'd used a condom every time. I'd counseled him on that too. Spreading knowledge around could be a fun and satisfying thing and I was sure the next girl he slept with would appreciate what I'd taught him – if he chose to use that knowledge.

***

The next morning, I called and accepted the job at the warehouse then I went down to the health clinic and got a prescription for the pill. I spent most of the day planning a strategy for our band. It seemed like we just had to get more experience and exposure with me as a front man of the band. I also thought there needed to be some leadership in our household so I slipped into level one, the personality that was a lean, mean, fighting machine.

When the rest of them came home from work, I lit into them. "Kevin, take out the fucking trash." I told him. "It's your responsibility and I don't want to have to remind you again."

Then I turned to Carol. "And it's your responsibility to do the grocery shopping. Keep a fucking list. You were also supposed to wash my clothes too. I don't fucking pay all the bills for you assholes not to be doing your share."

"Who died and made you boss around here?" she roared back at me.

"I did! And I've been resurrected!" I shot back. David and Kevin stood in the doorway watching and listening.

So now we were shouting about my sudden role as boss but my anger was larger and she was backing down. "So go do the grocery shopping!" I told her again.

"I don't have the fucking money!" she roared back at me.

"Then quit spending it on stuff you're not supposed to!" I said in a threatening voice as I was right in her face. I hadn't been the level one personality in quite a while and she reluctantly stepped back knowing I wasn't in a kidding mood. I stared at her just waiting for her to say one more word while the others watched wordlessly.

"Fine!" She said as she got her purse and slammed out of the house.

Rick had been taking a shower. He entered the room with tousled wet hair and wearing his jeans. "What the fuck is going on?" He remarked.

"It's time for y'all to step up and do your chores like we agreed upon." I told him.

"Oh, don't fucking start on me. I'm your guardian." He warned me.

"No. I'm YOUR fucking guardian. Get the vacuum cleaner out and vacuum these rugs and dust the furniture." I ordered him with extra warning in my voice.

He bristled so I stepped up into his face and he pushed me. With strength I didn't know I had, I knocked him to the floor so quickly that it even stunned me. He fell hard on his butt and it startled him.

"Hell, I'm going to sweep and mop the kitchen floor." David replied suddenly. "I'm not getting involved in your psycho mood."

Inside, that amused me but on the outside, I was still mean and dangerous. I saw Kevin disappear too. "Well, you'd better start supper right after that because I'm fucking starved!" I warned David's back as he was walking off.

I turned my attention back to Rick who was getting up off the floor. "Don't you ever fucking do anything like that to me again. I told you no fighting." He warned me.

He truly didn't know who he was talking to at that point. No longer was I the meek person that had just lost her dad and her life. I was the bully again and I'd do whatever the fuck I wanted to. I was the boss. "I'm going to do what it fucking takes, and if it takes knocking you down until you listen, then that's what I'm going to do." I warned him. Yeah, I had lost my spark for quite a while but now I was coming back as the whole damn fire.

"If you want me to call Bob and have him haul your ass back to South Carolina, I can do that." He informed me with his hands on his hips and anger in his eyes.

"If that's the way you want to play it, fine, but know this. I'm ready to move forward on becoming that band that makes it big and if you don't want to listen to me and play by my rules then I'll just move on. From now on, I'm going to be the front man of Rebel and Kevin is going to be our drummer. I can either force you to go along with this, or I can leave and find a more appreciative band, your choice."

Rick and I argued about the changes I wanted to make. He swore he absolutely was not going to deal with those changes. "Take a few days to get a grip with it." I told him. "In the meantime, get your ass working on the rugs and the dusting."

I saw his fist shoot out and I blocked it then I was down on the floor. I shot back up and I was faster as I socked him in the jaw and when he stumbled back I somehow managed to shove him down on the floor. Kevin and David came running in as we were about to go at it again. They pried us apart. "I told you no fighting, that we weren't doing this again." Rick spat at me.

"And you also told me with the agreement at Christmastime that if you got out of line, I was to put you back in line. You ARE going to listen to me or else, because I'm not backing down until you do. And just for the record, you threw the first fucking punch." I replied back coldly.

"I think you'd better fucking listen to her, man." David told Rick. "I think she's right about the band, and we've not held up our part of the agreement we made at Christmas. It's just fuckin' sad that the youngest and smallest one of us has to make us see the light, and it's truly fuckin' sad that she has to use violence to do it."

I saw some of the fight go out of Rick, not much, but some. "And what the fuck are you going to do?" He asked me.

"Once we do some practicing with me as the front man, I have some places I want us to audition for. As for the housework, the agreement says I foot the bill for the rent and the bills so that I don't have one lick of chores assigned to me. I fork out at least $1,000 every month, plus I have a job. My chore is to pay for our asses to live here." I replied as I pulled away from Kevin.

Rick shoved David away and stomped off.

"I'd better hear the vacuum cleaner running in the next fifteen minutes or I'll be dealing with you again. " I called after him.

As I was staring at Rick's back and burning a hole in it, David touched my arm and I jerked into a defensive stance ready to deal with him. "Hey, hey!" He said as he backed up ready to defend himself. "What the hell has gotten into you? You were more assertive when you first got back from South Carolina but now I think you've gone crazy. Did something bad happen to you there?"

I regarded him and I noticed that Kevin was eyeing me warily. "A LOT of things happened in South Carolina, none of which I want to talk about, and none of it was bad. The bad things happened here." I replied as I noticed his concern turn to pity. He knew what Carol had done and he had figured that I cared about Jace.

"Kick him to the curb." David told me, not mentioning Jace's name. "But as much as you want to, please don't fuck Carol up. I'm afraid you'll kill her and I sure the hell don't want you to go to jail even though I think we'd all appreciate her being off'd."

I just stared at him thinking because I realized that I did want to kill her but I knew I'd settle for killing Joseph and his goons. The time just wasn't right yet. It was the right time to start learning his schedule and to find out where he lived. He was going to regret the shit that he'd done to people. Yep, there was no doubt in my mind about that.

David persuaded me to come up to his room so we could talk. I wordlessly followed him and he shut and locked the door behind us. Then he proceeded to tell me in a sympathetic but serious voice that if I let my temper get the better of me that I was looking at a jail sentence. As he was talking, I was evaluating the energy of him and everyone else in the house. David was so scared of me right now that he was almost shaking although his voice and body looked calm. He knew I was a psychopath and he knew I'd actually thought of killing Carol. I wouldn't kill her but I'd thought about it. Kevin wasn't really as much scared of me as he was disappointed. He didn't think I'd ever hurt him because we were friends, however he was angry that I'd yelled at him. Rick's energy was a toss-up between wanting to kick my ass once and for all, or whether he should be scared that I was a psychopath and would I kill him in his sleep? He also entertained the thought that there was a shred of truth that the band would succeed if I were the front man. They were all correct and I liked it that way. All of them were beyond surprised at my sudden transformation back to the bully they knew in South Carolina. They just didn't know that this personality was a coping mechanism and that I could pull it out or put it away as I pleased. They'd learn though because I was going to pull it out a lot from now on. And from now on everyone was going to call me C. Angel. I was born again.

David put his hand on my arm and I jerked as I pulled myself back to the present. I probably hadn't heard half of what he'd said. "You can tell me what happened in South Carolina. I won't tell anyone." He was saying.

I guessed now that I was thinking back on it, that there had been incidents that that happened in South Carolina that I should have cried over but hadn't. The only thing I'd cried about was my dad's death.

Sometimes I wished there was someone I could trust and who would take care of and protect me since my dad was gone. Bob and Nancy had offered that to me but I'd decided that I wanted to be famous instead. I sighed and leaned towards David wondering if he'd give me what I needed. "Hold me." was all I said, and he did. As I relaxed into him, his energy leveled out into one of understanding and pity. I didn't care for the pity. I heard the vacuum cleaner start up which further soothed me so I put my arms around him. He pulled me onto his lap and tightened his grip, as I sighed softly. It reminded me of when daddy used to put me on his lap to assure me everything was okay. I was okay now but we stayed holding each other. He'd really needed this closeness too I realized, and I wondered what had happened in his personal life lately that had hurt him, but I was too self-centered to ask. The voice in my head told me to breathe in his pain and breathe it out, that it would soothe the both of us so I did.

Kevin knocked at the door. "There's someone here to see you, Baby. One of your admirers. I warned him that you're in a kick ass mood but he still wants to talk." He said through the door.

Both David and I had relaxed in the comfort of our embrace with me releasing our pain and I had almost started to doze. "I'll be there in a minute." I yelled back as I rousted myself awake.

I leaned back and looked at David who was staring at me curiously because he felt calmer now but he didn't know why. I ran my hand over his short hair and lightly grabbed a bit of it and then ran my hand down it in a gesture of affection as I stared into his eyes. His eyes widened as he considered it a gesture of passion and

I could tell that it had startled him. I hadn't meant to startle him. "Don't worry. This psycho isn't quite psycho enough to kill someone." I remarked as I gave him a little smirk. "Thanks for being a friend. If you want some more comfort, crawl in bed with me tonight."

He blinked in surprise at my last remark. "Uh, I can't have sex with you, you're a minor."

I smiled at him. "I didn't say I was going to have sex with you, but we could if we want to regardless of me being a minor. What I meant was that if you want to sleep next to me tonight to crawl in bed with me. I'll see you later, or not." I replied as I pushed myself off his lap.

When I got downstairs Rick was talking to Curt. I rolled my eyes in frustration seeing him then we went out to his truck at his insistence to talk. It was dark except for the streetlights. "What do you want, Curt?" I asked him. "We can't be hanging out like this. I told you last night was a one-time deal. And also at the moment, my band and I are having a meltdown. It's all I can do to keep it together right now."

"I'm sorry. It's just that I really like you. I know you like Jace but I know he wouldn't be faithful to you but I would be. Last night was incredible and I don't know how you can expect me to just put it on a shelf." He told me.

I looked at him, the street lights hardly giving us any light in his truck. "I know you're lonely, but if you do the things I told you to do, the women will be fighting over you. There are women that crowd around you after your gigs. Smile and flirt with them but don't outright say, "fuck me, Baby." like you have in the past. Compliment them, tell them how pretty they are, how sweet their voice is. Don't be creepy. Ask them what tv shows they like and then start talking about one of the episodes. After you have one talking for a few moments, ask them out. When you take them home after the first date, let them make the first move to kiss. If they don't, just ask for a hug and leave it at that. If you get to a third date, then kiss them or go further if they give you encouragement to do so. Just stop treating them like a piece of ass. Treat them like a friend with benefits. But as for me, I have too many problems right now to consider a relationship, plus you and I don't have anything in common."

He sighed. "Jace's a fucking idiot. If you ever reconsider, let me know."

"I know you don't know me well enough to know this, but I'm a fucking psychopath. Just ask any of my band members. And I'm stone serious about that. It's best that you find someone who isn't. Ain't nobody got time for that." I replied. Before he could reply I got out of his truck and stalked back up our stairs to our house. I'd thought at the time when I'd spent the night with Curt that I had been doing him a favor. Maybe I hadn't. At any rate, I'd taught him a lot and been satisfied in return.

About an hour later, the house was cleaner, the groceries had been bought, and David had made supper. We actually all sat at the supper table although not a whole lot was being said. The only sound was of the tv playing from the living room. All of them except David were angry at me. "Are you fucking happy now?" Rick asked, breaking the silence.

They all stared at me waiting for my answer. "Ecstatic, for the clean house. Now what about the changes to the band?" I asked back.

"No. I'm the front man."

"I'll compromise for now. You be the front man for one set and I'll be the front man for the second set."

Both Rick and Carol were arguing with me now.

I ignored them and continued eating as I let the negative waves roll off me.

"Fucking shut up!" David told them. "What could it hurt to give her a shot? She's a fucking good guitar player and we could use that exposure, and we sure ain't getting anywhere as a band right now."

"Yeah, give her a break. It might work out a hundred times better than you think it would." Kevin agreed.

Rick and Carol continued to argue but I wasn't joining in. I'd give them a few more days before I did something drastic.

Later that night when I was about to go to sleep, David hesitantly came into my room. I was glad he decided to sleep wearing briefs instead of being naked because a naked man lying against me just turned me on. It was a little awkward at first as we lay together on my bed holding each other. I wasn't one to actively seek comfort but I had invited him and here he was. And truth be told, even though he had on briefs I was still rather aroused. I reminded myself several times that he wasn't interested in having sex with me. Now if he started to seem interested, well I was going to be all about that.

He was trying to get me to tell him what happened in South Carolina that had made me come back as a different person. I wondered why he kept bugging me about it. I wasn't one to talk about stuff but the feeling I was getting from him was that it was important for him to know. I guessed that I would tell him then. "I was too lonely there mostly. I had to stay out of fights if I wanted to get Bob and Nancy to trust me, and you can only imagine how hard that was with everyone at school that I'd beaten up in the past. Being there forced me to deal with my dad being gone and having Bob and Nancy as parents. They were a lot stricter than my dad ever was. They wanted me to stay in South Carolina, and part of me really did want that because they were giving me a family and a ton of relatives. I never had a two-parent family or relatives. My dad wasn't your average parent. But they also wanted me to be a kid. I just couldn't do it. Shit from the past made me an adult a long time ago. I came back with the decision to be who I am, which some of the time is a psycho. Y'all can deal with it or not, doesn't matter to me anymore. I'm going to be true to myself."

"How do you find the strength to be true to yourself when you're so different from us? You know that psycho isn't going to get you any friends. You never had friends in school when we lived in South Carolina." He replied.

Yeah, but I'd made friends with him, Kevin, Rick, and Carol, and I had a lot of friends in the short time I'd gone to New Rochelle High School. "You're thinking about it wrong." I told him. "You'll have friends, maybe not many friends, but they'll be the friends that will stick with you no matter who or what you are. At times maybe I won't have any friends at all but I'm okay with that. In time the world is gonna find out that I'm a guitar legend. That's all that matters to me at this moment. Once I'm a guitar legend, I'll have friends out my ass, and if I don't, I'll buy them."

He snorted at that then was wistful. "I wish I had your strength." He murmured.

"Are you going to tell me what the problem is that you're dealing with so I can help you? Because I'm pretty sure I can help you." I asked him.

"No, but thanks for asking."

"So, you made me spill my guts but you're not spilling yours, huh?"

"Yeah." He agreed. "That's the way guys are."

"I'll honestly listen and try to help you. Daddy really did teach me those things. Deep inside me lie all the positive traits of my dad." I assured him as I looked at him lying beside me, the soft glow of the lamp illuminating us. "And I won't tell anyone."

"I'm not ready to talk about it."

"Okay." I replied as I reached over and switched off the lamp. The room fell into darkness then. I wondered if daddy had been alive, if David would have confided in him. "Well, snug up to me then. We both need to get some sleep so we can get up for work tomorrow morning." A moment later his face was up against my neck and a few moments later he was snoring on me. I liked him wrapped around me, and it hadn't taken much encouragement either. I smiled and shut my eyes. I was always going to get what I set out to get.

CHAPTER 14

I started work at the warehouse the next morning. There were about fifteen of us that helped unload and load the trucks, and we stocked the warehouse shelves but also picked items off shelves for orders. It was a physical job and I didn't mind it. Four other females worked there besides me and they were larger and more manly looking than me. Being my first day on the job, my co-workers were ready to scoff at me and placed bets if I'd stay because it was a very physically demanding job. They also made snide remarks to me and about me saying I was a spoiled pretty bitch who was going to get her ass kicked, but I didn't take it personally. I figured they did that to all the new employees. I rolled with it and kept on trucking as the trucks rolled in and out. I'd kept in shape by running and lifting weights so it didn't faze me much. However, when the five o'clock whistle blew I was more than ready to call it a day. I walked out the door with the rest of my co-workers as if I hadn't broken a sweat, although when I got home, I threw my clothes in the hamper and got into the shower, then thought maybe I'd flop in bed. The rest of them were downstairs either watching tv or making supper. I was starving, as usual and I hoped we weren't having spaghetti again.

I was sitting on my bed combing out my wet

hair when Jace appeared in my bedroom doorway. As I looked up, he walked in and shut the door behind him. "You're in the wrong fucking bedroom." I told him. "Carol's bedroom is down the hall."

"I didn't sleep with Carol."

I gave him a cold hard stare. "You were about to. You should have just fucking finished it, got your STD, and gone home."

He sat down on my bed uninvited. "I don't want to fight with you about that. I came over because Rick seems to think you've gone psycho. He said you went off on all of them last night, and you and he got into a punching match. He said that you want to be the front man of his band. He wants to know what's up with you."

I finished combing through my hair and I set the comb on my nightstand. "I'm gonna lay it out for you, so take notes. The truth is, I'm not who you think I am. I moved here when I was grieving my dad's death and then I had to deal with this sudden change in my life. What I am really is a psycho, and the personality that Rick witnessed last night is who I am. He's seen it before when we were younger, and most times I'll control my behavior, but those other times I won't. As for the band, it's about time that we made a change, and I intend to make us stars. Rick has taken us as far as he can, and I appreciate that, but now it's time for me to be the front man. And as for us, I like you. I've been waiting for you to only want me but who knows what the fuck you want. You come onto me and then nothing, you seem interested and then nothing, and then when I leave for a while you're ready to fuck Carol. I don't get along with Carol and sometimes I just plain hate her but you already know that and you still were about to fuck her.

That really hurts. I trusted you and I thought we were best friends. I know better now. Oh, and did you see the house is clean? Psycho will get you that, and believe me, the psycho is not going to stop. If there's anyone in the band that doesn't like it, they can get the fuck out. I'll pave my own way with or without them. In a year or so the world is going to know that I'm a fucking guitar legend. I'm gonna take along whoever is with me so they better get on board. Oh, and I might as well lay this on the line too – it's gonna be my way or the highway from this point forward. Take it or leave it. I might have only been a spark before but now I'm a fucking wildfire out of control."

He looked at me in wonder and seemed to have several things to say but didn't know which one to verbalize first. "Wow. You never talk about feelings but you sure said a mouthful there. I don't think you're psycho." I smiled a small smile at that because he was wrong. "I think you've just held your feelings in for so long that they just exploded. I told Rick that he should let you be the front man at least to try it out. But I don't know if your attitude is going to fly with anyone in the band or outside the band. And I'm really sorry about trying to sleep with Carol. You're right, I'm an asshole for letting her talk me into it and I do know how you feel about her. It was wrong and I'm sorry. We are best friends and I like you too but I don't want a serious relationship. I know you do, but I'm just not ready to have a serious relationship with any one woman yet."

"I'm glad you cleared all of that up because I've made a decision too. We're not friends, let alone best friends anymore. Any guy who would fuck someone he knows I hate should get out of my life." I told him evenly. "Get out."

"Are you serious? I don't say or react the way you want me to and so you're writing me off?" He asked in amazement.

"Yep, just fuckin' get out."

"You're right, you are a fucking psycho! And you're conceited as all hell. You think you're going to take the world by storm but what's going to happen is that it's going to take you by the balls and spit you out! You'll never be famous; you'll just be a nobody without any friends!" He spat out as he glared at me.

"If they're all going to be cheaters like you that stab me in the heart then fucking good riddance." I replied back coldly.

I watched his back and then my bedroom door as it slammed shut behind him. I was shaking in anger. The asshole had some nerve. I took a deep breath and blew him and his games out of my life. I had no time for that shit.

David stopped in my room after Jace had slammed his way out. "What did you tell him?" He wanted to know.

"I'm sure you heard every damn word." I scoffed as I glared at him. No doubt he'd had his ear to the door the entire time.

"Not all of it." He replied guiltily.

So, I told him every damn word.

"Are you sure you want to be burning bridges like that?" He asked with genuine concern over Jace.

"Yep, I'm so fuckin' sure. If he doesn't want only me, then fuck him! I don't need that in my life. He disrespected me!"

David swallowed hard; he thought I was being too

hard on Jace. "Uh, and so if I didn't like you being the front man of Rebel or your psycho-ness, you're going to throw me out?" He continued.

"What I mean is that you either follow Rick or you follow me. The band is mine now. If Rick can't deal with that, then I'm leaving. It's up to you who you follow. But yeah, I'm the front man now, and I have a psycho personality. I've never had a problem with you or Kevin. The both of you seem to deal with me fine. We'll still be friends even if you decide to follow Rick. But as for Jace, I don't need that crap in my life. I want a man that wants me, and he sure the fuck doesn't want me. I don't need any cheating sonofabitch."

"Can I sit down and we talk about this?" He asked hesitantly as though I might beat the crap out of him.

"Yeah, sure." I replied in an unconcerned voice. I observed him with interest as he shut my bedroom door and locked it. I wondered if he meant that in a threatening gesture. I felt his energy and he was just scared and wanted privacy. That was interesting.

"Can I be honest with you?" He asked as he sat on the bed.

I shrugged my shoulders. "I expect nothing less."

He seemed concerned that I was making more enemies than friends and that I was going to end up alone and friendless. He said that he didn't know who would take care of me if I left.

I rolled my eyes in exasperation at him. I'd always taken care of myself. Who had found the house we were renting? Who had outlined a budget for us? Who had bailed Rick and Carol out of jail? Who had sent the landlord the rent money the first month I was back in South Carolina? The list went on and on.

"Yeah, but who's gonna clean your room, or wash your clothes, or cook for you?" He asked. "Right now, I do most of that shit."

Inside, I smiled. Hell, if he wasn't around to take care of my needs, then some other clueless man would step up. There was no doubt in my mind about that. I was fucking good looking with some inner magnet that made men do things for me. "Hmm." I mumbled pretending to think about it.

When he'd finished explaining his view on the matter, I replied. "Duly noted. Are you sleeping with me tonight?"

"You're something else, you know that, right?" He asked as he seemed not sure whether he was aggravated at me or amused.

I smiled. "I get it, I really do. You want to stay friends with Rick and the bitch, and me too, but they want you to pick sides. Whatever. You do whatever you need to do. You're still my friend either way and I'm not going to be mad or huffy if you play their game. I'm not about this pettiness, I'm about us getting along and getting famous. This is just the only way I can deal with them. I mean, if you think you know of a better way then lay it on me and I'll give your idea a shot."

I felt his energy lighten. Yeah, Rick and Carol were making it hard on him and Kevin. I understood that even though that's not what he had talked about. That's what he had really wanted to say. The voices had told me.

He shook his head in the negative. "No, I don't have a clue of how else to handle our situation. I'm going to skip sleeping with you tonight. Carol has been on my case ever since she realized that I slept in your bed last night. She figures that if I'm fucking you than I should be fucking her too. Man, I wish she'd get off my fucking case."

He and I weren't having sex but I knew what he meant.

***

Work was harder the next day because my muscles were sore but I pushed through it. The exertion helped me to work off the stress of my lack of a relationship with Jace. A few people talked to me then. I noticed that warehouse workers were crasser in their conversation but I didn't really mind it. I seemed to be fitting in as they included me in their conversations now, and it was only my second day there. I hadn't put up with their shit the day before and I'd kept up a strong front. They'd just wanted to know if I'd break. Now they knew I wouldn't. I patted myself on the back for making such progress. I'd be leader of the pack soon. Daddy would have been impressed. And then, maybe he wouldn't have been.

After work, I surveyed our house and it was staying pretty clean. When certain people had started leaving dirty dishes and cups around the house, I'd lit into them about picking up after themselves. I also wanted my wash done regularly and that seemed to be working. David was doing nearly all of the cooking of our dinners now, and there were leftovers to take for lunch or there was lunchmeat to make a sandwich. I liked it that way. Carol had complained that there wasn't enough money for the groceries and so I gave her another twenty bucks. They traded off chores every week so she wouldn't always be going grocery shopping but I suspected that David would always be cooking.

We were supposed to practice as a band that night

and I wondered if we would. Rick and Carol were still angry at me. At the appointed time I was rather surprised when everyone was present and accounted for. I had my favorite white Gibson around my neck and Kevin had taken a place at the drums. I looked towards Rick because we were all silent. "Well, what song are you going to sing?" He finally asked.

I smiled inside. "ZZ Top. Can't Stop Rockin'." I replied back. They all nodded and Kevin started us off. We'd played that song before and several others, and it went well with me as the front man.

"This is just a trial." Rick reminded me.

I nodded back. That's what he thought and he was wrong. I knew they wouldn't leave a good thing, and that's what I was.

***

I was watching reruns of Speed Racer on the cartoon channel late Saturday morning when Kevin came downstairs and flopped across my lap. "I'm bored." He said as he looked up at me.

I observed him. He needed a haircut which I figured he didn't have the money for, and as I noted further, he probably needed some new clothes. I ran my hand through his sandy colored hair. "Are you hungry? We could start off at the Chinese place I like then see what's going on downtown."

"I dunno. I'm kind of low on funds." He replied with a sigh.

"I got it. While we're eating, we can discuss what to do next."

We took my truck. I let Kevin drive since he seemed to have been born with a sense of direction, and I didn't like to drive anyway. I watched the scenery go by as Motley Crue blasted on the radio. The mall loomed ahead. I knew it had a Chinese restaurant in it. "Let's go to the Chinese place in the mall." I grimaced to him.

Kevin thought that was funny. "Yeah, right. You haven't set foot into any kind of store since you were like five. You always make me and David go instead. I'm so sure you want to go to the mall."

"Um, hell froze over. Stop at the mall." I repeated.

He glanced at me once more then we were parked in front of the mall. I sat and stared at the building for a moment. It was an intimidating place. I knew that inside it would be all bright lights, announcements, mind boggling smells, and chaos. And it was Saturday so there would be loads of people wandering aimlessly like zombies through the place. And zombies tended to breed. The world was already beginning.....

"Are we going to eat in the truck or are we going in?" Kevin asked impatiently.

I took a deep breath. "We're going in." I agreed. "You know this is a breeding place for zombies, right?"

Kevin laughed a while at that. "Why is it exactly that you don't like stores?" he asked as we walked past several stores. Someone's kid was screaming from the second floor of the mall. The smell of baking cookies filled the air. A guy from a booth set up in the middle of the floor was promoting fingernail care and he wanted to demonstrate the product on me. "Oh my God, are you serious?" I asked Kevin after I declined the guy's offer. "How can you deal with all the mind-boggling shit going on here?"

After we talked about what shit I was referring to, he laughed at me as if I were being ridiculous. But he couldn't feel all the energy from these people, how it affected me. He didn't hear all the voices of the lives of these people as they invaded my mind. On stage I could tune them out as I performed, in regular life, not so much. I glanced over at several teenage boys lusting in their minds over me and sizing up who Kevin was to me. One of the boys was sizing up Kevin, thinking about doing him. I jerked to look at a woman and a baby clear across the mall. She was there to meet her lover. The baby was his, not her husband's. One guy had lost his job and was sitting on a bench staring at the floor. Several teenage girls were giggling. Two of them were planning on losing their virginity that night. And the energies and thoughts continued on - of course the voices had advice for all of them. It nudged me towards the guy who'd lost his job.

"What are you doing?" Kevin asked me as I changed direction.

"I gotta talk to this guy."

"But why? He's definitely too old for you, probably old enough to be your—" Kevin rambled as he changed direction and followed me.

The guy looked up and gave us an uninterested look.

"Have you ever thought of driving for UPS? They pay pretty good." I remarked to the guy.

"What?" He asked, clearly distracted and maybe a little wasted.

"I was just telling my friend that UPS is hiring some drivers and you looked like a capable and dependable guy. I just thought I'd mention it."

The guy stared at me. "Are you trying to be funny? Did someone set you up to do this?"

Well, yeah, they had but I wasn't going to mention that it had been the voice in my mind. "Um, no." I lied as I shrugged my shoulders. "I'm just sayin'. Sorry if I offended you." I replied as I turned to walk away. Kevin glanced at both of us, shrugged his shoulders and followed me. "What possessed you to say that?" he hissed to me. "Now that guy is suspicious of us."

"I hear voices, Kev. I'm just relaying messages." It's not like he hadn't heard me say that before.

"Voices talk to you in your head. Yeah, that will sound good whenever they're hauling you off to the funny farm."

"You have to remember that I didn't sign up for this." I reminded him. He dropped the subject then, mostly because he thought I was making it all up. That was another reason I didn't like going to the mall – I always had work to do when I got there, stuff that wasn't any of my business at all.

The food court had several different choices. I gave Kevin a twenty-dollar bill so he could buy a steak sandwich and fries, while I got my order of Chinese food. He'd keep the change. That was expected. We met in the middle and sat at the chairs provided. "So, what's on your mind? Why are we here?" He asked.

"We need shit. This is the place to buy all of it, plus I'd heard that this Chinese place was good, and it is." I remarked with a mouthful of lo Mein noodles. Man, I loved those! I was trying hard to block all the thoughts from all the others from invading my mind. It seemed to be working.

"I've brought you food from this place before."

I smiled at him in amusement, men doing things for me.

"What do we need?"

"Haircuts, clothes, and pictures. And maybe a new

guitar." I answered as I stared back at a two-year-old that kept staring at me from the next table. She was talking to me in her mind but I was ignoring her. She was going to visit her Nanna today. No one else could hear her so she would just assume that I couldn't either.

"I like how we're discussing what WE'RE going to do after we eat." Kevin remarked sarcastically. "Remember? We were supposed to discuss our plans together?"

"Did you really fucking think that I didn't already have a plan when we left the house?" I asked back. I was thinking that this Chinese food was even better than the place Kevin usually went to. It was too bad it was located in a place I planned never to visit again. Oh wait, I could pawn Kevin or David to bring take out to me.

"No."

"Surprise."

He smiled and shook his head. Then he went back to eating. He couldn't fool me. He liked these surprise trips.

"Rick was talking to Jace and he said that you told Jace to fuck off because he didn't want you as a girlfriend." He said as he glanced at me.

"Why is that so surprising to everyone?" I asked as I shook my head slightly in frustration.

"Because you told him straight up about a lot of things. I don't think I've ever heard you come right out and put your feelings on the line about anything."

"I don't want to talk about this. You're giving me indigestion. And what good did it do anyways for me to lay my cards out on the table? Notta, not a damn bit of good." I huffed.

"And what about David sleeping in your bed?"

I picked up my cup of soda and took a thoughtful drink. "What's that any business of yours?"

"Stop being this way. I don't like you this way. You're not usually so argumentative with me." Kevin griped as he looked away.

"I just don't like everyone knowing my business. Jace went and told Rick everything I said, and in turn he told everyone else."

"We're family. We live in the same house. We're bound to know just about everything about each other. You always seem to know our business yet we hardly know any of yours."

He was right, but it didn't make me feel less angry about everyone knowing that I'd lost. Jace didn't want me and he had cheated on me. And I did know a lot of personal things about the band, sometimes by hearing it, and sometimes the voices talked. Carol regularly asked her parents for money and they usually gave it to her. She was disgustingly descriptive about what her and Rick did in bed, how it felt, and how long it lasted. I was sure that David and Kevin had learned a lot from her. They'd both talked to her about her period and sex and she'd answered them but sometimes exaggerated which meant that they both in turn asked me – as if I wanted to talk about personal biology. She'd talked Kevin into letting her put make up on him. I knew he just liked the attention. But now that I thought about it, David and I had done the same. Rick sometimes wore briefs and sometimes wore boxers. I'd watched him and Carol have sex before, all of us had at some point. David liked sports and was a jock. He had sportsmanship though and wasn't all about winning. He also always had his damn camera aimed at me. He'd joined a camera club and sometimes those nerds invaded our space. I'd told him many times where I'd shove that camera if he didn't stop taking pictures of me. He always replied that he was priming me for the fame that I claimed I'd achieve one day. And that usually lessened my aggravation with him because he was right.

Neither Rick or Kevin liked David walking around naked because they thought David's dick was bigger than theirs. I was thinking that he was just hung better, however that worked. Rick liked to read mystery novels and playing video games, but it seemed that all guys liked playing video games. He was somewhat of an obsessive compulsive. Carol liked clothes, makeup, sex with any guy available, and acting like a teenage girl. When she got tired of tie dying everything then she painted stuff. Mostly she yakked on the phone in a high giggly voice with her friends and smoked a lot of pot. Kevin could draw really well. He liked to listen to public radio to a show called "car talk", and he could tell you every model of car on the road. We often had name-that-car contests. He couldn't wait until he had a garage of his own so he could restore an antique car.

David got along better with women than men unless they were a jock too. Kevin got along with everybody and was cuddly and likeable. He and David were pretty good friends. David was better friends with me then he was with Rick or Carol. Rick and Carol had more couple friends than single friends and most of their friends thought of me as a cute little brat. If Kevin was really upset, he sucked his thumb but only in our house. Outside, he tended to ball his hand into a fist and press it against his mouth. I tried not to judge. He wanted to be friends with everyone and didn't like conflict. And me? Sometimes I just wanted to be alone like when I'd been a kid. I'd been an only child and now it was like having a house full of siblings where everyone was in your business and helped themselves to your stuff. But another part was that I felt responsible for all of them except that I was the youngest. I was so different from everyone and sometimes I really hated that. I had my differences too. I tended to expect others to pick up after me, I constantly left drawers and cabinet doors open although I didn't know why. I hated partly open closet doors because that scared me but sometimes, I left my closet door partly open and that was really confusing. The part that seemed to really make me different was that people in general seemed to think similar thoughts and have similar reactions to situations, but me? Half the time I was on a whole different page. While they might run screaming or cower down from someone trying to rob them, I'd more likely roar into a rage and lay them flat. They made sure that they never came up behind me to deliberately scare me. And people, especially men were constantly drawn to me, asking me questions, hitting on me, wanting my time, wasting my time. I was damn good looking even when my hair was a mess and I hadn't slept for two days. But I sensed that wasn't all they approached me for. At times, strangers outright asked me for answers as if they already knew I was psychic. It was especially unnerving when they did this while I was surrounded by my band. The band asked for my advice a lot too but they didn't seem to connect it with me being psychic.

"Hey. Don't space out on me. And don't be mad." Kevin remarked as he nudged me.

I blinked out of my thoughts and looked at him.

Oh, and I sometimes tended to space out and think too much.

"Awe, c'mon." He said as he leaned forward and pulled me down towards him so he could touch his forehead against mine briefly. I wasn't sure why he liked to do that. It was weird.

I looked at his cute face. "What Jace didn't tell Rick was that he told me that I'm fucking conceited and that the world is going to kick me in the ass and I'd just be a nobody." I said as I pulled away. I still couldn't believe Jace had said that to me. Those were fighting words.

"Um, he did tell Rick."

I had nothing to say to that.

"You are conceited. But I believe in you. If you say you're gonna be famous then you will be."

I smiled, and pulled him down to touch foreheads. It was no wonder he was my best friend.

We visited one of the hair salons next and we both got our hair cut. Then we hit the clothing stores. I didn't have the patience to look through the racks of clothes so I sat on the bench outside the store while Kevin picked out several things. He came to the entrance of the store and I followed him in. I had wanted him to try them on since we were the same size but he was insulted by my suggestion and he also said the store, which stocked only women's clothes wouldn't let him in a dressing room alone. I thought that was kinda funny. I walked up to the girl minding the store and asked her if Kevin could come into the dressing room with me. The dressing rooms were one by one rather than one room with stalls.

"Why?" She asked with her eyes narrowed at me.

"Because I need help getting dressed. My shoulder is

messed up." I replied with a perfectly straight face. Kevin was looking at me with a deer in the headlights look.

She looked me up and down. "I guess so but no funny stuff or I'll call security." She finally replied. She unlocked one of the dressing rooms and let us in. Kevin was mortified at what I'd done.

"You gotta ask for what you want." I told him. "Sometimes you get it." After I'd tried on the clothes, he went to get more. The clerk checked on us. I showed her what I intended to buy and then she was ok. After two more times of trying stuff on, I paid for my purchases.

I left him in a men's clothing store while I put my new clothes in my truck. He was only going to buy a pair of jeans and a shirt but I sent him back in to try on other stuff. He ended up with five pairs of jeans, six shirts, a jacket, and some shoes. I added in socks, t-shirts, and underwear. "I don't know how I'm going to be able to repay you for this." He said as we stood at the checkout.

"I'm buying these for you. I don't want you to pay me back." I replied.

While he talked and talked and talked about that, we were now walking past a portrait studio. "Now we need our pictures made." I said interrupting his boring monologue.

"What? I thought you were kidding about that." He said as he stood looking at the store.

We walked in as the last customer was leaving. "We want some pictures of us taken outdoors." I told the girl photographer. Her name tag said "Jessica".

"This company only does studio shots but I get off in an hour. I'll take pictures of you for seventy-five dollars if you don't rat me out to my boss."

I looked at Kevin and smiled.

He had this puzzled look on his face. "Why are you paying for this? David would and does take hundreds of pictures of you – for free."

I knew he wouldn't like the answer. "Voices, Kev. I hear voices."

We met Jessica, the photographer, on a bridge that looked big enough for cars. It was a walking bridge which didn't allow anything except for bicycles and walkers on it. We were wearing our new duds and we'd both brought our guitars with us. "I want to do pictures like the Calvin Klein ads in magazines." I told her.

"That sounds cool." She nodded. And so, we did. I knew enough about posing from having worked as a model. I coached Kevin too, and then Jessica had some ideas that we liked. She took one of me standing in the middle of the bridge holding my guitar and the wind blowing my hair. I knew it would be a really cool picture. We took a lot of pictures on that bridge, most were of just me, but we did some with Kevin and I, and ones of just Kevin. As he stood there looking cool and uninterested with his guitar slung down, I smiled. He was a cute dude, and when he wanted to, he could rock it.

We went to a music store so I could look at new guitars. "What kind of guitar are you looking for, sweetie? Are you going to take lessons?" the older gentleman asked me. I was betting he was thirty if he was a day. I looked up as two guys who looked about eighteen entered the store. There was also a dad and his kid looking at drums.

"She's already a guitar legend." Kevin told him as he glanced at some starbursts.

The guy chuckled. "It just so happens that we have a special section for guitar legends."

"It would be cool to play the Fender Stratocaster that Jimi Hendrix once played." I remarked, ignoring his sarcasm.

The guy looked at me with a little more respect. "We'd all like that, sweetie. But I have some new Fenders that haven't been played yet if you'd like to try one out."

I accepted a white guitar thinking that white always sounded better. The guy plugged it in for me and I played a few chords from "Purple Haze". I scrunched my face and handed the guitar back as the guy commented that I was good on guitar. The two guys were standing there watching and listening to our interaction. "That was sweet!" one of them agreed.

"Thanks. That Stratocaster wasn't bad but I prefer Gibsons. How about that Les Paul Studio there in blue?"

"Good choice. That's Slash's favorite guitar." The guy agreed. Well, what could I do but play a riff from a Guns N Roses song? I noticed the two guys conferring amongst themselves and smiling. Oh, hell yeah! I was a master!

"But can you play the solo from "Freebird", little girl?" smirked one of the guys.

I closed my eyes in frustration at the jackass but only for a second. I swear everyone thought I was five years old. "Can you?" I asked back.

The guy snorted as if I were stupid. "Well hell yeah." He agreed.

I went to hand the guitar off to him and he shook his head. "I want to hear you play it." He told me. "I mean, if you think you can." He smirked.

"I might break a fingernail." I pouted to him. I had no

idea that I'd play that song a hundred thousand times in my lifetime because people thought no one really could play it, it was so hard.

The guys laughed and scoffed at me. Oh yeah! Show off time! I ripped into the solo and their wisecracks and laughing stopped. Kevin was laughing at how stupid they were. Then I closed my eyes.

"Holy shit! She can play it with her eyes closed. Mother fucker!" one of them exclaimed. The sales person asked them to watch their language. The volume increased and I imagined that Kevin had turned it up. Oh yeah!

When I'd finished, everyone in the store was standing around me and there was a sudden silence. "I'm a guitar legend. I'm bad, bad, super bad." I smirked.

"Oh my God!" the teenage guy with the dark hair exclaimed as he fell to his knees in front of me. "Will you have my baby?"

I was amused but I kept a neutral expression. "No." I replied. Then I turned to the old guy. "I'm ready to buy Slash's favorite guitar."

"Sure thing, guitar legend." He murmured back, smiling in appreciation at me.

So as everyone chuckled and I turned to follow the sales guy to the cash register, the teenage guy was following me on his knees begging me to reconsider. "How about giving me your number?" He pleaded.

I turned and looked down at him. "I'm only fifteen, dude. Daddy wouldn't like that." I lied. It hit me then that my guitar playing would get me laid anytime I wanted to by whomever I wanted. Wow. Kevin gave me a curious look while the other people around us made comments. I wondered if this was going to be my life from this point on. "I'm playing at Willie's Grill Wednesday night at 8pm with my band if you want to hear more." I added.

"Oh yeah!" the guy agreed.

"We have jam sessions on Saturday from ten to noon if you feel like joining us sometime. I'm sure everyone would love to hear you play. You're really talented." The old guy told me as he finished up my purchase.

"You sure are spending a lot of money today. Can you afford it?" Kevin asked as we got in my truck.

"Yeah, I made two thousand on that last photo shoot with Cardello. I haven't bought anything in a long time and I think it was overdue."

"What are you going to do when Rick and Carol are on your case after seeing everything you bought today?"

"I guess I'll give them some money to shut them up." I said as he started the truck and headed towards home. I hated to give them anything because they'd both been jerks so much of the time but yeah, I'd just bought a twelve-hundred-dollar guitar. I knew that I'd have to give them something.

"I'm going to Corner Red. I'd like you to go with me." I said to Kevin about 7pm that night.

"Why are you going there?"

"It's open mic night. I feel a need to perform."

"It's a comedy club. What are you planning to do? You don't know any jokes." Hell, I was a joke.

At 8pm, I was at Corner Red with Jessica, the photographer that we had met that afternoon. She had been excited when I'd asked her if she'd video my performance. Kevin had reluctantly come with me but he was afraid that I was going to bomb out and that we'd get tossed out of the place on our asses. I was thinking that we wouldn't.

I wanted to remember everything about this place and this night. I surveyed the dark room and the people, then I looked on stage where it was brightly lit. The vibe of the room was fairly open and accepting which was good because I intended on trying their patience. Oh yeah! They'd get a show tonight!

I was the fourth person to go in front of the mic. I was dressed in a white tank top which showed my toned arm muscles, and my favorite ripped blue jeans, and brown cowboy boots. Oh, and I'd brought Slash's favorite blue Gibson with me. "Hi y'all." I told the crowd. "I'm C. Angel. Are you ready for some jokes and bad ass guitar?"

"Hell yeah!" Someone shouted.

"That's cool. One person's pumped." I deadpanned as I looked out at the audience. There were maybe thirty people there. A few chuckled at my response.

I started on my first joke.

There's a blind guy sitting on a bar stool. He shouts to the bartender, "Wanna hear a blonde joke?"

In a hushed voice, the guy next to him says, "Before you tell that joke, you should know something."

Our bartender IS blonde, the bouncer is blonde. I'm a 6 foot tall, 200 lb. black belt. The guy sitting next to me is 6'2", weighs 225, and he's a rugby player. The fella to your right is 6'5" pushing 300 and he's a wrestler. Each one of us is blonde. Think about it, Mister. Do you still wanna tell that joke?"

The blind guy says, "Nah, not if I'm gonna have to explain it five times."

I smiled when most of the crowd laughed.

A guy took his blonde girlfriend to her first football

game. They had great seats right behind their team's bench. After the game, he asked her how she liked the experience.

"I really liked it," she replied, "especially the tight pants and all the big muscles, but I just couldn't understand why they were killing each other over 25 cents."

Dumbfounded, her date asked, 'What do you mean?'

'They flipped a coin, one team got it and then for the rest of the game, all they kept screaming was: 'Get the quarterback! Get the quarterback!' I'm like, Helloooooo? It's only 25 cents!

I'm really good at telling stories and jokes when I put an effort into it and I knew I'd sold the joke I'd just told even before the audience laughed.

"I have a dog." I continued. "He's part St. Bernard and part Pit Bull. He saves people then he kills them."

The crowd was howling over that one. I'd always liked that joke.

"I've been playing guitar since I was a kid." I told them.

"You're still a kid!" someone heckled.

"At least I'm not old like you." I replied back.

The audience laughed at that. A few people told the dude to shut up.

"As I was saying," I continued. "They start you off with simple songs." I started playing "Twinkle, Twinkle, Little Star" and I messed it up (on purpose).

A few people snickered. "Looks like you didn't learn shit!" the heckler shouted.

I pretended to look a little perturbed. "Now, give me a chance. This is open mic night, right?" I asked back. "Let me try another song." I said as I tried to play "Mary Had a Little Lamb". I played the right notes for a few seconds then messed it up.

"Awe, c'mon kid, get off the stage! You don't know what the fuck you're doing!" the heckler shouted.

"Let me play you a C chord." I played a G chord instead. I had told Jessica that when I started talking about my guitar to make sure she zoomed in on where my fingers were on the guitar when I said that I was going to play a C chord. I also told her that if no one spoke up about my playing the wrong chord that she should shout out that it was wrong.

"Hey, that's not a C chord!" Someone up front told me.

"It's not?" I asked as if I didn't have a clue. "My guitar teacher said it was."

"You've had your fun, now get off the stage and give someone else a chance!" someone else told me.

I smiled in amusement at them. "Now this is what I call audience participation!" I had been sitting on the stool the club had provided but now I stood up and took a cool stance. I pointed out at the guy who'd given me so much lip since I'd gotten to the mic. "This one's for you, old dude." I told him. Then I ripped into "Thunderstruck" by ACDC.

Two guys about my age jumped to their feet cheering and clapping. Three minutes and four seconds later when the last note died, several people in the audience raised their drinks to me. I reached over for my drink, which was a Sprite in a clear glass that I had taken on stage just for this moment, and held it out as a toast to them.

"What are you playing next?" the heckler shouted.

I took a sip of my Sprite and set it down, purposely giving a few second pause to that question so the room would be quiet. "Hell, that's the only song I know and

253

I've been practicing that fucking song my entire life." I quipped back with a straight face.

The audience roared with laughter on that one. Yeah, I was an entertainer. I could do this shit. It just took getting the timing right and the right attitude for whatever skit you were doing. I allowed myself a smile. "What do you want to hear, old dude?" I asked him.

The audience chuckled at that.

"Quit fucking calling me old dude!" He shouted.

"Lynyrd Skynyrd! Freebird! Play Freebird!" The two younger guys yelled. "We wanna hear you play Freebird! You're bad ass on that guitar!"

I shook my head as if I couldn't believe they were asking that. "Why does everyone fucking want to hear FreeBird?" I asked no one in particular.

The heckler was laughing loudly. "You can't fucking play it, can you? little girl, you're just a no talent little shit!"

"Hey!" someone yelled as they turned to face the heckler from across the room. "Shut the fuck up! We're tired of your shit! Give the kid a chance."

I motioned to the heckler. "C'mere, old man. Sit on stage with me and I'll show you how I do Freebird. And I do it good." I teased.

Now he was hesitant but the audience had taken my side and badgered him until he came up on stage. He looked kind of rough but maybe that was only because he was drunk. He was really old, maybe thirty-five, with scruffy long hair and stubble on his face. He sat down on the stool.

"What's your name, man?" I asked him.

"Lawrence." He said. "Are you going to fucking play or what?" He prodded as he figured I was stalling for time. And actually, I was. There's nothing like making a person uncomfortable on stage and building crowd anticipation.

"Lawrence, I'm C. Angel Devito. Remember that name because Buddy, I'm gonna rock your musical world with this fucking guitar. And in another year, I'm gonna rock the fucking world so the only name they scream out in the night will be mine!" I told him in a very conceited tone (and yeah, that was on purpose too). "C. Angel Devito. Remember that name and that you heard me first." Oh yeah! I wanted those words recorded on video.

"You're such a bullshitter! All I want from you is a blow job!" He laughed.

Before I could respond back, someone in the front yelled, "Shut your fucking mouth, man! Or I'll drag you off the fucking stage! None of us need to listen to your shit!"

"Just get off my stage if you're going to say shit like that." I told him. I was glad that I hadn't been able to respond quickly because I probably would have regretted what I had been about to say. I'd reminded myself that I was being filmed. I imagined that this video would be viewed long after I was famous and I sure didn't want it showing me being an ass.

"Bitch!" He muttered along with a few other words before he stumbled off stage with the help of the bouncer. A few people were saying shit to him as he walked away giving me the finger. The bouncer had been ready to take him down if he'd caused trouble but he was only being verbally abusive to me.

Okay, so he had almost ruined the mojo of my performance. It was time to move on. I put the microphone in the stand and started playing "FreeBird". The crowd hushed as I poured my heart and soul into that song. I had to admit that I could sing that song as well as I could play it. Maybe it would become my trademark. I'd always related to that song. Hell, that song totally represented me in the lyrics and the fact that I could laid down the guitar in it. I smiled at the two guys who had come to the edge of the stage to sit and get a better vantage point. "Come sing with me." I told them in between lines. I nodded my head at them. They jumped on stage with me then, one on either side of me and the three of us sang that song through. I got a standing ovation as that song ended too. I told the crowd that if they were interested in listening to live rock and roll to join me at "The Joint" where Rebel and I would be playing our next concert.

It amused me that the guys beside me were so thrilled by it all. They followed me to a table in the back where Kevin was sitting. They sat with us the entire night as we watched the next performers and as random people came over to chat. Jessica sat with us too and told me that I needed a website. She said that she could make us one so we were going to get together in a few days to discuss what she needed to make that happen. Oh yeah! I was a star.

"Your first two groupies." Kevin remarked as he drove us home.

Austin and Bart had asked us a ton of questions and been so enthusiastic about me and my band, that I had to admit that they were our first groupies. They said they wanted to be my roadies when I went on the road. I took that into consideration. They asked me for my phone number several times. Kevin finally gave them our home phone number to shut them up. Neither of us knew if that had been a good idea but it was done now. "Yep, this is our future." I replied as I looked at the dark scenery passing by as Kevin drove us home. I hoped to have a driver to drive me places when I got famous.

"I'm really surprised and impressed that you got up on stage tonight and told jokes. I can't say that I've ever seen that part of your personality. You were funny and so casual up there. I always knew you were funny but I've never seen you put yourself in the spotlight like that. You handled that heckler really well too. I knew you could sing and play guitar by yourself but I didn't know you could just get up on stage and entertain them like that. You were a talk show host in a way."

"Bad To The Bone" was playing on the radio and I thought it was an appropriate song for the moment. Oh yeah! "That person you saw? That's who I could be, who I may become down the line." I replied.

"Well, it's fucking impressive."

Oh yeah!

***

"Where's our new clothes and our guitar?" Carol asked me the next day after noticing that I had a new guitar and both Kevin and I were wearing new clothes. We were all sitting in the living room in front of the tv eating McDonalds which I had paid for.

"I'll give you two hundred each to shut up." I replied as I chewed on some French fries. All the other fast-food places could say they had the best fries but McDonalds was the winner in my opinion. I didn't even need ketchup.

"What about your guitar? That had to cost a pretty penny." Rick remarked as he pushed Carol's hand away from his fries.

"Yeah, it did. What about it? I still have enough for next month's rent and utilities."

"I think you should give us at least five hundred a piece. You must have spent that much on clothes and shoes for Kevin." He replied. David and Kevin looked for my reaction.

"Two hundred. Take it or leave it." I said as I ate the last bite of my Big Mac. I couldn't wait until we all lived in our own individual houses so Rick and Carol wouldn't be such pain in the asses.

The three of us got in an argument then with them saying I'd come from a rich family and I'd always had money. They knew that wasn't true. Sometimes my dad and I barely had enough to get by on let alone to buy new things. The first time I'd really had money was after he'd died and Bob had sold our ranch. I hadn't been spending any of that money until now, at least not on anything except rent, gas, my truck payment, and everyday expenses.

"It's five hundred a piece or else." Rick told me.

"Now I ain't giving you a cent. So sad, too bad. You had your chance and you blew it." I told him.

He got up to stand in front of me in a menacing stance. "You'd better listen to me." He warned.

"Okay, y'all, stop it." David told us.

"I'm not afraid of you. I will fucking lay you flat." I warned him back.

Rick yanked me up by my arm and I laid him flat but as I was on the floor ready to backhand him across the face, David stopped me. But then Carol had pushed David and we were all scuffling. Then Kevin got into it and was trying to hold me back.

"What the fuck?" yelled a guy's voice from across the room. It caused us all to stop and look up. It was David's friend, John. "You guys are all crazy! Get the fuck off the floor!" He said loudly as he walked towards us. John was a solid two hundred pounds and probably six feet or more tall and he walked like the Hulk. I knew I couldn't take him out but I didn't appreciate him refereeing.

"This is our house. We can do whatever the fuck we want here." Rick told him as he stood up and helped Carol to her feet as if nothing out of the ordinary had happened.

"From my vantage point, you were about to punch this kid. I know she's underage and from what I hear, you're her guardian. I have half a mind to call the police." He replied angrily. I had stood up and now he had walked in front of me like a shield even though Rick's temper was now mostly defused.

"Nobody invited you in. I could report you for trespassing." Rick answered back.

"Yeah." Carol agreed. She was standing there with her arms crossed but safely out of the way should anything else happen.

"Let's step outside and settle this." John told him.

"John, no. Leave it alone." David said as he put his hand on John's arm.

"Yeah, leave it alone." I agreed as I stepped to the side of John. "I'm his guardian and I don't need him beaten up or in jail."

They all looked at me strangely, especially John. He then turned his gaze to Rick to see his reaction. "Yeah, what she said." Rick agreed as he shrugged his shoulders. None of what we'd just said made any sense. It was obvious that I wasn't old enough to be anyone's guardian.

I wish you could have seen the expression on John's face because it was priceless. "All of you are fucked up. I swear I've never seen such a fucked-up mess before." He said in exasperation to me and Rick in particular, then he stomped out of the room with David running after him.

There was quite an awkwardness as Rick, Carol, Kevin, and I glanced at each other. If John reported us to the police we'd be in serious trouble. But in the meantime, I was ready to lay Rick flat again if that's what it took for him and Carol to see my point of view.

"In your fucked up mind you seriously think you're my guardian, don't you?" Rick said to me.

"I am the guardian. I've kept us all together. I found this house for us, I drew up a budget, I've been paying for this house, I've bailed the both of you out of jail, I've been trying to get us all to get our act together so we can be famous. So yeah, I'm the guardian." I replied.

"Then give us five hundred a piece."

"Two hundred or nothing." I replied as we stared each other down. The phone rang and Kevin who had been watching us went to answer it.

"This time."

I had four, one-hundred-dollar bills in my pocket. I pulled them out and handed two to Rick and two to Carol. "By the way, I got us a gig down at the River Rat on Friday night, and we're making seventy-five each instead of fifty." I remarked as they gave me a curious look. Yeah, I was the boss too. I made things happen. I got us raises.

"Hey. Phone's for you." Kevin announced.

It was Austin, one of my groupies. He wanted to talk

about guitars and when could we get together? "I gotta work, and then I got gigs." I told him. He was going to stop by for our concert at River Rat.

David stormed into my room as I was researching other clubs that might give us a chance to perform. "You nearly cost me my friendship with John!" He said angrily. "Do you have any idea how close he was to reporting Rick to the police? Do you know what would have happened if he'd called the police?"

"He walked into our house uninvited. He had no right to do that. We have the right to act like fools in our own fucking residence." I replied back.

He growled in frustration with me. "You and Rick have got to stop throwing punches! Do you know how insane that is?"

I shrugged my shoulders. After all, he knew I was a bully at heart.

"Fucking unbelievable." He muttered as he paced my room.

I reached over into my night stand and pulled out five hundred dollars. I held it out to him.

He gave me a confused look then took the money and looked at it. "And now you're bribing me?"

"I don't bribe anyone. I gave Rick and Carol money, so I'm giving it to you too."

"You gave them five hundred a piece?"

"No, two hundred a piece, like I said."

"How's it fair if you gave them two hundred and me five hundred?"

I leaned my head back against the wall as I sat on my bed and said in exasperation, "David, life ain't fucking fair. Deal with it, huh?"

CHAPTER 15

A few days later, I met up with Jessica and she gave me the photos she'd taken and the video of me at Corner Red. She'd really done a good job on both, and I'd been right about the photo of me on the bridge holding my guitar with the breeze blowing in my hair. I looked fucking awesome! I had a poster made of it and hung it in my room.

David saw it first. "WHY DID YOU HAVE SOMEONE ELSE TAKE YOUR PICTURE? I could have taken that same shot!" He remarked loudly and angrily.

"I was giving someone else a chance to capture my stardom." I replied. Plus, the voices had suggested it.

"And you paid her. You never pay me." He stood there with his hands on his hips.

"Would you take care of an expensive camera if you had one?" I asked back. I was thinking that it would be cool if David could take a lot of our pictures. I figured I'd still have to use Jessica at our gigs since David couldn't possibly take those shots, but other shots? He could take those. He had never done so though. He mostly took pictures of me and Kevin, and then everything else.

"Why?"

"I might buy you one."

He looked a little startled at that. "You know that I

take care of my car, right? So, I'd take care of a camera too." He replied back.

"I'll see what I can do."

Then he told me what model camera he wanted plus ten other things. "And you owe me another shoot because of this. As a matter of fact, there's no time like the present."

I supposed that I knew that had been coming.

He was in my closet now picking out clothes for me to wear.

We ended up at Huguenot Lake which was close to the high school. I guess I never minded being the object of a photoshoot but David tended to get carried away. I was done after thirty minutes but David had a hundred more shots he wanted to take. "Why do you need more shots?" I complained to him. "You've done a zillion shoots of me."

He checked a setting on his camera and mumbled, "As you well know, you have to practice at something to be good at it." He just as suddenly looked up. "No, forget that shit. You're the one that does something once and is an expert at it."

I just looked at him. Guys were so exasperating. I saw a small rock so I picked it up. Sometimes I had to study and practice at something before I was good at it. Hell, the school had made me take math every damn year and I still could hardly understand it. I huffed and skimmed the rock across the lake. But hell, a camera wasn't math. "Yeah, I'm fucking good at everything. Give me the camera. I'm taking YOUR picture." I replied.

It took some arguing but he finally handed it over. I was tempted to snap shots cutting off his head but after the first couple of shots like that, it wasn't fun anymore.

I took two more shots, one of him leaning against the little bridge and one of him sitting down and leaning against the railing. Then I gave the camera back.

"That's it? You're done?" He asked as if that was surprising.

I yawned real big. "Yeah, let's go."

Later, in my room I was in deep thought. I was thinking that I could invent something if I just put my mind to it. The minutes ticked by but nothing had come to mind except for an idea for a children's book. It involved a dog, and the dog's name was Sa...

"Hey!" Kevin exclaimed from the doorway.

I looked up.

"David needs help editing pictures. He says you're a know-it-all. He needs you to go help him."

I blinked at him.

"You know, Photoshop? That magical program?"

I shook my head in exasperation, thinking that I needed to get out of that bad habit. One head shake too many and all the expertise was apt to become mush. "So, in other words he's not going to shut up until I physically go in there and try to help him. And then he's going to be mad if I find that I have some skill at Photoshop."

"Yep, exactly. Hop to it, Little Bear."

I threw a pillow at him.

It was no use trying to argue. I appeared in David's room. "Show me." I remarked in a very unenthusiastic way. I watched him for a while. It truly didn't seem that difficult. I had started out with the intention of messing up an image for him and then him yelling and me going back to my room. But the whole spectrum of functions that he'd shown me were incredible! Hell,

I could transform him into a cyborg or a horse's ass for that matter! An hour or so later I'd finished editing the images from two of his photo shoots, and some of the shots of me as well. I found myself admitting that he was a decent photographer. Mostly he'd taken shots of men but there were two females that he'd taken an awful lot of shots with. I liked the ones he'd taken of me.

And David liked my work, well except for the one where I'd made him half donkey. I even showed him two better ways to improve on what he knew and he took it all in stride (which was a first for him).

"You really are good for something." He remarked in approval as he looked through the edited images. I huffed to myself. I'd totally fucked up. I'd totally been played.

***

The crowd at River Rat was a higher class crowd than we usually played to but they were receptive to us. Austin and Bart had shown up early and had helped us set up. They were hanging on my every word as I took it all in. Rick, David, and Kevin observed the interaction. Carol managed to get their attention for a while but obviously they were more interested in guitars and one petite, muscular dark-haired chick, than keyboards and one tall, anorexic, bleached blonde.

When we took a fifteen-minute break, a guy came up to me and introduced himself as Bo. He said he was a DJ for WAXQ 104.23FM. He said he liked my band and that I was so damn impressive on guitar. He wanted to know if I'd give him my phone number so we could talk about my band. I gave it to him. He looked to be about twenty-five and he seemed harmless enough. He said that he'd love to have me on the morning show one morning. Oh yeah!

Jessica showed up towards the end of our show and took pictures of us performing. I was really feeling like a star. David and her talked cameras for a while and I half listened. Afterward, she and I went to a diner and talked about a website. She was going to be the leader of our fan club. I was going to pay her a hundred a month to do so and she was ecstatic about that. She was also talking about having t-shirts made with a picture of the band on the front, and maybe some other promotional items. I was all about that.

I went back to the music store on Saturday to see what a jam session was like. I took my new blue Les Paul Studio guitar with me. I'd asked Kevin if he had wanted to join me but he'd made other plans. Now that he had wheels, he was popular.

I was the youngest musician. The energy from the five guys that had shown up to play music was a little cool, as if I were butting into their little group. I'm sure they expected me to be amateur but I was anything but. They played mostly classic rock but there was also a blues song and a country song or two. I could pretty much pick up anything and fit into the groove when it came to music so we were like a well-oiled machine by the time noon rolled around. I knew they'd thawed out towards me when they asked if I'd come back and play again. I told them where we'd be playing that next week and a few of them were thinking about stopping by. Oh yeah! We needed all the fans we could get.

***

"What are you looking for?" David's voice asked as I stood in front of my closet surveying my clothes. Carol had wanted the crazy clothes that Cathi had bought for me while I was in South Carolina. For the most part, they fit her and she had huffed about it as she was trying to be a size 3, but she'd taken what clothes she wanted. I didn't care. I sure didn't see myself wearing any of it in the future and I was fine being a size 5. As for clothes, I'd ruined some of them from working in the warehouse. A lot of my clothes were older and just needed tossed. What Kevin and I had bought not all that long ago only made a slight dent in my wardrobe. Mostly I'd bought clothes for him.

"I'm looking in here for something that I actually like and that I haven't ruined by working at my job." I replied.

"Buy something you do like." He replied in an off handed way as if that was an actual option.

"I think I'll just slap you in the head." I replied as I closed the closet door and stepped back, causing him to step back also.

"It's a bummer that you don't like stores." He said as he lay across my bed.

I stared at him. You know, people will just come into your room and make themselves at home. It's rude. "Get off my bed."

"Ya know, if you were willing to take say 30 or 40 pictures of me, I mean really truly put your talent to use in taking them, not goofing off, I would be willing to shop for some new clothes for you." He replied back. He hadn't moved from lying on my bed and he thought he was being amusing with his offer. When I didn't reply, he continued. "It sure would be nice to have some new jeans and maybe another stupid Aerosmith t-shirt, huh? Maybe some flowered underwear too."

The sad thing was that it was time to buy all the

clothes that he had mentioned. I needed some new bras too. But to have some punk kid go buy them for me? I'd be teased forever about that. I sighed in defeat. "Are you serious?" I asked him. "Are you really going to buy stuff I would like and not make a big deal of it in front of the others, especially about buying my underwear?"

I saw him jerk. He sat up, all seriousness then. "Uh, yeah. Does that mean you'll hold up your end of the deal without jerking me around or giving me a hard time?"

"Yeah." I grumbled in defeat.

"Well, make a list of what you want and what sizes."

He was whistling as he left my room with the list and my money.

At least two hours later, but more likely three, David was dropping bags on my bed. He also gave me back change from the money I'd given him. He'd been to the Goodwill store as well as one or two other places. "Isn't this the coolest jean jacket ever?" he gushed as he shook it out and held it up. I had to admit that it was. It was a washed out lighter colored denim and had been someone else's at one time. I slid it on and it fit pretty well. I nodded to him and took it back off. He'd bought me six pairs of jeans, four from Goodwill, and four shirts from there. One was red flannel and the others were t-shirts with logos. One was a walking advertisement for beer but it was a cool blue color. He'd only spent twenty-five dollars at the Goodwill. At Walmart, he'd bought me solid color panties, four bras, socks, and a pair of pajamas. Two pairs of jeans were Levi's button ups. I hadn't had a pair of those in ages and I loved them. I even accepted the other three regular shirts he'd bought. I noticed that one pair of jeans was a size smaller than I normally wore and one of the shirts was a large. He saw my face scrunch up at that. "Try them on. I bet they all fit."

So, I did. I tried everything on except for the bras and panties, and they did indeed fit.

He shrugged his shoulders as I looked at him. "I just held them up and looked at them. I know your size." He started folding up the jeans and hanging up the shirts. "It would help if you talked sometimes." I heard him mumble.

He finished putting away my clothes and then turned to me. "What? I did good, right?"

"Are you ready?" I asked.

"What?"

"You wanted pictures."

"Would it hurt you to compliment me, or anyone for that matter?" He asked as his mood darkened.

Hell, I didn't want to deal with that. "From now on you're in charge of buying clothes for me." I informed him.

"No, I'm not. I'm never doing anything for you again." He said as he brushed by me.

I watched his back as he exited my bedroom. He just didn't know how to handle me, that was for sure.

Kevin appeared as I was half watching a tv show but mostly thinking of chocolate milkshakes. "Why do you have to piss off David?" He wanted to know.

It was fun for me mostly. I shrugged.

Kevin went on to lecture me about how good David was to me, how he was good to me and that I should talk more and be more social. Obviously, he'd been talking to David. "Go tell him he did a good job, Baby."

He started hugging on me and trying to be cuddly. Kevin knew I wasn't cuddly. He knew how to handle me.

I pulled away and went to my room. I pulled out a pair of the Levi's and the cool beer shirt and changed into them. I stood at David's bedroom door and stared at him talking on the phone. He didn't take the hint so I stood in front of his closet and started pulling out clothes. He hung up the phone then. "What are you doing now?" He demanded.

"I'm ready to shoot you. I'm preparing your clothing." I replied holding out a shirt to him.

He was still trying to be angry with me but I knew Kevin had cooled him down. He stood there staring at me and not taking the shirt. But I noticed that he noticed that I was wearing the clothes he'd just bought me. We probably stood there two minutes not saying anything. "Tomorrow. 11am. In just a bit it's going to be too dark to take any pictures." He finally remarked.

I put the shirt back in his closet. "See you then." I replied as I headed out of his room.

"You live here too! What do you mean, see you then? I see you every fucking day!" He yelled after me.

Yeah, he was fun.

In case you're wondering, I did take about sixty pictures of him the next day using all of my expertise and more conversation. He wasn't angry then. I even edited them for him. He had performed some excellent shopping for me, you know.

***

Bo, the morning DJ from WAXQ 104.3FM left a voicemail on our home phone. I called him and he wanted to know if I could be on their morning show. I told him that I'd have to make arrangements with my work to come in late, but yeah, I wanted to. My boss was none too happy about me wanting to come to work late but I had the time off. I spent about forty-five minutes at the radio station. Before we went on the air, I asked him not to ask detailed questions about how I'd gotten from South Carolina to New York. I was just going to briefly explain that the band and I had gotten together in high school and then we'd come to New York. I also asked him not to ask how old I was. "Are you on the run?" He asked me.

"No, but all that stuff is irrelevant."

On air, Bo asked me about everything else including if I had a boyfriend. "No, I'm focusing on becoming a star right now. I don't have time for a relationship." I told him, although I was lying. I would have liked to have had Jace as a boyfriend.

He let people call in and talk to me and I avoided answering any personal questions. I was quite good at that. I did talk about our gigs and everything else though.

Two weeks later, the last catalog I had modeled for while working for Harris Company was sitting on the kitchen table while I was trying to make breakfast. David sat down and began thumbing through it. He began to aggravate me by getting in my way as I put a bowl of cereal together, and he was naked. I thought maybe he'd leave me alone if I got a bowl of cereal for him too. I did and it didn't help. Carol watched him aggravate me and get rather friendly with me, which he had never done before. He was sitting beside me with his hand on my leg as I was trying to eat. His hand was slowly working its way to my crotch. I'd had enough. "Dammit, David! Leave me alone and go put some clothes on while you're at it!" I yelled as I jerked away from him. I knew he didn't want sex. This was some sort of game to him.

"You know, Baby, you think you're such a big shot since you did all those catalogs and modeling jobs. They probably paid you a bundle."

I supposed giving concerts and having all sorts of fans hanging on you afterwards didn't account for anything. That happened at every gig. "I don't work for Harris Company anymore. I work for a warehouse. I don't make that much money." I replied.

"Cardello calls you sometimes to model." He mumbled as he made his way out of the kitchen. Well, hell, he was right about that. I made a bundle modeling.

I watched him leave all the while wondering what that had been all about.

"Baby." Carol said nudging me as I settled down at the table to finish eating. "What's with you and David? We all thought you two were fucking each other but obviously that's not the case. But now it looks like he wants something from you. Are you going to give it to him?" She said trying not to smile but failing miserably.

I was going to snap at her but for some reason I couldn't help smiling too and saying, "Yeah." Our life together was just so unreal sometimes, and I was more than willing to sleep with David if he wanted me.

She looked at me a moment debating whether to take me into her confidence. But before she said anything, I remarked, "I already know that you never fucked Jace. You wanted to. You even had him talked into it but then I walked in on you." I said almost verbatim what she would have told me. I had found out while I had been yelling at her that same day. Otherwise, I wouldn't have been able to be civil to her as I was doing now.

"Did he tell you?" She asked in a puzzled voice.

"No. I haven't talked to him or seen him in over two weeks. I just kind of guessed."

"Then just call him up and sleep with him. I know he's crazy about you."

I didn't know whether to believe her. "And that was why you had to seduce him? Why would you do that, Carol, especially if you thought I might care about him? And that you know I don't play around?"

She looked at me for a long moment as if she were seeing me for the first time. "You have everything. I wanted to take something away from you." She said rather tensely.

"Jace isn't mine. All you did was make me see how it would have been if we'd been a couple. That really sucks to know he wouldn't have been faithful. As for having everything, I don't feel like I do. I can teach you to play guitar or whatever. I can give you clothes or get you some of the perks of modeling. I don't know what else I can do there. You're very pretty and you're skinnier than I am. There's no reason you couldn't model too. You should have entered that first Cardello contest like I did." I replied. Winning that contest was how I'd gotten a contract with Cardello.

"Jace really isn't that way, Baby. Really." She said touching my arm."

She really didn't know him. "Yes, he is. He screws anything that moves."

"Maybe if he were in love he wouldn't."

I didn't have a come back to that.

"Are we over this?" She asked with a hint of a smile.

"Yeah, but I have a confession."

Her smile faded.

"I hit on Rick and we almost slept together." I replied wondering how she'd take the news.

She shook her head in an "oh well" gesture. "Yeah, I know. He told me. He said he just couldn't do it. But if you're both waiting for my permission, go ahead and do him. I'm ok with it."

I stood there with my mouth open.

"I'll still take the modeling perks though." She smiled, then looked at her watch. Before I could question her, she was dashing out the door. One thing was sure, I couldn't sleep with Rick and I wasn't about to call Jace. Instead, I headed upstairs to see if Rick was awake. I had to tell him about a modeling shoot I had been offered by Cardello that I had accepted. He was coming down the hallway wearing only a towel around his waist, fresh from out of the shower. "Can we talk?"

"Come on in." He said as he pushed open the door to their bedroom.

I hesitantly entered the room trying so hard to forget our moment of passion. He motioned for me to sit on the bed which I did. "I'm glad you stopped in. He told me. He picked up a comb and was fixing his hair in front of the mirror of the dresser, his back to me. He apparently had put the incident out of his mind. "I bought you a cell phone and I expect you to have it with you in the case I need to get a hold of you or vice versa. You're going to pay for the service and reimburse me for the phone."

I blinked in annoyance. They all had cell phones but I'd never gotten one. I didn't want to be bothered. We had a landline if I needed to call someone. "Seriously?" I asked him. "I don't wanna carry a fucking phone."

"Oh, but you're going to." He assured me.

We disagreed about it for a few minutes but somehow, I ended up on the losing end.

"Actually, I just came in here to say that I have to go out of town for two days on a photo shoot." I managed to say.

"What kind of shoot? And where at?" He asked as he put down the comb and then sat by me.

Now I felt really uncomfortable. Unpure thoughts were running through my head even though I didn't want them there. I wondered if he knew what I was thinking. "Probably jeans and a white shirt but who knows? It's in Florida this time."

He asked me if I would be okay by myself, which of course, I would. He told me to take someone with me if I thought it would be easier for me, and he had me write down all the flight information and where I could be reached at, etc. Then he ushered me out of their bedroom so he could get dressed and go to work. He was intentionally giving me the brush off. I didn't really know if it was because there was still sexual tension between us or because he really needed to get ready for work.

I stood in the hallway for a moment then headed to David's room. In a way, David was like me. He didn't hang around with the rest of the group much but he was one of us. Sometimes we'd all do something together or go someplace together, but most times not. He was that way about his personal life too. I knew a lot of different things about Kevin, Carol and Rick, but not much at all about David. I couldn't even say that I knew much about his family even though his brother had bothered me all through school. And although he said he didn't like housework; his room was as neat as a pin. He actually had been doing more housework lately.

I knocked on David's door. I heard muffled voices then he finally opened the door. A guy I'd never met sat on the bed. There also was some sort of tenseness in the energy that I didn't recognize. The energy I felt was sexual and something else. All I knew was that something wasn't quite right. I supposed that the two of them had been trading stories about sexual conquests or maybe they'd been looking at porn magazines that they'd stashed under the bed.

"I just thought I'd see what you were up to." I remarked.

"What's that supposed to mean?" David asked almost in alarm.

Again, there was that feeling that something was going on. "Nothing. Just wanted to hang out, that's all. We never hang out anymore." I replied.

"Oh..yeah. You're right." He said in what I thought was relief in his voice.

"I gotta be going anyhow." His friend said. He got up and walked to the door. "See ya later."

"Yeah, later." David replied.

I sat down on David's bed and stared at him.

"What?" He asked.

"What was that about?"

"What are you talking about?" He sat down beside me and nervously began flipping a magazine.

"I'm just getting this weird vibe." I replied.

"I have no idea what you're talking about. And why all the conversation all of the sudden? Usually, you have nothing to say." He protested.

I ignored that jab. "Was that guy giving you a hard time about something?"

"No."

"I'll kick his ass if he was." And I was serious. I had a long history of being a bully.

He gave me this incredulous look. "What the fuck, C. Angel? If he was giving me a hard time, I'm man enough to kick his ass. Why are you like this?" He said.

"Can't help myself, I guess." I smiled. "But the vibe was weird." I continued.

"Fucking stop analyzing me! Stop analyzing us! You don't have to know every damn thing or feeling we feel or vibe that we give off. We sure the fuck don't know anything you feel or think!" He huffed.

He was decidedly aggravated and frank. I sure didn't want to talk about my feelings or thoughts. An awkward silence descended upon us. I asked him how his job was going, and a few other things but he kept giving me one-word answers instead of keeping the conversation flowing. I finally just asked him what he wanted to watch on tv, and we began watching a movie. We decided the movie was boring so we decided to go to the park and run. He was trying to tire me out but what he didn't know was that I ran four to five miles nearly every day. It really helped me to keep my anger in check when I wasn't in level one. Later he was in my room helping me pack for my trip. I had a hard time understanding him. If we spent time together, then it was a whole day thing with him. You just couldn't do one thing and then be done with him. And truth be told, sometimes he didn't care if I had any conversation. That day ended with us wrapped around each other, but he still didn't want to have sex with me. "Get over yourself. " he told me. "Not every man wants to have sex with you."

CASSIDY A.STORM

I was really sorry to hear that because David was really buff and he was really well hung. "So, look and get excited but don't touch?" I asked him.

"Only if you want to torture yourself, because I'm never fucking you." He replied.

I noticed the energy around us. He was serious. He wasn't even entertaining the thought for future consideration. He wasn't hard either. That surprised me because I thought guys couldn't control those things, and I was so damn hot and bothered. All the guys wanted me. "Dammit!" I cursed softly. "I'll play some mean guitar for you." I added as a second thought. All the other guys that had heard me play guitar wanted me.

He smirked. "I can play guitar as well as you can."

"Oh yeah, right." I huffed sarcastically.

"Go to sleep, huh?"

Yeah, like I could really do that now.

CHAPTER 16

Arriving back in New York was always too real after being out of town on a modeling shoot. I had enjoyed Florida and the shoot. It had let me put my problems in a drawer so I didn't have to dwell on them. I knew how I wanted my life in New York to be and people to act but reality didn't reflect any of it. The house was a disaster area, and although the band hadn't done any drugs and rarely drank in front of me lately, I figured that they still did, especially while I had been gone. It was a shame I'd had to get on their case again. Not.

I talked to Jessica and she had created our website. Most of the pictures were of me and there was concert information. She'd researched the t-shirts and was going to take our picture for it. I really liked the website and that she seemed to have a head for business. She even had a place on the website where people could comment. She said she'd have to look at each comment as it came in and monitor whether it was something that should be posted or not. If there got to be too many, then she would stop the comments. She was also amazed that I modeled as well as played in a band. She wanted to put that on the website but I said no.

Streethart had a gig that night. I decided to go even though I had to go to work the next morning. Yeah, I'd told Jace to go to hell but now I was fucking missing him.

Some team had just won a ball game and everyone was out getting wasted. During the break, Greggie appeared backstage. As he hugged me, I was wishing that he didn't have a girlfriend. It irked me that all the guys I was interested in either weren't available or didn't want me. When he went to pull me onto his lap, I let him just to make Jace jealous. We talked and laughed until he had to go onstage again. The guys had been watching and teasing us, and warning me about his girlfriend but I let it roll right off of me.

I took a seat at the bar. As Streethart was tearing up a Rolling Stones song about fifteen minutes later I just couldn't stand the cigarette smoke one more minute. I walked outside to get some fresh air. For some reason I walked around the side of the club away from the parking lot. The club sat pretty close to a hill. It was dark but my eyes adjusted easily. I stopped and leaned against the building. It was cold and I wasn't sure how long I wanted to stay outside. Out of the corner of my eye I saw a couple come around the opposite end of the club towards me but they didn't see me in the darkness. They looked like lovers. One of them leaned against the building and the other leaned against him and they began kissing and groping each other. I squinted several times to see if I could get a better look. I didn't see any better but I heard a voice and I recognized it. Then I heard the other's voice. Both of them were guys! I gasped but not loud enough for either of them to hear me. I wanted to stop watching but I couldn't. I couldn't really see much more than shadows but I knew they were kissing and I knew they were groping each other. And I knew one of them was David. Shock washed over me but all the pieces of things he'd said or I had noticed began to fall into place. He might have dated girls for show but it was guys that he was into. Some louder voices were approaching from behind them so David and the guy quickly pulled apart and lit cigarettes as if they'd been smoking the whole time. I slipped back the way I'd come and went back inside.

It wasn't but a few minutes later that Streethart had finished their last song for the night. Some of the girls were waiting to talk to the guys in the band. I stood beside the ones waiting to talk to Curt and I smiled inside as I heard him flirting very nicely with them rather than using his usual repulsive come ons. The girls were responding in a positive way too. He wouldn't be lonely much longer. He noticed me and drew me over and hugged me. "You sure are looking sweet tonight." He remarked in almost a sincere tone. I thanked him and told the other girls how cool he was. I left them hanging onto his every word.

As the club closed down, I began to help them dismantle their equipment, Jace appeared beside me as if nothing had ever happened between us. After the gear was loaded, we watched the others leave. I would have liked to have walked and stayed outside somewhere like the park but it was cold and New York was crime ridden. I followed Jace to his apartment. "Did Greggie tell you that I'd meet you tonight after our gig was over?" He asked as we settled on the couch with the tv volume on low and his dog, Biscuit laying on my lap.

"No." I replied trying to discourage Biscuit from licking my face. I liked dogs but not dog kisses.

"Well, I want to apologize to you. I'm sorry that you

had to catch me trying to do something I shouldn't be doing. I didn't fuck Carol, you know."

"You would have if I hadn't walked in."

"She's been trying to get me in bed for a long time. She worked extra hard at it while you were gone."

I sighed. "You hurt me. I never thought you'd betray me like that."

He looked at me strangely. "I'm not your boyfriend and you're not my girlfriend, how did I betray you?"

"I do like you, Jace." I replied.

I jumped slightly as he nudged Biscuit off my lap and to the floor. Biscuit was not happy about it. Jace edged closer to me and in slow motion his lips came down on mine. "I'm sorry, Baby." He murmured breathlessly.

"I am too." I replied as we kissed some more. I wanted to believe that we could be a couple and that I'd be woman enough that he wouldn't cheat on me. It felt like he cared about me.

"He won't be faithful." I heard as Biscuit hit me on the leg with her paw. I broke away from Jace and the world refocused.

"What?" He asked in a puzzled voice.

"I don't want a fling, Jace. If I sleep with you, I want a relationship." I told him, which is not what I wanted to be saying.

"We're both too young for something serious. He replied.

"Maybe that's so but that's what I want."

He was about to say something and then reconsidered. I was glad he didn't say it. After a moment he said, "I don't want a steady relationship. I want my freedom."

"I want all or nothing." I replied.

"I guess all we have is friendship then. I really don't want to hurt you."

He at least was serious about not wanting to hurt me. I patted Biscuit on the head. "So, we're still friends?" I asked.

"Yeah." Jace replied.

"Okay, I guess I'd better get home. I have to be at work at 6am." I told him. He just looked at me and I supposed he knew the score. If he didn't want me there was always a man that did. I was going to put him out of my mind and see who else came down the line.

And, I had a new cell phone and I knew Curt's number. I called him and he answered on the second ring. "Are you busy?" I asked him.

"Nope, just waiting for a gorgeous chick like you to call." He replied.

"I was wondering if you've learned anything new lately that might interest me."

"Oh yeah, come on over and I'll show you. I think you'll like my new skills." He murmured.

"I'll be there in a few."

I was really amazed at what I'd taught Curt, so amazed that I did him twice. Then he told me that he really had to get some sleep because he was now working at the new job I'd suggested that he apply for. I might have done him a third time if he'd hadn't needed to go to sleep. I had never needed more than five hours of sleep a night. I'd always been that way. It seemed sad that he wasn't willing to give up another thirty minutes of sleep but I supposed it was 2am, a time when most people were asleep.

CHAPTER 17

At work the next morning I realized that some of my co-workers were into some interesting things. The most interesting was a guy named Santiago. He was a lanky dark-haired dude who had driven an old Camaro to work. I knew that I had seen him in a different car the day before, and even a different car a few days before that. I parked by his Camaro and I stood there looking at it. My curiosity was killing me and so I put my hand on it to catch the vibe. It didn't let me down. The car had been stolen. I was smiling about that when Santiago's voice startled me. "What are you doing?" He asked in a cold voice.

I took my hand off the stolen car and asked, "Can you teach me how to lift a car?"

He laughed. "What makes you think I know how to do that?"

I felt the energy around us. He wasn't dangerous, he was just in it for the kicks and someone had taught him. "Ahh, nothing. Forget it. I doubt you'd know how to do something illegal like that."

He looked me over. "Oh, I can teach you but it will come with a price."

I was willing.

Later that night he taught me some things in bed. He was about ten years older than I was and so far, he was the most experienced lover I'd ever had. I almost forgot about learning how to steal a car. I hadn't realized how much I'd missed having sex regularly. As I cooled down from having just come three times from our second sexual adventure, he told me we had to get going before his old lady came home and caught us. I looked at his hand but he wasn't wearing a ring. I stared at him for a moment. This wasn't how my life was supposed to go, finding every cheater in the world. Was there anyone that was faithful?

We went down to a garage a few miles away where there were several cars and he taught me how to break into each one of them without breaking a window. Each vehicle was a different year and model and I must admit that I was a fast learner. The next few nights we spent alternatively in the backseat of one of those vehicles, and then me breaking into them. I hadn't been so pumped about something since my dad let me learn motor cross. That night I broke into each of my band's vehicles just for practice and I didn't set off one alarm.

Another talent that Santiago had was picking locks. If I thought stealing a car came naturally to me, picking locks came even easier, probably because I could feel the energy of it. Who knew what skills I'd be learning next? I hadn't had so much fun in, well, ever. I was so happy that my life was finally feeling good to me.

***

I had gotten paid for my last modeling gig so I cashed the check and hit the local camera store. I told the guy that I wanted a camera that you could put different lenses on and also at some point could be used with studio lights. I spent nearly four thousand dollars buying a new camera and a used off brand fast lens.

I hadn't planned on it but it seemed like a good deal. I knew I'd have to watch my spending from there on. I guess my mind was still screwed up. I had plenty of money but for some reason I still thought I didn't.

I met David at his car as he came home from work. He gave me a curious look. "What did you do now to piss everyone off?" He asked.

"I bought you a camera and the glass you wanted." He was so damn on the mark though.

His eyes lit up. "You did? Whatcha buy? Can I see it?"

"It's under my bed."

We went to my room and he pulled out the boxes. "Oh my God! This is great!" He gushed as he looked the camera and the lens over. It was the camera and the glass he'd wanted. "This is some serious stuff! Thank you!" Then he hugged me and I went with it even though I wasn't a hugger. I was thinking it was too bad that he wouldn't pay me in sex. I would have been so willing to get paid that way.

Rick, Carol, and Kevin were angry that I'd bought David something and that it was an expensive purchase.

"We need pictures and he can take them. I didn't just buy it for him, I bought it because we need it." I argued back.

"But you bought it for him." Carol argued.

"Yeah, and he's going to take care of it. And don't worry, I'm sure he'll take glamorous pictures of you." I assured her. Well, I hoped he would.

"He'd better! He sure doesn't take many pictures of me now. It's all you, you, you, as if you deserve it." She huffed back with her hands on her hips. She was glaring at us. Well, I was the better looking of the two of us. And

I did model for magazines so obviously my picture was out there for everyone to see.

"Yeah, I'll take gorgeous pictures of you." He agreed.

"And of you." He added as he looked at me.

"I'm not doing any porno pictures." I griped back. I just knew that's what he had in mind.

"Did I say that?" He replied back, his voice laced with innocence. "All I need now is a tripod."

He was going to have to do without for a while because moneywise I was tapped out. Oh, I still had a lot of money but it was better not to spend every last dime of it.

When David was constantly in my face with the new camera, I realized that I hadn't really thought the whole camera thing through well enough. Sure, he'd taken pictures of me before then and I'd mostly been a bear about it but now that he had a new camera, he expected me to act differently. "You said that you bought this camera so I could take cool pictures of you. That means you have to cooperate. I found some really good locations too. Besides, I need the practice." He told me as I was trying to ignore him. I thought he'd had plenty of experience so far.

I groused in my mind at him but was really just hoping if I didn't answer he'd leave.

"C'mon, let me show you what I can do with this new lens. Huh? C'mon." He pleaded.

I sighed. Then we were standing in front of my closet and he was picking out what he wanted me to wear. "I get to wear what I want to wear this time." I informed him.

"At least put on the ripped jeans. I'll deal with the black t-shirt, and the cowboy boots are cool." He said. I changed into the ripped jeans.

We went downtown and he photographed me in an alley and against rugged looking wooden doors with paint peeling off, and in a small wooded area with me sitting on the tailgate of my truck with my guitar. I had grudgingly agreed to give him two hours only because we were going to several different locations. Every time I started to scowl; he reminded me that I'd said I'd cooperate. "You are a model, right?" He asked. I agreed that I was.

When he showed me the images later, I was impressed. "These are really fucking exceptional." I said in a confused voice. I hadn't really expected him to take any better shots of me than he had with his older camera. I had liked the locations too. In the back of my mind, I knew I'd end up editing the images.

"I told you I could do this." He smiled.

Yeah, that sounded like he needed chased through the house.

"You are so fucking weird!" He exclaimed over his shoulder as I ran after him. But hey, if he didn't like it, he wouldn't be running.

***

Our gigs were going really smoothly too. We still may not have been getting along famously at home but in our music, we were really together. I want to think it was because of the new fans we had. Austin and Bart showed up at nearly every gig, and from my jamming with the guys in the music store every now and again had brought us more fans. I'm not sure that the website was getting us more fans but it was there and I referred people to it. I'd even been back to Corner Red another time to tell jokes and stories, and to play a song or three on guitar. Jessica showed up sometimes and filmed us. The rest of the band had specific fans too. I was pleased the way things were moving along.

It was a Friday night and the band and I had a gig at the Rooster Bar and Grill. We'd performed there a few times before and it seemed to be working out well. I was looking good in my black jeans, cowboy boots, and black t-shirt advertising Aerosmith. As I belted out "Sharp Dressed Man" I surveyed the room. It was about 9pm and I loved the darkness in the place and the cool different colored lights that shone on us. A red light was shining on Kevin and a blue light was on David, while a yellow one was on Carol. The clothes that she wore were skimpy and skin tight but the yellow light didn't help any of that. My bare arms looked purple because of the purple spotlight shining down on me and I supposed that my face looked purple too. I was cranking out the guitar solo on my favorite white Gibson as I looked out at the crowd. I turned my attention to someone walking up to me. Yeah well, I missed a note when I saw Jordan glaring at me. He nodded his head at me then nodded towards the crowd. I took that to mean that he expected to talk to me on our break. I couldn't imagine what he was doing there or why he was angry. He stood to the side and leaned against the wall staring daggers at me until our break four songs later.

I put my guitar in its stand and he about yanked me outside. He looked around as if making sure no one else was in hearing distance. "Have you been in town all this time?" He demanded.

I shrugged my shoulders wondering what his deal was. "Uh, yeah. When I moved back to New York I went to see y'all at school and told you I'd moved back, remember?" I replied. I could still remember seeing him standing there with one of the cheerleaders possessively hanging onto him.

The look he gave me conveyed that he thought I was insane. "You said hi and bye and then you split. No one heard a word from you after that. You never enrolled in school again. We thought you went back to South Carolina."

"I didn't need school. I took a GED test, and no one said anything about wanting to hang out with me. Everyone seemed to have moved on so I moved on too. I found a full-time job and I do gigs with the band, and we still live where we've always lived."

"You could have given me your number or something."

"Our number at the house hasn't changed and its published, and I didn't know you wanted it anyway." I argued back. "It looked like you had something going on with Tracy so I cut my losses. I can't read your mind, dude. Besides, you could have asked Gabby. She had the number to the house."

"Sometimes you're just clueless, you know that?" He scowled. Since the conversation was taking a turn for the worse. I wondered if I should just let it drop. I would have liked a boyfriend but not a stupid one. He knew I played gigs with the band, and he knew where we'd played before. It's not like we had stopped playing at most of those places. Why hadn't he searched for me? Why hadn't he asked Gabby for our number? What would have given him the idea that I'd moved away again? Were all football players that stupid?

"Look, I gotta get back inside for our second set. Do you want my number?" I asked.

"No. Tracy is my girlfriend now. Have a good life." He remarked.

Then I was watching his back as he strode to the parking lot. I closed my eyes and shook my head in frustration. Why'd he even bother chewing me out tonight? I had been right about him being with Tracy. She was his fucking girlfriend! Men were so stupid and insensitive.

***

I came home and flopped on my bed closing the door behind me. It had been a bad day at work with trucks being late and tempers running high. I'd been happy to get away.

I groggily opened my eyes as the mattress sunk down as someone sat beside me. I hadn't meant to fall asleep.

"C. Angel, guess what?" David asked, all excited about something.

I growled. "What?" If he'd just walk back out the door, I could go back to sleep.

I talked with the photo club and they had a great idea for a photo shoot for you.

I closed my eyes again and he nudged me. I half listened to him as he described a big adventure where all the members of his photo club would get together and we'd go to someone's house who had a home studio and then downtown and do a photo shoot. "This is so exciting!" He exclaimed as if he didn't already play guitar in a rock and roll band, and as if he didn't already claim that he was as good a guitarist as I was. And if he hadn't already taken hundreds of thousands of pictures of me in the past couple of years.

"And I'm sure the rest of the band is ecstatic about

this?" I mumbled.

"The shoot is for you, not them. You're the photogenic one, not to mention beautiful."

I ignored his assessment of me. "It's for all of us. You can't leave them out. Rick and Carol already freak out about everything I do on my own. I don't need this to add to it."

He hesitated and I was thinking I could sleep now. "I guess they're invited too." He finally mumbled. He stayed sitting beside me.

I opened my eyes and rolled to my side. I looked up at his hopeful face. "Yeah, I'm in. I figure you guys want to do this on Saturday. You know that Rick and Carol probably have to be at work at 10am."

"We'll have to start at 8am then although I doubt they'll get up that early."

"Yeah, okay, and not my problem, just invite them."

I was the only one that made it on time to the guy's house who had an in-home studio. Kevin, Rick, and Carol had trouble getting out of bed. It was annoying that the photo geeks all looked awake and perky so early in the morning. David was especially perky looking.

"We'll start with you and David." His photo friend, Brian announced. David had told me to bring some clothing changes. I had on ripped blue jeans, a gray t-shirt advertising Ford trucks, and my cool brown cowboy boots. David was wearing a plain white t-shirt, blue jeans, and cowboy boots.

I looked around at his studio. Brian had speedlights on light stands, reflectors, and a spackled blue background. Three other guys were in the studio with us and they looked at me hungrily. It felt more like they were more giddy to take my picture than them wanting to fuck me. Whatever.

"You should be wearing something sexier. I knew I should have picked out your clothes instead of letting you do it." David told me.

"I look fine." I replied as I caught a glance at one of the guys.

The guy nodded appreciatively. "You probably have been told this at least a thousand times but you are metal melting hot. And I can vouch for myself that men become weak kneed and stupid when they see you, especially when you're burning up the strings on that guitar. It's a wonder we're not all melted puddles right now."

While I didn't have a quick reaction or comment to that statement, David burst in. "I told you NOT to make her head any bigger, Dirk! She's already full of herself."

"Yeah Dirk, what were you thinkin"? I smiled back.

"Ah man, you know I can't help myself." Dirk replied back. They went on trading comments while I decided to fluff out my hair a little. Ha. I didn't feel that I looked metal melting hot but it was early and one could aspire.

Brian posed us holding our guitars, then he took some of David by himself, and then me by myself. The other guys suggested poses and voiced their approval. I hadn't told them anything about myself but they knew a lot about me. I was afraid that David had told them everything. They asked me about the modeling I did, and they were psyched about my guitar playing which they hadn't even heard yet. And one of them remarked, "She looks pretty harmless."

I glanced at David. Yeah, I could be scary. "Seriously, David, did you have to blab everything about me?"

"They were interested and you're a model,

remember?" He replied.

The guys were chuckling amongst themselves.

"Wear this." David said as he nudged me. He'd gone out to his car and had come back. I took the shirt that he was handing to me and looked at it. It was a peach-colored spaghetti strap knit top that looked like it would cover my stomach. I had brought a pair of jeans that were a lighter color and I supposed I could change. "How do you know it will fit?" I asked him.

"I do your freaking laundry. I looked at the labels on your shirts. I know what size bra you wear and what size panties. And I know you won't wear anything that shows any skin." He quipped back, but his tone wasn't angry. Hmmm, a drawback to having someone do your laundry. Who would have thought? The guys snickered. But then I remembered – he'd bought some clothes for me. I guessed I wasn't quite awake enough yet.

I looked in the bathroom mirror to evaluate the peach top. It was a short top that came to the top of my jeans but it was snug. I supposed you could call it a corset. I walked back out in that top knowing that it hugged my every curve. Even my boobs looked bigger but I supposed it was because it had a built-in shelf bra. I was okay with it though because it hardly showed any cleavage. I brushed my hand down my faded blue jeans. They felt soft and I knew they looked good on me.

The guys drooled their appreciation as their eyes sized up my body but it was David that blushed.

"Oh yeah, let's get some more shots of you and that white guitar." Brian remarked. So, they did, and then we redid the same poses of David and I, except now he had his shirt off. He was buff.

"You two do make a good couple." One of the guys

remarked.

I heard the doorbell ring and one of the guys went to answer it.

I jerked to look at David. "Are we a couple?" I asked. "I don't remember us talking about that."

"Well, one could hope." He replied back, which only confused me. Maybe he was bi-sexual. I could only hope.

Carol, Rick, and Kevin walked in. They were thirty minutes late.

"Well, look at you all slutty looking." Carol remarked.

I really hated her. She was wearing an off the shoulder top which showed everything, and tight skinny jeans with stilettos. It wasn't what she was wearing that made me hate her, it was just her attitude. The guys could hardly hold their cameras after looking at her.

"She's MY girlfriend." Rick informed them. They nodded their heads as if to congratulate him. If they'd known that she fucked other guys more than she fucked her own boyfriend, they would have invited her into the bathroom with them for a quickie. There was still a chance that Carol would initiate it herself. Rick didn't like it but he mostly kept his mouth shut and slept with other women to justify her cheating to himself. I'd told him once that he would one day regret wasting his life with her. "Mind your own damn business." Had been his reply.

Somehow, we settled down and the guys took pictures of us as a band. They took a bunch of Carol. It made me realize that I liked it better when the spotlight was just on me.

Then we headed downtown for the urban shoot. It

was cold outside and Carol complained and complained then she and Rick left to go to work. Kevin bugged out on us immediately afterward. One of the guys remarked that he was glad that she'd left because she'd complained so much. Then he brushed his hand past my cheek and flirted with me. I moved backward. "I bite. You only get this one warning." I told him seriously. David affirmed that while the other guys laughed.

David had his camera and it became a photo shoot of me and my guitar. In some shots I had my jean jacket on over the peach top but in others I was without the jacket. I posed suggestively against the column of a building in one shot then I wondered if I'd regret it. Then they were in my face with close ups, but hey, I was metal melting hot.

We ducked into one of the buildings about fifteen minutes later because it was too cold but it was one of them that complained, not me. We tried some more shots outside then called it quits. The guys thanked me for modeling for them. They'd all had their pictures taken with me individually and all of them had had their arms around me. David gave me a look that said, "deal with it" and I grudgingly did.

As David drove us back home, he remarked, "I really thought you were going to lose it when Gary touched your cheek, but you didn't. Thank you for behaving. You were great."

I wasn't sure why I had behaved. I'd been about to have a tantrum three different times and I had been so done with the picture taking more than thirty minutes before. I supposed I'd had patience because the Cardello photo shoots took forever too. The photographer was forever changing his camera settings or talking about the light quality or wanting us to wait for some reason or another. It was always hurry up then wait. "Why did you tell them we were a couple? You sure don't want to fuck me so why would we be a couple?" I remarked back.

"Uh yeah, about that – I shouldn't have told them that but when I started talking about you and how you were such a great guitarist and that you were a Cardello model, their eyes were bugging out. And I realized that you'd somehow already reached star status. I just wanted to be part of it so before I knew it, I'd told them that you were my girlfriend. Sorry about that." He said as he looked over and gave me an apologetic look.

Since we were boyfriend/girlfriend now, I felt it best to fight with him. "Why did you tell them every damn thing about me? I don't want people knowing half that shit. I'm not proud of where I came from or my fucked-up childhood, and they talked about all of that stuff!"

"I didn't tell them any part of your childhood. I hardly know anything about it."

"Then how did they know that I know how to bushhog?"

His face reddened. "Well, ok, maybe I did say something."

I rolled my eyes in exasperation. "Please don't tell anyone anything about me anymore, okay? As far as you know I was beamed down from a spaceship and I'm a kick ass guitarist, that's it. You know nothing else about me."

David snorted. "Yeah, I forgot that you were an alien."

I certainly didn't want that fact known. "Shut up, David."

"Our first fight, wow."

Oh my God! Was he really going to continue telling people that we were a couple when we really weren't??

***

Cardello wanted me to do a product ad shoot which happened to coincide with a day that the warehouse was closed. I'd been having exceptional luck juggling both jobs. The shoot was in New York City and I didn't care for the traffic there but I agreed to it. The shoot turned out to be for some type of shampoo and so they were looking for me spinning around with my hair blowing. They also did some with a fan. It took like three hours for them to get what they wanted. They'd washed and dried my hair three times. I wondered as I was driving back home if this was the way I wanted to be seen. I was looking to be famous as a front man of a band. What were people going to think if they saw my face in a magazine advertising shampoo? I thought my face was rather plain but I did have gorgeous hair. Could I be a pretty thing and a bad ass guitar front man of a band? Did that even go together?

CHAPTER 18

December 2006

I woke up one abnormally frigid morning thinking that it was time for revenge on Joseph and his goons. It had been months since they had bothered any of us and it was time for payback. I'd followed Joseph several times in the past months and I knew where he worked out nearly every day and where he lived. Sometimes I snickered to myself that the situation had reversed itself and that the prey was now the predator.

I clocked in at work at 6am and asked Santiago right before 8am if he could cover for me for an hour. He seemed to know that I was up to something but I steered him into thinking that I was taking time off for some woman problem. His face had turned ashen as he probably thought I was going in for a pregnancy test. I didn't tell him any differently. My story had to be solid.

I parked down the street from the gym that Joseph visited at 8am sharp every morning. I noted that he was about the only dumb ass out in the weather but that was to my advantage. Most people had opted to stay home where it was warm instead of working out. I saw him pull his Lexus into the parking lot and him walk towards the building as if he were a king. When he was out of sight, I shimmied underneath his car. Damn, that ground was cold! I bucked up and concentrated at what

I was there to do. I damaged his brake cable so it would break in the near future. Then I went back to work.

"Why are your hands so dirty and you have grease on your cheek?" Santiago asked me.

"Had a flat. Had to change the tire." I replied.

"But you're not pregnant?" He whispered close to my face.

"No. Dodged that bullet. I'll be back in a minute and then I'll get to work." Yeah, I was thinking that the pregnancy test rouse had worked to my advantage.

***

As it were, David's family decided to visit us at Christmas since David hadn't made a trip to South Carolina to see them. "Oh shit, oh shit, oh shit!" He fretted as he walked into my bedroom. Kevin and I were sitting on my bed. Kevin had his guitar and we had been singing some song that he liked. He truly was a better drummer than a guitarist but he wasn't a bad vocalist, not that he'd ever want to be in the spotlight.

"What's the matter?" Kevin asked as he stopped playing.

David looked at us as if we should have already known. "What's the matter? I've been talking to y'all about this for days. My freakin' family is driving here as we speak! What the hell am I going to do?" He said breathlessly as if he'd just run a few miles. He was pacing around the room. Well, like he'd said, we'd all known this for days now. Some of us had gotten tired of him talking about it and had tuned him out.

"Oh, you mean about all the screwing, drinking and pot smoking?" I asked in an unconcerned voice.

"Yes! That's exactly what I fucking mean!" He exclaimed as he stopped his pacing to stand in front of us. He could be such a drama queen.

Kevin and I looked at each other and giggled. "Offer them a toke." Kevin snorted, then he fell back on the bed laughing.

"That's not funny! You two have no fucking compassion because you have nothing to fear. You don't have parents. You don't know how they are!" David huffed. Then he looked at Kevin, who'd stopped laughing and had told him to fuck off. "I'm sorry, I didn't mean it that way." He said to us. "You know your dad would blow a gasket if he were here." He added, speaking about my dad.

He was absolutely right about that. "Well, it's just your parents and your asshole brother, right?" I asked, ignoring his remarks.

"Just? You know how they are! They only like my brother." He said as he stood there with his hands on his hips.

"Um, if they're driving up here, they kind of like you too." I remarked. I happened to glance across the room towards the window but instead I noticed all the clothes that I'd discarded on the floor. Someone would have to pick those up, not me, but someone.

David huffed. "Well what little bit they like me will be gone once they leave here knowing all the shit that goes on in this house."

I nodded my head towards the clothes on the floor. "Hey, could you wash my clothes for me?" I asked him.

"You're not listening to me at all." He replied. He sighed and began picking up my clothes and putting them into the clothes basket in the corner as he muttered bad things about us, me in particular.

"What do you want us to do about them?" Kevin

asked.

David paused and looked at us. "What I want is for no one to be drinking, smoking, or having sex while they're here. I want to show them a nice time even if they've been piss poor parents to me."

"I don't have a problem with that." I remarked. "Wash my clothes and I'll plan some nice things for them to do while they're here and one nice restaurant to go to. I'll pay for most of it too."

"Oh really, like what? And don't say rock climbing. I know you and I like to do that sometimes but we're talking about my parents here." David asked. He put down the clothes basket and sat on the edge of my bed. We had gone rock climbing at The Wall a few times.

"How about a nice helicopter tour of the statue of liberty and that area? The tv has been advertising that like crazy." I asked. Now that I thought about it, a helicopter ride sounded like just the thing to make my Christmas.

"My mom will never go up in a helicopter." David snorted.

"Well, even if she doesn't it will be something to offer. She'll like World Of Wings with all the butterflies, and then there's a bunch of museums to go to. And to top it off, how about a nice steak restaurant and a nice Broadway show?"

"And you've got enough money to pay for that?" David stated.

"Yeah. But you're going to pretend that you're paying for all of it. I'll toss in the helicopter ride."

"How much money do you have?" He pressed.

"A couple bucks." I replied in a non-committed way. I wasn't about to tell him my net worth.

Both of them looked at me. "Seriously, how much money do you have in your bank account?" David asked.

"I work a full-time job, I play gigs with you guys, I model for Cardello, and I'm paying for your parents to have a nice visit. That's all I'm saying."

"But I think you have a lot more money than from your jobs." David remarked.

"You might ought to remember the circumstances of most of my money. It's not like MY dad will be coming to visit." I said as I glared at him.

An awkward silence settled in as I thought about another holiday season without daddy.

"Daddy would want me to do this. He liked you, David. He liked you and Kevin a lot, and in a roundabout way he got us away from that one horse town that we hated." I added.

So, we talked about my dad for a while.

"Okay, I'll wash your clothes, even though Carol's supposed to do them." David relented.

"But first and foremost, you'll need to keep your perverted idiot brother away from me." I added.

David's mom and dad and brother drove in about seven that night. "Baby, how are you?" His brother Alan said to me sweetly as he went to hug me. I turned my head and didn't respond back. "Don't do that. You know I don't like you. And don't call me Baby."

I felt David's elbow in my ribs and I jerked.

"I see your manners haven't improved since the last time we saw you." David's dad remarked. I remembered that I wasn't fond of his dad.

"Excuse her, she's not housebroken yet." Kevin piped up. I turned and glared at him. If it had been just us and the band, I would have run after him and wrestled him to the floor.

"Come in and have a seat." Rick told them.

"Are you hungry?" David asked. I wondered how long it would be before Carol and Rick were screwing on the couch or lighting up a doobie. Hell, if Alan was still a virgin, she'd take that away from him before their visit was over. He was fifteen now.

David warmed up some BBQ and made some sandwiches for them and they talked about their trip. David told them all the activities we had planned and they perked up. I lightly kicked him under the table and smiled.

I wasn't sure if any of us were aware that David's parents were shacking up with us for their stay. David gave his room up to his parents and said he was bunking with Kevin. Alan was going to sleep on the couch. I conferred with Kevin in his bedroom. "I don't trust Alan. I'm not sleeping by myself tonight."

"You can sleep with me." Kevin offered.

I looked towards the door then turned back to him. "No, I think David ought to sleep with me." I pulled on thermal bottoms and a matching thermal top to sleep in.

"Why? Are you fucking him?"

"I would if he'd do me but he won't so no, but I think that people are going to see the real Alan during this visit."

When David finally came into Kevin's bedroom, I told him that he needed to sleep with me.

Once in my bedroom, he was messed up about that and had to talk about it for almost thirty minutes. "I'm tired, can we just do this?" I asked him as I observed his sleep pants which had a chili pepper design on them. He was wearing a black thermal shirt with it.

"This doesn't feel right with my parents here." He told me as he lay in bed with me a few moments later.

"Shut up already!" I whined as I rolled over. I was snoring before he finished whining to me.

"What the fuck?" I heard him exclaim suddenly.

I jerked awake at his movement thinking I'd just fallen asleep and now he was rudely awakening me. "What now?" I whined.

"What the fuck are you doing here?" Another voice demanded.

I reached over and turned on the lamp on my nightstand. Alan was standing there in his briefs. His erection preceded him.

"Get OUT of my bedroom!" I yelled.

"Shhh!" You'll wake up the whole fucking house." David shot back.

"You fucking get out of her room." Alan loudly told David.

"I fucking live here. And she invited me into her bed, you dumbass!" He shot back.

The argument got louder. I was hoping for that because now everyone was standing outside my door. The door opened and Rick and Carol stepped in followed by David's parents.

"What are you yelling about?" Rick asked wearily.

"This jerk came in my room to do who knows what to me! My door was shut. I didn't know I'd have to LOCK IT!" I replied loudly and angrily.

David's parents stepped forward trying to defend Alan. Rick reminded them that he was my guardian and that Alan needed to stay on the couch, that I hadn't asked him into my room. They started on David and his illicit affair with me. "You'd think you could wait until we'd gone home before you had relations with her." His mom huffed.

"I told you this was a bad idea." David replied, loud enough for everyone to hear, and glancing at me.

I blinked at him not sure where he was going with this, because he seemed like he was going somewhere other than where I originally thought he was going.

David looked back at his parents. "We wanted to tell you we were together but we knew you wouldn't approve because Alan has had a thing for her in the past."

"Aw don't believe that shit! He's a gay boy, he aint' screwin' her!" Alan snorted.

"Shut the fuck up!" David retorted and they started shoving each other angrily. It was obvious they'd gotten into some fist fights in the past. It surprised me that their parents didn't seem fazed by it. There was some real hate between the brothers. If I'd had a sibling and had been fighting like this, daddy would never have tolerated it.

"Ah boys, lets settle down. Let's all go back to our rooms and get a good night's sleep. This was all just a big misunderstanding." David's dad said. A big smile almost crossed my face when I saw his dad wink at David but I managed to keep it in. "C'mon." His dad tapped Alan on the arm. Alan shrugged him off, gave me a dirty look then exited the room. "And her guardian lets this go on under their roof." His mom murmured loud enough for us to hear.

Most of us except for David were holding our laughter in. He was just angry.

"So, you two are together, huh?" Carol remarked

thoughtfully. I was surprised that she hadn't ruined the whole charade by busting us out.

"No, but you're gonna pretend we are." David told her. I wondered if we could pull this off. Someone would screw up or maybe one of their friends would stop by and blow the charade.

There were a few comments but then Rick said, "I guess so. If that's the way you want to play it."

"Are we all better now?" Carol asked. To me she said, "You should have had a threesome with them. I've never done two brothers before."

I wondered why Rick put up with her shit. They supposedly were in a serious relationship.

"Shhh! Can you fucking say that any louder?" David complained. "Fucking go back to bed, huh?"

"Thanks for defending my honor, guardian." I called to Rick as he was exiting my room taking Carol with him. I was really surprised that he had stood up for me.

"Now how can I still stay here and sleep?" David complained as Kevin stood by.

"Please don't make me hurt you. Your dad obviously approves by that wink I saw him give you." I situated myself under the covers. "Go back to your own fucking room and sleep with your parents if you want to. Kevin will stay here. He's a big boy unlike you."

"When I fuck you silly, you're gonna regret saying that." David informed me.

"Bring it on, Big Dave." I chuckled. He was never going to do me and I knew it.

"Shut up!" He huffed. He turned to Kevin. "If we're pretending to be together, you can't stay in her room." They grumbled to each other about what was right.

"Look." David said wearily to Kevin. "Can you just go

along with this charade, huh? Please?"

I locked my door after the both of them exited my bedroom to sleep in Kevin's room.

Breakfast would have been awkward the next morning but amazingly, ha! I had to work. It was a Friday – three days before Christmas. Work had a tasty buffet lunch catered in for us. For that hour I forgot all about the house guests and that David was pretending that we were a couple. I stashed several food items aside to take home later.

CHAPTER 19

We were extra busy at the warehouse. Instead of working 6am to 3pm, we put in another two hours. All of us were dragging but happy for the long weekend as we left work.

I hoped to never hear Alan's voice in my house but he was right there when I rolled in the door all sweaty and dirty. "Where in the world do you work that you look and smell like that coming home?" He wanted to know.

"I'll tell you about it at dinner, after I get a shower." I said as nicely as I could as his parents were right there too. I would have liked to just punched him in the mouth. I doubted that he would ever have a job where he worked as hard as I did, and hell, I liked my job. It gave me a good work out. I had arms and legs of steel because of that job. I could have easily knocked him out with one punch.

The door on the main bathroom upstairs didn't lock very well so I took my stuff into Rick and Carol's private bathroom and showered. I knew their door locked. I also knew they'd get all messed up about me using their shower but shit, I wasn't letting Alan walk in on me. I knew if Alan busted in on my shower that I would have to kill him. I normally was pretty lax about getting totally dressed from the bathroom to my bedroom but given the circumstances, I was totally dressed as I walked out of their bathroom. I was wearing a clean pair of black jeans and red sweater because I knew we were all going out to dinner. I'd borrowed the sweater from Carol. Truthfully, David had borrowed the sweater for me. It's a good thing I was dressed because Alan was sitting on my bed as I came into my bedroom.

"Get out!" I told him angrily. "I don't want you in my bedroom, ever."

"Ah Sugarplums, you don't mean that." He smirked.

"I do mean that." I snapped as I tossed my clothes in a heap in the corner, then put my toiletries on my dresser.

"You're not really fucking my brother, are you?" He said in a know-it-all tone.

"Believe me, I am fucking him, up down and sideways. He's fucking hot and wild!"

"That's bullshit and you know it. How about you give me some of that pussy? I can't help but jack off every time I think about the time you let me feel your titties." He smirked.

I wanted to smack that smirk right off his face into tomorrow. Regretfully, I had let him feel my breast in order to borrow his dad's cell phone a long time ago in what seemed like an emergency. I just wanted to forget that unfortunate choice. "Shut the fuck up!" I warned him. To hell with keeping peace, I was going to walk up to him and bust his face in. I took a step towards him.

"Quit bugging her." David demanded as he walked into my room. I stopped and turned back to look at David.

"Tell him how you let me feel your titties." Alan taunted.

I hated when guys talked the smut he was talking. I wished that his parents had been out somewhere because I wanted so badly to set him straight. Instead, the actress in me took over. "Not even in your fucking dreams."

"Stop talking shit." David warned him. "You're fucking aggravating her and you don't want to see her mad. I can't keep her under control if she gets mad. And I wouldn't want too. I'm just warning you."

"Whatever, she knows the truth even if she isn't admitting it. Give her a big fat kiss and prove that you're together."

"You're such an annoying fucker. Fall off the earth and die." David shot back. And then they said a lot more cruder things to each other. I put my hands up in defeat and walked out. By that time punches were being thrown. Carol ran in and pried them apart. I would have just helped David sock it to Alan if I had helped. Then for sure I'd been in the dog house.

When all of us were in the living room ready to leave, David surprised me by putting his arm protectively around my back. "Honey, why don't you wear that nice coat you have? It would be warmer than that jean jacket you're wearing." He said to me in a soothing tone.

"Yeah, that jacket looks kinda ratty for going out on the town." Kevin remarked. I gave him a dirty look and bit back the smart remark on my tongue. I was itching to knock him back and for us to roll around on the floor like two angry siblings. I thought he wanted that too. We'd done that a lot since we'd moved in together. All of us squabbled but with Kevin it was mostly play.

The coat David was talking about belonged to Carol

so I supposed he had asked her if I could wear it. I also supposed that he wanted me to look more dressed up than I was, but he was right. It was too cold to be wearing the jean jacket with the sweatshirt material in it. I glanced at Carol and she nodded so I went into the coat closet and got the coat out that he wanted me to wear. I couldn't help notice that she was on her best behavior too. Normally she would have given me shit about borrowing the coat. I wondered what price he was paying her to keep her from being her asshole self. No doubt it was high.

I sat in the back seat of David's car with his dad and Alan so that his mom could sit up front. Kevin, Rick, and Carol were riding in Rick's car.

At the restaurant, David pulled out a chair for his mom and then he pulled out one for me. He kissed the side of my head before he sat down. I smiled at him as if he always did that. I had said that I was going to behave and I did even when Alan and his parents said stuff that was setting me off. It was so incredibly hard. The restaurant was upper class and his parents were impressed. They were more impressed when he paid for it. I'd given him five hundred dollars the night before. This was the one nice restaurant that I'd said I'd pay for. After this we weren't eating anywhere half as expensive and David was paying for most of it. Our bill came to right over four hundred dollars. Rick and Carol gave me suspicious looks. No doubt they knew I was paying for the night out. They didn't make any stupid remarks though because I was paying for their meals too. I supposed too that David had bribed them to keep their mouths shut.

We went out looking at Christmas lights after that.

When we stopped at one display and were standing in front of it, David gathered me up for a hug and we stood there holding each other as we gazed happily at the lights. It was easy for me to smile about that. So, David's mom and dad did the same, and so did Rick and Carol after noticing us. Yep, good times even if it was pretend.

Rick's cell phone rang about an hour later as we were about to call our outing to a close. He walked away from us so he could talk privately. "Can I talk to you a minute?" He asked me after he hung up and walked back to us. The rest of them got in the car. "That was Jace. One of his band members saw us and he wanted to know if it's true that you and David are together."

I rolled my eyes at him. "And?"

"I told him the score. I just wanted you to know."

"Whatever" I replied. So Jace didn't want me but he was going to get messed up if I was with someone else? That was fucked up.

I was also surprised that night when David came into my room to share my bed for the night. I gave him a wary look. I didn't want to spend my night listening to him gripe about his family or to talk about feelings.

He shook his head and said, "Dad said that if we're already having sex that there's no reason for me to pretend that I sleep in my room."

"Cool, don't hog the bed. I need a lot of sleeping room." I replied. I wished that he wanted to have sex but there was no reason torturing myself by suggesting it or dwelling on it.

"Thank you for pretending with me, and thank you for being on your best behavior." He murmured as I was falling asleep. He was spooned against my back. He gave me a little squeeze then I felt him kiss my cheek. It had been hard to behave and also hard to know that the times that David was so huggy with me was just to spite his brother.

The next day we all went sightseeing. David was attentive and considerate to me and I found myself feeling really weird about it because I liked it. I liked his attention and consideration. I wished that it wasn't all an act. When we had a moment alone, I asked him if that's how he would really treat a girlfriend. "Yeah." He replied.

"Lucky girl." I murmured back. I couldn't read the look on his face but if I had to guess, it was regret that I was wishing for something that was never going to happen. I mostly accepted that. Guys were always throwing themselves at my feet but it seemed like the ones I was interested in were the ones that didn't want me.

***

"Let's go up in the helicopter." I suggested to his parents on another outing. His dad and Alan perked up at that. "Oh man! That sounds great!" Alan exclaimed.

And David was right about his mom, she didn't want to do it. Then they were fretting about the cost for such a frivolous activity. "I'm paying for it. Enjoy yourselves." I told them. After some protesting, they agreed to go up. Well, his mom wasn't going. She was going to stay and chat with another mom that wouldn't get in the helicopter.

It was a really cool ride. I'd paid for Rick, Carol, and Kevin to go up too. It was only fifteen minutes but so awesome, and cold too.

We went to a museum after that and we ate at iconic places that weren't too expensive. It wasn't a half bad weekend. The only thing that could have messed us up was that a friend of Rick's dropped by and talked about partying. Luckily David's parents were upstairs and didn't hear that conversation.

Monday was Christmas Eve and we had a high paying gig at the River Rat. David's parents and brother came with us and sat in the audience. It was basically a bar, one of the larger ones in the area, and it was funny to see his parents sitting at one of the tables drinking martinis. I started us out with Paint it Black by The Rolling Stones. By the time I got to the guitar solo in Ozzie Osborne's Crazy Train, his family was looking adoringly at me. At break, they were introducing me to people they'd just met. They introduced David too but I got more attention. I smirked to myself remembering his dad scoffing at me when I was fifteen when I'd said that I was going to be a famous rock star. I wasn't famous yet but one day I would be. I was already famous in the nightclubs and other places where we played. People always wanted to hang out with us. A lot of the regulars came over to acknowledge us and chat on our breaks.

"Wow, y'all aren't proud of me at all. I drop a week's pay on a fancy restaurant and show you the town, and I get nothin'." David huffed to them somewhat seriously.

"We're proud of you son." His dad replied. "But your girlfriend is one talented, sweet girl. You gotta love that!"

I cracked up laughing. I just knew David was biting his tongue to tell them how I wasn't sweet at all. He talked to me about it later saying that he was happy that they were finally acknowledging him but that he might have to off me because I was stealing away his limelight.

"You might ought to wait until you're a beneficiary on my insurance first." He socked me with a pillow. He kept on about his parents and brother gushing over me.

I regarded him thoughtfully. It was going to be a rare moment. I was going to talk about the past. "Now you know how I felt when you and Kevin used to visit and talk to my dad. He always griped at me after you guys left, asking why I couldn't be more like y'all were. Why couldn't I be easy going and why couldn't I do the chores he assigned to me? Why couldn't he have had sons like you instead of a daughter? They were more cooperative. Yeah, he'd actually said that to me one time.

"Really? Your dad said that to you?"

"Yeah, you guys made me look bad and it made me jealous that you bonded with him so easily. He liked male company and he was all ready for both of you to become part of the family. He was afraid that I'd run y'all off. Him saying that, hurt my feelings."

David's eyes glazed over thinking about the past. "Wow." He remarked as his gaze focused back on me. "I miss him. He treated me more like a son than my own dad does." He blinked as the emotion of that hit him. "I'm sure your dad didn't mean it the way he said it. I know he loved you dearly by the way he talked about you. You really were his everything." He remarked as he remembered what I'd said. He went on to talk about some fun things that they'd done together and some of the conversations where daddy had praised them. He was chuckling because daddy had talked to them about sex and being responsible with birth control and generous with a woman. I knew it was mostly because daddy didn't want me to end up pregnant. My mother getting pregnant and dying of a drug overdose had really shadowed his life. I wished that he had been able to let that go.

Several scenes of my dad and Kevin and David flashed through my mind. Then I thought of my dog, Yellow who had passed away some months before my dad had. You just never knew when your world might be shattered, that was for sure. I sighed softly.

"I really am sorry. I know you miss him." David added. "Can I hold you a moment?"

I had been looking downward at nothing really as I thought of the past. I looked over at him. "Yeah."

***

At Christmas, David presented me with a sweater and a heart shaped necklace. I found that I had bought him a coat. I was as surprised as he was because I hadn't bought anyone a gift. I supposed that either him or Kevin had bought it and labeled it from me. He smiled broadly, gathered me into a hug and smacked his lips against mine, and it wasn't a short kiss either. I went with it wishing I'd had a moment to prepare. I heard Carol muffle whatever response she normally would have blasted out. I hoped my face didn't show surprise. But he'd looked at me then, and I was ready when he kissed me again. Afterward I noticed everyone else in the room pretty much stopped everything they were doing to gawk at us. Carol, especially was evaluating whether she get him in bed soon. I could tell by the look on her face. I glanced at Alan. He looked like he was bursting with a secret. No doubt Carol had fucked him without his parents knowing. I'd seen that coming. Outside, it started snowing.

Somehow, I got stuck going to the grocery store with David even though I normally avoided stores like the plague. I noticed at least one other couple shopping. Then when we both reached for the same package of hamburger at the same time, we looked at each other and I blushed. "I like this. I like us." I found my mouth saying.

Several different emotions crossed his face like a breeze blowing through. "It's just pretend." He told me.

I was still staring at him. "But I don't want it to be." I found my mouth saying. I couldn't believe that it was me saying them. I'd always had a stone-cold heart and I never voluntarily talked about feelings.

He gave me a sympathetic yet sad look. "I can't give you what you need. I care about you as a friend and family but I just don't feel the way you do. I'm sorry, and I really mean that because you really are a treasure. I wish it could be different. I really, really wish that." He replied.

I looked downward and he put the hamburger meat in the cart.

"I'm sorry." He said. "I really am. I'm not trying to lead you on or make you mad. It's just the way it is. I can't explain it any better and I wish it were different. You've been so great as a pretend girlfriend. I never thought that you could pull this off but wow, you're just perfect with my parents, Alan, and me."

"Yeah." I murmured as I swallowed the rejection, but then I decided to let it go. I had to. I knew why he couldn't. I also knew he didn't want to acknowledge the reason why.

"That was hard for me to say, especially knowing that you could just stop this charade with my parents at any moment." He murmured.

"Life works better on truth for me. I'm glad you're

being truthful. The charade won't stop just because you were truthful." I replied.

"Thanks. I really do consider you a good friend, and family."

Hmm. A lot of different thoughts bounced around in my head then. We finished our shopping in a sad awkwardness but then it passed once we got back home.

Since I was going to be leaving for work at 6am the next morning, David's parents said goodbye to me the night before. They had warmed up to me by then. "We're so glad that David has such a nice girlfriend. Maybe one day he'll be giving you a ring and you can be part of our family." His mom gushed to me. She meant it and inside I was rather blown away.

It was hard because I knew that it would never happen but I blushed and gushed right back. All I could think of was how that would have been nice to have a family welcoming me and to be marrying a considerate, attentive man who loved me. In our everyday life, David and I squabbled and wrestled like siblings. I thought about all of that for a long time as I lay awake that night with David pressed up against me. He'd go back to his own room and his life with his male friends once his parents had ended their visit but for now, I was going to lay there and feel his warmth. I'd had a good Christmas but I was wishing the boyfriend part had been true. Having a new love would have been the ultimate Christmas gift.

***

Through one of Rick's friends, we managed to get a gig at a well-known club in New York City. I had talked to a local radio station and they let me come on their early show and talk about my band. It was hard to get up so early in order to be at the radio station at 6am but I did it. They let me play a guitar solo and they were so impressed with me that I got extra time on air with them. I hoped that people were listening and would show up at our concert. One of the DJ's and I really hit it off. Later I wondered if he was just a groupie.

We were so excited about being able to perform at the upscale club and we gave an excellent performance. The crowd was the wildest I'd ever seen, even the others thought so too. I had guys hanging all over me between sets and after our performance. Security had to physically remove one of them. It scared me a little because I had been the front man that night and the crowd was wild. It seemed that me being the front man was really working out. I'd gotten Austin and Bart in by saying they were our roadies since they'd advised me beforehand that the cover to get into this particular club was too much for their pocketbooks. Those two cracked me up but I appreciated them being devoted fans.

We all went home afterwards instead of going off in different directions. Rick and Carol had been fighting and they both had a date beside them to make the other jealous. Kevin and David had dates with them too. I watched David and noticed that he never kissed his date or did anything remotely affectionate. I immediately thought back to when his parents had visited and he had been affectionate with me. I sighed to myself.

Jace had been in the audience at the club and had followed us home. He'd heard me on the radio advertising our concert. I hadn't seen him or talked to him since the day we'd kissed and Biscuit told me he wouldn't be faithful. I wondered if he'd really missed me, or if he'd missed Carol. At any rate, he was by my side. Austin and Bart had bargained their way in too. They were just happy to have tagged along and to party like the rock stars they knew. There were three chicks there that I didn't even know. They'd latched onto Austin and Bart but were also eying Rick and Jace.

We gathered in the living room. Beer was being drunk like water and someone had lit up a joint. "Come on Baby, take a drag." Kevin urged. He showed me how to smoke it and then handed it to me. Jace shot me a questioning glance. I handed the joint to him. He took it, looked at me, then passed it on. The others started to harass us. As they began talking about playing strip poker, Jace and I went up to my room and shut the door to drown out the noise. It didn't help much.

Jace seemed instantly comfortable lying on my bed. "Would you have taken a hit off that joint if I wasn't with you?" He asked.

I flipped on a little tv that sat on the dresser close to my bed. "Nah." I replied sitting cross-legged beside him. "Would you have?"

"Sometimes I smoke." He replied. I guess I'd already known that.

"My mother died from a drug overdose. At least once a week my dad talked to me about the dangers of drugs and alcohol. He said I could do anything else besides that so I never did drink or smoke pot. I cussed a lot, fought a lot, hung out with the band, lost my virginity. My dad used to lecture the band. He was so great. Everyone loved him.

Jace looked at me taking it all in. He seemed just a bit jealous. He wished he could have grown up with us. "Why did your dad like Kevin so much? He's such a baby sometimes."

I smiled. "Kevin was my first close friend." I admitted. "I had all this anger and all I could do was fight with people. The girls were afraid of me as were most of the guys. If you crossed me, I punched you. I couldn't relate to anyone and I didn't have any friends. I had decided that I was a superhero at one point and so I started looking for fights. I saved Kevin from getting beat up after school one day. That's how I met him. Then he kept following me and talking to me. He wanted me to teach him to ride my motorcycle and that's actually what made me put my guard down. After we became friends, he introduced me to his friends. But I really had to make an effort with them. I can't tell you how hard it was. But now we all live together."

Jace was staring at me in amazement. "It's few and far between when you really tell me personal stuff about your life."

My face stiffened as I realized he was right.

"So, are you still a superhero?" He grinned.

"No, but I'm a bully when it's needed, and sometimes in this house it's needed." My smile froze as the realization came over me.

A sudden howling of laughter roared from downstairs. We both looked towards the door. The others were sure having a blast.

"Do they still party a lot like this?" Jace asked.

"When Bob first brought me back to New York they didn't, but that didn't last long."

"How much worse does it get?"

"Stick around and see, if you want to." I was surprised when he did.

At 2:30 a.m. one of the neighbors asked us to shut

up. At 3:00 a.m. we were warned again. I was afraid that if the police showed up, everyone would be busted for drugs. Neither Jace or I wanted to spend the rest of the night in jail. We crashed the party and things settled down. "I guess that's it." Jace remarked sleepily.

"Hardly. For the full effect, you have to stay the night. We'll finish watching this movie." He wasn't acting amorous and I had long given up that we'd be a couple. He decided that he could lose some sleep so we went back to watching the movie that was on.

"Seems quiet." Jace told me.

I knew it wouldn't be long. I fell asleep in time for the fighting to start. Rick had made a pass at Kevin's date (or vice versa) so he and Kevin were arguing. Carol woke up and then they were all arguing. Kevin threw his date out and then argued some more with Rick and Carol. I looked over at Jace who must have been startled awake too. I giggled at his sleepy face.

We listened to the commotion. About ten minutes after the noise quit, I was almost asleep again when Rick barged into my room. He took a look at Jace who was half asleep laying against me and then at me. "I'll be damned." He muttered. "Don't get her pregnant."

"Get out of my room!" I growled at him.

He slammed the door on his way out.

Jace's face darkened. "You didn't sleep with Rick at first but now you are, aren't you?" He asked evenly.

"No. Rick is back to being like a guardian to me."

"Then why did he just come into your room in the middle of the night?"

"To argue with me about something. I almost expect it to happen when he gets high. It's like a ritual. Wake Angel up. Argue with her and get her mad, then leave." I replied.

"Have you honestly never slept with Rick?"

"No, I have never slept with Rick. I can't ever sleep with him." I replied.

"Why?" Jace asked in a puzzled voice.

"Do you remember how I know things? Well, this is something I know. It would break up the band if I did." I was really hoping he didn't ask any more about it.

"Why does Rick think we're sleeping together?"

"You're in my bed, aren't you?" I replied rolling my eyes.

A sound like glass breaking echoed from downstairs.

"How in the world do you live like this?"

"Lord only knows." I replied wearily. "If I know they're getting wasted before I go to bed, I lock the door." I remarked as an afterthought. "It sure doesn't block the noise out though."

He sat up and rubbed his eyes. "I can't take any more of it. I've got a headache from being woken up so many times. I'm going to hit the road. Do you want to sleep at my place?"

There was no way I was going to his place. The chemistry would kick in when we were alone then he'd fuck me and forget me like he did every other woman. "No. I'm good. They're about done for the night."

After he left, I locked my door.

I was downstairs by 9am. The living room looked disastrous. Bart was asleep on the couch and Austin was sacked out in the recliner. Someone was in the downstairs bathroom vomiting.

I didn't feel like dealing with any of that so I headed out. I found myself knocking on Jace's door.

"Oh hi. What's up?" He said standing in the doorway with that just out of bed look. I liked that look on him. It turned me on. Maybe I was wrong about holding out on him. Maybe if we just got the sex out of the way things would happen for us.

"Do you want to go grab breakfast with me?" I asked. I was thinking that after breakfast that maybe I'd allow myself to sleep with him. *I want you so bad! Why do you have to look so sexy in the morning, dude?*

"Uh, I wish you would have called first." He said nervously.

"Who is it?" a female voice called out.

I know I had this incredulous look on my face as I remarked, "You left my house at fucking 4am and you still managed to pick some chick up to screw at your place?"

"Baby." He whined slowly drawing my nickname out. And now he was calling me, "Baby"?

"I guess I'm just that fucking naïve." I replied as I turned away from his door.

I sat in my truck getting colder and colder as I listened to "Still the Same" on repeat. On top of that, it was snowing. I cursed the snowflakes as they landed on my truck. I called Smith then. He invited me to have breakfast with him and Carrie. So over bacon and eggs he asked me what I was upset about.

"I want to be a rock star but it seems like it's going to be a lonely and fucked up gig." I remarked as I played with a piece of bacon on my plate.

"Maybe things will fall in place when that happens." He replied thoughtfully as he chewed. "I understand what you mean, though. Your living situation is chaos. I've heard that you and Rick punch each other. And I

don't know how you stand Carol. David is okay but he
has no ambition, and Kevin is such a baby."

"Do you know everyone in my band?" I asked,
surprised.

"Yeah, I've met them and talked to them before. Jace
has also told me a lot about them." He agreed.

"Do you not like bacon?" Carrie asked me.

I shook my head as she'd brought my thoughts back
to the present. "Uh, I like it. Thanks for cooking." I
answered as I finally took a bite of the bacon.

"So, what happened? You don't usually call us." She
replied.

I relayed how the night and the early morning had
gone down. "I'd like to tell you that all of that is going to
change, but I can't. I don't think it will." She said as she
poured Smith more orange juice then offered me some
more.

They shared a look that made me wonder what was
up. "Word has it that you taught Curt a thing or two
recently. And now he has a new job too." They were
smirking at me.

Man, I hated that Curt had blabbed but I could
handle my emotional reactions.   I swallowed the
mouthful of yummy eggs that Carrie had made then I
glanced at them. "Yeah, I did. I'm a fucking rock star
now." I smirked back.

We laughed. But then they wanted me to talk about
it. "I don't kiss and tell, unlike Curt."

"Apparently your sex and personality lessons have
paid off for him. He's getting laid left and right now. We
get to hear all about his conquests." Smith remarked as
he finished off his toast.

"Does Jace know I did that?" I asked.

"Not yet but you know he'll find out, right? He'll be hot when he does. You know that Curt can't keep a secret to save his life."

Yeah, well, it served Jace right.

"Sooo, I was wondering, Angel, since you have so much insight, what do you see in my future?" Carrie asked.

Crap. She was asking me to be a dime store psychic. That had been my fault for telling Curt where to look for a better paying job. I looked up in surprise. "You're pregnant."

She smiled. "Yeah, three months. What's she going to be like?"

I shook my head. "Not a she, a he, and I don't know. He'll just be a regular kid." Then I turned to Smith. "But you're doing really well at your job and they're going to offer you a higher salary if you move to West Virginia. That will be about six months from now. I think you should take it because there's a good school there where Carrie can study to be a teacher like she's always wanted to. And you'll meet someone there that will be a good nanny."

They were excited about what I'd foreseen and we talked a little while longer about it. I went with them while they ran some errands after that to kill more time until it felt safer to go home.

That night David was excited to show me the pictures that he and the guys had taken. A bunch of them were great. I was getting hot just looking at myself in print. "You like them." He smiled. It was about 10pm and we were sitting on my bed in our pajamas.

"I'm so hot!" I smirked. Inside, I felt a twinge of sadness at the pictures of the two of us – a visual image of the couple we would never be.

"Yeah, you are, and you're so conceited too." He smiled back. We looked at all the shots then he put them on my night stand. "Take your top off." He said as he turned back to me.

"What?" I asked. Whenever any other guy had made that statement to me, there was sexual tension or sexual energy. I didn't feel either from him at that moment.

"Take your top off. I want to see your sexy body. The guys were totally drooling over you at the photo shoot. And you've seen me naked a hundred times. It's only fair."

He often walked around the house naked. I wondered if my being naked would make him want me. It was worth a try. I pulled my pajama top off. Just imagining having sex with David turned me on. He was staring at my breasts so I took off everything else.

"You're as buff as I am." He remarked in an approving tone as he ran his hand down the side of my body. "Are you sleeping with anyone?"

"I'd sleep with you." I told him as I took his hand and put it on my breast. Desire surged through me. He had to be feeling that, right? He was changing his mind about me, right?

He slowly removed his hand. "I can't sleep with you. You know that. You're like my little sister."

"Stop it! You're fucking confusing me!" I griped as I pulled my pajamas back on. "You tell your friends and family that I'm your girlfriend, you want to see me naked, but then you don't want sex. I don't know what the fuck to think!"

"I'm sorry but us sleeping together just isn't a good

idea. I guess I'm confused too."

I knew it wasn't going to go any further even if we talked more. I was going to have to get myself off after he fell asleep. Dammit.

CHAPTER 20

A few days later, I found out the identity of one of Carol's lovers. It was about 7 a.m. when I woke up. I was hungrier than usual that morning so I went downstairs to find something to eat. As I walked into the kitchen, I found that Carol was already eating her breakfast. Kevin was perched on a kitchen chair, naked as usual, and Carol, wearing a skimpy teddy was giving him a blow job. I walked around the table as he came. Wordlessly I pulled out a chair and sat down. I handed Kevin a napkin to wipe up his spill. "You guys know this wasn't a good idea, right?" I asked them. "You know it could have been Rick instead of me walking in on you."

They traded glances. "Rick wouldn't have cared. He knows that I've slept with Kevin before." Carol replied.

I raised my eyebrows at Kevin. *Seriously? Did he not have a lick of sense in him??*

Kevin got up and stood in front of me. He moved his hand up my thigh. My arousal shot upward even more than it had when I'd walked in on them. "Why don't you take off your nightgown? You don't even have to do anything to me." He said as he licked his lips. He looked for my reaction and then began to push my nightshirt up. I stopped him only because I didn't want Carol as an audience. "Not here." I remarked.

He nodded and we went to my room and locked the

door behind us, not that I imagined that Carol wasn't right outside the door listening. I knew she was. It was easy for him to make me feel better, twice even. I hadn't been hanging around with him all that much, with all the car theft I was doing, and I realized that I'd missed him. He was so damn good in bed.

CHAPTER 21

January 2007

I went to an eye doctor appointment a few days later. As I sat in the waiting room, I saw that the girl sitting across from me had deep emerald-colored eyes. I got up and went into the bathroom to look at my eye color. They were my dad's eyes, really amazing blue. As I sat in the chair as the doctor examined my eyes, I told him I wanted colored contact lenses. He assured me there were many different and wonderful color shades to choose from. "I want purple."

He brought his face out from behind the tool he was using and looked at me. "Purple?" He asked. "That's not one of our color shades. Maybe you could go with a nice aquamarine."

"I want them a nice shade of purple so people will notice them. Can you make them?"

"You're eyes are amazing, I'm not sure why you'd want to change them."

"Thanks, but I want to change them sometimes. Can you make them purple?"

"It will cost extra, but if that's what you really want, we can do it."

This was going to be so cool!

***

A week later I had the purple eyes I wanted. I

showed up at work wearing them. I thought they were the coolest thing ever. "What the fuck?" Brandon, one of my co-workers exclaimed to me. "Are you a fuckin' alien?"

I smiled. "Yeah, I am." I agreed.

"That is so fucking weird. You really do look like a fucking alien."

I smiled. "You'd better watch your step, earthling." I replied back with an evil laugh.

Throughout the day I got similar reactions from people. They thought I looked weird.

"Take those out, they look ridiculous!" Rick told me but that was the new thing for me and I wasn't removing them.

"I think they're cool. "Kevin added.

David wanted to put them in but he couldn't deal with putting something in his eyes. He took some close ups with my purple eyes. The three of us thought my purple eyes were awesome! Rick thought they were weird but Carol liked them too.

Santiago thought they were weird too. Later that night we went out breaking into cars. We drove around in a really plush Crown Vic then we had sex in the back seat, then dumped it. We'd both had a lot of fun.

When I got home it was nearly eleven. I got a coke out of the fridge and sat on the couch with Rick and Kevin who were watching the end of a movie. I yawned a big yawn as the news came on. Rick was talking about an upcoming gig as I half listened. I just wanted to go to bed.

"Hey! Isn't that Joseph?" Kevin interrupted as he pointed towards the tv. The scene was of a crashed Lexus and there was a small picture of Joseph in the corner. Kevin turned up the volume and we listened to the reporter say that Joseph's car had veered out of control and crashed and he was now in intensive care in serious condition. The police were investigating to whether there had been foul play involved. I'd made sure that I'd not left any fingerprints so I wasn't concerned.

Rick dramatically put his head in his hands. "Oh my God! We can finally rest! Someone gave him what he deserved."

No, they hadn't. I had been hoping he'd be dead. He was an evil man who'd harassed and harmed a lot of people. He deserved to die.

Rick jumped up and ran upstairs to tell Carol the good news.

"The world is fair after all." Kevin decided.

I knew it was only as fair as you made it. "Sometimes it is." I agreed.

David came bounding downstairs. "Is it true? Did the news really say someone might have tampered with Joseph's car?"

"Yeah. Heard it ourselves." Kevin smiled.

"Now you don't have to get revenge." David told me. "It's good that you didn't do anything to him or you'd be in jail right now."

I gave him an aggravated look. My revenge hadn't gone half as well as I'd planned it. I knew I could do better if I tried again... Nah, I'd just let it go. Now if he or his goons bothered us again, his ass was gone. I could see huge flames in my mind burning his house with him in it to ashes. I'd always liked fire.

***

Another club that I had scouted out had agreed to

have us perform a few shows for them. I kept my purple contacts in for the concert. Austin and Bart thought my purple eyes were the coolest thing ever. I wondered if they'd really tour with us when we made it big. They had started dropping by more often and visiting whoever was home at our house. Jessica never did say if she liked my purple eyes. She took some close ups of me playing guitar that showed my eye color. I thought it all was so fucking cool!

We did an awesome show for the club with me being the front man. We had started out a few weeks ago with me being front man for one set and for Rick to be front man for the other set. Now he had stepped back and we had showcased my bad ass guitar playing, and kept me as the front man. We had more fans now than we'd ever had. It was especially easy to play the animal circuit - The Elks, The Bear Lodge, etc. As long as people were dancing, they bought drinks and that made the management happy. People loved to dance to our music and they always crowded around the stage to be close to us. We always had people wanting to talk to us during our breaks. It was a lot of fun but I felt it wasn't the atmosphere we needed to play in. Rick and the others were happy because we were getting paid pretty decently while I knew we'd came and conquered, and now we needed to move on.

It seemed like I needed to write some songs so the next morning after I'd had sex with Kevin, and the rest of them had finally gotten out of bed and made breakfast, I set to writing some songs. While they had slept, I had picked an artist and listened to the style of his music. I settled on Eric Clapton and then I let his style lead me where I needed to go. I wrote a song about a man on the run from the cops and I titled it "On the Loose." I had broken into a car the night before and had almost gotten caught and that's really where the lyrics came from.

Jace appeared in front of me as I was finishing up the song. He hadn't knocked, he had just invited himself in and I supposed that was okay. We talked about the song I was writing, but not the story behind it, and I got the impression that he had begun to miss me. It served him right. I loved him and he didn't want me. I didn't want him either. "Are you avoiding me?" He asked.

"Yep." I replied. "Tired of my heart breaking." He didn't realize that I'd been avoiding him pretty much since I'd come back from South Carolina, and my heart jerked knowing that.

He sat down but didn't say anything. I strummed my Gibson just feeling the song I'd just written when I heard the front door slam. Kevin appeared a moment or two later and when I looked up at him, he kissed me. He was talking about a movie that was playing at the theatre and he wanted me to go with him. He was also totally ignoring Jace. I glanced at Jace and he was definitely not ignoring that Kevin had just kissed me. "Are you sleeping with him?" He asked in irritation.

"Seems so." I replied.

Kevin took that as a hint to sit down by me and put his arm around me. "You're loss, my gain." Kevin smiled at him.

"I ought to knock your fucking block off." Jace told him.

"I gave you a chance. You didn't want it." I reminded Jace.

"Yeah, but I could just as well fuck you as he could."

He argued back.

"I don't have time for this shit. If you don't want a one-on-one relationship with me, I don't want you." I replied back angrily. "I'm not going to fight with you about it."

"You know, I really hate those purple eyes of yours." He remarked. He gave me a dirty look then he walked out.

"You're only seventeen. Why do you want something so serious with him?" Kevin asked after Jace had left.

Some years later I'd ask myself the same thing.

***

I got up the next morning knowing that I needed to go talk to the neighbor. The voices had told me so. It was always interesting when the voices would tell me to do something but not tell me what I was supposed to do or say, what the point was to my mission. I headed out the front door and crossed the lawn. The couple next door was older, probably in their late forties. They kept to themselves but had been angry with us before about our music being too loud. I wondered what in the world I was supposed to say to them.

As I rounded the hedges, the man was getting out of his car. He looked perturbed. "What's the matter?" I asked him for lack of anything better to ask.

"Damn transmission is having trouble." He muttered slamming the car door.

"I know about cars; I probably can fix it."

He looked at me and frowned. "You're like twelve. What do you know about cars?"

After a lot of explaining which, I hated to do, we talked about the car and he showed me what was going on. I'd known at least one person that had had the same problem. I rode with him to an auto service shop and they confirmed my suspicions. "That's gonna cost a good two thousand or more at the shop." The mechanic remarked.

"How much are the parts?" I asked.

"You're looking at around a thousand."

The neighbor turned to leave. "Wait." I told him. "Would you let me work on it?"

"I don't have the money for the parts let alone to have anyone work on it."

"I have the money and I can do the work." I turned back to the parts guy. "Go ahead and order the parts."

The neighbor argued with me but I went ahead and paid for the parts. They had to order them so they wouldn't be in until the next day. He rambled on the drive home that he couldn't pay me and he rambled on about me being twelve and about the band being lousy neighbors. It was hard helping people sometimes.

"He's reported us to the police before. Why are you helping him?" Rick asked me the next day as Kevin, David, and I were walking out the door to work on the car.

"I'm supposed to."

"What the hell does that mean?" He asked back in exasperation.

"The voice in my head told me to. Maybe they'll quit calling the cops on us now."

So as Rick stood in our doorway watching us walk to the neighbor's house, Kevin and David were teasing me about the voices in my head. I ignored them. They thought I was kidding.

"Are you sure you know what you're doing?" the

neighbor asked as Kevin and I were lying under his car putting the parts in. David was nagging us from above.

"I'm pretty sure." I yelled back.

"She's kidding. She's fixed my car before. Both of them know what they're doing." David assured him. He and David were talking now. The neighbor was apologizing for calling the cops on us.

"No biggie." David assured him. "Just say something to us next time. We don't realize how loud we are at times."

The neighbor's wife came out and brought us iced tea. Soon half the neighborhood was hovering over the car and giving us advice. "Don't snap." Kevin murmured to me. "Just ignore them." I was sure he couldn't see me rolling my eyes at him. He started singing "Still the Same" to me and I had to smile.

A few hours later we were finished. The others had since left. Kevin and I were dirty and greasy and my neck hurt as well as my arms. We let the neighbor take the car for a test drive. David went with him. Kevin and I sat on his porch steps and talked to his wife. She was crying because I'd paid for the parts and Kevin and I had fixed the car. Her mom had been having health problems and they had paid for her hospital bill. That was why they were so broke. The voices tapped me on the head. "Can I meet her?" I asked.

"Oh honey, she's pretty sick." She remarked while Kevin looked at me curiously.

"I'd really like to meet her."

"She's in a coma. She can't communicate."

"I feel like I need to visit with her." I replied

She wiped her eye with the tissue she was holding. "Okay." She finally agreed. "Why don't you clean up and then come back over for supper? It's the least that I can do."

Oh yeah. I could eat supper.

"So why do you want to see her mother?" Kevin asked me that night.

"I think I'm supposed to heal her."

He gave me a strange look then sobered. "Oh, the voices, right." He remarked.

"Yep."

A few nights later Kevin and I got in the neighbor's car with them. We were going to see the neighbor's mom, and I supposed that Kevin wanted to see what I'd do. Her mom was still in the hospital. They were right, she was really ill. I wondered if I could really do anything for her because she was unconscious. "You're only the vessel. Thy will be done." The voices reminded me. I stood by her hospital bed and put my hands on her arm. I found myself singing a song I'd never heard before. Even as I sang, I wondered how that could be.

"She's crying." The neighbor gasped. They eagerly called the doctor in. We stayed a while longer then Kevin and I took a taxi home because the neighbors had decided to stay at the hospital.

"What did you do to her?" Kevin wanted to know.

"I don't know. I was the vessel for healing that's all. God did the rest, but I don't know exactly what he did." I could tell that didn't answer his question but I couldn't explain it any better even to myself. He asked a lot of other questions about it afterward and I answered as best as I could.

She was released from the hospital a few days later. She cooked supper for us about a month later. I wasn't sure if she was totally healed but she was doing a lot better.

***

At our gigs, the guys tended to loiter around me when we had our break and after we finished for the night. "You are such a dick magnet. Guys are always gawking at you or trying to talk to you even when you tell them to fuck off." David remarked one night as we loaded up our gear. "I think if I advertised that you'd be picking your nose that the guys would line up to watch."

"Oh, shut up." I replied in irritation. At times some of those guys were psycho, even more than I was. A good bit of the time they were crude telling me what they'd do to me sexually. And sometimes those guys were men, old men. Gross. If I ever gave birth to a male child, I was going to teach him to be a gentleman around women.

"No, it's true." Kevin added. "None of us guys have that many girls hanging on us as you do guys. The guys don't hang on Carol even though she'd give them a blow job as sure as talk to them. People have always followed you ever since we were in high school together."

Guys had followed me even when I was a kid. It seemed irrelevant to mention that.

"Dick magnet. I'm a dick magnet too! Blow jobs. Hahaha." Carol giggled. She was high as usual.

"I'm gonna make some money off you." David told me. I'd stopped listening to him, to all of them. He and Kevin were talking about what they were going to do. I was thinking about big fucking trucks.

"We need to get to the club at least 90 minutes before our gig tonight." David advised me about a week or so later.

"Why?" I had just gotten home from work and I was thinking of a nap before then. If we had to leave earlier then there would only be time for a shower.

"You have fans waiting."

I gave him an angry look then went upstairs to the bath. I heard the door squeak open as I washed. "Who the fuck is in here? I locked the damn door. This is supposed to be a private room for God's sake! What if I were in here using the bathroom?" I growled. I swore one day that I was going to fix that damn door so it stayed locked like it was supposed to. The landlord sure wasn't fixing it.

"Calm down, Grouchy Bear. I heard the shower running so I knew you weren't taking a shit." David replied.

"Get the fuck out! And stop calling me Grouchy Bear! I'm gonna knock you in the head when I'm done showering just for that remark alone." I yelled back.

He was ignoring me. He was teasing me that he'd put up a sign at the club that he was charging thirty dollars a person for people to be able to talk to me and get my autograph, and a kiss with tongue.

"Oh, shut the fuck up! You did not! I'm gonna rearrange your face if you really did that!" I growled back in undisguised annoyance. What I really needed was a nap, not to be leaving even earlier than usual.

"I'm bigger and stronger than you, Grouchy Bear. When you're done in here, me and Kevin are going to dress you appropriately for tonight so hurry up and wash."

"What the hell does that mean?" I yelled back, but he had already exited the bathroom. He'd totally ruined my night talking shit. My temper steamed hotter than the water from the shower as I washed. I was totally gonna rearrange his face.

I poked my head out the shower curtain to make sure I was alone. As I dried off, I looked for my clothes. I had figured he'd taken my underwear or something as a prank but my clothes were still there. I got dressed and dried my hair, then I headed for my bedroom, only to find him and Kevin sitting on my bed talking. Clothes were laid out on the bed between them. "You know, I should clobber the both of you, you jerks." I told them.

"Get out of those raggedy old jeans and put these on." David commanded as he held out a new pair of black jeans.

"No. Now get lost." I replied with emphasis as I placed my brush on my dresser and fluffed up my hair as I looked in the mirror. I turned around and stood in front of them. "Why aren't you gone yet?"

"We warned you." David replied, then he and Kevin wrestled me to the bed and were trying to get my jeans off.

"RICK!" I yelled at the top of my lungs. "Get these jerks off of me!" I kept fighting the both of them and screaming.

"What, are you doing?" Rick calmly asked them from the doorway.

They released me. They hadn't been hurting me and I wasn't scared, just angry.

"We asked her nicely to change into the cool clothes we bought for her but she's so damn uncooperative and grouchy." Kevin remarked.

Rick laughed. "Awe Jesus, Baby. It wouldn't hurt for you to dress up for once." He remarked. "Good luck, guys." He said to Kevin and David. I couldn't believe that I was now watching his back as he exited my bedroom. He was supposed to be my guardian. He was supposed to protect me from thugs. This was disturbing.

"YOU are the guardian." The voices in my head reminded me. I ignored them.

"WHY, are you doing this?" I demanded.

"Look at this." Kevin told me soothingly as he waved his arm over the clothes on the bed. "These black jeans and this pink shirt are gonna look so hot on you. And look at the jewelry. And you can wear your cool black cowboy boots with them. And David will let you wear his black cowboy hat. Black is your favorite color, right? And you'll be holding your favorite white guitar. You're gonna be the picture of hotness! Guys will have to jack off in the parking lot!"

Both of them were a hundred times better at putting an outfit together than I was. I knew I'd look good in what they had laid out for me but I didn't want them to know that. They'd commented in the past that I dressed in a "homeless woman" type of look and that one day I'd be a cat lady with a hundred cats. I stared at the clothes. "What are you gonna do for me if I go along with you?" I replied noticing that the new black jeans were super black, and I loved black.

"Nothing. You don't need the money but we do." David replied.

"I need you to bake that scrumptious chocolate cake for me that you've baked before, except I'm gonna eat it all. And I need back massages from you." They argued back but then decided that they'd do what I asked if I dressed in what they'd selected.

They were right. I looked HOT! I loved my black cowboy boots, and the pink shirt really popped the outfit. It fit snugger than the t-shirts I usually wore so it showed off my body. I would look ten times hotter when

I was holding my favorite white Gibson. Guitars were like that. The guys were teasing me about my arrogance and I was tempted to snap at them until I saw the lust in their eyes. Yep, I was fucking hot! As I admired myself in the mirror with Kevin standing on one side gawking too, David came up from the other side and plopped his black cowboy hat with the silver metal work on it, on my head. "Damn." Kevin growled. Oh yeah! Then David was snapping pictures of me... double yeah!

When we rolled up to the club, only an hour before our gig – yes, late even for a regular gig, we had to double park at the back door because the parking lot was packed. We'd taken two vehicles. "They must be offering a combo meal or something on special." I remarked as I saw all the cars. "And that would be good because I could go for one of their double cheeseburgers. Those cheeseburgers are the bomb!"

"You just ate! Enough for two people, I might add." Rick exclaimed in exasperation. "How can you eat so much and be so thin?"

"Soon you'll be a fat cow. You're already bigger than me." Carol piped up.

I ignored them both. There was no way I was about to fight them while I was looking so hot. They were so jealous. And Carol was the one who'd been starving herself to fit in a size three. I was still a size five. I worked out, plus my job worked off my calories. There was only muscle on me, no fat to be found.

"Oh my God!" David exclaimed. "This can't be real."

"Why are all those people here?" Carol asked. She had dressed in something hot after she'd seen how good I'd looked.

"Get your guitar." David commanded to me.

"What did you do?"

"I told you, you're a dick magnet and you already have groupies. I advertised with your fan club and at this club that you'd sign autographs and take pictures with people for thirty bucks a pop. I didn't really think anyone would show up. I thought that maybe one or two people would be stupid enough to pay to talk to you, not seventy-five!"

"No, that can't be it." Carol murmured, so we walked around to the front of the club.

"There she is!" I heard a few people shout, and then the crowd was running towards me. I felt like running but I was pretty sure I couldn't outrun them all. And David was right, those people couldn't all be there paying thirty bucks a pop to have a picture with me and to get my autograph, right? I strengthened my stance and wiped the surprise off my face. I was a bad ass guitar legend, and a bully at heart. I'd fight any storm, or at least stand strong as the crowd bowled us over and trampled us.

There had to be fifty or more teenagers running at me. And as they came closer, I noticed that some of them were actually little kids, and there were a few older men and women trailing behind them. It didn't make any sense. I'd never had that reaction before from a crowd. People came up and gushed over me at every gig but we never really had time to do pictures or such, and I never gave autographs. I recognized some of the fans. I'd met several of them at the guitar shop, and a few others from our past gigs and the comedy club. They were smiling, and excited, and calling out different greetings to me. All of them wanted to be first in line.

David elbowed me. "Smile, These are your FANS." He whispered loudly to me. So, I did. Hey, I was still recovering from the surprise of it. The band had constantly teased me that I was so full of myself but obviously these people were full of me too. Oh yeah!

Part of the deal was that these people wanted pictures with me as I was playing my guitar. They wanted the action shots, and some wanted a kiss. We ended up inside the club and plugged in the amp. And as people came up, David took their thirty bucks and they got a picture with me as I looked cool and played my guitar. A lot of them got pictures with me just standing there with my guitar, and they had their arm around me. Then they wanted hugs because I wasn't handing out kisses. OH MY GOD. But I rolled with it because David leaned over and whispered in my ear that we needed this for the publicity. He also said that I needed to be warmer and a lot flirtier. He had the nerve to tell me that he'd teach me about that later, said the jerk that wouldn't fuck me. Rick and Kevin were left to set up our equipment. Bart and Austin were going to help them but they had to be bribed with having their picture taken with me for free. Carol should have been helping set up equipment but she was trying her best to get some of my attention. Jessica stood around taking pictures of the event. I was glad that I'd found her. She was so good at everything she'd done for me.

I also signed autographs which I swore I'd never do. We were almost an hour late starting our set because of the fans. The management was okay with it because nearly all the fans stayed and ate or drank something as they listened to us play. And David had made nearly two thousand dollars. Rick and Carol weren't happy at all about the whole thing, but that was normal when it was something that was happening for me.

"That guitar and your looks will get you the world by the tail. If only I could be that fortunate." David lamented as if he wasn't good looking and played guitar.

"And you and Kevin are keeping the money for me doing all of this, right? You weren't going to give me any of it." I asked back.

"I bet you that you were a dick magnet and you accepted that bet. So yeah, you're not getting any of this cash." He smirked back. I wasn't sure how I felt about any of that because I hardly remembered the conversation. I certainly didn't remember accepting his bet. "Oh, cheer up. You just learned that your guitar will get you laid, and that you can make a hellava lot of money with it. That was worth the lesson." He added.

I rolled my eyes because it hadn't made me any money, only him and Kevin. Did he realize the irony of what he'd said? "I learned that when I was nine years old. And you're just as good looking as I am and you can play guitar. There's no reason you can't make the same money."

He gave me a strange look then. I supposed he thought I'd gotten laid when I was nine but that wasn't what I had meant. Although I'd realized at age nine that my guitar playing could get me sex, it had only been recently that I'd realized it wouldn't get me love. Jace was proof of that. And the guitar playing wasn't a guaranteed lay – David was proof of that. And yeah, I'd gotten several offers that night to get laid, and some had been willing to pay if I reconsidered. One guy had offered me a thousand dollars. "I'm not a prostitute." I'd told him as David looked on wide-eyed. David's expression alone was worth that remark. I wondered if he would have taken that offer if someone had asked it of him. He'd told the guy in a serious tone that he shouldn't be soliciting a minor or any other woman either. I was tempted to offer David a thousand dollars just to see if he'd do me.

"You still don't get it, do you? You dense little girl." David remarked as he was driving my truck home with Kevin and I after our gig. By the tone of his voice, he obviously thought I was the stupidest person on earth. I didn't appreciate that.

"No, I don't get it at all." I reluctantly replied, reliving the crowd running towards me.

"It worked because we advertised that you'd meet with people and cooperate with them. Normally you won't give them the time of day. And they liked that you had dressed up for them. A lot of people complimented you on your outfit."

"That's not true. I talk to people." I replied back. I'd talked to people before. Hell, words were coming out of my mouth right now. It's not like I'd just learned to talk earlier that day.

"Mostly you're tweaking the sound system on our breaks. You're that super cool chick that plays amazing guitar and is just out of reach of every guy in the place. Everyone wants you but no one can have you. And you don't really talk to them, you say "yeah" a lot and half listen. Mostly you look bored at their conversation." Kevin informed me.

I truly didn't understand that. There was no one person that I was that gaga over that I'd pay thirty bucks to hug them and get my picture made with them, not even my cartoon crush, Speed Racer. Yeah, sorry Speed.

As for their conversation, after the initial compliment they mostly wanted sex or to talk about themselves. I wasn't interested in either conversation.

CHAPTER 22

It was a lazy Sunday and I had just come home from jamming with some people at the music store. Kevin was the only one home. He was in his room watching tv. We made small talk for a while. I was feeling hate for Jace and that he didn't want me. "Kevin, do you want to go for a world record for sex?"

He looked curiously at me as we hadn't slept together since our move to New York. "Oh yeah, I'm down for that." He was laying on the bed with his head propped up with a pillow.

I rolled towards him and slid myself across his chest to look him in the eyes. I hovered over him. "Remember the time we were learning about sex in my room when we were fifteen?" I asked softly.

It only took that sentence to heighten the desire in his eyes. "Oh, yeah." He replied as he pulled me down for a kiss. "I remember."

We both had just come so good and were barely apart when Carol stuck her head into the room. "You're fucking Kevin." She remarked as if it was a revelation to her.

I guess I had kind of gotten used to all of us being half naked most of the time or in one another's beds so I hardly flinched when I saw her. Besides that, the sex had been so good and I was still feeling great so I didn't even bother to cover up. "Yeah. You would have to walk in on us." I smirked.

"I'm so glad. You can be fun when you relax." She murmured as she began undressing. I wasn't paying attention until she got into bed with us.

"What do you think you're doing?" I asked.

"I want to have fun too." Carol replied as she pushed her nakedness between Kevin and me. "Light one up, Kev." She urged.

I don't know exactly why but I didn't feel that weird about what was happening. When she asked me to take a hit from the joint and then showed me how to smoke it, I went ahead and took a toke. Although it hurt my throat I continued smoking and got high for the first time – something I swore I'd never do.

I woke up an hour or so later as Carol was getting up. "That was way cool, Baby." She remarked as she deliberately brushed her hand against my breast. "Oh man." I muttered. "That really happened."

"Yeah." She giggled. She reached under my chin and brought my dizzy head up to hers and kissed me.

I moved my head away. "I'm not like that. I'm into guys." I complained although I immediately thought of David and his homosexual tendencies, and of how Cathi had seduced me when I'd stayed with Bob and Nancy. I didn't want to be gay.

"Oh, me neither. It's fun to experiment though, ain't it? Or it was fun a while ago, wasn't it?" She laughed as she began getting dressed.

Kevin giggled from the other side of the bed.

I ignored him and didn't answer her. I hadn't even begun to think about it. I got dressed and went to my room for a while.

Carol made supper but I was too embarrassed to come down and eat. I knew she'd tell the rest of them what we'd done. A few minutes later David yelled up the stairs for me to come down. "Everybody knows what you did and nobody cares!" He yelled.

I yelled back that I was staying in my room. I heard them giggling. A few minutes later Rick appeared and shut the door behind us acting every bit of a guardian. "I know Carol is embarrassing you, but you and I have to talk about this." He said as he sat on the bed with me.

I am sure my face was so red. I couldn't even look at him. "I really fucked up. I got high and I said I'd never do that. I promised my dad I wouldn't do drugs. And I had group sex." I told him.

"Is that what you wanted to do?"

I went to answer but he cut me off by saying, "No. Tell me the truth. How could you really help it either? You're around sex and drugs all the time."

I took a deep breath. I had been going to say that I didn't want to do two of the three things I'd done, but I realized that I did want to be part of the group and have fun and I had done everything on my own free will. And I also realized that Rick was sounding like a guardian. "Yeah." I agreed as I met his eyes.

"Then I'd say you're normal. There's nothing wrong with anything you've done. Carol probably has never done anything like that either. She just wants to freak you out. But please tell me you're on the pill or something and you're not going to get pregnant. I really should have talked to you about this a long time ago."

I probably should have been mad at Carol but what Rick said made me smile even though he had told me several times that I'd better be on the pill. "Yeah, the joke's on me. And yeah, I'm on the pill. Don't worry."

"What about Jace? Are you sleeping with him?"

My face reddened yet again as I looked into Rick's eyes. "No."

"Really?" He thought I was lying. "Why not?"

I stared at him a moment deciding to spill my guts. "I don't lie. I only want him if he'll be mine. He just wants his freedom."

I could tell that my response wasn't what Rick had expected to hear. "It might be better if you sowed your oats too. Get it out of your system while you can."

I felt he wasn't taking me seriously. "What about love? I don't want him screwing everyone else."

"Love isn't all it's cracked up to be." He replied as he held my gaze.

My first thought went to his and Carol's relationship. "Is it not working out with you and Carol?" I asked almost dreading his answer. If they were breaking up then what would happen to the band?

He didn't answer right away. He looked at me as if he didn't think he should confide in me then he said. "Look, all I'm saying is that a relationship takes work from both people to keep it going. Carol and I have our ups and downs but we still love each other. Most of the time our fucking other people doesn't get in the way. We're too young to get married so we're doing the only thing we can do. But you're way too young for a serious relationship with a guy. Don't get so hung up on Jace. He's too old for you for one thing, and for another he's probably a lifetime cheater. Believe me, there are other guys you are going to be attracted to besides Jace. I mean, I thought that no woman would ever turn my head after I fell in love with Carol. Man, was I wrong."

He was talking in general about a lot of women but in the back of his mind he was particularly thinking of me and that was really weird considering that we punched each other sometimes. I couldn't let on that I knew. "So, I'm thinking about this whole situation in the wrong way, huh?" I asked.

"Yeah. I mean, was it so hard to sleep with Kevin today? You don't love him but you slept with him." He rationalized.

I cracked a smile. "Kevin and I have slept together before."

Rick didn't seem surprised. "What made you sleep with him today?"

"Are you guys coming down to eat or what? You're not fucking my guy are you, Baby?" Carol yelled from downstairs.

We both looked towards the door. I stood up and was going to ignore his question but he took hold of my arm and I faced him.

"Well?" He asked.

"Jace pissed me off. He'll never be mine. He's just interested in screwing every girl that walks by." I replied as I looked at the floor.

Rick tipped my chin so I was looking at him. "Then I'd say either sleep with him or move on." He replied seriously.

I didn't know what to say to that. I wondered if daddy would have said the same thing.

He stood up. "Well, think about it. Let's go eat."

We walked downstairs to the dinner table where David, Kevin and Carol were eating. "So did ya have the talk?" Carol giggled at us. "Yeah." I replied red faced but I couldn't help but laugh too as I fixed myself a plate. We giggled over it for a while longer then went on to other subjects. In the back of my mind, I kept thinking about everything that Rick had said to me. It wasn't until a while later when Carol was washing dishes that I talked to her alone. Her hands were in the soapy water as I came up behind her. She must have thought I was Rick. She was a few inches taller than me. I reached around her and cupped my hands under her breasts and when she turned towards me, I pulled her head down towards me and kissed her startled lips.

"Oh my God" She said as she moved back and her soapy hands came out of the water to drip on the floor.

I just smiled and gave her a knowing wink. "Yeah, that was fun." I murmured. I left her standing there speechless and that was the most fun of all.

***

I had parked myself on the couch and was watching tv when Kevin came downstairs. "I'm going to the motor cross at the arena. Do you want to go with me?" He asked.

I wasn't used to any of the band asking me to go anywhere with them so I was a little surprised at first. "Yeah, I'll go."

"I'm ready to leave if you are." He replied grabbing his jacket which was hanging over the couch beside me.

We arrived at the arena all psyched up to watch the motor cross. We were both remembering our dirt bike riding, and motor cross dreams, which seemed to have happened a lifetime ago. Since we had moved to New York I hadn't much thought about those dreams.

We managed to find some good seats and settled in. We watched the motorcycles go around and around and jump and skid around curves. At pretty much the same moment Kevin and I turned to each other and whined, "I want to ride again!" Then we collapsed together laughing. On our way out of the arena we talked nonstop to my truck about how we'd buy a motorcycle and be big bad riders. At my truck he picked me up and spun me around. "We're going straight to the dealership, right?" I laughed as he set me back down on my feet. "You betcha. Get in." He replied.

We did go to the dealership but there wasn't a whole lot we could see being it was late at night and dark. So, we headed home. Right before we parted ways to go to our respective bedrooms he remarked, "Tonight was a lot of fun, like we used to have. Do you want to hang out together sometimes?"

"Yeah, it was cool. I'd like that." I replied. Before I knew it he was climbing in bed with me. After another great romp in the sack, we fell asleep together.

CHAPTER 23

Kevin, David, and I were lying on David's bed one night watching a movie that was sure to give me nightmares. "You'd better cover your eyes because they're gonna whack that chick." Kevin advised me.

"Shut up! You keep telling us what's gonna happen and you're ruining it." David remarked in irritation. Then Kevin was reaching over and smacking David in the head, and then they were fighting over top of me.

"Stop it, you jerks!" I exclaimed as I batted them out of my space.

A piercing scream came from the tv and I jumped. They laughed at me. We alternately talked, laughed and scuffled throughout the movie.

"We really are like brothers and sisters." Kevin remarked as he observed us at one point.

"Except when you fuck her." David smirked.

"Yeah, well we're really bad kids." He replied back as we laughed. David was channel surfing to see what else was on.

"Did you tell her?" Kevin asked.

"Tell me what?" I remarked as I shifted my pillow into a better position against the headboard of the bed.

"Since you asked – we were talking with Jessica and we're going to set up a little concert with just you playing for a small crowd of people. We'd charge thirty bucks a person and you can play your guitar and sing unplugged, maybe like an hour or so, then you'd hang around for another hour and get pictures made and mingle with them. I mean, if you think you could do that. I don't know, you might not be able to handle the pressure of being a one-man band."

"Hell, she couldn't handle the talking to people part." Kevin quipped.

"Shut up! Of course, I can handle it. I could have handled it when I was nine years old. And I can talk to people. Words are coming out of my mouth right now." I griped. "And you're so fucking stupid! It would be plugged, not unplugged. I play electric not acoustic."

"So, you'll do it?"

"And you guys will get all the money?" Yeah, I'd played right into that one all right.

"Well, yeah." David agreed. "What are you good for anyhow, right?" I wrestled with him then and we both fell on the floor with an "owww!" and a crash.

"You're gonna kill me, you ape!" I complained.

"Not if you don't kill me first, you jackal!"

Now Kevin was on the floor with us trying to tickle us. I wished then that I'd had a brother or sister when I was growing up. It would have been nice to have had a companion.

Three weeks later after a few heated arguments with Rick and Carol, I arrived with Kevin and David at the VFW. Rick and Carol were right behind us. They had to cash in on this too and they were going to do crowd control and sell soda and chips. David and Kevin had sold one hundred and fifty tickets at thirty bucks a pop. I had suggested the venue because you didn't have to be twenty-one to get in and there was no alcohol being served. It was also two o-clock in the afternoon so the rental was cheap. Kevin had set up his drums. He was planning to supply the beat. They had dressed me in some cool duds to go with my cool brown cowboy boots. I had forgone the hat though. Although I liked a cowboy hat, I was a rock star not a country star. I had even dressed willingly in the cool, tricked out clothes they'd laid out for me. I knew I looked hot! Both of them knew super cool clothes when they saw them and I absolutely loved what they'd bought.

David welcomed the crowd and then introduced me. I walked out from a room that we had deemed as the dressing room although I had been dressed before I got to the VFW. The crowd cheered as they saw me approach. I took the microphone and looked out at them. "Are you ready for some soothing soft rock?" I asked them in a DJ voice.

"No!" several people yelled. Some were asking their neighbors, "What the fuck?" Even Kevin and David were giving me strange looks.

I put the microphone in its holder. "Soft rock? HELL NO! I'm gonna tear this joint down!" I yelled then I launched into "The Kid is Hot Tonight" by Loverboy. I changed the kid from a he to a she. The crowd cheered and clapped as I played and sang. I performed "Jumping Jack Flash" with the Rolling Stones as a follow up. As the cheering died down from that, I took the microphone. I welcomed everyone out, and introduced the rest of the band even though they weren't all on stage with me. "But you guys came here to hear me, right? Not these dudes!" The crowd yelled and cheered while David gave me the finger. I noticed Bart and Austin in the second row. They were yelling "Freebird,

Freebird!" It didn't take but a few seconds for everyone else to start yelling "Freebird" too.

"Y'all are killing me." I smiled about how many times I'd played that song in my lifetime. It had become my anthem. I nodded at Kevin and he took a seat at the drums while David walked off to the side. When the guitar solo was about over, I called Bart and Austin to come up and sing with me. They about jumped over the people in front of them to get to the mike. They weren't half bad vocalists. When the song ended, I introduced them as my roadies. I laughed as they were high fiving each other. "Hey, this is my show." I laughed at them. I high fived them and they melted back into the crowd. I saw them accepting high fives from various people. I played several of my favorite rockin' songs, all were upbeat songs. David set a root beer down by my guitar stand as I wound down a song. I picked up the root beer which was in a brown bottle which looked like a standard beer bottle. The crowd stepped their cheering up a notch. They thought I was drinking beer. I looked out at the crowd. It was made up of mostly men in their twenties and thirties. The other twenty percent were older men, and women and kids of various ages. I was still holding the root beer in my hand. "It's root beer, dudes." I informed them. A few booed me. I just smirked and took another swig. They settled down and I put the bottle back down by my guitar stand. "Y'all want to hear a song I wrote?" There were whistles and agreement to that. "I wrote this song when I was about nine. It's called "Another Day." Several people laughed and I ignored that. "I wrote it because my dad was always lecturing me about the dangers of drugs. I got tired of listening to him so I wrote this song and told him it was because

I saw a documentary on tv." The crowd laughed and whistled.

"Y'all might think that's funny but he sure didn't. He grounded me for two weeks and I wasn't allowed to play this song ever again."

Kevin hit the drum with one thump to get my attention. I glanced at him. He shrugged his shoulders at me. Yeah, we hadn't rehearsed this. He'd never heard this song before. I gave him a quick chin up gesture which meant just go with it, no biggie if it wasn't perfect. He could fake the drumming. Who'd really know if he was drumming correctly or not? Not half of the people in the room. He gave me an exasperated look.

As I sang, I thought about how angry my dad had been about the song I was singing. I doubted he believed that I'd written it because of a documentary.

The crowd seemed to like my song. It had a great melody and was upbeat, and now I could admit that I had gotten most of the information from a spirit that had died from a drug overdose. But mostly I'd written the song because I was so tired of my dad lecturing me about drugs.

I played a few more songs then wound her down. I had told David and Kevin that they'd better be right there with me if over a hundred fans were going to bowl me over afterward. They walked to me as I nodded to them when I was finishing up the last song. Each person or family was going to get to snap a picture on their cell phone or camera with me. Some people weren't going to wait for an hour for their turn and left. Several of the guys commented on how buff I was. I flexed my arm muscles for some of them. A few offered to sleep with me even with all the people right there listening, including Kevin and David. "Move along." David instructed. "She's jail bait."

Another guy had his hand in my long wavy hair. "Dude, hands off the guitar legend." I remarked to him in irritation which I was faking.

"Smack him." Kevin remarked.

"It would be worth it even if she smacked me." The dude remarked. I reached out and as he flinched, I gave him a solid pat on the cheek. He blushed but moved on, but he was just one of the men blushing and stammering as they talked to me or hugged me to them as someone took our picture. Kevin and David were going to owe me big time for all of this hugging that I was enduring.

I looked up to find Smith and Carrie standing in front of me. When they went to hug me, I went with it. We had a little reunion there, then they had their picture taken with me, and they moved on. And they weren't the only band members that had been in the crowd. Several other people I recognized from local bands had shown up too. Maybe I was big time now.

The band had to clean up the place afterward. There were about twenty guys still milling around. Bart and Austin were among them. They talked to me while the rest of the band loaded up the drum set, picked up the trash, and swept the floor. "Are we keeping you from cleaning up?" One guy asked.

I smirked at him like that was the funniest thing I'd heard that day. And yeah, it pretty much was. "No. I'm a fucking guitar legend. I don't have to clean up anything." I replied. I wasn't getting any of the money from the concert. Oh, I could have insisted on my share but I had plenty of money.

"You're so fucking conceited." One guy told me as the others nodded their heads in agreement.

"There's the door if you don't like my attitude." I knew he'd fuck me if I gave him the chance. They all would have.

He snorted but didn't leave either. Most of them shot me a look as if they couldn't believe my attitude while a few of them thought it was funny. "Do you have a boyfriend?" Another of them asked. That made them laugh.

"Me and Kevin are trying the couple thing." I replied as I nodded towards Kevin. We hadn't talked about it but we seemed to be a couple.

"And he puts up with you being so conceited?"

"It's not conceit, if you're that fucking good, and I AM THAT fucking good, a guitar legend."

"That still sounds like conceit to me." One of them remarked.

I stretched and yawned. "Y'all are boring me." I replied, then I turned to walk away.

"Wait, wait! We can talk about something else." Several of them exclaimed.

I looked back at them. "I'll be back, I gotta pee."

When I came out of the restroom Carol was talking to them. I stopped by Kevin who was sacking up the trash they'd swept up. "Did Carol steal your groupies?" He asked.

I was about to say something snarky when a voice from behind me said, "There you are."

Kevin and I both turned to the voice to see the entire group of them walking up behind us.

"Hey! I was talking to you." Carol said loudly from nearly across the room. They'd all just left her standing there.

"Awe dudes, I'm gonna have to listen to her cry now. I wish you wouldn't have done that." I remarked. I smiled inside although I still thought that they'd been rude to her.

"How do you deal with her?" one of the groupies asked Kevin.

"I've learned to handle her."

"Seems like she's handling you. You're cleaning up and she's bullshitting with us." One guy laughed and the rest of them did too. I guess they thought they'd put Kevin in his place but I didn't butt in because I wanted Kevin to stand up for himself. I tipped my head to him as a signal.

"You can laugh about that all you want but after we get out of here, I'll be the one she's doing all night." He quipped back.

That stopped their laughing but now they glanced at me. "Oh yeah. That's a big 10-4." I smiled.

"But you're supposedly jail bait." One objected.

"I'm a month younger than she is." Kevin told them and several of them nodded or snorted.

***

"I'm mad at you." Kevin informed me as David drove us home.

"Why? What the fuck did I do besides just make you a shit load of money?" I asked as I pushed repeat on the CD player to play "Still the Same".

"I can't believe you just said that." He replied back in disgust.

I looked at David for a clue.

"Seriously?" He said instead. Wow, he was no help.

I turned the volume up as the CD player played "Still

the Same".

Kevin grimaced and David turned the volume back down and pushed the button to stop it from playing again. "In all the years I've known you I don't remember you ever singing "Another Day" before or even mentioning anything about that song, and then today you tell a crowd of over one hundred people that you wrote it to spite your dad when you were nine. Total strangers – you told that to total strangers but you never said anything to us. What the fuck, Baby? Why haven't you told us everything about your life?" He asked in exasperation.

"I forgot about it, actually. And I was probably a lot older than nine when I wrote it, maybe I was ten." I pushed the back button on the CD player to play "Still the Same" again.

"Stop playing that fucking song!" David suddenly yelled at me. "We're fucking mad at you!" He shut the radio/CD player off and it was now silent except for the sound of the road. It wasn't often that they yelled at me and meant it. I could now hear the sound of the V8 engine in my truck. I thought about mentioning it but then bit back the observation. There was nothing like the sound of a powerful V8 engine. It had the same effect as my favorite guitar chord.

"I can't really tell you a lot about my life." I growled back. "It's not that I'm keeping it from you, it was just hard and I don't want to think about it again, ever."

"All I know about you is from when I met you when we were fourteen. I don't know anything that happened to you before then." Kevin complained.

"Me neither." David agreed.

"Nothing happened before I met you guys." I replied

as I eyed the CD player thinking that I sure would like for Still the Same to be playing.

"Ohhh! You're so exasperating sometimes! So fucking exasperating!" Kevin loudly exclaimed.

I shrugged my shoulders.

"Okay, so why do you have an obsession with "Still the Same"? Why do you have to hear that fucking song over and over?"

"Because daddy used to sing it to me when I was a kid. It was his favorite song. It's all I have left of him." I murmured.

"You have a real gift of getting people to shut up, you know that?" David remarked as he took a turn rather quickly. I saw that the light had turned red as we'd passed under it. Oh yeah, it was a tactic I employed when I didn't want to talk about my life.

"Pay attention, huh? I like being in one piece and not splattered all over the road." I griped.

"What?" I asked as they both glared at me. Apparently the conversation wasn't over like I had hoped. I sighed. "I'm telling the truth. Daddy used to sing that song to me, mostly before I was a teenager. He said that song calmed me down. And it does. That's the truth. I mostly listen to it over and over to calm myself down not to piss you off, mostly."

Kevin began talking about my dad and I let him. That was enough to get them off my back, and I didn't have to reveal anything about my past to them. I'd become a master of avoiding answering questions that I didn't want to answer. Yep, it was a gift.

May 2007

I went back to crafting new songs in the style of

The Rolling Stones. I had five songs written and three of them sounded like hits to me. I had since put stealing cars on the back burner much to Santiago's dismay. He still wanted to hang out and screw and lift cars. I'd had enough of that for a while, and now I had Kevin to screw. The day my boss made me quit wearing my purple contacts was also the first time that someone recognized me from a modeling ad I'd done for a magazine. "She looks a lot like you." One of my co-workers told me as she handed the magazine to me to look at. With my hair styled differently in the photo, and a more glamorous edit to my face, I was having trouble recognizing myself. I liked the shot though. "It is me." I replied.

"You're fucking shitting me." Her mouth was open in surprise and I hoped no flies were nearby. "What the hell are you doing working here then?" By then she had attracted the attention of several other co-workers. They were looking at the magazine ad and staring at me.

"I just needed a job. I'm a front man of Rebel and until we make it big, we need jobs to support ourselves. Modeling and working here are my jobs." Now they wanted to know where my band played. I was seriously afraid of these two worlds colliding, but if they did, it was my fault. Now several of them had their phones out and wanted pictures of me holding the magazine with the ad. I couldn't do much except let them take a picture. I was going to have to quit Cordello but my contract wasn't up for a few months.

We were playing more gigs than ever now. There were several reasons why. One reason was that I jammed with the group at the music store every

Saturday that I could. The group had told their friends and those people had told their friends. It had gotten to be standing room only in that store, and those people would go to our concerts. I'd gone to different radio stations and they'd put me on the air and I'd tell people where we'd be playing. Some of those people knew the owners of clubs, and the clubs hired us.

Austin and Bart came to almost all of our concerts and they took it upon themselves to act like roadies. It worked out for them because they got into the clubs for free and it worked out for us because we had their help with the equipment and anything else we needed. Sometimes they dropped by our house and hung out. I had never paid them an excessive amount of attention but they didn't seem to mind. They just latched onto whoever was around. As soon as we became famous, I was going to offer them jobs as roadies.

Later that night, the band and I practiced the songs that I'd written. They were surprised that I had some talent at song writing because they really liked them. I'd mostly written the songs to showcase my guitar playing but they were rock and roll songs that were upbeat. I wanted to stay away from dark and brooding songs because they had to be one in a million to be a real hit.

We finished about 11pm and by then some guy was knocking on the door looking for Carol. I observed Carol greet him with a kiss and a squeeze. I glanced at Rick but he was getting ready to leave. I went out the door with him. "Tell me this cheating between you and Carol isn't going to break up our band." I remarked to him.

"Oh, it's not." He smiled at me, then before I could react, he leaned down and kissed me on the lips. As I was standing there in shock, he smiled at me, then turned and walked to his car. I felt the energy around me because that interaction had confused me. They were both pumped about fucking someone else. That confused me too but it was better energy then them cussing and screaming at each other. I went back inside.

Carol and her guy friend, Hunter were cuddled on the couch and the tv was on. I went into the kitchen where Kevin was pouring some soda. He gave me the glass and I took a drink. "What do you think about that?" I asked him referring to Rick and Carol and their weird agreement.

"Let's join them." He smiled. "Might as well, right? "Umm hmmm." I agreed with him. He was so good in bed.

So as Kevin and I cuddled on the couch opposite of the one where Carol and Hunter were, they started making out. Kevin slid his hands down my body and I turned into him and we started making out too. I'm not sure who started having intercourse first but I had vaguely heard David come into the room and I knew he was watching. I was tuned into the sexual vibe going on between all of us and it shot my arousal up several notches. I immediately climaxed with Kevin not far behind. As we pulled apart, David was walking over to us. I glanced at Kevin who murmured, "Do him Baby."

I was all about that and so I looked for David's reaction. "No, I can't." He replied.

I knew why he couldn't and I thought Kevin did too. I licked my lips at him at what I intended to do, and pulled him down to sit on the couch between us. He wordlessly let me undo his fly and everyone watched me give David a blow job. I figured that's what he had wanted to begin with. He was hard as a rock from watching the live porn around him and he came fast. Carol wanted to do him afterward but he remarked that we'd all blown his mind and he disappeared upstairs. "What about you? Are you up for another round?" she asked Kevin. Kevin looked at me for confirmation and I shrugged my shoulders at him. Hunter, who I'd never met until thirty minutes before was wanting a turn with me. I was still hot from David so I walked my naked self over to him and we began making out. We ended up with me sitting on him and coming twice. I had insisted he use a condom but I wasn't sure he'd used one with Carol. I wondered how old he was. He was definitely committing delinquency of a minor with me but I wasn't going to hold that against him. Yeah, we had game for the rock stars we were going to be.

Carol had a grand time after Hunter left, teasing me and talking of how Kevin and I were finally getting it. She still wanted to do David though. "He isn't into women, Carol. Surely you get that, right?" She was about to go upstairs and talk to him. She was sure she could make him straight.

"Please don't do that. He's messed up about not being into women. I'm afraid you'll knock him over the edge." She was still wanting to do what she wanted to do. "Seriously, if you have an ounce of restraint in you, don't press him to have sex with you. Don't make a big deal about it."

She gave me a mean look and went upstairs. He'd let her blow him but that was all. I was thankful that she hadn't pushed him too hard for sex.

The next day when Rick came home from work, he chewed my ass out for the group sex I'd had the night before. "What are you yelling at me for?" I demanded. "You gave me the go-ahead last night before you left to screw someone. And what about Kevin? He's seventeen too. Did you chew his ass out? And Carol was all for me fucking all of them. Does she get any blame for this?"

When it came down to it, no. No one else was to blame but me he said. He was responsible for me and he wasn't going to let me become a juvenile delinquent. I thought about how many cars I'd broken into lately and all the other sex I'd had. I hadn't taken any joyrides lately but maybe that was coming. "You haven't seen anything yet." I told him. I knew the rest of them were listening to our argument from the living room.

He was going to shake me then.

"Hey, if you want to get physical, we can do that. I say we all do our household chores right now before I freak out." I turned towards the living room and yelled, "Okay, everyone do your chores. The beast is about to freak!"

I felt Rick grab me and the next thing I knew I was on the floor but that was okay. I wasn't about to really hurt him by kicking him in the nuts but I kneed him in the chest and threw him off me, and as we were tossing each other around trying to control the other, the rest of the band was trying to pull us apart. Now I was angry. "Seriously, let's do our chores now. I hold up my part of our bargain and fuckin' pay for everything every month."

They took a look at my demeanor and they wordlessly went to work cleaning the house. Carol deliberately ruined a white shirt of mine by putting something red in with it in the wash and I slammed her against the wall until she got the message. Rick had gone to do the grocery shopping so he wasn't there to protect her. Kevin and David let me man handle her. "I'm the boss." I told her. "Do you get that? I will hurt you."

"Leave." I ordered Kevin and David. It wasn't a request; it was an order and they heard it in my voice.

"Don't kill her. There's no place close to bury her." David replied under his breath as I saw them walk out of the room.

I let the evil in me show through as I told her not to cross me anymore, that in the end I would always get my way. If all of us as a group worked together everyone would be okay. We'd all end up rich and certain things might not always go the way she wanted them to but it was for the best. She also wasn't to tell Rick about our talk. "Do you agree to this?" I asked as I pressed off her airway, then I stopped. I was satisfied when I saw real fear in her eyes. "Yeah, you fucking psycho, I agree." She sputtered, coughing.

"Cool, now try and make my white shirt white again. I love that fucking shirt." I replied as I let her up. I liked that I could turn vicious at the drop of a hat.

Since I had gotten kind of tense with what had happened, I agreed to meet Santiago to lift a sweet, sweet ride that he'd had his eye on. I hadn't been out with him in a while and he had been feeling hurt. I was thinking that was the reason he was tempting me with a tricked-out Chevy Silverado. Man, there was nothing better than a tricked-out truck! The whole escapade was even wilder because we were lifting the truck in broad daylight. We pulled it off too and the head rush was even better than the best pot around! It was a four-wheel drive and so we took it four wheeling, then we had sex in it and abandoned it. Life just didn't get any better than this.

When I got back home, I was in my room trying to come up with a song that would really put us over the edge as a number one hit. I was getting vibes about the fight that we'd just had and I realized the song had to be about people not getting along and how we all got fired up. I was going to call the song, "On Fire." I had been working on it for about an hour and it was really coming together. It had a good drum beat and a small drum solo as well as a great guitar solo. The chorus was hot and the song rocked the way I wanted it to. I loved the hook, I just needed to come up with some more lyrics.

Kevin came in and sat on my bed with me. I knew he wasn't happy with me. "You're a bully." He told me in disgust.

"I was a bully in South Carolina. You knew that. I saved you from other bullies. Now I'm a psycho bully."

"The others sent me up here to talk to you because they're all afraid of you. They want to kick you out." He said hesitantly.

I smiled in amusement. "Yeah, that's funny."

"No, I'm serious. What the hell am I going to do if they kick you out? I have nowhere to go and I'm not sure I'd want to go with you, because you're right, you are psycho, and you don't give a fuck about punching any of us. What the hell would happen to me? Where would I go?"

I had really been hoping that the construction job that Kevin had would toughen him up, and it had to some extent but underneath he still had some toughening up to do. But I also understood what he meant about not having any place to go. Other than his parents who didn't want him and were nowhere to be found anyway, he had an uncle who he didn't like. I had no family to go back to either, and no other life, and neither did he. I sighed softly as I slid out of level one. "C'mere." I said to him as I held out my arms. As we leaned up against the headboard of my bed holding each other I told him how it was. "Baby, this is mostly an act, okay? I need for us to work together but Rick and Carol want to control everything. They're always on my case and I can't take it anymore. I hate the house being a mess and we did make a deal. I pay for absolutely fucking everything so I don't have to do chores. I've kept up my end and you all need to keep up yours. We all need to get on the same page and work together both in our personal lives and in our music. Rick wants the band to go a certain way but if we do that, we'll never be famous. If we do it my way, which may not always be easy, we're going to be famous within the next year. They have to decide which way they want it. If they want to kick me out, I'll just find another band that wants to be famous, and I'm taking you with me. I care about you, I always have. I don't know that we'll ever be a couple, but we'll always be friends and family, and I'd never punch you. I have to be a bully with Rick because he's bigger and stronger than me. He won't listen to me otherwise. If he's at least somewhat scared that I can kick his ass, then that's the way I have to deal with him. If it were ever just me and you, we'd get along fine. Heck, me, you and David could coexist without a problem. Add Rick and Carol to the mix and it's a mess."

We talked some more and I listened to him. He said his life was okay but he was all messed up inside that our little non-related dysfunctional family wasn't working out. He didn't want another broken family. I gave him a sweet kiss, assured him that we'd all be just fine, then we went downstairs to talk to the others.

There we were, sitting in the living room. "We're tired of you fist fighting with us and bossing us around." Rick told me. "We want you out."

"I'm tired of y'all not doing the chores you're supposed to do when I pay for every fucking thing around here. And I want to be famous. If we work together and do the things I need for us to do, we'll be famous within six months to a year." I replied in a non-threatening tone.

He was arguing with me asking why I thought my way would work when his wouldn't.

They all were quiet looking for that answer.

"Because I've known that we'd be famous from the time I was fifteen or I wouldn't have followed you here to New York. I just know things. I feel them, I dream them, I see visions, etc, etc, etc. Do you want me to be a dime store psychic tonight and prove that to you?"

"Yeah." David agreed.

"Research Martin Jones, the race car driver then talk to your boss about what a great driver he is and pretty soon he'll be giving you a raise."

I looked at Rick. "Don't park near the post office tomorrow, park farther away because someone is going to ram their car into whoever's car is sitting right in front of the building."

I looked at Carol. "You're going to be at Ray's bar one night this week and a guy with a red shirt is going to look really good to you. You'd better watch your drink because he's going to slip a roofie into it."

I turned to Kevin. "You're interested in a girl named Cheryl but you don't think she'd go out with you. She is interested in you. You just have to take the chance and talk to her. Butter her up a little bit then ask her out. I think you're going to marry her."

As they all buzzed about everything I'd predicted, I went on. "We have to be at the right club at the right time to be noticed by someone that owns a record company. I don't know how we're going to get into this club but this chance is coming up soon. Y'all just have to be open to what I tell you to do."

"What club?" Rick asked.

"The Starlight."

His eyes widened. "And just how are we going to get into that club to play? That's big time."

"I don't know yet.....but I will soon. But first we have to really practice three certain songs.

Rick ran his hand through his hair in exasperation. "Baby, you're just guessing. Do you think we're just supposed to do this because you say we'll be stars? You don't know."

"What if I do? What's this one thing going to hurt?"

We talked about it. I'd never outright told them any psychic predictions and so they were leery too. They were still thinking that all the things I'd told them wouldn't come true. We talked about that for a while and also about why they wanted to kick me out of the house. I wondered how in the world they would be able to support themselves if I didn't pay for everything, but I agreed to calm down and they agreed to get on board with doing their chores and acting more like a team than they had been doing previously.

I was gearing up on my song writing too. I'd had a

few songs written but we needed more. I got my guitar and plucked out the song I'd written when Daddy had taken away my motorcycle. I had called it "The Angry Song." I worked on the lyrics so that it was more of a song about people letting you down. I ran it past Kevin and he liked it. I changed the song title to "Ain't It A Bitch."

I called my favorite radio station and they invited me to be on the radio the morning we were to play at the Caterpillar Lounge. I wore my purple contacts and the two DJs were all about that. They wanted to hear me play a riff on my guitar so I did. They gave me plenty of air time and I appreciated it.

From there I went to a Cardello studio shoot where they had me wear a clingy dress with more cleavage than I would have liked. I was advertising some brand of lipstick. I was thinking that people would hardly recognize me anyways because I never wore makeup. I sure looked hot though and it was a plus that we were done within an hour. I thought that had to be the quickest I'd ever gotten done with a shoot. I had forewarned my boss that I'd be late for work. I had to make up that time by working two hours later. I supposed that was the price I had to pay.

CHAPTER 24

The next night, we had a performance to give at the Caterpillar Lounge. Shortly after our second set began, I spotted Jace and a few others walk in. Our band had gone onto some different songs with the more advanced guitar solos, and Rick had taken a bolder approach to his singing, while I was just over the top as a front man. Even if I was the front man from now on, I would always let Rick sing a song or two. I noticed that Jace reacted to it immediately. The crowd seemed to be enjoying it more too. The DJs from the radio showed up and I invited them to sing with us so they would brag on us the next day. The club was packed so I knew that we'd done well on the air. We also played "Ain't It A Bitch" and we got a good response from the crowd so we played two more of the songs I'd written and people seemed to like them. That just motivated me to write more songs.

After our performance, Curt told me that they were going to another club and asked if I wanted to go with them.

"Yeah. sure." I agreed.

Kevin just wanted to go home and crash so I told the others that I was leaving with Streethart and followed Curt out to his car. Curt and his date sat in the front seat. "Cool set tonight, Baby. You and that guitar are so awesome."

"Thanks, Curt."

Jace seemed mad at me right off the bat and I hadn't even said hi to him yet. He had already gotten in Curt's car. Jace, his date, Greggie, and I sat in the back seat. Since the front had bucket seats and there was only room for three passengers in the back seat, I ended up on Greggie's lap. I could tell Jace was aggravated about it.

"How about a kiss, girlie?" Greggie remarked in a sexy voice. "I mean you are sitting on my lap."

"Get rid of your girlfriend and I'll give you that kiss."

"Awe, come on. You can give me one kiss." He pleaded.

"Yeah, and maybe we all could have an orgy." Jace remarked with quite a sharp edge to his voice.

"Now, you're talking!" Greggie laughed. I was glad it was dark because my face was suddenly red. I should have figured one of my band would tell Jace about Carol, Kevin and I fooling around.

"Why don't you tell all of us how something like that happens, Baby?" Jace said over the hoots and laughter in the car.

The car was almost silent then. "What?" Greggie and several others asked in unison. They prodded until I answered.

"Hey, you guys do stuff. Why should I be any different?" I asked.

"I can't believe you fucked Kevin!" Jace spat at me. Even though he was sitting two over from me the fury in his voice pierced me sharply.

"What do you care who she fucks?" his date spat back at him. And then the shouting went on between them. Curt and Greggie were trying to calm them down.

"Curt, stop the car. I want out right here." I demanded. I was totally embarrassed.

"But Angel...."

"Just do it."

He pulled the car to the edge of the road. I opened the door and exited the car. I was just glad to be away from Jace's date who was still cussing at him in a high shrieking voice that sounded almost like Carol's. Then suddenly Jace was tumbling out the door behind me.

"Just get us the fuck out of here!" Jace's date screamed at Curt.

"Leave." I replied to Curt. Jace made no move to get back into the car. Curt gave him a moment to see what he'd do then he drove away.

"That's just fucking great! All because of you we're walking." Jace said angrily as he kicked at the dirt.

It was pretty dark but a town was maybe a mile or so in the horizon. We weren't that bad off. Maybe we'd just fight the whole way there. I had a tiny flashlight hooked to my house keys and there was a street light here and there so we'd manage.

"You could have gotten back in the car. I didn't tell you to stay." I told his dark shape.

"What the fuck!" He replied angrily. "Why did you have to fuck around with Kevin and Carol? And Miss Holy, what about how you got high with them? What happened to, oh I'll never do that? What, did hell freeze over and make it a special day?"

"Like I said in the car, why is it a crime for me to do anything? I'll fuck whomever I want to. I was tired of never doing anything. I never get on your shit about fucking all those women. I don't tell you not to drink or get high. Besides I've fucked Kevin before. You knew that. He was practically my first."

Out of the darkness he managed to grab my arm. I tried to yank away but he held me tight. "Because you never do that stuff, that's why I'm so pissed. What's gotten into you lately? You've been a totally different person ever since you came back from South Carolina."

"This person is who I am. The person you saw before that wasn't me. And like you're so fucking fond of saying, we're not a couple. You've always made that quite clear, we're just friends but right now I don't think we're that either. Was I supposed to ask your permission first before I got high and had sex?" His grip loosened and I pulled away.

"Maybe you should have. Did Rick say anything at all to you?! You're 16. Do you want to end up pregnant?" Jace yelled.

"I'm 17! In 5 months, I'll be 18! Jesus! You'd think someone would know how old I am! And good God, I know how to take birth control pills. Do you think I'm stupid, like one of your groupie bitches? Well, fuck you, Jace." I spat back.

"Fuck you, Jace? Since when have you ever talked to me like that?"

I wished that I could see his face but there was just the darkness and we were over a mile away from town. "I really hate you right now. The sex and drugs are a two-way street. You do them. What's the difference if I do them too?" I replied in an even voice. "Let's get walking." I felt like I was in the twilight zone. We had had fights before but we had never had a fight where we were so hateful to each other. "Damn double standards." I muttered under my breath.

"Well, you know something? I hate you too." he replied, as he bumped into me in the darkness.

We walked in silence for quite a while sometimes brushing against each other in the darkness then pulling away, sometimes stumbling on uneven ground. I hated fighting with him. I knew he was right about some things he'd said but I was right too.

I broke the silence. "I was tired of being so fucking good. I was tired of being the responsible one. Rick was supposed to be the guardian, not me! I wanted to have fun too. Believe it or not me and the band are a lot closer now, no pun intended. They talk to me more. Kevin and I are together now."

I heard Jace gasp a little. "You're in a real relationship?"

"Yeah."

The lights ahead were getting brighter and it looked like it wouldn't be all that much longer before we reached town. Very few cars had passed us by.

"Did I ever tell you what the first thing a boyfriend of mine has to be?" I remarked.

"I'm sure you have."

"The first thing is that he has to be faithful. I don't want any guy saying he's mine then running around on me. I want him also to be my friend. Kevin will be faithful and he's a friend......... I don't hate you anymore. Do you still hate me?"

"Yeah." He replied with resignation.

"Wow. What happened to us?"

"Read my mind if you want to know."

"I can't and I wouldn't if I could." I kept walking.

The town was within a few yards of us and now the light was falling on us. I could see Jace's face now. He looked hurt. "I don't know Baby, what did happen to us?"

"There never was an "us because you didn't want an us." It sounded like a break up speech to me but I had rarely hung out with him in the past two months. I saw a phone booth which was a rarity nowadays and Jace followed me as I walked up to it. It just happened that my cell phone that I was supposed to carry at all times was on the dresser in my bedroom, and the battery was dead in Jace's cell phone. I should have taken that into consideration when I'd gotten out of the car on a deserted road.

"Who are you calling?" He asked.

"The cab company. None of my band is reliable enough to come get us." I replied.

He fell silent. He thought I'd been about to call Kevin. I would have called him but he'd have too many questions.

We stood silently waiting for the cab. I started to feel bad about everything. "Can we get over this? I'm hurt that we're so mad at each other." I remarked as the cab pulled up to us.

"I guess we'll see." Jace remarked as he opened the cab door and waited for me to get in.

I wished the two of us could be together. It was him that I wanted. But he treated his women so badly. Why couldn't he treat them better? If I slept with him, he'd probably still go on sleeping with other women. That would kill me. Why couldn't he see that Mr. Right could be him?

The cab took off. We were silent most of the ten miles home. I was crying before we got to my place although I had tried not to. The cab came to a stop.

"I'm sorry about tonight. I'm sorry for a lot of things. I shouldn't have talked to you like that." I told him through my tears. I leaned over and hugged him and although he didn't respond at first, he did finally hug me back. I hurriedly gave the driver a twenty and ran out of the cab. I ignored Jace's voice demanding I come back and get my money.

I guess I moped around for a few days afterward. I knew Jace wouldn't call. He'd never been the kind to call right away after a fight. The band asked me what I was so down about and I had told them that Jace and I were fighting because they couldn't keep a secret from him. "He's so fucking jealous of Kevin." Carol replied.

"Yes, I know that but he needs to get rid of all the other women before anything at all could happen with us." I replied in exasperation. I knew that she'd been the one that had told Jace everything but I wasn't mad at her but I should have wondered when she'd seen him in order to tell him our business.

Somewhat later as Carol lay with her head on my shoulder, a creeping sad realization came over me because I had unconsciously read her without meaning to. But it wasn't really an angry realization and that rather surprised me. I knew I didn't need to look into her eyes when I asked her for the truth. I already knew the truth. "You know I've never fucked Jace. So, how was he in bed, Carol? Any good?" Even I noticed how dead my voice sounded.

Okay, so when her body jerked in response to my question I would have known anyway. Ouch. She raised up into a sitting position looking very surprised at my calm question. She didn't know how I knew. The tears were suddenly in my eyes and I put my hands over my face.

"Oh my God, you're not just playing with him, you love him! I never thought you loved him." She cried touching her hands over my hands.

I brushed my hands over my face trying to sop up my tears. "We talked about this. So please tell me why did you still have to fuck him?"

She slowly took her hands back. "I thought you'd sleep with Rick and we'd be even. I didn't know you'd never fuck Rick. I slept with Greggie and Curt too."

Yeah, it figured.

Later, I penned the lyrics to "Things I'd Never Do." Even though it was based on the group sex that Kevin, Carol, and I had done, the lyrics were so vague that I could have been talking about anything. I would never tell anyone what the song was really about.

Sometime later I was in my room watching a tv show that no one else wanted to watch. The band was watching some horror flick in the living room. I never really cared for horror flicks. I had thought about calling Curt and having sex with him but I was just too depressed to do it. Mostly I'd just thought about bad things as I pretended to watch tv. Maybe some grand theft auto would make me feel better. Hell, I didn't know.

The credits were rolling when David came in to see me. My door had been mostly closed but not shut. I didn't think anything about it when he closed it behind him. "Whatcha watchin'?" He asked as he rolled onto the bed and lay beside me.

I gazed at him and wondered why he wasn't out with one of his guy friends. "Nothing now. You can pick something out." I replied handing him the remote.

He flipped channels for a while and then settled on "Mash 4077".

We started talking about everyday stuff while we half watched the show. David could be a really funny guy. He had us cracking up about something that had happened to him at work. He and his boss were becoming pretty good friends and he'd gotten a raise. Kevin and Carol came in and joined us for a while. Horniness hit me and I had my hand on Kevin's dick. Then somehow the three of us were having sex. Kevin fucked us both and got us off with one hard on. He wasn't even sure how he'd done that. David was lying there and had been masturbating because I'd heard him sigh as he was coming. There wasn't even much self-consciousness between us. I was glad that Carol hadn't bugged David about having sex with her. Kevin and Carol decided that they were going out on the town. Rick poked his head in my door not long afterward saying he was also going out. He said he'd lock the door on his way out. He was rarely forthcoming about leaving the house so I knew he just wanted to see what we were up to.

"Don't you have some place you want to go too?" I asked David.

"Uh, no." He replied still staring at the tv. "Hey thank you for telling me how to get a raise at work. I like going to work more now since the boss likes me."

"You're welcome." I replied. I guess I shouldn't have been lying down because I dozed off. I jerked awake when I felt someone's hands touching me inappropriately. "What are you doing?"

"Just feeling you out." He blushed guiltily as he removed his hand from my breast.

"You've heard stories and seen the movie, haven't you?" I kidded in a huffy voice.

"Yeah. Want to fool around?"

I wasn't anything but curious so I moved closer and we kissed. We made out for a while until I wanted to go further, then he didn't want to. We were both nearly naked and physically ready and there wasn't a reason to stop in my mind. David was trying to get dressed but I pulled him back down on the bed. "Don't get dressed. We can just talk, okay? What's wrong?" I asked him. It was hard to say that because the only thing I wanted to do was fuck. I guess I put up a good front because he finally quit getting dressed and sat down on the bed. But he said nothing.

"Does it seem like incest?" I kidded.

"No." He replied looking down at the bed.

More silence.

"Whatever it is, I'm okay with it." It dawned on me then that David had come to me to find out if he really could get into women. The voices explained. I didn't know it until that moment but he had always been into men. The night I'd seen him at the club making out with another guy was how he really was. It wasn't just an experiment. He had come to me because he couldn't help but know what I'd done with Carol and Kevin. He thought that if anyone could help him it would be me. But it hadn't turned out like he'd thought it would. He thought we'd go all the way and he'd begin liking women, the past would be gone.

"You know, you don't have to be like everyone else." I told him. "It's okay to be who you are. Be true to yourself. I'll always be there for you. I promise."

David stared at me then. "What's that supposed to

mean?"

I sat up and pulled my shirt on. He was still staring at me. "It means that you don't have to be into women. If you have urges for guys that's fine. You have to be true to yourself."

"I'm not into men!" David said angrily as he gathered up his clothes. "I just didn't feel like fucking you, that's all!"

"Okay. You're still cool with me." I remarked as I watched him pick up the last of his clothes.

"Don't be telling everyone I like guys!" He said angrily as he intended on stomping out of my room.

I jumped up and caught his arm. He looked at me angrily but he stopped. "I won't say a word about anything. I wouldn't have anyway."

With that he yanked his arm back and started out my door.

"Don't be mad at me, David." I yelled after him. I heard his footsteps down the hall and then his door closing.

When Kevin climbed in my bed later, he told me that we couldn't sleep together anymore. He had it bad for Cheryl. Well, we hadn't been the best at trying to be boyfriend and girlfriend and I knew it would come down to this sooner or later. We agreed that we would always be friends and family but I still felt a little let down. It didn't make sense that I felt that way either. Did I think I could just keep Kevin on the side forever? Maybe.

¤ ¤ ¤

Cordello wanted me on a photo shoot in Georgia. Several of us would be filmed on and around a train. It was a fashion shoot for some clothes company and the pictures would end up in a catalog and in some magazines. That meant that after I got off work at the warehouse, I had to rush to the airport to get on a plane. It was around midnight when I finally arrived at the hotel.

A lot of the models were tall. I was not. Emily was younger than I was and was easily six foot tall in heels. I'd met her some time ago and had seen her at various shoots. She often said things at inappropriate times but most of the other models didn't hold it against her. She talked to me sometimes but it was mostly about makeup and wondering when she was going to meet some rich dude who would spoil her. "Good luck with that." I told her. I wasn't sure if there was such a thing. She was way too young for a relationship anyway.

We did an early shoot and then I was running to catch a plane to make it back to New York for our music gig that night. In a way, that all was exciting but, in a way, it was also nerve wracking. I had wanted to stay and party down with the other models after the shoot but I didn't have time. They thought I was just blowing them off because I'd never mentioned my other life as a fame seeking rock star. Santiago was also angry because he thought I was blowing him off. Rick was angry because he didn't like worrying that I wouldn't make it in time for our gig at the club. I did make it in time for our music gig and I calmed everyone down in the band. We went on stage on time and I blew that audience away. I had noticed that our band was drawing more of a crowd and it was cool to notice that. Girls and guys wanted to hang on us afterwards. The guys were all about me and my guitar. They flirted and carried on with me which fed my ego. The guys that couldn't get close to me, flocked around Carol with her fake blond hair and sexy clothes. If this many people wanted a piece of us, I couldn't imagine what it would be like when we performed concerts in front of tens of thousands of people. It felt like that reality was coming up quickly and I wondered if I was ready for it. I was already having time crunch problems with the Cardello shoots, working at the warehouse and then performing at our gigs.

The next Monday when I got to work at the warehouse, I turned in my one-week notice. The boss offered me more money to stay but I told him that I was about to become a rock and roll star. He accepted my resignation but laughed at me. He pretty much laughed at me all week so I wore my purple contacts. Hell, the entire company laughed at me all week. Their laughter and teasing angered me to an extent but in the end, I knew I'd have the last laugh.

I was in the break room on our lunch break minding my own business while my co-workers sat at the tables around me talking and eating. The break room had a tv and a few people were watching some soap opera. One girl who really didn't like me was laying into me about how stupid I was to think I'd become a rock star. She was being loud as she tried to embarrass me.

"Well, I wanted to be a model and I did that, so why wouldn't I be able to be a rock star?" I asked her.

"Yeah, you're really a model." She replied back loudly and sarcastically.

I happened to look up as the scene on the tv changed to a commercial. I shrugged my shoulders at her and nodded to the tv screen. Everyone that had been watching us turned to look too. She turned around to see me on tv in a shampoo commercial tossing my hair and saying something seductive to the viewers. Even I had to admit that I looked like a million bucks, and a little bit not like myself with all that makeup. And my hair was gorgeous, so fucking gorgeous, but then it always was. My co-workers kept looking at the tv screen then back at me.

"Holy fucking shit!" someone gasped as they looked back at me with their mouth open. "That's you! You're in a fucking tv commercial!"

"And pretty soon I'm gonna be a fucking rock legend." I replied back with a smirk on my face.

Most of them hated on me for the rest of the week after that incident. Santiago was less than pleased that I was leaving, but hey, he had never been part of my plan. I didn't care in the least that he was willing to leave his wife for me. Now I just needed to get out of my Cardello contract.

At supper I was pretty distracted. I knew our chance for the band was here and I was nervous. I kept thinking that we had to perform at the Starlight on Friday which was a week away if we were to catch a break. I just didn't know how we were to get on that stage. We had no contacts at that club. I didn't know if I should just go in and talk with the manager or what. We had practiced the new songs I'd written and the band seemed to really like them.

"Angel! C. Angel! I'm talking to you." Rick said banging on the table.

"What?" I asked. None of them knew that my last working day with the warehouse had been today.

All of them looked at me with interest. "What's with you?" Carol asked. "Yeah." David replied. He was back to treating me normally again.

"We have to play at the Starlight next Friday. I just don't know how we are going to get ourselves in to do that."

None of them understood why I was so determined that we had to play at that club in particular. They thought it was a notion I'd thought up even though everything I'd predicted for them had come true. Kevin had asked Cheryl out and they were dating, Rick saw someone ram into a car parked in front of the post office, and Carol had gotten drugged by the roofie but a friend of hers saved her from being assaulted.

By the time Friday had rolled around Rick and I had talked to the manager of the Starlight and gotten nowhere. I desperately grasped for some idea of how we were supposed to get in. I kept telling the others that something would come up to get us in. I had to believe that. We were down to the wire that Friday and still nothing. Whatever band was playing would be going on at nine. Rick was sure that we'd missed our chance and actually I was too, but I didn't say it. At 6:30, I told them that we were going to load up our equipment and sit in their parking lot. It took all my effort to get them to agree with me and to get us there. Then it was about 7:30. Rick and I were arguing about the whole deal. He was walking behind the club so he could light up a joint. I followed him. We were still bickering when we rounded the corner. We stopped as we happened upon two guys that looked like bouncers. "What the hell do you want?" one of them asked us.

"To be the band that plays here tonight." I told them.

"We ain't got no fuckin' band tonight for you to play with!" The bouncer spat at me. "Their bus broke down in Buffalo Springs.

Rick and I looked at each other in amazement. "We have a band. Our band is here and we're ready to go!" I replied eagerly.

"Don't be fuckin' with me chickee." He replied.

"We're not fucking with you." Rick told him. "The rest of the band is in the parking lot with our equipment. We're good and we're ready."

The bouncers talked a few minutes amongst themselves and then threatened us to stay put. They disappeared into the club. A few minutes later the manager came out. He remembered us and reluctantly told us to come in, get ready and to get with it.

The atmosphere wasn't what I expected. It was tense and I could tell that they were all ready to be thoroughly pissed at us if we didn't work out. When we were out of earshot, I told Rick to forget their attitude because it didn't matter what they thought. It wasn't them we were going to get a record deal from. It was someone that would be in the audience this night. I thought that he would keep questioning me about that but he didn't. He took it at face value. We were both psyched up by the time we got to Carol, David and Kevin. We psyched them up too and told them if they ever had needed to play like their lives were on the line, tonight was that night, and to ignore any negative thing that happened that night.

Just by the amazement that everyone had argued with me about coming to the Starlight and waiting even though we didn't have a gig, they were all on board when we went inside and set up. I took up my place beside Rick with my guitar and we started off with one of the songs with the best guitar solo. I sensed that the crowd was used to a band that played a bit more toned-down music. I didn't care. We were there to tear that place apart and that's what I told the others to do. I guess when you gear yourselves up on something and practice, that it falls into place if it's meant to be. We played a stellar performance which brought that crowd to its feet. By the second set that place was on fire. I'd played three rocking guitar solos including "Brownstone", which I'd written. The crowd had gotten considerably larger. I was amazed that the crowd screamed for an encore after we were through. We went back onstage and played two more songs. I ended with a guitar solo that Jimi Hendrix had once played.

Everyone in the band had felt the buzz, and really felt it click. I don't think I'll ever forget that night. We were winding down backstage when the manager came to talk with us. He tried to talk to us as though we hadn't done much for the club that night, but the fans were still screaming and yelling beyond us which made his talk unbelievable. Rick dealt with him. I wasn't listening. I noticed another man off to the side watching us. As the manager handed Rick our pay for the night, and Rick was walking towards the rest of us, the man came out of the shadows. He introduced himself as Adam Greer, one of the owners of Harmony Horizon Records. Everyone in the band suddenly became quiet because this was a well-known record company. Adam looked intently at me and said, "How would you like to sign on with Harmony Horizon Records?"

Rick and I met with Adam the next Monday to discuss details. They were signing me up, not the entire band but I wanted Rebel with me and so that's what we finally agreed upon. At any point I could use a different band. Rick wasn't happy about that but there was no other way to seal the deal. We were going to cut an album and we were going to do videos of the hits! We'd record one song first and release it and we would also film the video to it and it would be played at the same time. "Maybe you don't know it, but you're going to be a legend with that guitar." Adam remarked. "I don't think I've ever heard a guitarist as good as you."

"I've been a guitar legend since I was seven."

He laughed. I just knew what I'd said was true.

We were thrilled to be discovered. Rick talked to me a hundred times about how did I know? There wasn't much to say on that. I got tired of him asking. I certainly got a new respect out of him that I hadn't had before. In the back of my mind, I wondered about Jace and I.

CHAPTER 25

It had been over two weeks since Jace and I had walked along the roadside cursing each other in the middle of the night. In another week it would be September and the band and I would be leaving for California to shoot a video. Kevin was getting serious with Cheryl even though they'd only known each other a short while. It was Jace that I wanted to clear the slate with regardless of whether we ever became a couple.

As I sat at the kitchen table that Sunday afternoon it occurred to me that if I wanted to clear the air with him, I had to take the first step.

Ignoring the voice in my head, I drove over to his apartment and stood in front of his door wanting to knock but also wanting to run away. What if he never wanted to see me again? We'd both made each other jealous and done hurtful things. I wanted so badly to have him with me as I became famous.

Finally, I knocked. He opened the door and I felt relieved just to see him.

"Are you alone?" I asked.

"Yeah."

"Can I come in?"

He stepped back so I could enter.

I hated that we were acting like strangers. He sat on a recliner and I sat on the couch.

"The band and I are going to be leaving New York in a few days. We got a record deal. After that it looks like we won't be around much. This is probably the only time I'll get to see you before we leave. I wanted to clear the air with you before we left." I paused for a moment.

"You got a record deal? You and Rebel, rock stars?" Jace gasped. I felt him remember that I had told him at Christmas that we'd be rock stars.

"Yeah." I smiled and felt destiny smile too.

Jace sat down, overcome by the news. We talked about it for a while but then it was time to clear the air.

"We've done some hurtful things to each other." I remarked to him.

"Yeah, thanks for fucking Curt." He replied angrily.

I shrugged my shoulders. "Back at you for fucking Carol."

We stared angrily at each other for a moment. "For the most part it's been nice knowing you. Have a nice life." I replied as I stood up to leave. When he didn't reply I got up and walked towards the door.

I was surprised when he suddenly was there at the door with me as I opened it. "Wait." He said. It felt like the words were burning his mouth as he said them. "I don't want us to end this way."

I shut the door then smirked at him. "Really? We hate each other right now. There's no denying that for either of us."

"Yeah, but we need to get over that." He sighed. "Are you still with Kevin?"

"He met someone and they're already pretty serious about each other. I think he's going to marry her."

"Wow."

A moment of silence went by. "I really want us to

be friends again." I finally said. "We used to have good times together."

Jace was tracing his finger along the coffee table. "I want that too but where does that leave us with you and the band leaving to travel and getting famous?"

"We won't be gone long to shoot the video and record a song. Then we'll be back every couple of weeks. Can we start over then?"

"Yeah, I'd like that. Maybe it will be different for us." He replied. I was thinking that if we played basketball or did whatever without fighting then we'd have some memories that we'd been friends before we dropped out of each other's lives. Yeah, that's what I was thinking. There was no way that anything else would happen. If it had never happened before then why would it now? It was best that I understood that.

***

Cardello hadn't let me out of my contract, and I was going on another photo shoot. In another month, my contract would be over. And it wasn't that I minded being a model, it was just that if I wanted to create a certain image of a rock star, my model image just wasn't going to work.

The shoot however, was with Mobey which was the coolest thing ever. I got to wear the coolest jeans and jean jacket over a white knit shirt. And best of all, I got to work with a gorgeous male model named Sylvester. There were shots of each of us separately, and then couple shots. One, I was staring in the distance as he was looking at me like he was going to ravish me. It was so hot! It was the best shoot I'd ever had in regard to everything! I looked hot, he looked hot, we also looked cool and sexy, and yet nothing was bared, on me at least. Sylvester and I worked well together although it was a bummer that he didn't want to fool around. All he wanted to do was get high. I wasn't into that since I was by myself. We met up with some other models at a club but I didn't click well with them because they had all snorted cocaine and I wasn't going there. It was funny because a few of them were cheering me on to snort it too and I just laughed at them. Peer pressure, I didn't have to go there.

***

In September, Rebel and I flew to California to shoot our first video. The song was titled "On Fire". It was the song I'd written about us having trouble getting along, and it was also the title of our album. The video was mostly of us performing onstage.

During the last week of September, Rebel and I had a three-day tour in the New Jersey area as the opening act for a bigger band. Harmony Horizon Records wanted us to try out some of the songs I'd written. We rock and rolled them and then headed back to home sweet home. I was pretty tired so I laid down for a nap. I guess I went right into dream mode. I dreamt that David and I were home alone watching cartoons. David ever so casually moved closer to me and before long we were into some heavy making out. I was so hot for him. We were just about to go farther when someone patted me on the shoulder waking me up. "Wake up sleepy head." Jace said as he nudged me over and sat on the bed.

"Mmmmm." I replied still feeling the lust from the dream. I smiled just thinking about it. "I can't believe riffraff can just walk in off the street and wake a person out of a dream." I remarked.

"Were you dreaming about me?"

"No." I replied stretching past him in a big yawn.

"You were dreaming about Kevin?" He asked in an irritated voice.

"Lighten up, Jace," I replied as I propped myself up in a sitting position. "I was dreaming about watching cartoons."

"Where is Kevin? He shares a bed with you, doesn't he?" He said accusingly.

I stared for a moment. He had on jeans and a nice t-shirt. "I told you before that he'd met someone, so no, he isn't sharing my bed. And no, I haven't slept with him since he met this girl." I replied getting irritated.

"I bet he's lousy in bed."

"Jace, just go beat him up or something, okay? Just quit being so jealous of him." I replied in exasperation. Before he could say anything, I had to take that back. "No, wait. Don't beat him up. Make friends with him. No matter what happens Kevin is always going to be around. We're family. We're in a band together. I can't avoid him because you're jealous of him."

Jace glared at me. "Kicking his ass sounds better to me."

"You know, if this is how our conversation is going to continue, I'll just roll over and go back to sleep and you can go home." With that I rolled away from him.

Jace was silent for a moment but he didn't move to leave.

"Why did you wake me up?" I asked over my shoulder.

After a moment he said, "I just thought we could hang out today if you're not doing anything."

I rolled over and sat up to look him in the eye. "I guess it's come down to this. Today we either start over with a clean slate or we decide to end everything. I hate that it's come to this but I can't do this anymore, you know?"

Apparently, he had been thinking the same thoughts. "Yeah, I can't take it anymore either."

"So do you want to end this, or do you want to start over?" I asked taking his hand.

His eyes had a different attitude in them as he squeezed my hand and said, "Let's start over, ok?" I felt his hurt but he had to make the first move. I don't know why I couldn't make the first move but I just couldn't.

"Yeah, sure. Just let me take a quick shower and we can take off." I replied as I dug through my dresser looking for some clean clothes.

He went downstairs to wait while I showered and dressed. When I walked down the stairs I saw him and David watching a Tom and Jerry cartoon. "Hey David, is Rick home? I wanted to tell him something."

"No. I'm it." He replied not moving his eyes from the tv.

"Okay. Well, I guess we'll see you later then." I replied. Oh dreams....

As we got into Jace's car I remarked, "I really need to work off some energy. Let's get your basketball or something."

His basketball was in the trunk so soon we were at the court. Jace never let me win so it was always a competition with us. I liked it that way. When I'd get the better of him, he'd carry on as though it was really making him mad but I knew it wasn't. We laughed and caught up on what everyone was doing. I was a little surprised that we were having so much fun. The last times we'd gotten together I hadn't had much fun at all.

Jace had been mad about something or fighting with his women. This time he didn't say one word about anyone else, not even Kevin. In the back of my mind, I kept telling myself that I needed to tell him how I felt about him.

We stopped at the video store and rented a movie and then drove through the drive thru of a fast-food place and got some burgers to go with the movie. Once back at Jace's apartment I greeted Biscuit and we put her outside for a while. Jace put in the video and we spread our food out on the coffee table. I don't know if it was the video that steamed with passion or just me but that was all I felt as the movie progressed. "Do you want to watch the rest of this?" I asked.

"You're the one that picked this movie." He kidded as he nudged me trying to push me over. I didn't move much and he just leaned on me then. "We'll watch for just a little bit longer and see how it goes, okay?"

"Okay." I agreed. Jace's one leg was stretched across the couch. I really liked him leaning against me. If only he would have let me sleep, then the passion would have left. Or if it hadn't, I could have got rid of it in other ways.

The couple in the movie was making out now. "I love you so much." The guy said to the girl right before he began undressing her.

I would just have to leave. I guessed we would just have to end everything. As much as I had good intentions on revealing my feelings, I still couldn't do it and I was really upset with myself. "I have some stuff I have to do." I told Jace as I pushed him into a more upright position. I was trying to stand up when he laughed and pulled me back down towards him and said, "But Baby, I love you so much."

I sat back down never taking my eyes from his. It felt like the color had drained from my face. His face had turned serious again. "Do you?" I barely breathed.

"Yeah." He replied breathlessly.

I took in a small sharp breath. "I love you too. I've always loved you."

He looked at me for what seemed like forever.

We fell together kissing passionately and tugging off our clothes. We came together hot and quick within hardly five minutes but what an ecstasy filled five minutes. "Wow, that was awesome!" I exclaimed contentedly as I lay against him.

"I can't believe we did this." He remarked in awe as he surveyed our naked bodies and our clothes strewn everywhere.

"Do you want to take it back and forget it all happened?" I asked. I figured he didn't.

"No." Jace said tenderly. "I just want to go back and relive it slowly so I know everything we said and did was real."

"Then, let's do that." I replied pulling him closer. Suddenly I didn't care anymore if he was faithful or not. I just wanted him to be mine.

Afterwards lying in his arms, I told him, "I really do love you."

"I really love you too."

"Why didn't you ever tell me?"

"We've always had a weird relationship, you know? We started out as friends but then we kept right on the edge of sleeping together, and then we just started hurting each other with the things we did. I've been wanting to say something to you all day. I'm glad the movie caught us off guard because I wasn't doing any good in getting the words out that I wanted to say. I meant to tell you this morning, especially when you told me that you couldn't deal with this anymore."

"I've been wanting to tell you all day that I loved you. I couldn't get the words out either. I'm so glad you finally did." I replied as I hugged Jace tighter.

We napped for a while then decided we needed to get out of bed. Jace was half dressed when he stopped and sat back down. "Angel?"

"Yeah?" I smiled as I zipped up my jeans.

He patted the bed for me to sit by him. "It really hurt when I found out that you slept with Curt."

"It really hurt when I found out you slept with Carol."

"So, what are we doing here?"

"You tell me. All I know is that the band and I will be recording an album in Los Angeles and then going on tour. Now we're talking about moving there. We're all tired of this frigid weather and snow. Either me and you just slept together and this is goodbye, or we're going to do a long-distance relationship. I don't know what else we can do." I replied.

Jace leaned toward me with his face close to mine. "I don't want to say goodbye. I'm not sure that I can live without you. Can't I be a roadie for your band or something so we could be together? I only want you and I'm going to give you that serious relationship you've wanted for so long now. Let's agree to be faithful, okay?"

I jerked a little in surprise and I suddenly felt like I was going to cry. "So, we just slept together for the first time and now we're going to move in together and have a faithful, serious relationship?" I asked.

"Yeah. We love each other. Why not? We can make this work, right?" He smiled.

"Oh yeah!" I replied as I hugged him tight and a tear slipped down my face. This moment was everything that I'd ever wanted. Everything would be fine.... except for that twinge that I had just felt that said, "are you sure about this?" I was sure.

Later that night at home the band was having a party amongst themselves. I smelled pot and the stale smell of beer. I had a bad feeling about it. I was tired of them drinking and smoking pot. I had told them many times that they didn't have to be wasted to have a good time. Mostly my words had gone on deaf ears. They invited me to join them but I went up to my room.

I turned on my tv and started watching a movie. I must have dozed off because the next thing I knew Carol was screaming. I stumbled out of bed and ran downstairs. I gasped as I saw that David was lying on the floor unconscious. Kevin was calling an ambulance and Rick was attempting to wake David up.

I didn't realize that I was crying until the paramedics came. They bundled David up and rushed away with him. Rick and Carol went with them.

At the hospital, Rick was pacing while the rest of us sat in shock, sometimes crying, but all of us wondering what had happened.

Rick stopped in front of me. "Baby, is he going to make it?" He asked.

"Why are you asking me?" I replied through my tears. "Because you always know too much." He said as he sat by me.

I looked at him and after a moment I said, "I don't

know!"

He put his arms around me and I hugged him close. He began brushing my hair back with his hand in a comforting way. "This is really important. Can you find some way to find out?" He asked softly.

"I'm afraid to know. What if it's not good news?" I cried.

"But what if it is good news? Wouldn't you want to know?"

I tried to block out everything else that was happening so that I could clear my mind. I felt the others standing there waiting. Suddenly it was there. I relaxed and moved out of Rick's embrace. I turned to face them. "David is okay. They pumped his stomach and he's going to be in the hospital for a while but he's going to be okay. The mix of drugs and alcohol he took almost killed him." I turned back to Rick and asked him to take a walk with me.

As we walked down the hall and out of the hearing range of the others I said to him, "I can't be sure because I'm really kind of unclear about this but I think that David was trying to kill himself."

Rick stopped in his tracks. "Why Baby? Why would he do it? He has everything going for him. We just made our first music video!"

I led Rick over to the windows where we were out of the others' sight. "He doesn't have everything going for him. He's fighting something inside him. The world wants him to be heterosexual but his mind says that he is homosexual. He doesn't think that we relate to him. He has a lot of problems. They're just not in the open."

Rick drew a deep breath. "I kind of knew he liked

guys. I guess everybody did. It's just that we never said anything. What do we do now?"

I leaned against the cool glass of the window and looked out. "We don't need to do anything. David will decide." I replied distantly.

We walked back to the others. It was an hour later before we heard from the doctor that David was okay.

By noon of the next day, most of the world knew that David had nearly died of an overdose and was in the hospital. It was something that we all would have rather kept quiet. We stood around his hospital bed talking small talk. I thought that he looked different somehow. He was alert and in the frame of mind to talk. "I have something important to tell you all." He started. "You may not understand why I'm doing this but that's okay. I've decided to quit the band. I just need some time to sort out some things. For the time being I'm going back to South Carolina."

"Are you coming back to the band?" Carol asked.

David paused a moment. "No." He replied with finality.

I took his hand. "But you're part of our family. Do you have to go?"

"Yes. I do. But don't worry. I'll keep in touch." He said as he gripped my hand.

We talked some more about his leaving then the nurse told us that visiting hours were over. He asked the nurse if he could talk to me alone for a minute. I was stumped as to why. She told him that it was okay.

I watched her leave and then turned to him. "What David?" I asked.

"You tried to talk to me about being true to myself.

You said it was okay and that I was still cool with you. You said you'd always be there for me."

I strummed my fingers nervously on the bed. "Yeah. I meant it, and I'll always be your friend."

"I don't know why I couldn't accept that I was gay then. I was screwing guys all the time."

I felt my face redden. "I said that because I had seen you one night making out with some guy behind a club."

His expression was one of shame. "You never said anything about it, Baby. Not to me and not to the others. I didn't know that you knew. But I'm glad you didn't say anything."

He had never called me "Baby" before. This was weird. "It wasn't any of my business." I replied.

He looked out the window. "The night that we were watching tv in your room, I thought I could sleep with you. I really thought I could. I got mad because I couldn't. I thought if I was a real man that I could enjoy women."

I sat on the edge of the hospital bed and took his hand. "David, you are a real man. We love you for who you are. But I'm afraid for you. Even if the doctors don't know it, I know that you took that overdose on purpose. Why did you do that? Did something else happen?"

"Yeah. There was someone I fell in love with. I made a pass at him and he freaked on me. He started calling me a gay boy and a gay bastard. I guess I never admitted to myself that I'm gay until now. I can still hear him." David replied sniffling and hanging his head.

"That's rough." I replied hugging him to me.

We sat in silence for a few minutes. "Do you still feel like hurting yourself?"

"No. It was stupid. I should have more self-worth than that." He wiped his eyes.

The nurse came through the door interrupting our conversation. She was upset at me for upsetting David and asked me to leave.

"It's not her fault. It's mine." he told her.

"Do you want us to stay here at the hospital tonight in case you need us?" I asked as I paused at the door.

"No. I'll call if I need you. Promise." He replied.

I felt he was being honest. "Okay, bye." I said as the nurse began pushing the door shut on me.

On the way home, the band wanted to know what David had to talk to me about. A few months ago, I wouldn't have told them. Now, I didn't see any reason not to. It wasn't anything new to them, Rick had told them some time ago. The only thing was that no one had believed it until now.

***

We went back on tour without David. We didn't want to replace him until we found out for sure that he was really quitting the band. The first place we played at was in Connecticut. We opened for a band called "The Rovers". One of the backup musicians agreed to fill in for David for the week. We had four concerts and then two free days when we would fly home and check on David.

I talked again with David. "I'm moving back to South Carolina." He told me.

"Why? You don't get along with your parents or your brothers so why would you move back there?"

"I'm going to live with my uncle until I get a place of my own, but I'm not going to live in Whitmire. I'll probably live in Greenville or some other town.

Somewhere away from my parents, and Alan." He replied.

"Why can't you stay with us? We're moving too. Even if you wanted to quit the band, you could still be a roadie or something."

"It just feels like I should go back to South Carolina right now. I can't explain it."

I wanted to talk him out of it but instead I just dropped it. His mind was made up. I still hoped he'd come back one day.

I found that his overdose came as a turning point for the others. We had finished the first show and were in the dressing room where the partying usually started. Some of the road crew were already on a roll. I happened to see someone start to hand Rick a beer. I did a double take when Rick told him that he'd given up the stuff. I suppose Carol and Kevin had gotten scared enough too, because neither of them accepted any alcohol or anything else.

Hours later we were at the hotel. We were all feeling the loss of David's presence. I knocked on Rick and Carol's door. Rick invited me in. Everything was pretty quiet. Kevin and Carol were downstairs socializing.

Rick turned down the tv but then lay across the bed on his stomach as though he was still going to watch it. I sat beside him. "I feel sad." I told him.

"We all do." He replied as he flipped channels.

I felt more than sad, I felt empty. I lay down too.

"What's going to happen?" He asked me.

"I'm not a dime store psychic. I don't know everything, Rick." I said wearily.

We heard a key turn in the lock and then Carol walked in. "What's up?" She asked us.

"Nothing much." I told her.

She sat on the bed with us and gave us a report on the going ons in the lobby. "So Baby, is David going to stick with the band, or what?" She asked.

"No. He was serious. He's not coming back. He realizes that he has some problems that he can't deal with and I really think that he'll start seeing a counselor. It will probably be the best thing that's ever happened to him too."

"I can't believe he's throwing his chance at stardom away." She muttered. I didn't bother commenting. I knew she'd never understand.

That night I thought about a lot of things. David's decision to go back to his roots inspired me to write a country song called "A Country Day". It was about the simpler things in life. The song itself seemed to come to life even though I wondered why it had ended up as a country song. We only played rock music, not country. We couldn't even record it. I was thinking it would be a top ten hit. My inner guidance was pushing me to sell it to a publishing company. Maybe some country artist would record it and become famous. In fact, I was sure they would and I felt really happy about that.

I also penned another song called "Just Say Goodbye". David had inspired it but the song was actually about a couple that was breaking up and how they would always remember being together. It was a heart wrenching love story, also which we would never record. I would sell that song too.

Rick came to my room to talk to me about a replacement for David. "Well, you're the boss of Rebel, so are you going to give David's spot in the band to Jace now that you two are a couple?"

I regarded Rick's mood and he seemed okay with that move.

"Do you think I should?" I asked.

"I don't have a problem with it unless you break up, then what?"

"I could say the same about you and Carol." I replied back.

"You could but what I want you to do right now is to ask yourself what you would do if you broke up with Jace. Could you work with him or would you throw him out? You might as well face it now just in case."

I pondered it a moment while Rick watched me think. "I'd kick him out of the band." I decided.

***

When we got back to New York, David was pretty much ready to leave. He had already moved out his stuff into the moving van. We had a few hours together and then he was gone.

I called Jace but he wasn't home. I let Carol drag me to the mall with her.

A few hours later I dropped her off at the house and then I went over to see if Jace was home. He was looking especially good when he answered the door. "Hi." I smiled.

"Hi yourself." He replied in irritation.

I walked in and he shut the door behind me. "I've only been back for about six hours, what could I have done wrong?" I asked.

"You could have asked me yourself instead of pawning it on Rick."

"I have no idea what you're talking about. What did Rick do now?"

"He asked me if I'd take David's place in the band."

I smiled. "I'm glad he asked you. What did you tell him?"

Jace turned to me. "Well, if you weren't going to ask me, who were you going to ask to replace David?" He asked angrily.

I touched his arm. "You got it wrong. It was something that was just understood between us that you would be asked to replace David. I just didn't expect Rick to beat me to it. I'm supposed to be the boss of Rebel. But you know how hard it is for him."

When he didn't reply, I moved into his arms and hugged him. "I love you, Jace."

He pulled me close and we kissed.

Somewhat later, I lay beside his warm body. I drew the sheet over me and smiled. Getting into a relationship with Jace and our band being discovered were the best things that had happened to me so far. It was a good feeling. I just knew that a lot of things were going to work out.

He saw me smiling and he smiled too. "Hey C. Angel Devito of Rebel."

"Yeah, lover?" I smiled.

"About me joining your band..."

"Yeah?"

He leaned over and kissed me. Then he had the sweetest look on his face. "I can't wait." He murmured.

www.ingramcontent.com/pod-product-compliance
Lightning Source LLC
Chambersburg PA
CBHW072256020726
47501CB00002B/292